BEYOND ICEFALL

Guy Hallowes

National Library of Australia Cataloguing-in-Publication entry

Creator: Hallowes, Guy, 1941- author.

Title: Beyond Icefall: Conflict in a new Australia / Guy Rupert Hallowes.

ISBN: 9780648148500 (pbk.)
ISBN: 9780648148517 (ebk.)
ISBN: 9780648148524 (POD)

Subjects: Australian fiction.
Australia--History--Fiction.
Australia--History--21st century--Fiction.

Layout by OMNE Author Solutions www.authorsolutions.com.au
Cover design by Designerbility www.designerbility.com.au
Published by OMNE www.omne.com.au

Available in print, POD and eBook formats.

In '*ICEFALL*', David Bower determined the relentless progress of global warming would result in the collapse of the Ross Ice Shelf in the Antarctic, resulting in a catastrophic15-metre tsunami travelling at speed around the world. David forecast that all major ports and most oil refineries in the world would consequently be destroyed, resulting in the collapse of human society.

Tanya Bower, David's daughter-in-law rescued herself from her poor drug dealing background to become a partner in one of Sydney's leading law practices. It seems that nothing could stop Tanya and merchant banking husband Mark from reaching the very top of Sydney society. Following David's seismic revelation, however, and after much introspection Tanya committed herself and persuaded a reluctant Mark to support his father. She put her heart and soul into the project as she and David became the driving force behind the establishment of an enclave in the Blue Mountains with the sole purpose of surviving the impending catastrophe.

Despite many challenges, violent public scepticism and destructive military interference, The Settlement endured. When the ice shelf finally collapsed, the decision was made end and the only entrance though the gorge was blown up, effectively isolating the community from the rest of the world.

The Settlement soon realised that their worst nightmares had come true as reports came filtering through of wholesale destruction from all around the world. Human civilisation, for all intents and purposes, had been effectively destroyed.

After a raid by a neighbouring community, was ruthlessly repulsed, Tanya spearheaded numerous missions to determine whether how many other communities had survived. Their explorations unearthed a variety of competing groups, including the Vikings, an ex-bikie group and the Amazons, a women's only group. With resources already stretched and supplies dwindling, the war for survival was ignited .

Following David's untimely death, Tanya assumed leadership of the Settlement Although anointed as her father-in-law's successor, her rise to power was not welcomed by all. The Settlement was faced with an uncertain future, threatened from outside and within.

Beyond Icefall awaits.

BEYOND ICEFALL
MAP

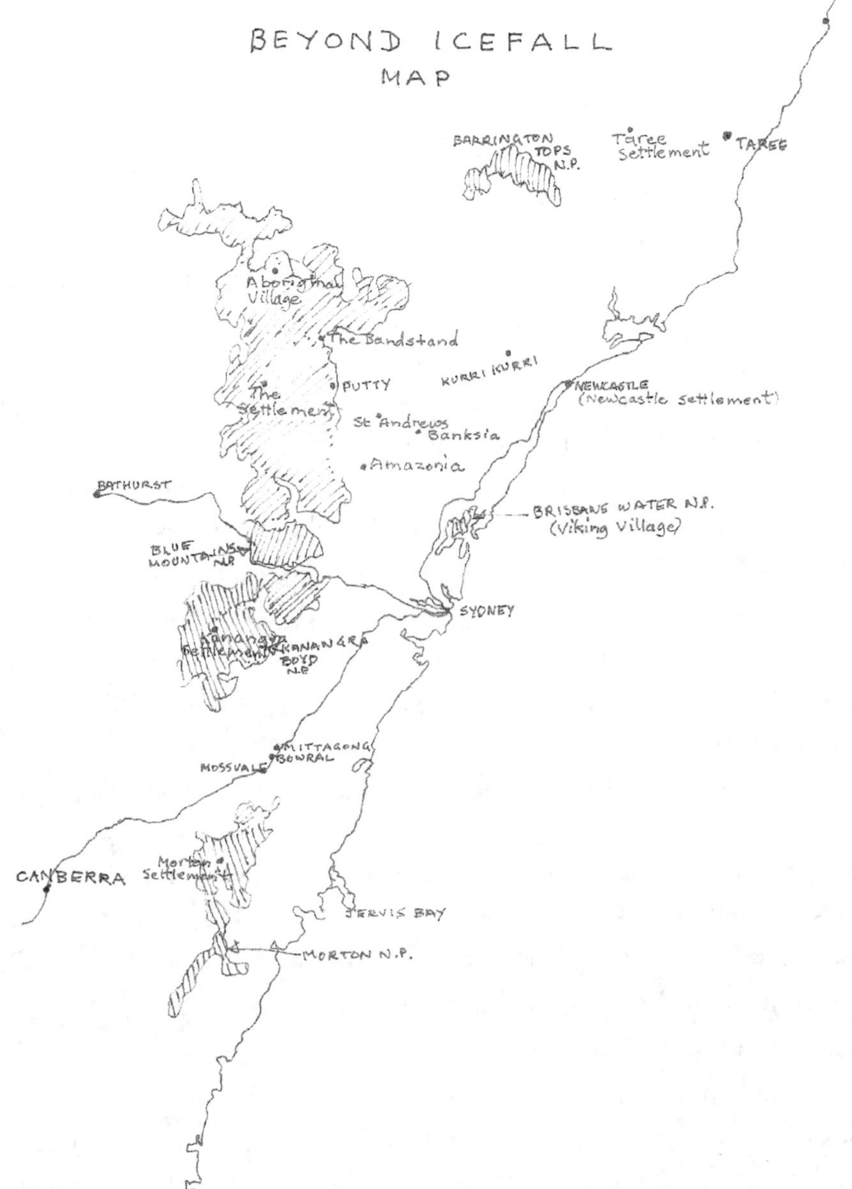

David Bower. The original leader of The Settlement. Deceased.

Tanya Bower. Current leader of The Settlement.

Mark Bower. Tanya's husband. Head of The Settlement Academy. Son of David and Chloe.

Derain. Leader of a local Aboriginal group. Responsible for teaching The Settlement people about the bush and how to survive in it.

General Jonathan Bower. Mark Bower's younger brother. Head of the elements of the Australian military to have survived the aftermath of the tsunami and the consequential flood.

Stephanie. Talented young woman in charge of the development of the Amazon establishment and further developments east of there.

Patricia. David Bower's daughter. Married to Joe.

Joe. The technical genius behind the developments at The Settlement, particularly the application of solar power.

Virginia. Elected leader of the Kanangra settlement. Was Mark Bower's mistress.

Chloe. Was David Bower's wife. Now living in the Viking village and is Thor's mistress.

Roger. Much trusted long-term resident of The Settlement. Second-in-Command at the Academy.

Kim. Joe and Patricia's daughter. Tanya's niece.

Jason. Joe and Patricia's son. Tanya's nephew.

Thor. Head of the Viking establishment.

Hercules. Thor's son.

Susan. Now married to Hercules. Kim and Chloe rescued her in the bush during their escape from Sydney at the time of the flood. During the journey she found out she was pregnant. Her young child, Barry, was murdered.

Venus. Thor's daughter. Jason's wife.

Louis. Leader of the Taree village.

Colonel Jacobs. Part of the military establishment.

Chas. Tanya and Mark's eldest son.

Didier. Tanya and Mark's younger son.

Eustace Thornbury. American helicopter pilot. Rescued by an Aboriginal group.

Contents

Chapter 1: Transition 11

Chapter 2: Kanangra 33

Chapter 3: Morton 59

Chapter 4: Expansion 93

Chapter 5: Chloe 103

Chapter 6: The Battle with the Vikings 129

Chapter 7: Louis 165

Chapter 8: Development 199

Chapter 9: Warship 215

Chapter 10: More Ships 229

Chapter 11: Taree again 235

Chapter 12: Election 245

Chapter 13: The Frigate to Newcastle 255

Chapter 14: Military Coup 267

Chapter 15: Newcastle and Kanangra 279

Chapter 16: Wentworth 293

Chapter 17: The Reverse Coup 311

Chapter 18: Consolidation 335

Chapter 19: The Wedding 341

CHAPTER 1
Transition
(September 2036)

TANYA

Since David's death, both before and after his funeral, Tanya often revisited all parts of what had, over the previous 25 years, become known as The Settlement during her early morning rides. She had always loved the place; the clean fresh air, tinged with the faint whiff of eucalypt from the swathes of surrounding gum trees. She, together with her father-in-law and mentor David, had been instrumental in creating the haven and ensuring its survival. She would often ride to David's Hill, at the eastern side of the establishment, passing the extensive stables housing several hundred horses, and pause not far from his gravestone, admiring the familiar scene. Below her lay 250 cottages, with their solar panels glinting in the sun. The cottages housed the more than 700 residents of The Settlement, many of whom could be seen busily going about their daily chores. There was her small Bell 206 Jetranger helicopter on the parade ground nearby, together with one of the much larger Merlin machines rescued since the flood. To the south of the village the sun reflected on AVCAT storage tanks.

On a ridge and uphill across rough terrain was the eastern gate, some three hours ride from the village. It was their main access point to the outside world and the other establishments that had come under the security umbrella provided by The Settlement. To the west, the stream, dammed in three places, enfolded a large pocket of land, a sheltered haven for the livestock— the cattle and sheep which had become the lifeblood of The Settlement.

She remembered helping to develop the large cultivated area, separated from the livestock by a sturdy fence, now often seen with solar powered tractors busy on some essential activity. In the distance, just visible was the three-metre-high fence and the occasionally used western gate, which delineated their western boundary. When riding up to the northern, forested end of the property, she smiled at the memory of David's negative reaction when she had included the area, illegally at the time, within Settlement boundaries; it had proved to be a wise move and had gone unchallenged by the authorities.

Sometimes during these rides, Tanya reflected, "This place, these people are my *raison d'être*; my whole being is consumed with their survival and nothing is more important than that. I have and will continue to dedicate my whole life to that end."

Tanya, as she often did, had been on an early morning ride. She sat down to breakfast, provided by Nanny, who still lived with them although her duties regarding the children were long past. Tanya's eldest son Chas, dressed in military fatigues, came tearing past muttering, "Academy exercise," as he rushed out. Didier, her younger son, was already seated at the table. Tanya asked, "Anything interesting on today?" Didier was training as a doctor at The Settlement hospital. "Always, there always is," he answered with enthusiasm, "I'll tell you later."

By seven in the morning, Tanya was seated at her rough but solid utilitarian desk, made by a resident from local timber. She was in her neat Settlement office set-up on the top floor of the community centre. She cherished this part of her morning routine—a pause where she could settle herself in readiness for the business of the day. She looked around the well-ordered room: the mixed bag of furniture, some locally made and some rescued during re-supply expeditions from various Sydney warehouses; tables laden with Settlement documents; the comms station, where the transceiver for the jury-rigged phone line had been set up; and the small conference table near the windows, where she would sit during frequent Settlement meetings, often gazing abstractedly out over the parade ground while supposedly listening to droning complaints about water supply, the food supply, and the minutiae of comfort and survival.

The sound of footfalls climbing the winding wooden stairs signalled the arrival of her brother-in-law, General Jonathan Bower, Chief of Defence, who was head of the still-formidable remnants of the Australian Defence Force. Jonathan was tall, athletic, passably handsome, still in his mid-forties and, as he often was, dressed in his military uniform. He eased himself into Tanya's office. "Penny for your thoughts?" he said smiling, noticing Tanya staring off into the distance before she acknowledged his presence.

"They're worth a bloody sight more than that," she smiled. "We'll talk about that later. There's a list of things here I need advice on."

An hour into the meeting with Jonathan, where they discussed the population growth at the neighbouring settlement of the Bandstand and another more distant village of Amazonia, Tanya added, "The success of these operations, apart from their own work ethic, is largely due to our re-supply expeditions for equipment they didn't have, like access to solar power. There are now more than 700 in each place."

"There is also a possible threat from a group settled west of Taree, where members of another group migrated to after an earlier clash with us," she added, waiting for a response; there wasn't any. She could see Jonathan was fully engaged in the conversation despite his reticence, so she continued, "Fuel supplies: we need to talk about fuel…" but before Jonathan could answer, the jury-rigged phone connecting The Settlement with the Bandstand rang. Tanya glanced at the instrument, rarely used now David was no longer there. Some years earlier, David had moved to the Bandstand, firstly to be with Caroline, the leader of the Bandstand group, but also to allow Tanya to grow into the job of running The Settlement, with him out of the way, but still accessible.

She grabbed the phone saying, "Caroline, how nice to hear from you…"

"It's not Caroline. Tanya, we need help!" a male voice yelled. "Don Owens and a mob have taken over here. Caroline has been locked up." Tanya listened for a few minutes to the details. Then "…Aarrgh." The line went dead.

Tanya stood frozen with shock for a few seconds. "Mark, I must get hold of Mark!" she said as she rushed past a confused looking Jonathan. "Takeover, there's a fucking takeover at the Bandstand!"

Tanya ran down the stairs and onto the parade ground, hardly noticing the army Sikorsky S 92 A helicopter and The Settlement's Augusta/Westland Merlin AW 101 parked alongside her own much smaller Bell. She ran past some of the neat rows of cottages to her own cottage where she found her husband Mark, just finishing his breakfast. "Major problem at the bandstand," she said breathlessly. She told him about the interrupted phone call. "We'll need troops…"

"Okay." Mark quickly absorbed what Tanya was telling him; he finished his coffee saying, "I'll get hold of Roger."

Half an hour later, Mark and Tanya, now dressed in flying gear, returned to her office. "There's a major security problem at the Bandstand; the line is now disconnected," she said to Jonathan as she picked up the phone, waving it about. "Dead," she said. "We've scrambled two platoons of our Academy and we need your big Sikorsky to help get them there. Okay?"

Jonathan nodded, "I'll just get ready."

40 troops, including two medics in each platoon, were assembled on the parade ground. Mark, Roger and the platoon commanders helped with inspection checks of weapons and equipment. During the briefing, Tanya said, "Listen-up. That unbalanced fucking clown, Don Owens, is leading a small crew trying to take over the Bandstand. Our mission is to re-take the Bandstand. Take out anyone who is armed."

Mark and Rebecca, Tanya and Jonathan's helicopter pilot, and one of the platoon commanders were scanning a map of the area surrounding the Bandstand village. "Fast rope the troops down to the ground here," she said, jabbing her finger at the map, "well away from the village and go in on foot."

As they took off, Tanya said to Jonathan, who was sitting in the right-hand seat of the chopper, "Roger is organising another platoon. The choppers can drop us all off and return for reinforcements. I'm not going to stuff around; we have to nip this thing in the bud. Any hint of success might give Thor ideas."

Within an hour of the phone call, the two large helicopters had taken off on the 20-minute flight eastwards. Jonathan accompanied Tanya, and Mark was in the Sikorsky to direct the army pilot. The troops assembled a few hundred metres from the Bandstand village and were rapidly organised to move into the settled area. The Settlement Merlin, piloted by Eustace, an American pilot and maintenance engineer they had rescued some years earlier, returned for reinforcements. The army Sikorsky remained on the ground.

Tanya, with Jonathan in tow now dressed in his battledress, and Mark led the Academy troops through the bush quickly and quietly to the village. As they neared their destination they halted the advancing troops as Tanya, Mark, and a three-man fire team crept towards the outskirts of the village. They managed to work their way silently through the village, without being seen, right to the village centre where most of the citizens were gathered.

Tanya said to Mark, "Get the rest of the troops. Spread out. Surround this place, make sure nobody escapes; I need to surprise Owens," she added, as he rushed off.

Tanya approached the gathering in the centre of the village, through the cottages, which had been built in a haphazard, unplanned way, making it easier for Tanya disguise her approach, moving from cottage to cottage. The horror of what was unfolding soon became evident. A group of armed men in the centre were trying to control the terrified villagers by shouting at them and firing shots into the air; there was no real sense of any kind of plan though. Caroline and three others, all naked, were kneeling in front of them. Their hands were tied behind their backs. One man, Geoff, also naked, whom Tanya knew well, sat on a horse with his hands bound behind his back and a noose around his neck. Don Owens' brother, Dave, was vainly trying to throw the other end of the rope over a nearby tree branch while Don was reading a litany of supposed misdemeanours relating to Geoff. With all the noise, Tanya was unable make out the detail of what was being said. The naked body of a woman, Fiona, again someone Tanya knew well, lay nearby. Tanya knew the key to every-thing was Owens himself, and she had to act decisively and quickly; it was all up to her.

Tanya and her detail continued to creep up unseen on the gathering, moving from cottage to cottage. Owens had established himself in a clear area to the side of the community centre in a large thatched area with a concrete base and open sides. An attempt was being made to herd some of the villagers into the centre, which gave Tanya an opportunity to further conceal her movements whilst moving through the gathering. She was aware that Jonathan had hung back a little to stay out of what was a probable firefight, but he remained close enough to witness how Tanya handled herself and the situation. Tanya was just about to move into place to get a clear view of Owens when she spotted Tim in the crowd. Tanya put her finger to her lips and, moving behind Tim, got herself quietly into a position where she had a clear shot at Owens. Tim whispered, "The gangsters are the only ones with weapons." Owens continued droning on:

"You collaborated with Tanya Bower and The Settlement people to enslave us.

"You encouraged more settlers to increase the population here, which reduced our own situation very badly.

"You stopped us developing our own security, making us more and more dependent on The Settlement..." Suddenly, he stopped. Dave had finally got the rope into position. Tanya glanced at her companions, who had moved into position alongside her. All were outwardly calm. Other people in the centre saw what was about to happen and tried to move away causing a surge of movement in the crowd.

Tanya knew she had to act quickly otherwise all would be lost. She pointed: One to the man with the rope, herself to Don Owens and the other two to the remaining members of the insurrection. Holding her breath, she quickly took aim and fired along with her three companions. Four shots cracked out in near unison. Owens flopped to the ground and lay still. Dave's head burst into a halo of pink mist. The other two fired shot after shot into the group of rebels. The horse bolted, with the intended victim, Geoff, falling heavily to the ground. He sensibly kept still. There was a shout from Mark, who had approached with all the Academy troops, reinforced with the second batch of personnel from The Settlement, who were able to disembark much closer to the village. The troops had quickly surrounded the village. "Down! Down! Down!" Mark yelled. Luckily most of the villagers understood the instruction; they dropped to the ground and stayed where they were. Three, in a panic, tried running away, and one was felled by a stray bullet. Tanya and her detail ran up to Owens and kicked away the weapon he was vainly trying to point at her. "Another move and I'll plug you," Tanya growled.

The horse was recaptured by one of her detail. Tanya removed the rope from around Geoff's neck; he was badly shaken and had a broken arm from the fall but she knew the medics would quickly tend to him without being instructed. She tied a monkey fist to the end of the rope and flung it expertly over the tree branch. She yelled to her companions, pointing at Owens, "Get the bastard onto that horse!" Tanya fixed the noose around Owens' neck, and asked one of her companions to tie the end of the rope to a nearby tree, while another bound his hands behind his back with a cable tie. "I'm wounded," gasped Owens. Tanya shrugged.

She ran over to Caroline and her fellow prisoners. Some of Mark's troops had already cut their bonds. "Clothes!" Tanya yelled, "Bring clothes!" She removed her leather jacket and helped Caroline struggle into it. More clothes were brought for Caroline and her companions who, too shaken to say much, quietly sat on chairs that had been brought out for them and the medical team who had advanced with the Academy troops attended where needed.

It took another hour to round up the remaining rebels. Rebecca and her platoon had seen three rebels trying to escape on horseback. They had anticipated the move and set an ambush among a group of trees on the one exit route from the village. Rebecca held her fire until the rebels were within ten metres and then let fly, giving the rest of her group permission to fire. The three rebels hardly knew what hit them and they were all dead before they hit the ground. The horses were recaptured and Rebecca and her platoon returned to the village.

Mark had seen another group trying to organise resistance from one of the nearby houses. He instructed a platoon to surround the house and a hail of bullets poured into the house until a white sheet was thrown from one of the windows. Mark yelled, "Come out with your hands in the air!" Five people emerged into the sunlight with their hands up and were restrained with cable ties. The platoon commander threw a stun grenade and a smoke bomb into the house; a minute later three troops rushed into the house firing blindly as they went in. They emerged a minute later with one dead body.

Several rebels abandoned their weapons and tried to pretend they had had nothing to do with the insurrection. Tanya knew what they were up to and asked several members of the citizenry to help identify anyone who had been part of the rebel group. She also suggested to Mark that a careful house to house search be conducted. Tanya shouted, "Everyone to remain outside! We'll assume anyone found in a house is a rebel!"

Two of the platoons were directed to this task; most of the houses were indeed empty. There was, however, an almighty firefight in two of the houses on the periphery of the village; two soldiers were severely wounded and three more rebel bodies were produced. The troops apprehended a further seven people assumed to be part of the rebel group.

Jonathan

Once the firefight appeared to be over, Jonathan walked into what was still an unstable situation but he was well experienced and knew how to look after himself. In his youth Jonathan had seen a great deal of action with the Australian Army. He was, however, horrified that people who had lived together for years could perpetrate such violence on each other. He was also surprised how well Settlement Academy troops had accounted for themselves, but he thought he could see some weaknesses, which he kept to himself. He had never seen them in live action before. He said to Tanya, "Your troops are well-led and well-directed. I'm impressed." Privately, he thought the fact that there had been an attempt from some of the people in the Bandstand created an area of vulnerability in the areas The Settlement claimed to control.

From the very first time Jonathan met Tanya, when Mark introduced her to the Bower household, he had had mixed feelings about her. He admired her beauty and obvious ability, but distrusted her background; that of a poor migrant family living in what Jonathan considered to be the less than salubrious suburb of Cabramatta in western Sydney. Jonathan had never set foot in Cabramatta. He continued to ponder whether Tanya was as well accepted as she claimed throughout the domains controlled by The Settlement. He thought she was more vulnerable than his father had been and he also wondered if Mark might be a more pliable leader.

TANYA

The stretcher bearers loaded the several wounded Academy troopers into The Settlement chopper. Mark pointed to one, "Serious injury, here, should be treated as a priority."

Tanya said to Caroline, "What do you want done with that animal?" pointing at Owens, still sitting on the horse with noose around his neck.

"No, no more hanging," was the tearful answer, from a pale and shaking Caroline, who was trying to come to terms with what had occurred to the people and the organisation she considered herself responsible for. "Let him down. I suppose he should be attended to."

Tanya nodded, telling the troopers holding Owens to remove him from the horse. She directed a medical team to treat his wounds. Those members of the Bandstand needing attention were separated into citizens and rebels. The citizens were helicoptered to The Settlement hospital where necessary, otherwise they were attended to by the Academy medical teams.

"What do we do with the rebel wounded and the other rebel captives?" asked Tanya of Mark who was standing nearby.

"Serious rebel wounded will have to go to The Settlement hospital," Mark reported. "As for the others, we'll have to try them here; anyone who is found guilty may have a jail sentence imposed." He looked expectantly at Jonathan. "Jonathan,' he said, "as you know, we have no facility to hold prisoners, so is it possible for you to hold those found guilty in prison in Canberra? We're not asking you to run trials or anything," he added hastily, "their fates will be sealed before they come to you."

"What's the alternative?" asked Jonathan, thinking he was being led into a trap. However, he didn't think he could refuse. He could see doing The Settlement such a favour would put them further in debt to him and the military, which suited his wider ambition.

"The only alternative is execution," replied Mark.

There was some whimpering from nearby prisoners, who were within earshot.

"Okay, we'll take them to Canberra," said Jonathan.

"We'll have to try them here and impose the sentences," repeated Mark.

Tanya nodded, "One week. We don't have time to bugger around; this is going to be a very swift process. Jonathan, what are you going to do, stay here or return to Canberra?" She then added, "We'll need your chopper to ship people to jail in Canberra."

"The chopper will have to stay," answered Jonathan.

The Settlement medical teams carefully examined every member of the Bandstand who needed medical attention, including wounded rebels. Caroline refused to go to The Settlement hospital. "I was not actually hurt in any way," she said, "so the priorities should be reserved for those who really need the attention." She helped the medics decide who was to go where. Geoff, the man who fell off the horse, had already been transferred along with six others. Tanya made a note of three rebel wounded who were on the transfer list. "The bastards aren't going to get away with what they did just because they are getting admitted to the hospital. We'll try them in absentia. I have plenty of dope on them here." She waved a sheaf of papers.

It took Tanya another half day to sort out who had been part of the rebel group. She decided to start with two of the lesser lights of the rebel gang. The trials were held in the Bandstand's community centre, so it was open to all who wished to attend. Those awaiting trial were held in a separate house out of sight and earshot of the centre.

"Fred Atkins," began Tanya in a neutral, friendly voice, "perhaps you'll tell me why you decided to join Don Owens on this murderous rampage to try to take over the running of this well-run establishment. What did you hope to gain?"

Fred, a small, slightly overweight middle-aged man with greying hair, blinked in confusion. Tanya hoped her manner would encourage this man and others to confess to participation.

"It's not well run," blustered Atkins. "As Don says…"

"So you admit to being part of the group of people trying to take over?"

"We need a change. It's the only way."

"So you willingly participated?"

"Yes. As Don said, we were being dudded."

"Fred Atkins, you have now admitted participation in this scheme. I will see if I can mitigate your sentence if you give me some more information."

Atkins looked dumbfounded and suspicious.

"What information? I didn't hurt anyone," he said, starting to defend himself.

"I need the names of all the people who were part of Don Owens' scheme."

Atkins gave her the names of people who were already held in custody.

"Not fucking good enough, Mr Atkins, we already have those names. It's beginning to look like 25 years for you, up from 20."

"You don't have the right to do this!" Atkins yelled angrily.

"Oh yes I do, and I will. Those names please."

He gave her a few more names, which Tanya wrote down. She gave the names to Mark.

"Okay, I'll get them picked up," Mark said.

"Fred Atkins, you have admitted complicity in this affair. I sentence you to 20 years in prison. If you were to give me more names, I could reduce it further."

There was no further response from Atkins. He was led away in tears. The next person to be tried was Marge Scobie. Tanya tried the same tactic on her. Marge, a good-looking woman in her early thirties, glared at Tanya.

"Silly cow," she said. "If you think I'm going to fall for that one, think again. Fuck off. I admit nothing."

Tanya didn't hesitate. "Marge Scobie, we have evidence here telling us you shot and killed one James Scobie, your husband. I hereby sentence you to 25 years in prison. Take her away," she said to the guards.

"My children! You can't do this!" yelled a struggling Marge.

"Next," said Tanya.

Two more prisoners were dealt with in the same manner.

"Bring Don Owens," Tanya instructed the guards. They carried him in.

Don Owens, a tall good-looking man in his early forties, had a convincing, confident style about him which Tanya had always distrusted. Obviously still in pain, although his wounds had been bound up, he looked at Tanya from the chair provided. "I should be in hospital, like some of the others. You have no rights in this matter."

Tanya ignored the outburst.

"Don Owens, you have been brought before this court to be tried on very serious charges."

"You have no jurisdiction. I do not recognise your authority."

Tanya hesitated for a moment and then read out a list of the charges against Owens, provided to her by Caroline and another member of the Bandstand staff. Mark had checked it. Owens tried to drown her out by shouting obscenities. Tanya had him gagged. When she had finished she said,

"Don Owens, based on the evidence presented, you have been convicted of three counts of murder. I am also cognisant of the fact that your activities put the lives of many of the people here at the Bandstand at risk. I therefore sentence you to death by firing squad. Sentence to be imposed as soon as possible. There is no right of appeal."

Owens was silent for a moment as reality struck home. He was locked up in isolation, under guard.

Over the next week, under the same regime, the rest of the rebel group were tried, some individually and some in batches, including those in The Settlement hospital who were tried in absentia. All were sentenced to 20 years or more in a military prison. Tanya thought Jonathan seemed happy to be seen as a significant resource in terms of being able to house the people sentenced to prison. He looked on, as those sentenced were all sent to Canberra in the army helicopter, under Settlement Academy guard.

"How are we going to handle Owens?" asked Mark.

"He's been sentenced to death," answered Tanya. "We should not back off on that one. Jonathan, maybe you could carry out the sentence in Canberra?"

Jonathan didn't hesitate. Looking at her he said, "You imposed the sentence. You carry it out. It should be done immediately, in public."

"Mark, detail a squad. I'll command," responded Tanya, without hesitation.

Mark barked, "Sergeant, I need eight members from your squad. You are to remove their weapons. You are to load five rifles with one live round each and three with blank rounds and then return the weapons to each trooper. Once the execution is complete you are to again remove the weapons from each trooper and you will personally clean them before returning them. Is that clear?" "Yes, Sir," he replied.

Owens was brought out and tied to a tree. Tanya marched the eight troopers (four men and four women) to the execution site. Caroline, Mark, and Jonathan were in attendance as well as all the Bandstand villagers. All Settlement troops were lined up on parade, including two medics. Tanya had armed herself with a .45 Webley revolver which she kept in the Merlin.

Tanya said to him, "Don Owens, you have been sentenced to death for murder by firing squad by a legally constituted court. Do you have anything to say?"

Owens was silent, but Tanya could see a wet patch spread over the front of his trousers. Tanya lined the troopers up fifteen metres from Owens.

"Aim for the heart, you will each fire one shot."

"READY!" The squad levelled their rifles at Owens chest.

"AIM!" Muscles braced, breaths were slowly expelled and held.

"FIRE!" Tanya called and dropped her arm. Triggers were squeezed in unison. Owens slumped against his bonds as the shots were fired.

A grim-faced Tanya marched up to the body and tested for signs of life. There were none. She gave instructions for the body to be cut down and the burial party organised beforehand took over. Tanya had instructed that the gravesite be located in a remote place, so it could not be found. She marched the firing squad back to their platoon.

With all the activity going on and given Caroline's fragile state of mind, Tanya had not been able to have a sensible conversation with her regarding the nightmare they had all just participated in. The day before Tanya and The Settlement crew were due to return home, and when the situation at the Bandstand had started to return to normal, Tanya managed to get Caroline on her own. Trying to keep the edge out of her voice, she asked her, "Do you have any inkling why any of this happened? I thought the Bandstand was the last place where we would have trouble."

Caroline looked miserable. "You warned me about Owens," she said. "I took no notice. I really thought we had everyone under control, even after David died. It seems Owens was spared by Demetriou at the time of the raid, perhaps as some sort of insurance, if Demetriou ever came back. [Demetriou had led a raid on the Bandstand, some years back. Tanya had led a posse which ruthlessly killed Demetriou and all his men] I dismissed him as a crank. I should have known better. I suppose he thought that with David gone it would be easy to take over and impose control. Anyway, we'll soldier on. Four of us died in this fracas," she let slip a few tears, "all of them good people and that's not including a dozen or more rebels who died and a further 15 who will spend most of the rest of their lives in jail in Canberra."

"Do you need any further assistance from us?" asked Tanya. "I've had the phone line restored."

"If you could leave a few Settlement troops here for two months, I think we would all feel a bit safer. They could also help with some of the rebuilding."

"Okay, 20 troops for two months it is," responded Tanya. "Anything else?"

Caroline stood up and hugged Tanya. "You've saved us twice now. I don't know how to say thank you enough. I hope it won't be necessary again."

Tanya organised a gathering of the whole Settlement community to celebrate their homecoming and the successful operation to save the Bandstand from destruction. As was often the case a barbecue was held on the parade ground, having first removed the helicopters to safety. The crowd gathered was silent as she addressed them.

"You are all to be congratulated; the discipline and professionalism of the Academy is unrivalled. General Bower, who has never seen us in action before, was, I am sure, impressed, as was I. As a community, this latest clash tells us how critical the Academy continues to be to our own survival, and how important it remains in terms of upholding the values we all hold dear."

After the speech, she and Mark pinned medals onto each participant in the Bandstand campaign. She pinned a medal onto Mark and then Jonathan, to his surprise. Mark pinned a medal onto Tanya. Earlier, she had visited the wounded in hospital and spent time with their families. She satisfied herself that all would make a complete recovery in time.

Once routines had been re-established at The Settlement, two days after returning from dealing with the nightmare at the Bandstand, Tanya and Jonathan returned to her office to continue their discussions on Settlement issues, almost as if nothing had happened.

"Fuel, we were talking about fuel," said Tanya. "As you know we have no facility to replenish the fuel tanks here, because there is no road. The big Merlins, based in Newcastle, often dump most of what they have on board, into our tanks, which is just enough to keep the Jetranger going."

"I have some thoughts on the matter, but I will discuss that with you at a later date, when we have resolved a few other issues first."

Tanya looked at Jonathan speculatively wondering if he was hiding something.

"Ten of our Academy personnel are coming to you to train with your elite battalion," Tanya said. "Looking to the future I wonder if five of them could be included in an engineering group and five in the elite battalion."

Jonathan shrugged, "Certainly, makes perfect sense to me."

As far as Tanya was concerned the discussions were fruitful and helpful. Before the discussion was complete it appeared to Tanya that Jonathan still had something on his mind, so she waited to see if he would unburden himself. She said to him, "I think our troops did a wonderful job in dealing with the Bandstand."

He shrugged, "Mark seems to do a good job at maintaining standards."

She changed tack to see if she could prise out of him what was on his mind, saying, "I also need to talk a bit more about Mark." Jonathan nodded uncomfortably, "What about him?"

"He had an affair with Virginia."

"Yes."

"He also took advantage of Susan's vulnerability after her child was murdered. He made her pregnant. The situation was saved when Hercules took a fancy to her and, with some urging from Chloe and me, Susan agreed to marry him. Her child, Mars, was fathered by Mark though."

"Mnn, I wish I didn't know that."

"Part of the trouble is that he is somewhat frustrated by the role he occupies here. He knows I'm the right person to run the show, but the fact he is not in charge irks him, it makes him feel inadequate."

"What do you want me to do?" asked Jonathan after a moment's hesitation.

"He does a very good job on the security here, but I wondered if, with your help, his remit could somehow be extended, beyond just the interests of The Settlement."

"Do you want him out of the way?"

"No, he does a good job here. The Academy people revere him. His peccadilloes started when David made it clear to him that it was me and not him who would eventually take over the leadership."

"You call them peccadilloes; aren't they more serious than that?"

"I don't think so," she responded with a degree of uncertainty.

"I see," Jonathan said noncommittally. "I can always use a person with Mark's capabilities." He wondered if a rift between Mark and Tanya could serve his own purposes, where a possibly recalcitrant Tanya would be replaced by a 'real' member of the Bower family and a man at that. He continued, "What do you want me to do? There is the Kanangra Boyd settlement, which could benefit from some improvement in the security there, but that raises the question of

Virginia who, as I have already told you, lives there and in fact is one of the leading lights in that community."

"Virginia has the model of how we established the Academy here. Why didn't they just copy that?" asked Tanya.

"Partly resources, I think," said Jonathan. "They started their settlement a long time after ours was set up and had other priorities. They are now beginning to wish they had paid more attention to that aspect. There is a hostile group west of Nowra, in the Morton National Park, south of where they are, who they think will cause them trouble in the not too distant future."

"Your main base is much closer than we are." Tanya noted Jonathan's use of the word 'ours', which she supposed indicated some sort of ownership of the creation and survival of The Settlement.

"Our priority remains the Northern Command area and holding the line up there. And as you know, our doctrine with regards to disputes of this kind is that they be resolved locally. We could help if things became desperate, I suppose."

"We also have to worry about our own security," said Tanya. "In the near future we'll have to deal with those threats to our north; we think some of those assholes we chased out of Barrington Tops have joined up with another wild bunch somewhere between Taree and Port Macquarie. You saw what happened with that fuckwit Owens at the Bandstand. We must also keep an eye on smartass Thor who, given half a chance, may try something on. Either way, we have Chloe there who would alert us to any shenanigans Thor might be planning."

"Thor! I thought you had all that sewn up with all the inter-marriage caper and so on."

"We have. I still don't completely trust the bastard though. Different values..."

"Okay," said Jonathan finally, "we both have plenty to think about. How do you want to go from here?"

"I'll have a discussion with Mark and then maybe we could meet at Kanangra," replied Tanya. She got up and as she had always done kissed Jonathan chastely on the cheek as he left.

While it was on her mind, Tanya sought Chas out. "I've included you and another nine of our best from the Academy to train with and be embedded with Jonathan's elite troops in Canberra. I do not want there to be any overt association with The Settlement, so I will enlist you under name of Bolt. Mark and I are in the process of submitting a full proposal to Jonathan, which will include your complete training regime. My expectation is that you and two others will be commissioned as 2nd Lieutenants."

Seeing Mark was relaxed and at ease one evening after dinner Tanya decided to raise the question of extending Mark's responsibilities beyond his duties at The Settlement.

"Mark, I can see that you are still somewhat, err, frustrated by the role you play here, with David no longer with us and me in charge."

"We've had this discussion before. I've accepted the role I play, I don't know why you keep raising it," he said.

"Well, I was talking to Jonathan the other day, just using him as a sounding board on various Settlement issues. When we had finished he asked casually how the Academy was going and if there were any major security threats on the horizon."

Mark glared at her saying nothing.

"I told him he should talk to you on the subject; we all know those Taree assholes are going to be a problem at some stage," continued Tanya. "The Bandstand malarkey took us by surprise, where you and the Academy did brilliantly by the way. I know Jonathan was very surprised by the discipline and high standard of our troops."

Mark visibly relaxed but again remained silent. Tanya could see he was pleased with the compliment.

"He then asked if I thought it would be manageable from our point of view for your security remit to extend beyond the immediate boundaries of the wider Settlement; he obviously knows your security responsibilities include Newcastle and the Vikings."

"What did you tell him?"

"I said I would discuss the idea with you but, subject to anything you might say, I thought it might be a good idea."

"Do you know what he has in mind?' asked Mark, leaning forward.

"He mentioned the Kanangra place, saying they have similar values to ours."

"Yes, yes."

"Jonathan thinks their security is inadequate, and this is a real problem since there is a threat from another wild bunch to the south of them."

"Why doesn't he sort it out himself? He's much closer than we are." Mark sounded disappointed.

"You know the reasons. I suggest we meet him there, at the Kanangra settlement, to understand what is needed and go from there."

They continued an animated discussion for another half hour, almost like it was in the past, thought Tanya. She knew she should tell Mark about Virginia's presence and her role at the Kanangra settlement, but she held back, savouring the apparent renewal of her relationship with Mark.

CHAPTER 2

Kanangra

TANYA

Within a few days, Tanya arranged to meet Jonathan at the Kanangra settlement. She used the recently jury-rigged line connecting The Settlement, Jonathan's office in Canberra and The Settlement's developing base in the port of Newcastle. When she discussed the proposed meeting with Mark, he said, "Great. I think we should also include Stephanie in this. From what you say, she has done a great job with the Amazons and with Thor and the Vikings. She therefore has experience in how to deal with other independent surviving places. She is also very smart."

"It's just an exploratory visit. If we need to we can include her later."

"If we are going to include her at all it might as well be from the start."

"Okay we'll pick her up on the way," said Tanya, not wishing to prolong the argument.

During the intervening days, Tanya tried to find an opportunity to tell Mark about Virginia's role at the Kanangra settlement; but whenever the opportunity arose, courage always failed her.

"It's only about only about 60 ks as the crow flies to Kanangra," Tanya told Mark as they took off in the Bell which had recently been completely rebuilt by Eustace, "but we need to divert to Amazonia to pick up Stephanie. You can brief Stephanie and I'll talk to Irene. She gets all uptight if we just rush in there and rush out again."

Amazonia was one of several establishments falling under the security blanket provided by The Settlement. The 'women only' mantra of the place had gradually disintegrated. There were now a dozen families from The Settlement ensconced there as permanent residents; many of the single Amazon women had married men from The Settlement and even from the Viking establishment. As they came in to land, Tanya was able to admire the clean neat setup, with small cottages surrounding a newly mown green space, the extensive cultivated area and, beyond that, the substantial flock of merino sheep. Despite the original suspicions of Irene and the leadership of what became known as Amazonia, Tanya reflected on how the Amazon village had gained immeasurably from the association with The Settlement with solar power throughout the establishment. The re-supply expeditions provided them with solar powered tractors, computers, milking machines, dishwashers and washing machines to name but a few.

Irene always took great pride in showing Tanya around the Amazon establishment, almost as if all the new development was entirely her own idea; the help from The Settlement was almost never mentioned, so any visit always took longer than anticipated and this visit was no exception. The place was indeed a spectacular example of what had been achieved by the combination of the technical innovations provided by The Settlement and the real work ethic of the members of Amazonia, as it was still called.

"The next job is to make the dairy more productive," Irene announced. "I need help from your fellow at The Settlement to help me make butter and cheese from our dairy produce."

Taking off in the late afternoon, Tanya said, "There'll just be enough light to allow us to land safely at Kanangra."

The open areas between Amazonia and the southern Blue Mountains were, as expected, deserted; roads were still littered with the rusting wrecks of old vehicles. They crossed what had been the main road over the Blue Mountains, from Sydney to the outback towns of Orange and Bathurst and beyond, and passed over Warragamba dam, which in the past was the main source of fresh water for Sydney and was almost the same size as Sydney Harbour, now always full to overflowing since there was no offtake. Tanya wondered for how many years the dam wall would hold; she thought it would be generations before the facility would ever be needed again. A further few minutes were spent flying over the beautiful pristine bush, with its faint tinge of blue. Before landing Tanya circled the village which she could see consisted of a neat cluster of about 30 houses perched on the side of a hill and paddocks with contented looking animals stretched out below the houses to an extensive cultivated area. The whole area was surrounded by thick native bush. As far as Tanya could see there was no sign of any kind of access road. "Sensible," she thought, "one of the reasons for their survival." The army Sikorsky was already parked. "Jonathan," said Mark pointing. They landed on a small parade ground next to the community centre.

With the engine switched off and the rotors stilled, the helicopter door was opened. Tanya, followed by Mark and Stephanie, clambered out of the machine to be warmly greeted by a smiling Virginia and several others with Jonathan in the background. Tanya noticed Mark's increased interest and his flushed face when he saw the small reception committee was headed by Virginia. He glanced curiously in her direction.

Tanya tried not to notice the looks and the slightly longer-than-necessary handshake between Virginia and Mark. Stephanie was introduced, "Oh yes," laughed Virginia, "I remember you, during my visits to The Settlement." Mark and Tanya were shown to a cottage in the centre of the village.

STEPHANIE

"Stephanie, I have a spare room in my cottage for you. We'll have dinner at seven, which gives you time to have a shower. A hot shower, thanks to what I learnt about solar from my visits to your place," commented Virginia.

On the short walk over to Virginia's cottage, Stephanie kept her eyes and ears open, saying little but listening intently to what Virginia was telling her. She remembered the competent likeable person Virginia seemed to be, during her visits to The Settlement now more than ten years previous. "Well here we are," said Virginia smiling, as she opened her unlocked door and walked in. Stephanie noticed the cottage was much the same size as the other cottages in the village. In the dusk, she was unable to see much of her surroundings, a deficiency she would rectify in the morning.

Stephanie looked around with admiration at the modest but serviceable cottage belonging to Virginia: the lounge with a small dining table at one end and an open plan kitchen as part of the set-up. There appeared to be three bedrooms and a bathroom with a separate toilet down the passage. She was shown to her room. After showering, while relaxing in Virginia's small comfortable lounge, a boy who Stephanie determined was aged about ten came bustling in. "Stephanie, this is my son, Mark. Mark this is Stephanie, who was brought up in the place I have often talked about, called The Settlement." He greeted her politely. "Good trip down?" Virginia asked Stephanie. "Yes, it was easy, no problem with the weather. They had to fetch me from Amazonia; I don't live at The Settlement." She briefly explained the origins of Amazonia. The small talk continued mainly about the deserted pristine native bush on the way, while young Mark ate his dinner.

"Finish your homework and go to bed in good time," said Virginia.

"Yes, Mum," he said, almost tiredly, but he looked up smiling as Stephanie and Virginia stepped out on their way to the community centre and dinner.

TANYA

At dinner, which included the whole community, Virginia stood up saying, "I would like to introduce you all to Tanya Bower, who is the leader of a place called The Settlement which I have often mentioned, her husband Mark, who is responsible for security there, General Jonathan Bower, from the Australian Military, and last but not least I would also like to introduce you to Stephanie, who is responsible for a village falling under The Settlement's security blanket, called Amazonia. Please make them all welcome."

There was enthusiastic clapping from the assembled throng.

"The reason for this high-powered visit is the danger now posed to our own security. I can assure our visitors that there is a great deal of interest in their visit."

During the meal Tanya asked, "Virginia, could give us a brief history of the settlement here, as background for us."

"Of course." As they ate she began, "This place was founded by the Dunstan family, just the father and his two sons, only about five years before the flood. I joined them a few months before the flood and because of my army background, I took on the responsibility for security. We formed an Academy on much the same lines as you have. A few years after the flood, when the boys had grown up and were in their 20s, they started to take control and they ran everything on behalf of the Dunstan family trying to relegate the rest of us to the level of serfs. The father tried to stop this but he was getting old and then he suddenly died, under suspicious circumstances. Meanwhile,

I was still running the Academy so with a few people I trusted, and I staged what can only be described as a coup. One night after a drunken rampage when the Dunstans were asleep we surrounded their house and the boys were arrested and tied up. I had the body of the old man exhumed and, despite decomposition, we found his neck had been broken. We do not have the facilities for the niceties of a trial. Many in the community wanted to execute them immediately, but I managed to persuade them otherwise. So, a half-dozen of us took the boys to the boundaries of what was known as the Kanangra Boyd National Park and they were left with a horse and a rifle each and told that if they ever came near the Kanangra settlement again they would be shot on sight. We now know they joined a group in the Morton National Park. There have been a few incursions from those people in past months and they pose a significant threat to our community so we need help in dealing with them. Those boys are bent on control. Any dissent is dealt with ruthlessly. We have one settler here who objected to the way the community over there was being manipulated; he heard they were going to eliminate him so he ran away, with his wife and two children, leaving everything."

"When did the Dunstans leave?" asked Tanya.

"Five years at least," answered Virginia.

"Have you ever visited the Morton people?"

"No; we had no knowledge of any establishment there until two years or so ago. We have been very busy developing this place, making sure of our survival. Something we have most definitely achieved," said Virginia proudly. "Our biggest problem now is the bloody people in Morton."

"I think it would be useful if we could meet the people who escaped from Morton," offered Mark.

Virginia smiled at a man with an Arab appearance sitting at another table, "They are here. We'll make more formal introductions tomorrow."

Nothing was said regarding expectations of how The Settlement could help Kanangra. Neither operation had any real knowledge of the other. Jonathan was the catalyst bringing both parties together. Tanya sought to clarify the situation by asking Virginia, "How do you run this place?

"Mnn, maybe we are one step ahead of you in that regard," Virginia smiled. "We run on wholly democratic lines. There is an election for a mayor and six councillors, every four years, who are obliged to work with each other. I have now been elected mayor twice. The election is run very rigorously and independently by a man who brooks no interference and who is not on council. Everyone over the age of 18 is required to vote; we only have about 100 voters. We also have a quarterly meeting in the community centre where there is a report back on activities to the community and we answer any questions that arise. There is no secrecy about anything anyway, so most people know what's going on, on a daily basis. The most pressing issue now is security. I can assure you that there is considerable anticipation and interest in your visit."

The discussion continued around the security risk to the Kanangra settlement and what could be done about it.

"What do we know about the Morton village? How many people live there, and how well armed they are? In the morning, we can talk to the family that escaped," Tanya said as she brought the discussion to a close. "Okay. We'll sleep on it."

As they were preparing for bed, Mark said to Tanya, "Did you know that Virginia was part of the set-up here?"

Tanya shrugged saying, "Jonathan mentioned it, before David's funeral."

"And you didn't think to tell me?"

"I didn't think it was that important."

Mark shrugged and glared at her without saying anything further.

STEPHANIE

Once the dinner was over Stephanie walked with Virginia back to her cottage. The sky was clear and there was a half moon. Stephanie reflected to herself on the peace and tranquil beauty of the place.

They spent a few minutes in Virginia's lounge, chatting before they went to bed. Stephanie was intrigued with young Mark; to her his paternity was obvious but she hesitated to ask a direct personal question, so instead she asked, "What influenced you to call your son Mark?"

Virginia laughed, looked Stephanie straight in the eye and said, "It's pretty obvious, isn't it? I named him after his father."

Stephanie blushed despite herself. "Yes, I suppose it is. Does Mark Bower know?"

"No, he doesn't even know young Mark exists. I never told him. I only realised I was pregnant a month or two after what turned out to be my last visit to The Settlement and by that time I was committed to coming here. I decided I could deal with the situation by myself; I always felt a bit guilty about the relationship anyway, with Mark being married to Tanya. Nobody here turned a hair when they found I was pregnant. I have always more than pulled my weight of course."

"As soon as Tanya sets eyes on the boy, she will know who the father is. What are you going to do then?"

"We'll see how it pans out," she said. "She knew Mark and I were having an affair," she added wistfully.

"Are you in love with him?"

"I was; it's been such a long time since I saw him. I don't know any more. Turning to you," said Virginia, squirming. "Two questions: One, what do you do at The Settlement? And two, since we are being so personal, are there any men in your life?"

"When The Settlement took responsibility for security at Amazonia, Tanya asked me to be responsible for developments there. I am a qualified vet, by the way, so that in itself helps. It was a fairly ticklish situation; I needed to get things done without upsetting Irene, who set the operation up and still is the boss there. We have been nothing but constructive; our re-supply operations have provided them with all sorts of solar powered equipment, which has transformed the place. We have also used the operation as a jumping off point for development to unoccupied areas to our east. We are also a bit closer to Thor and the Vikings, which means I can keep an eye on what they are up to." She hesitated for a moment. "The Vikings have very different values to the ones espoused by The Settlement."

"Sounds wonderful; you always were a great talent," said Virginia. "What about the men in your life?"

"Before I answer that, how do you feel about Tanya?" asked Stephanie,

"I am in awe of her competence and ruthlessness. She made it quite clear to me that she knew Mark and I were having an affair, but she has never been unfair or unkind to me. She seems to take it all in her stride. Has there been any hint of another man in her life?"

"No, I'm certain she has had no involvement with any other men at The Settlement. I know of at least one who made an approach but came off second best. We would have known if there was any other liaison but there has never been so much as a hint of impropriety, if that's the right word," Stephanie continued.

"What about me and Mark?"

"Oh yes, we all knew about that, you couldn't keep your eyes off each other during your visits, and all those unnecessary trips to Canberra, it added up to one thing. We didn't discuss it much; it really had nothing to do with any of us."

"Why did Tanya put up with it?"

"Don't really know. Her priority has always been The Settlement and her children, of course. If it didn't suit her I am sure she would have dumped him years ago."

"And the men in your life?"

Stephanie laughed. "You keep saying men in the plural as if they are all running around me with their tongues hanging out. Nothing could be further from the truth. I seem to scare them all off. I'm not a nun, in case you wanted to know, but I most definitely have not found anyone who I would want to spend much time with," she added, "married or unmarried."

"Where do you see yourself going, in the future, as far as The Settlement is concerned?" asked Virginia.

"Don't know. I'm stretched where I am, and I think I've done a very good job. We all need to recognise our survival as a community is far from guaranteed; in fact, it's under threat. So to answer the question, all my efforts will be directed to strengthening our community and I now include you in that; we do have to tame or get rid of the thuggish elements around us. They have the potential to destroy us and themselves just as effectively as any tsunami. I've mentioned the Vikings and Thor, they seem to be under control right now, but I don't trust the bastard. If he saw a chance to shaft us I think he would, marriage alliances notwithstanding."

"Marriage alliances?"

Stephanie briefly explained the two marriage alliances between the Vikings and the Bowers. Stephanie hesitated, looking at Virginia, wondering how much she should tell her.

"Go on," said Virginia.

"Susan's marriage to Hercules, Thor's son, was a bit too rushed and her baby appeared rather too quickly. I am sure Hercules is not the father. They call him Mars, by the way."

"Who is the father, then?"

"I see the child every couple of weeks. There is no doubt Mark is the father."

Virginia looked devastated, but said, "Poor Tanya; she knows about this?"

"I'm sure she does. The pragmatic arrangements for the wedding and the speed at which it was done have Tanya's fingerprints all over it. Chloe was and remains very close to Susan, I expect she was a party to it all as well. I'm not close to Chloe, so I have not dared broach the subject with her."

They embraced briefly before going to their respective rooms.

"Thank you for telling me all that," said Virginia, "I won't breathe a word to anyone of course."

Before she went to sleep Stephanie spent a few minutes thinking about Virginia. She felt slightly uneasy about her revelations regarding Mark and Susan's son Mars. "What is done is done," she thought. "Virginia's obviously smart and strong. She wouldn't have been accepted as an officer in the Australian Army if that wasn't the case." She smiled to herself in the dark. "If we can keep her on side she will be a wonderful addition to the wider Settlement family," was her final thought as sleep took over.

Tanya

The next morning, the meeting was held in the community centre as soon as breakfast had been cleared away. To Tanya's surprise, Jonathan took it upon himself to chair the meeting. He opened the meeting by asking Virginia, "Perhaps you could tell us what first prize is, as far as you are concerned?" Virginia included and re-introduced Kanangra's six councillors to the meeting. Tanya took an instinctive dislike to councillor Bruno Saunders.

Tanya noticed Virginia moved herself to the other side of the table when Mark plonked himself next to her, as he rushed in, just before the meeting started, "Went riding with some of the kids; great fun," he explained.

"All we really want is to eliminate the threat and to live in peace with our neighbours," answered Virginia. "If we, with your help, blasted them out of existence." She hesitated and added thoughtfully,

"It sorts of reduces us to their level, and somehow, if we did that, I'm certain it would come back to haunt us."

"Virginia, could you ask the fellow who escaped from Morton to join us?" asked Tanya.

"Already arranged, as you suggested earlier. He's just outside," said Virginia.

Jonathan looked surprised at the interruption and tried to hide his irritation. He said nothing though.

"What resources do we have to deal with these Morton people?" Tanya continued, "Virginia, why don't we start with you."

"We have a platoon of 30 in our small Academy, but we only have two file of mounts; that's 20 mounted, well-armed and trained," she replied.

"Jonathan, what about you?"

Jonathan replied, glaring at Tanya, "Colonel Bower, I would rather this issue was dealt with locally, with local resources," he said, unable to hide his irritation. "I don't think the military should be involved in every local dispute anyway. If you got into trouble we would certainly come to your rescue, of course."

Tanya took no notice of his attitude.

"Mark, what about us?"

"Say 250 max, with all our other commitments. We have to realise they would be away for two or three months."

"What about the helicopters?" asked Tanya.

"If we wanted to blast them out of existence we could use them. Two armed with machine guns would do the job."

Darkly handsome Suleiman Ahmed was ushered into the room. He was drying his hands on his trousers.

"I was working in the gardens," he explained.

"Suleiman's skill has helped to transform our vegetable production," explained Virginia. "Please tell us the story you told us when you first got here," she asked.

"Well, everything was fine in the Morton settlement. We went there a few months before the flood. The place worked in much the same way as this one does. There was a man, Arthur, who funded the whole operation and we all mucked in and really got everything going. These Dunstan boys arrived a few years after the flood. To start with they seemed very nice, although I thought it was rather odd that they refused to tell us anything about where they had come from. They made all sorts of suggestions as to how we might improve things, some of which worked, but it gave them more and more control; they removed everyone's firearms, for example. Then one day, Arthur just disappeared and there was no explanation. By then the Dunstan boys were very much in charge. Some of us asked a few too many questions, I suppose, and one of those with whom I had cooperated also disappeared without explanation. I realised what was happening, so one night I took my family, stole four horses and after almost two weeks on the run, we stumbled across this place. We had no idea it was here. We had to hide in a cave for two days when the Dunstans almost caught up with us. Naturally enough, Virginia was very suspicious about who we were, especially when I mentioned the Dunstans, but I think by now we've proved our worth." He smiled at Virginia.

"If the Dunstans left what would happen?" asked Tanya.

"The people there would probably need some help. They have all been so used to obeying orders from whoever was in charge, but there is no basic evil in the place. People are grateful to have survived the flood and want to make sure that can continue. They certainly need some leadership though."

"Could you provide that leadership?' Tanya continued.

"Maybe, but like we had in Shepparton—if there was a genuine democratic process in place I am sure that would throw up appropriate leadership and they could move on from there."

"You don't see yourself as part of that community anymore?" asked a surprised Tanya.

Suleiman shrugged. "One can only uproot a plant and replant it so many times before it withers and dies. I could help, but we are well settled here and would choose to stay, if we are allowed."

"You can certainly stay here. I am sure there is nobody in Kanangra who would disagree with me," said Virginia.

"So if the Dunstans were removed, the place would probably return to its old way of doing things?" Tanya persisted.

"Some others seem to have taken up the Dunstan way of doing things. One would have to make sure that they were happy to be part of a new regime," replied Suleiman.

Tanya noticed Bruno Saunders, leaning forward and paying far too much attention to the point.

"How many in the Morton settlement?" asked Tanya.

Bruno cut in to answer the question, waving Suleiman away.

"Less than 50 adults and 40 or so children; one doesn't have to worry about many of the adults, few have any sort of military training or background. The only people worth worrying about are the Dunstans and four or five of the rest," he said.

Tanya summarised, after further discussion, "We'll send you 30 of our people, under Stephanie; they will then be joined by your 20 Academy people, Virginia. You can then lead the whole group to Morton, arrest the Dunstans, leave some of our people at Morton under Stephanie to make sure there is no unrest there, and I think that should do it."

Mark started to say something but Tanya gave him a nudge under the table, so he remained silent. All the while Tanya had been looking at Suleiman, almost with an attitude of 'do you approve?' She noticed Suleiman looking thoroughly disconcerted at the proposal, but he remained silent. Bruno dashed off as the meeting broke up and people went on to deal with their respective duties.

As they left the community centre Tanya took Virginia by the arm and said, "A quiet word, with Stephanie." Mark looking offended, saying stiffly, "I arranged to play football with some of the kids." Tanya held his arm and whispered, "I'll see you after the game." Mark had a surprised, but happier, look on his face as he walked off.

"Mnn," Tanya said to Virginia and Stephanie as they walked outside, "Lets watch the football." She directed them towards where Mark was organising two teams of both boys and girls. As they watched the kick-off from the centre line, she asked, "Tell me about the other councillors, particularly Bruno?"

"They have all been here since the beginning, including Bruno."

"So they all knew the Dunstan brothers?"

"Yes, why do you want to know?" asked Virginia defensively.

"There is something pretty odd going on," said Tanya, "I'm getting a feeling that Suleiman, Bruno, or both of them know a shit-load more than they are letting on. Why did Bruno answer the question of the numbers at Morton, when it was directed at Suleiman?"

"There have been several discussions on the number of people at Morton. The figure is no surprise to me," Virginia growled.

"50 adults? Bullshit! Too small to survive. And all that crap about firearms. Most people don't come and settle in the bush without some knowledge of firearms, for God's sake, or if they are unprepared they very rapidly address that deficiency." Tanya rattled off her concerns. "What do you think, Stephanie?

"Suleiman's elaborate story of his trip through the bush to here is a bit too perfect," Stephanie responded. "Did he ride straight here with directions from the Dunstan boys? There is clearly some sort of competition or struggle between Suleiman and Bruno. Also, both failed to mention anything about avoiding a conflict between the two establishments. There seems to be an assumption that there will be conflict."

"I watched both of them during the meeting," Stephanie added thoughtfully. "There is no love lost between the pair, I can tell you that. I agree there is something going on. If I could speculate, Bruno has remained in touch with the Dunstans since they were expelled from here. The appearance of Suleiman has possibly put a spoke in Bruno's ambitions. It's also just possible that Suleiman was sent here as a plant. We need to find out more before we finalise our plans."

Virginia stood there momentarily dumbstruck. When she recovered her composure she said, "Okay, I don't believe any of that, but if you're right we'll need another plan." They watched the football for several more minutes. Tanya started watching the game more closely; to her intense distress she noticed a ten-year-old boy who was the spitting image of Mark. She looked again; there was no doubt. She stepped away from the others. A hollow feeling invaded her stomach. With an enormous effort, she pulled herself together. She returned to the other two taking Virginia by the arm and moving away from Stephanie. She said sharply, "That boy, the one who looks like Mark, he's your son isn't he? What's his name?"

"Mark Andrews," answered Virginia shakily.

Tanya continued, in the same vein, trying to disregard her churning emotions, "I ignored a letter I received from one of the army officers who came up to train our Academy people about ten years ago, telling me you were pregnant. As always Settlement issues took precedence, and Settlement issues will take precedence now."

Tanya and a shaken Virginia rejoined Stephanie. Guided by Tanya, they started to walk back towards Virginia's cottage, having lost interest in the football. She went on, noticing that Virginia had gone deathly pale. "We'll need another plan. The only conversation we'll have, Virginia, for the time being, is about the plan we agreed. If I'm right and I'm sure I am, there is something pretty odd going on."

"What are we going to do? We need to be sure you are not mistaken," said a very worried Virginia.

"Put Suleiman and Bruno and their teenage children under surveillance," responded Tanya. "If they're working with the Dunstans, one or both of them will eventually have to make contact, and we will be there when they do. Have you got a real bushman who you trust and who can be relied on to keep his mouth shut? We need three recon teams; one for each surveillance target and one to scout Morton."

Tanya could see Virginia was in a bit of a state. She said to herself, "She must have realised I would get to know about young Mark; yet she still agreed to invite us here: interesting! What is done is done, I'll get everyone to focus on the threat to this place. We can't afford to fail here."

When they got to Virginia's cottage, there was an uneasy silence as they all sat down. Tanya said, "I must emphasise that there should be no discussion regarding the fact that we have realised there may be a problem here, which may require a change to the plan we agreed earlier." She glanced out of the window and saw that the football game had come to an end. Mark Bower had a few brief words with his son who ran over towards the cottage. A shudder went through Tanya, which she unsuccessfully tried to hide from the others. Young Mark burst through the door. Tanya got up signalling Stephanie to follow her, leaving the cottage as young Mark assailed his mother with an account of the wonderful afternoon he and the other children had had with 'that nice man Mark'.

"Dinner at seven, the same as last night," said a nervous Virginia to their retreating backs. Tanya waved acknowledgement.

"So, obviously you know about young Mark?" asked Stephanie, as they walked the short distance to the cottage Tanya and Mark were sharing.

Tanya nodded, trying to hide her churning emotions, "Yes, but as always the absolute priority is the survival and development of The Settlement, nothing else matters."

"What are we going to do about Morton?"

"We'll discuss it on the way home. Anyone who bears us ill will is going to be fucked out of sight, just watch me."

"Tanya," said Stephanie, carefully, "Virginia will be in a bit of a state about what you seem to have unearthed. At best, she will feel you've made a fool of her; at worst, she may try to undermine you somehow." She added after hesitating for a moment, "She needs some reassurance especially in view of the situation with Mark."

Tanya stopped walking. She looked at Stephanie, "Thank you. I was just thinking about how to resolve the position we find ourselves in with regards to the problem with Morton and not worrying too much about people's feelings. Virginia needs time to establish that someone here is playing a double game. Reinforcing that will keep her on side. She needs us more than we need her at the moment." A cold shiver went through her at the mention of Mark, and Virginia's relationship with him.

Stephanie walked back to Virginia's cottage. Tanya met Mark in their cottage and said, "We've got a fucking problem." She explained the byplay between Bruno and Suleiman.

"Virginia is going to run surveillance. We'll need a much more robust plan. Only you, me, Stephanie and Jonathan will know the details," she said.

"Really!" said a surprised looking Mark. "I had better go and find him." He hurried off.

A few minutes later Mark was back. Tanya met him outside their cottage. "I've told Jonathan," said Mark, "and he's decided to go home tonight since they can land there at night. He'll be over here in a second before he goes. What's all this about?"

Just then Jonathan strode over, allowing Tanya to explain Suleiman's and possibly Bruno's duplicity to both of them together.

"How did you suss all this out?" asked Jonathan.

"Body language. The solution we came up with would have enabled the Morton people to cope with our small force." She added,

"I'll come up with another plan which may mean that we're going to need some help from you."

"What help?" asked Jonathan suspiciously, "You know my position on that."

"Just prison. Once we have settled the issue we may have to put some people in prison."

"Prison!" said a relieved Jonathan, "No problem."

Jonathan walked over to Virginia's cottage and after a brief goodbye on her doorstep left to join his pilot who was busy arranging for take-off.

JONATHAN

It started to dawn on Jonathan that he really needed Tanya around to help fulfil his own ambitions. None of the others had worked out what she had understood about the Kanangra situation. He knew he would have to try to keep her on board somehow. Jonathan, deep in thought on the short flight home, said to himself, half in admiration, half in contemplation, "Tanya again. I suppose this is what it was like with Dad; she would sniff out impending trouble which they would then use to enable them to navigate their way through." He had intended to speak to Mark just to get a feeling of how he felt about his position vis-à-vis Tanya. "The stupid bastard was only interested in Virginia and her attitude towards him. I'll have to get to him some other time," he muttered to himself. Jonathan had always acted on his own, and relied on his own intellect. There was nobody he could talk to.

Jonathan also briefly reflected on the military hierarchy in Canberra. He was becoming more and more concerned about how to continue to motivate the people under his command. He thought about the vigilant border security regime he had set up, in Northern Australia, now steadily degrading under the perceived lack of threat. He knew if the vigilance established over past years was relaxed this would soon result in major incursions from Australia's northern neighbours and, if that happened, his dream of a united Australia would be lost forever.

From the very early days, Jonathan had paid attention to and, when possible, visited the bases he had set up in the north of the country. Most of the time there was also regular radio contact with the bases as well. Within the past month, he had been forced to close a base near Derby. In previous weeks, Jonathan had flown to the large base he had established in Darwin. He then accompanied the commander responsible for all the northern bases, Colonel Imhof, in a chopper used for accessing the smaller outposts scattered across Australia's northern coast.

He had been told the base near Derby had lost people, but what confronted him, as he stepped out of his chopper, had shocked him to the core. The base seemed to be idyllically situated near a fresh water stream. Of the dozen or so huts, most of which were comfortably shaded by large trees, he could see only two were occupied. There were a few scraggy looking cattle about despite a viable looking vegetable patch nearby, and he could see the solar powered water pump operating correctly.

The personnel at the base had been advised of Jonathan's visit so all four of the people (two men and their wives) remaining in the base stood to attention as the chopper landed. Jonathan was greeted by a smart salute as he descended from the aircraft.

"Corporal Greg Holmes, at your service, Sir," intoned one of the men.

From what Jonathan could see, the two families still there appeared to spend all their time merely surviving. While they were supplied regularly from a major base in Darwin, they were separated from their children, who were at school in Darwin. Jonathan asked the remaining two men and their wives and families what had happened.

"Well, Sir, there is a surviving settlement quite close by and one by one our people have left to go there," answered Greg.

"Why, what's the attraction?"

"They live a traditional lifestyle. We don't have the skills or the inclination to join them. The people that have left mostly have an Aboriginal background, so are able to cope."

"If I were to send reinforcements to you, in order for them to stay here, would it be better to send people with a non-Aboriginal background?"

"Yes, although we need Aborigines here because of their skills in the bush. Maybe people from other parts of Australia would be less inclined to join the local group. The group here all have a Yamatji heritage."

"How much patrolling are you able to conduct?"

There was an embarrassed silence.

"Well?"

"Virtually none sir. We can't leave the women on their own for very long, sir, for security reasons and two people have to go out on patrol together in case one gets hurt. All the local Aboriginal groups have been asked to tell us of incursions, of course."

At the conclusion of the visit, Jonathan arranged to close the base and the personnel were transferred to Darwin.

"This is not an unusual situation," said Colonel Imhof on the return flight back to Darwin. "This one is the neediest. What we really need is more people from your establishment in Canberra, Sir."

"Yes, I see," responded Jonathan noncommittally.

"If I can get people from The Settlement under control that will help solve the problem. They have plenty of people," thought Jonathan.

Almost as if reading Jonathan's thoughts and mood, the pilot said to him, "Things have changed a bit over the past few years, Sir, and not for the better." Jonathan was taken aback and almost dismissed the pilot's thoughts out of hand. He respected the man's integrity though and knew the man well since he was Jonathan's regular pilot. So, he asked, "What are you referring to?"

"Well, Sir, there seem to be a lot of drunken parties at the base, something that never happened in earlier times."

"Anything else?"

"I see even some mid-ranked officers running about in reconditioned fancy four-wheel drive SUVs, and some senior officers taking unnecessary helicopter flights, even at night."

"Mnn," said Jonathan.

"My observation, Sir, is that there is too much of this. We have survived the catastrophe, but are we going to survive the aftermath?"

"I see." Jonathan was aware of some of the abuse, but all this coming from just a pilot, disturbed him greatly.

"A friend of my daughter, who is a young, recently promoted sergeant, claimed she was raped at a party a month or so back." The pilot said, encouraged by Jonathan's silence.

"Did she make a formal complaint?"

"No, she was told by a senior officer, not involved with the rape in any way, that if she did, she would regret it bitterly, so she ducked the issue saying she would handle it another way."

"Who was the senior officer? And who are taking these night flights?" asked Jonathan.

"Sir, we're about to land," the pilot said, avoiding the questions.

The pilot skilfully landed the machine as near to the hangars as possible.

As he disembarked Jonathan thought about the conversation he had just had with the pilot. He knew it was all true, and wondered what he could possibly do about it. He also reflected with envy upon the hard-working, disciplined approach that had been created and maintained in The Settlement, now driven, as much as anything, by the example set by Tanya herself. Jonathan was directed to a new looking pristine Range Rover, as he disembarked the chopper, reinforcing the discomfort of the conversation with his pilot.

Tanya

Virginia had arranged for the visitors to be seated separately among local residents at dinner. Tanya noticed Stephanie sitting uncomfortably next to Bruno, and Mark was having an animated conversation with one of the other councillors. She spent time talking to an unresponsive and nervous Suleiman. She surprised herself by not allowing any feelings of resentment against Virginia to take over. The whole community had retired by 9 pm.

The next morning, after an early breakfast in the community centre, Tanya walked over to Virginia's cottage in order to be well out of earshot of everyone else. There was no sign of young Mark. "We'll need an update on the surveillance before we can finalise our plans," Tanya said without any kind of greeting. "I'll be putting updated provisional plans into place in the meanwhile."

"The surveillance is already in place," responded Virginia.

"Okay, we'll be off now. I'll be in touch," said Tanya as she turned away and made her way to the helicopter.

On the way home, in the Bell, Tanya, Mark and Stephanie talked briefly about their visit through the headphones. "We should spend an hour or two on the ground, while we're all together," suggested Tanya, "putting the bones of another plan into place, assuming there'll be more than just the 50 residents at Morton." Tanya landed the Bell at Amazonia and they all quickly made their way to Stephanie's cottage. "I'll just pop over to see Irene," said Stephanie. "She gets all uptight if she thinks she's being ignored."

Stephanie was back a few minutes later. "I told her you would both pop in before you left for home," she said.

"We need to make it look as if we are going to keep to the original plan," said Tanya, "that is 30 of our troops will arrive at Kanangra, whatever else we do. We need to wait until we are quite sure of the strength and preparedness of the Morton village."

"We are almost certainly going to need a lot more troops," said Mark. "How many from here?" he asked Stephanie.

"Say five, at the most," was the response.

Mark nodded, "I'll mobilise another four platoons from The Settlement; hopefully that will be sufficient."

"We need to work out a route for the additional troops to take, bypassing the Kanangra village, so they won't be spotted by messengers running to and from Morton and Kanangra," said Tanya.

"We have some old maps at home, I'll work on a route tomorrow," said Mark.

"Okay," said Tanya. "Stephanie, we'll expect to see you at The Settlement in five days, with the five people you indicated. By then we should understand more about the setup and strength of the Morton place."

A buoyant Mark noticed Tanya was unusually silent on their return to The Settlement.

On arrival, realising that Nanny and her sons were absent, Tanya put the kettle on and said to him, "We need to have a chat."

Tanya got straight to the point.

"Did you enjoy the football game at Kanangra?" she asked.

Mark knew Tanya well enough to know that this was no idle question, but he still had no idea what Tanya was driving at. "Well yes, of course, we all had fun."

"How did you get on with your son?"

With a puzzled look on his face Mark said, "My son? What are you talking about?"

"There was a young boy of about ten there, called Mark. He's Virginia's son. I'm bloody sure you're the father. Blind Freddy can see he looks exactly like you."

"What?"

"Mark, he's your son, wake up for God's sake."

"I had no idea. Virginia has never said anything. I didn't even know she was pregnant." Mark sat down muttering to himself, "she should have told me." He was completely absorbed in his own thoughts; it was as if Tanya's feelings were non-existent.

"Who else knows about this?" Mark eventually asked.

"Certainly Stephanie. Most of the Kanangra community would have noticed young Mark's likeness to you, now hoping against hope that we don't abandon them and leave them to their fate."

Mark was stunned into silence.

Tanya eventually said to him, "I've had enough of all this crap. You lied to me about Virginia in the first place and even after you denied the affair you carried on with it. Then there was the business with Susan. Tonight, you can sleep in the spare room, and tomorrow you can move into Jonathan's cottage."

"It was such a long time ago, I'd almost forgotten about Virginia," said Mark plaintively.

"Mark, it's all over, for Christ's sake!" she shouted at him, letting go of her emotions in a rare display of temper. "Your behaviour has made sure of that. I was prepared to overlook some things, but I saw the way you behaved around Virginia over the past few days. As far as I'm concerned you are free to pursue her and anyone else you fancy."

The conversation stopped abruptly when the boys and Nanny arrived.

Nanny said, "I expect you are both tired, so I've arranged an early dinner."

"How was the Academy training over the past few days?" Mark asked Chas.

"Great," answered Chas, "as a group we seem to be getting better and better."

Before they went to bed Tanya took Mark aside and, looking him in the eye, said, "I want every vestige of you and your belongings out of here first thing in the morning. You'll need to explain the situation to our children, as I will." She then added, "We both still have enormous responsibilities and people's very existence depends on how you and I behave. As far as I'm concerned, the absolute priority is The Settlement and rebuilding the civilisation we once had, so we must not let any of our other feelings get in the way of that."

CHAPTER 3
Morton

-MORTON 1. PREPARATION
MARK

While Tanya was out for her usual early morning run, Mark finished his breakfast and went to have a look at the cottage his father built years earlier for Jonathan, where he normally stayed on his periodic but infrequent visits to The Settlement. The cottage was furnished but had very little of Jonathan there. Mark returned, sadly, to the cottage that had been his home in The Settlement for 26 years, having first engaged the services of two colleagues from the Academy saying to them, "I just need a few things moved over to Jonathan's cottage please."

They spent most of the rest of the day carrying all Mark's possessions over to the cottage. Little was said, with Mark appearing to be operating almost on autopilot. Mark had a brief word with Nanny saying, "I'm moving out."

She answered, "Tanya told me. What about meals?"

Mark shrugged. He hadn't thought about it. Later in the day, when there was a break, he had a word with his two sons.

"As you can see I'm moving to Jonathan's cottage. I'm sorry to say it's not working out between Mum and me. I can't help it." He had yet to come to terms with the fact he had another son living at Kanangra, so was quite unable to discuss that with his two precious children or anyone else for that matter.

TANYA

Jonathan, anxiously wondering what The Settlement plans were in respect of Kanangra, called Tanya knowing she would be in her office by seven am. After the usual greetings he asked, "Is there an update on Kanangra? I just wondered what new plans had been put in place…"

"Nothing finalised; I'm waiting for Virginia."

"How long do you expect that to take?"

"Coupla days. I'm glad you phoned, there have been some developments here." She continued before Jonathan could say anything. "Young Mark, Virginia's son. Blind Freddy can see who his father is. You must have been aware of the situation from one of your earlier visits. Why the hell didn't you tell me?"

"It had nothing to do with me."

"Horseshit!" said Tanya. "Jonathan, it has every fucking thing to do with the relationship of trust between you and this place. I should have been told."

Jonathan remained silent. He wondered if Tanya's new knowledge would help drive a wedge between Tanya and Mark, thereby serving his own selfish agenda.

"I've told Mark to move into your cottage, I've had enough of all this crap. I still need him as head of security. The priority is the security of the wider Settlement."

"Okay, I agree with that."

"Mark will run the campaign against Morton and any aftermath. Gets him out of the way. I've told him he's free."

"Tanya, be very careful. Whilst I understand how you feel, don't marginalise him completely. He has been very effective at running your security and if he starts to undermine your authority it will weaken the organisation considerably," said Jonathan.

"Damnation!" Jonathan thought to himself. "Damn, Damn, Damn, Damn! Maybe inadvertently or otherwise this is the first step towards marginalising Mark. I don't like it and may have to think of another plan."

"Okay, we'll see," muttered Tanya.

"Changing the subject," said Jonathan, "what plans do you have for my brother Evan? He seemed to be at a bit of a loose end when I last spoke to him."

"Mnn," replied Tanya, happy with the change of subject. "He and Beryl are pretty tough and have done well with their Academy training. Evan told me that they spent some years both in Italy, and then later in Iran, growing grapes and making wine during their journey back here. We're in the process of setting them up to see if they can re-establish the industry in one of the old wineries in Pokolbin. There is an awful lot of work involved."

"The wine industry, is that really a priority? Surely there are more important things to focus on."

"It's what he wants to do; I would rather he committed himself to something he's passionate about and he's persuaded me that he has the skills to do what he's suggested. We have been to the area and he has provided me with a plan. It all makes sense."

"Be it on your own head," muttered Jonathan.

Glad to close the conversation down she said to him, "They have been telling me about some of the more lurid adventures they had on their journey back here. They are very tough and very lucky; you should ask them to repeat some of those stories to you."

Jonathan grunted and they rang off.

Privately, Tanya had concluded that neither Evan nor his wife would be able to accept the discipline established at The Settlement. They had spent too much time, especially during their journey home, merely surviving; she could see they both found it difficult to trust people. On more than one occasion she had noticed the sweet smell of dope when walking past their cottage, reminding her of her lucky escape from her Cabramatta upbringing. So she accelerated the process and, within six months of their arrival at The Settlement, had relocated them with three other families to the Hunter Valley. She personally destroyed the few marijuana plants left behind without telling anyone. She made sure that the couple were provided with the resources to enable them to survive and, if they put their hearts into the situation, to make a success of the venture.

From time to time, during short respites during the day, Tanya reflected on the very disturbed night she had had where she had cried herself to sleep, trying to put out of her mind the many highs and lows of her marriage to Mark. Several times, while tossing and turning, she had muttered to herself, "It's over, get used to the idea." Two days later Tanya, on her own, in the Jetstar, paid a surprise visit to Kanangra.

Virginia saw the helicopter and hurried to meet it as Tanya stilled the rotors. "This is a bit of a surprise," she said to Tanya as the helicopter door was opened. She still had her suspicions about Tanya's motives.

Tanya nodded as they walked over to Virginia's cottage, "I need an hour. Anything to report?"

"Yes, we've tracked Bruno's son to Morton, twice now. There are also more than 100 adults and quite a few children in that establishment." Virginia looked at Tanya, who didn't respond. "I just needed to be sure," she said.

Tanya nodded, "What about Suleiman?"

"He's worked his backside off. He's definitely not moving from this place at any time soon. He seems to be completely committed to us."

"Very good," said Tanya. "We can now finalise our plans. I can assure you we'll have enough troops to deal with the situation here. Just a couple of other issues…"

"Yes?" A wary Virginia still had some concerns about Tanya's motives.

"I realise I could have dealt with the situation here more sensitively than I did and you may have felt threatened by the way I acted. Once the situation with Morton has been resolved you will be left to manage your affairs much as you always have—I hope that's clear. We are of course in the position to help you in many ways, especially with our re-supply initiatives; if that's what you want."

Virginia visibly relaxed as the conversation continued. "You can thank Stephanie for much of what I have just said," Tanya concluded and, hesitating for a moment, said, "Just one final thing…I want you to know I've separated from Mark."

The two women awkwardly hugged each other before Tanya walked over to her machine and climbed in. Virginia realised what it must have cost Tanya to say what she did, especially the fact that she had dumped Mark. She now felt more comfortable with the situation as she watched the helicopter disappear northeast. "She didn't even mention the question of Mark's affair with Susan," she thought, "let alone my Mark's paternity. Amazing."

Later Bruno approached her as she walked from her cottage to the community centre, asking what the visit was all about. Virginia noticed Bruno had made sure there was nobody else within earshot. She played it with a straight bat saying, "Just confirming what we discussed during their last visit. Settlement troops will be here in a few days I expect. Everything is just as we planned."

On the way home Tanya reflected on the conversation with Virginia. She knew she had now given Virginia virtual carte blanche to renew her relationship with Mark. One side of her deeply regretted her action; in many ways, how she had dealt with Virginia was against all her instincts, part of her wanted to continue to fight for the survival of her marriage. She pulled herself together, "Get real," she said to herself, "you know your marriage was over some time ago and to go on fighting to preserve it achieves nothing. The most important thing is the survival of The Settlement and all it represents. I must make sure nothing gets in the way of that." A sad and unusually withdrawn Tanya returned to her cottage on her return having completed all the usual post flight checks on the helicopter.

Within a week, Stephanie arrived at The Settlement accompanied by five of her Academy trained people. Tanya, Mark and Stephanie spent two days finalising their plans.

"It'll take ten days to ride to Kanangra and another four or five to be in place near the Morton settlement," said Mark summarising. They agreed on a date when the helicopters would be required. "We've included a dozen homing pigeons in our plans," he continued. "As we have done in the past, we will duplicate messages by sending the same message with two birds. It is obviously very important to coordinate dates correctly. Derain has also asked one of his people to guide us, just to make sure we don't bump into messengers going to and from Kanangra and Morton."

Two weeks later Stephanie arrived at the Kanangra village with 30 troops from The Settlement, who were made comfortable in a campsite on the outskirts of the village. Bruno's son was again tracked to and from the Morton settlement. In her cottage, Virginia had a private meeting with Stephanie giving her details of the revised real plans. They then spent an hour making quite certain that all their actions reinforced the arrangements for the original plan relating to the now 50 troops from Kanangra (30 from the settlement and 20 from Kanangra itself). The 50 were integrated as one unit and they completed two short exercises ensuring that all understood how they fitted into the scheme of things. Stephanie had individually briefed all her troops that there was to be absolutely no discussion with anybody about the real plans.

For the 24 hours before the departure of the 50 troops from Kanangra, Virginia ensured a watch was kept on the Saunders household. At four in the morning there was a knock on her window. One of the guards reported to Virginia, "Bruno himself left on horseback about an hour ago, he's being tracked, but I'm sure his destination is Morton."

An hour later Stephanie and ten others surrounded the Saunders house and, as dawn broke, they smashed the front door down. Three female Settlement troopers rushed into Bruno's wife's bedroom and overpowered her. Amid her shrieks of, "Just wait until Rudolf Dunstan hears about this!" she was made to dress and was taken outside. Four Settlement troops had more trouble with the big burly figure of Bruno's teenage son. Between them they completely wrecked his bedroom and smashed the bed before the boy was subdued and tied up.

Shortly afterwards in the half light of dawn, they heard the rattle of rotors as the prearranged military helicopter landed. The two captives were secured, gagged and bundled into the machine, together with three sacks of weapons and assorted other incriminating evidence against the Saunders family. Stephanie and three others had systematically stripped the Saunders cottage, "Keep all this safe," she told the army officer in charge, "it's enough to incriminate the lot of them for years to come."

Before they departed for the expedition to Morton, Virginia had had a brief discussion with her fellow councillors, two of whom were in any event part of the Kanangra troops going on the expedition. "You'll have to trust me on this one," she said. "This issue has a long way to play out and it will all be explained to you in due course. Just keep the place safe and keep everything going."

By seven the same morning, the 50 mounted troops left Kanangra with Virginia and Stephanie leading them. Two days later they rendezvoused with the 80 troops led by Mark in the deserted town of Moss Vale. Mark, with the help of his Aboriginal guide, had made sure that he took a roundabout route to the town, making certain his large troop didn't cross paths with Bruno or any messengers moving between Kanangra and the Morton village. Mark and Stephanie took time to explore the deserted town. Virginia didn't join them making it clear that she wanted nothing to do with Mark except for essential communication.

Before the flood, the once prosperous small town of Moss Vale had an existence of its own by supporting the local area. It had benefitted significantly from its proximity to Sydney, being less than two hours away by car. Moss Vale, together with the nearby towns of Bowral and Mittagong, stood at an elevation of almost 700 metres above sea level which ensured a temperate climate. Now the area was completely overgrown with many of the houses barely visible through the vines clinging to their walls and roofs. Surrounding land and previously open spaces were a jungle of untended trees, shrubs and weeds. The roads were broken up; the tarmac cracked and potholed; and grass and weeds had invaded wherever they could find root. Adding to the unhappy chaos were the usual rusted wrecks of cars in every spare corner. Often the vehicles and houses contained skeletons of people together with signs that many of them had died violently.

"Most of these cars would have escaped Sydney adding to the chaos, and the higher rainfall we've had since the flood has accelerated growth everywhere," observed Stephanie, looking around, and speaking to Mark, "but this place is obviously more fertile than Virginia's place at Kanangra. I wonder if they wouldn't be better off moving here. There are plenty of houses which could be cleaned up and made habitable again; having sorted the security situation, of course. With solar power and a couple of solar tractors…" Mark nodded, "First things first, but we should have a look at all that. Good thinking though," he said.

Mark

The troops, consisting of Mark's 80 and the 50 under Virginia and Stephanie, were now, as had been agreed earlier with Tanya, consolidated under Mark's leadership. They were camped in nearby bushland and had posted sentries on the outskirts of the camp visible to one another. He called Virginia, Stephanie and the platoon commanders to a conference, standing next to a small cooking fire. "Your rules of engagement are: One; we need any info we can get, so the capture of prisoners is our first priority; Two; unless instructed otherwise nobody is to leave camp; Three; keep as quiet as possible. You will hear more from me tomorrow," he said.

He asked Stephanie and Virginia to remain behind. "From what we understand they'll be waiting for us in their own settled area, but you never know. Those Dunstans are canny people and might try something unexpected. So Virginia, I want two patrols to scout the Morton village," instructed Mark, "and Stephanie, thank you for arranging the army helicopter to pay us a visit tomorrow, we may need it."

So far, they had not seen any of the people from Morton beyond their village area. Mark doubled the number of sentries outside their camp. No fires were allowed. The horses were corralled keeping the camp between the horses and the Morton settlement. Mark, sleeping in a bedroll next to the fire, was woken by Virginia in the hours when the night was at its darkest. Amidst the sound of a scuffle and a lot of swearing, two men were brought into the firelight which was boosted to give more light. The men, both in their mid-30s, were unkempt and dressed in rags. In contrast, as far as Mark could see, they appeared to be in reasonable shape physically.

"The patrol found them on the edge of camp creeping about," Virginia reported. "Initially the patrol found their horses, tied to a tree about 200 metres away. I was alerted and then we found these two…"

"Thank you," said Mark. Stephanie joined them as did the platoon commander.

"I want information and I want it now," Mark said to the prisoners. "Cooperate and you won't be harmed; there might even be a place for you in the new set-up. Mess me around and you won't see the dawn."

One of the men started swearing and struggling against his bonds. "Strip him," ordered Mark. He sent the other captive, under guard, to the far side of the campsite, out of earshot. Watching apprehensively, the prisoner saw Mark place a sharp long bladed knife into the flame. Mark waited silently until the blade was red hot. "Tell me what they are up to over there in the village and I won't touch you," said Mark. The man was silent for a minute. "You can fuck off," he said. "If you think your mob..." Mark signalled to one of the nearby troopers, who gagged the man. Mark picked up the red-hot knife making as if to touch him in the leg, but he didn't actually make contact. The victim grinned crookedly and grunted, looking contemptuously at Mark.

Stephanie quickly stepped forward, snatched the knife from Mark and pressed the red-hot blade against the inside of the man's thigh. The prisoner, held firm by the trooper, jerked about in hideous pain and tried to leap away, grunting incoherently through his gag, as he voided his bowels. A look of sheer terror now covered the prisoner's face. The smell of seared and burning flesh wafted over the gathering.

A surprised Mark glanced at Stephanie as she placed the knife back in the fire. Mark then reasserted himself. "If you want to go on with this, the next time the knife will be on your prick. What's it to be?" he said to the prisoner. The trooper removed the gag.

"I'll tell you, I'll tell you," the surprised and now weeping prisoner said, who had fallen to his knees, casting a troubled glance in Stephanie's direction. "Your 50 people will be invited into our village in a show of friendship. They'll be told to leave their arms outside. We'll have a meal together. Dunno what's planned then...no bloody way a group led by two women..." He stopped talking, casting another venomous glance in Stephanie's direction.

"Maybe you know better now," said Mark. "Your friend's next. If you have lied to us or left anything out, I will have you executed." The still-naked the man was led away looking terrified.

The second man was dragged into the firelight. He needed no encouragement and told the same story as the first man. "Wun uvver fing," he said, "each Dunstan an' ten men hidden; very well-armed. If trubble will kill you."

"Tell me exactly where these houses are," instructed Mark. The man drew a map in the sand with a stick.

"Okay, bring the first one here," he said. "You didn't tell us everything," said Mark when the first man, still naked, was dragged into the firelight. "You will be executed right now."

The man was gibbering incoherently, "No, no…hadn't finished… I was going to tell you…"

"What were you going to tell me?"

"The Dunstans have a number of men in three different houses in the centre of the village. They've been instructed to shoot you all."

"Three? Bring that other fellow back here."

"You stupid bloody fool!" yelled the first man to his compatriot. "Why did you say anything at all?"

His companion merely whimpered.

"So, this seems a bit confusing," said Mark aggressively. "Repeat what was just said," he ordered, looking at both men. He also looked at Virginia for some sort of approval. She looked away.

"Sum talk abaat a meal an' show of frenship," said the second man, "Two hasses where people hidden…"

Mark, waited to see if any more info emerged. None did. He then instructed two of his troops to take the first man off into the bush. There was the sound of a single rifle shot. Stephanie looked at Mark with raised eyebrows. He silently and almost unobtrusively shook his head.

"Your turn next," Mark said to the second man who, having heard the shot, was crying and whimpering in fright. He would have collapsed onto the ground but was held upright by two troopers. "Unless you have other things to say."

"No, no, nuffink."

Mark made him redraw, with the aid of a pencil and paper, a plan of the village with all the houses. He then carefully identified the three houses which were part of the planned ambush.

As arranged by Stephanie during her stay at Kanangra, knowing they would not have the facility to hold prisoners, the military helicopter landed at Mark's camp just after dawn. Mark looked at Stephanie gratefully, acknowledging her foresight. Mark spent ten minutes talking to Tanya on the military radio, "We're more than a half day's ride from the Morton village." He told her about the two captured spies. "We'll see you in two days," and he cut the call. The two Morton 'spies' were loaded into the helicopter, firmly tied up. When he saw his companion the second man looked at him as if he was some sort of a ghost "I fort, I fort..."

The first man shook his head and a tear escaped, "Done for... I thought...fired shot into ground."

The helicopter returned to Canberra.

While the camp was being packed up Mark conferred with Virginia and Stephanie.

"When those two goons don't arrive back at the village, they may send out more patrols to see what's happened to them. So we need some patrols of our own to go post haste to the village and report back to us. I think ten patrols with three in each patrol," said Mark. "The rest of us need to be in place surrounding the village an hour before dawn the day after tomorrow. It will take us most of tomorrow to get into place."

"Thank heaven for Mark," Virginia said to Stephanie later when they were out of earshot, "I wonder what we'd have done without him."

There was further brief conversation and Stephanie was directed to organise and despatch the patrols. One by one she directed each patrol and indicated to them on rough copies of maps she handed out the whereabouts of the village and where the main body of the force would camp. She reverted to military terminology, "Your RE is to avoid direct engagement where possible, avoid any kind of fire-fight. We're looking for info. Capture members of their patrols as a priority. Be back in camp by three am, the day after tomorrow, no later. We'll have surrounded the village by first light." Her briefing sparked apprehensive looks on the faces of some members of the patrols. Others looked more determined than ever.

Once the patrols had been sent on their way Mark briefed the remaining platoon commanders; none of the details of what was planned for the next day had been shared with any member of the ten patrols just despatched. "Just a precaution," said Mark by way of explanation, "in the unlikely event that any of them are captured, none of them know anything of our plans, so can't divulge anything."

Just as the first shafts of sunlight emerged over the eastern horizon Mark directed the 100 remaining members of the troop, platoon by platoon, to saddle up and move out. There were a few muffled words and the rattle of bridles amid the occasional nervous snort of horses as they were saddled. Mark checked each platoon before they moved off. "Just walk, there is no hurry," he admonished. Each platoon consisted of a platoon commander, a sergeant, three corporals and a three-man medical team.

They made camp within a mile of the Morton village and had a cold meal, since they were not permitted to make any fires. Everybody was resting by four in the afternoon. Virginia was asked by Mark to post pickets to be relieved every two hours. There was no talking except for essential orders.

"I want everyone mounted and in full battle gear by three am," Mark told his platoon commanders. There were some brief discussions regarding each platoon's precise role. "We'll be in place surrounding the village by five am."

- Morton 2. The Battle for Morton

Stephanie

Nine of the patrols returned by three in the morning. One patrol had a captive, a young girl of about 18; Stephanie spent a few minutes interrogating her.

"She knows nothing and pees in her pants every time I go near her. For some reason, she had wandered outside the village perimeter in the early evening," she told Mark. The girl was left firmly tied up under the care of one of the older female troopers.

"One patrol, still missing," said Stephanie, to Mark, "from The Settlement."

Two of the returning patrols reported to Stephanie that they had seen glimpses of what appeared to be groups of armed men purpose-fully leaving the village and going into the surrounding bushland. Stephanie questioned them as to the precise location of the new threats. After a brief discussion with Virginia and Stephanie, Mark instructed three sections of ten men each, under the command of a corporal, to withdraw into three separate reserve areas where they would be able to cover any fire from the positions the armed men had been seen to retire to.

The balance of the joint Settlement/Kanangra force was in place by five in the morning. All the troopers were on foot, the horses having been corralled nearby. Mark, Stephanie and Virginia each patrolled their section making sure all were aware exactly where their respon-sibilities lay and what actions were expected of them. They started to move, in good order, towards the village. Just as dawn broke, an inhuman wail came from inside the village which was clearly heard by every one of The Settlement's troops.

"Shit. It's the missing patrol. Steady," said Mark, "this'll be a trap. We must hold the line." As the sounds of torture wafted over the force, there were bursts of rifle fire from the north, south, east and west of the village all directed at the barely visible attackers. With the first shots, the whole force dropped to the ground, as their training dictated. Three of the force were hit. Undistracted, the rest of the force crawled and ran, crouching, the last few hundred metres to the outskirts of the village.

The Settlement reserve force, from their hidden positions, identified the sources of the hostile fire, mainly from muzzle flashes. Soon there was the sound of battle from all around Morton village. During the height of the battle there was a shout from one of the groups near the village, "Virginia's been hit, she's badly wounded!" The nearest medical team rushed to the spot. A traumatised Mark appeared from close by wondering what to do, he was completely distracted. Within a few minutes Virginia had been stabilised. Mark could see what appeared to be devastating wounds in her upper left leg and lower torso, as the medics cut away her bloodied clothing. She whispered to Mark before lapsing into unconsciousness, "Nail... bastards. Okay...medics. Finish it off..."

Mark pulled himself together and ran off to find Stephanie.

Stephanie's first glimpse of the Morton village in the half-light was a disorderly, higgledy-piggledy shambles situated in a partially cleared glade, with houses constructed from old pieces of corrugated iron and tree branches from nearby woodland. Paddocks for horses and cattle and what looked like a vegetable patch were visible. Stephanie ordered a small detachment to release the Morton village horses into nearby bushland. At precisely 6:30, to the great surprise and relief of the ground forces, they heard the whup-whup of rotor blades as two Settlement Merlins advanced on the Morton Village.

During the previous week, Eustace and Tanya, piloting the two large choppers, had performed several practice runs outside the boundaries of The Settlement. Eustace, whom The Settlement had rescued some years earlier, was now in charge of the helicopter facility in Newcastle, responsible for the maintenance and servicing of the whole helicopter fleet. He was also responsible for adding to the fleet where possible. Each chopper had two 5.56 minimi belt-fed machine guns installed, one on each side, and each machine carried two sharp-shooters. "It'll take us about two hours to Morton Village," Tanya informed both crews before take-off.

Stephanie saw both helicopters, at speed, flying back and forth over the village pouring a murderous fire into all the houses.

"Stand fast," Stephanie ordered the platoon commanders, having had a brief discussion with a still-distracted Mark. "Take down anyone that leaves the village, they won't be able to hold on there for long now," she added.

As she spoke people started to flee the doomed village, rushing out of their shacks into the nearby open spaces to be captured by Settlement forces and bound with cable ties, as Stephanie had instructed.

From her vantage point Stephanie could see a continuous fire being directed at the choppers from four houses in the village. Almost immediately she saw the helicopter gunners redirecting their fire with burst after burst into the new targets. One of the houses burst into flames, and then the occupants of another went running into an open space within the village; anyone still holding a firearm was shot by the chopper's door gunners.

Stephanie and the troops outside heard Tanya yell into a loud hailer, "Drop your weapons and leave the village now if you want to live! Anyone who disregards this order will be shot!" She heard the message repeated twice and some of the villagers, scattered about, surprised and terrified by the sight of the two giant machines hovering in the sky above threw their weapons down and ran out of the village to be taken down by the troops outside.

By this time Stephanie had moved the bulk of her force to the very edge of the village. She had left four troopers to guard the wholly intimidated and terrified prisoners. She could see six men continuing to resist, hiding behind houses and firing at the helicopters. She saw a hit on one of the sharpshooters in Tanya's machine. The Morton men were completely focussed on the choppers so Stephanie directed a ten-man section to take them out. They crept around the houses and two of the resisters were shot dead. The other four saw what was going on and briefly turned their fire on Settlement troops, before trying to run away. One by one, Settlement troops took them down.

After another half hour, when it appeared the people in the village had been subdued and having secured their 60 or so prisoners, Stephanie ordered The Settlement ground force into the village. They quickly and silently swept in. Three groups made beelines for the individual houses previously identified as having people hidden in them to ambush any intruders. Amid brief torrid bursts of fire, the front doors were kicked in almost simultaneously and smoke bombs and stun grenades were flung through the open doors.

Some of The Settlement force kicked the villagers' weapons into piles in the middle of the village square well out of reach. A villager who made a grab for his rifle was shot dead. The rest of The Settlement force rapidly moved from house to house to ensure there was no further resistance. Stephanie ordered the prisoners held outside be returned to the village. Seeing Stephanie had the attack on the village well under control, Mark, trying to forget what had happened to Virginia, pulled himself together and directed his efforts to subduing the continuous sniping from Morton forces outside the village. He sent two sections to locations north and east of the village under one of the platoon commanders and personally took charge of another section to tackle the fire emanating from the south and west of the village.

Mark directed his machine gunner to pour fire into one position where he could see continuous muzzle flashes; he then led the rest of the troop to circle around the side of the position and when they were within 20 metres rushed in, all firing as they charged the enemy. Mark personally tackled one of the Morton rabble. Three men still standing dropped their weapons and surrendered. They found two dead and three others wounded in the prepared position. Leaving two men to supervise the prisoners and tend to the wounded as best they could, Mark then led his section to the other remaining position from where the occasional desultory shot was emanating. "What happened to your colleagues?" asked Mark, as they rushed the position finding just one wounded man there. There was a shrug and a grimace from the man. "Scarpered," was all he would say.

"Leave all the dead," Mark instructed, "get the wounded back to the village, ours first."

One of Mark's men came up to him waving a rifle, "Mark, just take a look at this." The rifle was a Steyr, the same model used by Settlement troops.

"It was among the arms we've picked up, in the first position we attacked," he added.

"I wonder where it came from?" asked a very surprised and worried Mark.

"There's only one possible source, and we know we have not lost a single one of ours in years," was the response.

On their way back to the village, Mark's detachment saw two Morton men trying to make a run for it to join their colleagues outside. They were unceremoniously shot dead.

Back in the village five people from each of the two 'ambush' houses staggered, disoriented, out into the weak sunlight. They were immediately taken down by the troops surrounding the doorways, disarmed, identified and tied up. The third 'ambush' house was completely empty. A heavy burst of fire was directed at the troops dealing with the 'ambush' houses from another house nearby. Three of the troops went down, but discipline was maintained and, under Stephanie's direction, most of the attacking force took cover whilst another group rapidly surrounded the house. Stun grenades and smoke bombs were thrown in and five men with large amounts of blood on their clothing staggered out into the weak sunlight, to be taken down, subdued and tied up.

TANYA

Tanya landed her helicopter in the village, with the door gunners and sharpshooters jumping out of the machine as soon as its wheels touched the ground, forming a protective cordon around the machine. Eustace remained on station, circling and keeping a watchful eye out for any further problems. Tanya immediately made sure a nearby medical orderly attended her wounded trooper. Two each from the troops who had apprehended the potential ambushers dived into the first two houses once the smoke had cleared, firing a few shots into the gloom. They were clean, 'Clear!' they shouted.

There was a wail of anguish from the last 'ambush' house, "Call Mark, quick, oh my God look what the bastards have done…" yelled one of the troopers as he staggered back out of the house and was violently sick. Mark appeared, having just returned from dealing with the Morton people outside the village and, taking one look into the house quickly emerged calling Tanya who, after seeing the mutilated bodies rushed outside also. "Three stretchers, quick!" yelled Tanya, "And line all these fucking people up; they need to see this!" Three stretchers were produced and the bodies of the missing patrolmen were gently placed on to them.

"Put them in the middle of the square, make sure every single bloody person from Morton village gets a good look at what has been done in their name," instructed Tanya.

Stephanie, after having had a brief discussion with Mark, instructed one of the patrol leaders to conduct an extensive search of the surrounding bushland. "Pick up stragglers and collect any dead and wounded."

In the meanwhile, the surviving villagers, having been returned to the village, were forced to file past and look at the slaughtered corpses. Some turned their heads away, others covered their eyes, but all cringed in horror. Several of The Settlement contingent had now become aware of what had been done to their colleagues and friends; they moved closer to the ghastly scene.

All three bodies were naked. Charlotte was covered in blood, her groin showing signs of being repeatedly raped, her breasts slashed and her throat cut. The female troopers looked on in horror; Charlotte was one of the leading lights in the Academy, she had helped and mentored many of the younger women. She was popular with the men as well, always cheerful and helpful. There was growing anger among Settlement troops, some of whom started muttering revenge. Joe and Michael had had their genitals removed and stuck in their mouths; they were covered in burn marks and their throats had also been cut. Deirdre, Michael's partner, was nearby and collapsed screaming in anguish when she saw what had happened to him. He had proposed marriage to her just before the expedition to Kanangra. She was led away by a colleague to the medics who gave her a sedative.

Understanding the emotion that was now swirling around the group, Tanya knew she had to act quickly to avoid a further catastrophe, "This has been done in your name," she said angrily to the villagers, "I can promise you, you will all pay for this!"

"We should hang them all now!" yelled a voice.

"NO, absolutely NO!" yelled Tanya. "That reduces us to the level of wild animals."

Mark now seeing the worst was over as far as the battle was concerned, ran over to where Virginia was lying, near where she had fallen, under the care of the medics, "She's lost a lot of blood, we need to get her to hospital quickly," he was told. She was brought into the village and Mark rushed over to Tanya saying, "It's Virginia…"

-3. Morton-The Cleanup
Tanya

Tanya saw the sheer panic enveloping Mark. "Okay, we'll take her and as many of the wounded as we can back to The Settlement hospital. Our people first." By now Stephanie had taken control of all the ground forces. She made sure the ten wounded Settlement/Kanangra troops were brought into the village. The military Sikorsky landed in the village as pre-arranged by Stephanie when it had picked up the two prisoners from the Moss Vale camp, a few days earlier.

Tanya assessed the situation; she could see Settlement forces were now well in control of the situation and the next phase would be to deal with the wounded and dead and then the Morton prisoners. The prisoners were all huddled together, with their hands tied behind their backs, in a corner of the clearing, under guard. There were the wounded, from both Settlement and Morton, being attended to by the various medical teams, as they lay or sat in the village square. She returned briefly to her Merlin and on the radio link told Eustace to land.

"Virginia and one other badly wounded are priorities," said Tanya, as she walked back to the middle of the square, looking at both Mark and Stephanie, "and we'll take as many of our other wounded as possible back to hospital."

One of the Morton village prisoners, from the huddle in the corner of the square, attracted Tanya's attention, "What about our people? We have 20, badly wounded."

Tanya looked at him, saying with considerable anger, "Our own are our priorities. I'll see what I can do, little as you deserve it." She walked over and raised Jonathan on the Sikorsky radio.

"Military hospital in Canberra," she told the man, when she returned from the call, who was looking at her anxiously, "then jail."

"Jail?" the man exclaimed.

Without saying anything further, Tanya walked away to supervise the loading of the Settlement/Kanangra wounded onto Eustace's helicopter. Mark helped with Virginia's stretcher and followed it into the machine. Tanya looked at him. Part of her was irritated with him as he just seemed to be abandoning his position for personal reasons. She bit her tongue knowing a heated public argument would achieve nothing and would detract from what the troops had achieved. "Mark, come back when you can. We'll need you here," she said firmly. He barely acknowledged her.

Tanya and Stephanie watched for a minute as the Merlin took off north-east into the now clear blue sky. The 15 men involved in the ambush houses were rounded up and isolated. "We have all their details, like their names and which house they were in. They each need to be kept in isolation and those with blood all over their clothes need special attention; those clothes should be stripped from them and protected as they will form an important part of the upcoming trial for these bastards," said Tanya to Stephanie who had now taken charge of all the ground troops.

Stephanie meanwhile had gently wrapped the bodies of the three torture victims in blankets and had them loaded into Tanya's helicopter, together with the four dead Settlement troops whose bodies had been retrieved.

"I'll get them home as soon as I can," said Tanya to Stephanie, standing next to the Merlin.

"Where is bloody Bruno?" asked Tanya, moving towards the group of prisoners, "And the Dunstans?"

"Here's Rudolf Dunstan," answered one of the platoon leaders. He was firmly gripping a short, innocuous looking man by the arm. "His elder brother is isolated with those murdering bastards." He indicated the house where the 'ambushers' were being held.

"Where's Bruno?" Tanya asked the younger Dunstan.

"Who...?" Tanya smashed the butt of her rifle into the man's face, knocking out some of his teeth.

"I'm sick of this shit!" yelled Tanya. "Cooperate, or I'll fucking string you up, now..." She pointed at a nearby tree.

"Is this who you mean?" asked a Kanangra trooper, dragging a struggling Bruno into the gathering. "He was trying to get away on a horse."

Tanya nodded. "So they get to know each other a little better, tie them up face to face as tightly as you can."

STEPHANIE

Stephanie, addressing the villagers, said, "You're to stay out here and remain visible until I say the word. Nobody, and I mean nobody, is to return to their cottages before I say you can. I will arrange water to drink."

"What about food?" asked a voice.

"Yes, for the children only. Meanwhile there are some discussions we need to have with you all."

"You should stay here and organise what we do with these villagers; we certainly can't let them go on as they are," Tanya said to Stephanie as she watched her quietly and competently deal with what was needed, despite the fact that her two senior colleagues were no longer around. "We could think about splitting the villagers up and moving them to the settlements we have around the place. Some of them will have cooperated with the Dunstan crew. We need to identify them and they should be prosecuted in Canberra. We'll need Mark to return here..."

"Okay," said Stephanie, wondering what Tanya had in mind, "I'll keep the troops here until we have everything under control."

They walked around the village, which consisted of about 55 shacks, some built from local timber, while others consisted of corrugated iron. Stephanie wondered if any of the shacks were truly waterproof. There was a vegetable garden protected by wire netting and a herd of cows in a nearby paddock. Troopers were busy having recaptured some of the Morton horses, a little way outside the village, returning them to their paddock. The whole village had a seedy and unkempt appearance, with no mechanisation of any kind.

"I wonder how much longer this place would have been able to survive," Stephanie observed. "I can see why they wanted to take over Virginia's place in Kanangra. Most of the people look half-starved." Tanya nodded.

Tanya left for home in her Merlin, with her grisly burden. "I'll be back tomorrow," she told Stephanie.

In the meantime, Stephanie made arrangements for every one of the villagers to be interrogated individually by a senior member of The Settlement entourage. "We need to include some of the older children in these interviews," she said to the platoon commanders involved in the process. The balance of the force was directed to make another thorough search of every house and cottage and all the communal facilities. "Firearms, you're primarily looking for firearms, but also knives, bombs and drugs; you must clearly identify the cottages in which any suspicious items are found and we will then link them up with the people who lived there. We seem to have identified most of the 'bad eggs' but my guess is that there may be one or two more still here."

By late afternoon all the interviews and searches had been completed. Six people had been isolated and were locked in one of the cottages under armed guard. The remaining villagers were told to prepare food for themselves.

"We will, for the time being, use our own supplies," said Stephanie, standing in the centre of the village addressing her troops, and those Morton villagers, not under arrest.

"Just as well," said one of the village women who was more forth-coming than the rest, "we can barely feed ourselves." Settlement troops had already started to set up their own cooking facilities in a corner of the square.

TANYA

Back at home, once she had secured the machine, Tanya steeled herself for the forthcoming discussions with the parents of her casualties, thinking about what to say and concerned about how they would react to her news. She knocked on the door of Charlotte Lee's modest, but neat and tidy cottage, situated in a row with a number of other similar dwellings, typical of The Settlement. There was an apprehensive look on their faces as they opened the door to Tanya. "It's about Charlotte, isn't it?" asked the middle-aged woman, hurriedly and anxiously.

"I'm terribly sorry," said Tanya, "but there's no way to break this gently. Charlotte was killed in the raid on the Morton village. She was very brave and her actions saved many lives." There were immediate tears and the couple clung to each other for a few moments.

"We'll show you her room," said Mrs Lee, once the couple had partially recovered their composure. They led the way down the short passage to a small bedroom. The room was festooned with Academy paraphernalia and numerous photographs of Charlotte with her platoon on the parade ground, on various exercises in the bush and, a recent one, in pride of place, showing off her Corporal's stripes. With an effort Tanya maintained her composure.

"Can we see her please?" asked a tearful Mr Lee.

"You can," said Tanya. "I brought her and six others back with me, but I warn you it's not pretty; she was captured and tortured before she was killed. I know this doesn't help but the some of those Morton people were truly evil and that evil has now been eliminated."

Still standing in Charlotte's room, the couple remained tearfully silent for a moment before Charlotte's mother said to Tanya, "Thank you for coming to tell us. As you can see she really loved the Academy and all it stood for, especially the equality of women. She knew she might be killed or captured. It doesn't make it any easier though." She burst into another flood of tears.

"Give me half an hour," said Tanya.

"One at a time please," said Tanya, to the seven families whose children had been killed in the raid on Morton. Charlotte's parents were the first to be admitted. Charlotte's body had been placed on a gurney in the morgue of The Settlement's small hospital.

Tanya pulled back the sheet to display Charlotte's face.

"Unless you insist, I will only show you the face; the rest is too ghastly to contemplate." Her advice was accepted.

There were more tears as the Lees spent a few minutes gazing at their daughter's still-pretty face, looking like she was just in a deep sleep. Mr and Mrs Lee nodded gratefully at Tanya as they left the scene. They glanced with sympathy at the other six families now waiting sadly and silently to see the faces of their children for the last time.

"We would like to acknowledge your children publicly with a full Settlement funeral, if that is acceptable to you. We should wait until the bulk of the force returns which may not be for a month or so. There will of course be obituary notices in the paper which you can discuss with the editor," Tanya said to the seven families. All of the families decided to wait for the full funeral and within a few days suitable obituaries would be published in the paper.

At the end of the day Tanya, completely drained by the experience, returned to her cottage. Nanny said very little, merely patting Tanya on her arm to show sympathy. Chas and the other nine Academy personnel had already moved to Canberra as part of arrangements made with Jonathan. Didier, training to be a doctor, was working flat out in the hospital, helping to deal with the casualties from the Morton expedition. Tanya spent a sleepless night, with nobody she could turn to.

The next day Tanya returned to the Morton village in the small Bell Jetranger, knowing that Stephanie would need her help. Stephanie had determined that 60 or so adults were relatively blameless for what had happened at the Morton settlement.

"All they suffer from is weakness and stupidity," Stephanie explained as she tried to summarise the situation for Tanya on her return. "The fact they allowed themselves to be bamboozled and intimidated into allowing the Dunstans to take over is difficult to believe. Anyway, I don't think there's much harm in many of them and they may make good settlers in the longer term," said Stephanie, adding, "Another problem is that we have ten children here belonging to the people in prison. In most cases both parents were involved with the nefarious activities of the Dunstans and I think will spend a long time in jail. If we leave the children here, they will probably be harmed by the people remaining. We have no choice but to take them to Kanangra."

The villagers were directed to bury the 11 of their own dead found in the village and in the surrounding bushland. Eight more people, including Rudolf Dunstan and Bruno, tied uncomfortably together face to face, plus the 15 ambush people, were transferred to Canberra for prosecution in the military's Sikorsky, once it had dealt with the 20 Morton wounded.

Mark and Virginia

Virginia, still groggy, became aware of Mark quietly sitting by her bedside; whenever she woke, there he was. She had been moved from The Settlement hospital's single ICU bed, to a small general ward, where there were three other patients.

"Will she be alright?" Mark asked. He couldn't bear the thought of Virginia dying or being crippled. "I think so," was the response from the chief surgeon, who was surprised by Mark's obvious emotional engagement with the situation. "She lost a lot of blood and the bone in her leg was shattered so it will take a while for her to recover; she will always have a bit of a limp I expect."

"No vital organs?"

"No, she was very lucky."

"How long will you have to keep her here?"

"A couple of months, but she will need attention for a while after that."

Within a few days Virginia was able to sit up in bed and talk. She was happy and surprised at the attention Mark was paying her. As far as she was concerned, while she slipped in and out of consciousness, his presence was the one constant during her nightmare. Mark arranged for their son to be picked up in one of the now frequent helicopter trips between Kanangra and The Settlement.

Young Mark rushed into the ward and as gently as he could he hugged Virginia for a good five minutes. "Oh Mum," was all he could say as the tears streamed down his face.

"Where is he staying?" Virginia asked eventually.

"With me, his father." Mark smiled.

"Come here, of course he is," said Virginia as she kissed him full on the lips.

Young Mark had dozens of questions as he became used to visiting Virginia every day. Mark soon enrolled him in The Settlement school. Mark explained to her what he knew of the developments resulting from the clash with the Morton village.

"Don't they need you at Morton?" Virginia asked him once it was clear to her Mark was not going anywhere.

"Virginia," he said, "as far as I am concerned, what happens to you is more important than anything, absolutely anything." He leant over and kissed her on the lips. Her arms went around his neck and she hugged him. A tear slipped out. The other women in the ward tried not to notice.

During her trip back home with The Settlement dead, Tanya had slipped in to see how Virginia was faring. She had a brief word with Dr Jane Wickremasinghe, the chief surgeon, and managed to spend five minutes with Virginia when Mark was briefly absent. She kissed Virginia on the forehead. "Jane says you'll make a full recovery," said Tanya, "but please don't worry, everything is under control." Virginia was pleased and happy that Tanya made no reference to Mark's obvious presence.

When Virginia was able to understand some of what had occurred, she said to Mark, "I really need to get back to Kanangra. For some time, I've been thinking we should move our base to the Southern Highlands before anyone else does. The problems with Morton prevented me from doing anything but now the immediate security issues have been resolved we can move on that initiative. What are we going to do with the Morton village? I don't want anyone else to steal a march on us."

"You'll be in hospital, here, for a few weeks yet. Your health is the most important issue. I don't yet know what we're going to do with the Morton village. However, if you agree, I'll base myself at Kanangra to look after the community's interests and make sure everything is okay. Hopefully your people will accept me in such a role."

Virginia raised her arms, and Mark responded by leaning down to kiss her, as he was now doing at every opportunity. She looked at him gratefully. "Thank you, thank you, my darling," she said. "That takes a great weight off my shoulders. I can now relax a bit and concentrate on getting better, with these marvellous facilities you have here." The previous bond between the pair was rapidly re-establishing itself.

"Jane says she's organised a full rehab programme for you, which you could start in another couple of weeks. It's really critical you take advantage of that. Please don't worry about Kanangra, I will make sure our interests are well taken care of."

Virginia said nothing but noticed the use of the word 'our'.

"Are you taking young Mark with you?" asked Virginia.

"No, for the moment I'll leave him here. I've spoken to Nanny and he can stay at Tanya's place while I'm away. Tanya is not spending much time here anyway, so Nanny only has to cope with Didier and herself of course."

TANYA

With Mark spending most of his time at The Settlement, Tanya had returned to Morton to help Stephanie to decide what to do with the Morton village and its erstwhile inhabitants. They walked around the Morton village together. "The cattle are in poor shape—lack of decent grazing," observed Stephanie. "The vegetable garden looks a mess," she added. "Maybe lack of fertiliser. The local wildlife seems to be the major beneficiaries anyway."

"Is this fucking place worth maintaining at all?" asked Tanya, looking around critically. "Moss Vale and Bowral will be more productive and are currently deserted. There are plenty of houses. A couple of solar tractors and solar power all round would make them self-sufficient. It's an option for the Kanangra people too, who might be better off moving to the more open areas."

STEPHANIE

"In view of the recent history, we may not want the Morton and Kanangra people to be so close to each other. At least not all of them," explained Stephanie. "We should split them up and send them to several different locations. Some people from The Settlement and even the Vikings and a couple from Amazonia could come to Kanangra, or wherever we move the centre of gravity to. But I agree, we should demolish or burn all the buildings here and let it go back to the bush."

Stephanie and the platoon commanders started to talk individually to the Morton villagers regarding their aspirations. About half of them indicated they would be happy to move to another location. After having determined a feel for the situation, she broached the subject in a mass meeting with the villagers about moving to the Moss Vale/ Bowral area. "We would set you up with solar power in your houses and there would be at least two solar powered tractors available as well," she told them. "You would have the support of the Kanangra people and we are going to ask others from some of the other settlements who come under our security blanket if they want to move down here. Maybe you could discuss it amongst yourselves and come back to me with any issues."

"What happens to this place?" Stephanie was asked, by a man named Jerry, whom she was beginning to distrust.

"We are going to abandon it. Sooner or later it will revert to a National Park, once everyone has been adequately settled. The cattle will probably remain part of the local settlement, but we may need the horses to get people to their new homes."

"Are we going to be compensated for any losses we sustain, for being forced to leave here?" asked Jerry.

"Compensation? You stupid fuckwit—the fact that you're still alive is a bonus for most of you. Frankly, with what you had planned, we were totally justified in coming in here and wiping you all out, and I mean all of you. If you want to go on in that vein, I'll happily transfer you to Canberra. I'm sure we could find some transgression that will enable you to cool your heels in jail for a few years. So, no, there won't be a skerrick of compensation for you or anyone else."

Another Morton man asked what would happen to the people taken to Canberra.

"They will be tried in a military court. I expect the prosecution will demand the death penalty for murder and rape for starters. As I have already told you, most of you are lucky to be alive at all," responded Stephanie.

"Death penalty? The death penalty was abolished in Australia years ago."

"Australia?" said Stephanie. "What's that then? We are Australia— The Settlement and the military. And if you threaten Australia the penalty is death. We've done it before and we'll do it again," said Stephanie firmly. There were no further questions.

Within a week, Stephanie had the remaining Morton villagers where she wanted them. Once they could see that she was fair but abided no nonsense, they started to go out of their way to cooperate. Tanya returned with Mark and the three had many long discussions deciding who should go where and when. Mark discussed the details with a recovering Virginia, still bedridden in The Settlement hospital.

"There are 40 adults who are happy to leave here, plus about the same number of children, varying in age from a few months old to mid-teens," Stephanie reported. "The children under ten need to be transferred either by road or in the chopper together with one parent."

Tanya took three adults and three infants scheduled to be moved to The Settlement in the Bell Jetranger when she left, promising to return the next day with one of the big Merlins.

After three long weeks of riding, Stephanie was beginning to regret her decision to bypass the outskirts of western Sydney, taking longer than the more direct route. They had avoided the usual clutter of rusted, broken down vehicles which always seemed, to Stephanie, such sad reminders of all that had been lost, but three weeks in the saddle had left her stiff, sore and irritable. It was with some relief that, late in the day, she spotted a group of three riders silhouetted on the horizon, slowly growing larger as they approached. Stephanie urged her party on to, her conviction increasing as they grew nearer, until finally she was within hailing distance of Roger, riding high in the saddle and flanked by two companions.

"Roger, you really are a sight for sore eyes."

"Hey Stephanie. You look rooted."

"Exhausted, yes. Rooted! Well, not for a while…" She smiled at Roger's mild look of embarrassment. "I'll see if I can get a ride in one of the choppers back to Kanangra/Bowral, when all this is over."

"Half for The Settlement and half for Amazonia," Stephanie continued. "For their sakes the sooner the better, most are in worse shape than I am."

The whole group had camped for the night before they were directed to their respective destinations. Stephanie managed to have a quiet word with Roger, out of earshot of the group. "Just watch that bloody man, Jerry." She was able to point him out without anyone noticing. "He seems to have slipped through the net somehow. I can't decide whether he's just a barrack room lawyer-type or something much more sinister." She shrugged.

CHAPTER 4

Expansion

MARK

Mark had by now established himself at Kanangra, having convinced the residents he had Virginia's full support. He still flitted backwards and forwards to The Settlement and Virginia's bedside, usually with his son, young Mark, in tow. He took several parties of Kanangra residents to the Southern Highlands where people excitedly identified some of the better areas. "I think we should have the pick of the areas though, rather than the Morton people," he told them. The use of the word 'we' was not lost on his new companions.

"The skill levels of the Morton people are quite low; I think of the ones that are left, many of them would probably be thrilled to be given places in Kanangra allowing your people to move to Moss Vale, or wherever," Stephanie told Mark on her return from the northern expedition.

Over the next few weeks Mark, Stephanie and some of the Kanangra people developed a plan. Suleiman was most active during these discussions, making sure any doubts regarding his loyalty to the Kanangra settlement were well and truly dispelled. Most of the remaining Morton villagers were given places at Kanangra. Ten families from The Settlement moved to Bowral and gradually many of the Kanangra residents also moved to the better areas. Roger provided three solar tractors with appropriate implements as part of his 're-supply' programme. Three people from The Settlement arrived to install solar power in the houses planned for occupation. After the people left the Morton village, Stephanie and part of the Settlement force demolished all the cottages there and had several bonfires to burn what they could.

By the time Virginia was ready to return home, Stephanie, with the help of Settlement troops, had turned their attention to what had been the small town of Bowral. Many houses had been cleaned up ready for the installation of solar power. A vegetable garden had been started. Some of the local cattle, gone wild since the flood, had been partially tamed. Mark helped move most of the existing population of the Kanangra village to Bowral, with energetic help from Suleiman. Mark made doubly sure that one of the Bowral houses was properly cleaned up for Virginia's return and that solar power had been installed so there was light, cooking facilities and a source of water.

"I've cleaned up a house in Bowral for you and young Mark…" Mark said to Virginia as he was making plans for her and Mark to return to their home base. A look of disappointment, almost devastation, came across Virginia's face. She allowed a tear to slip out, which she impatiently swept away. "What about you?" she whispered. "With all that has gone on I thought…"

"I'll be right next door."

Virginia realised what was being said, so smiling wanly through her tears she said, "I don't want you next door. I want you there with me and our son. With you in my bed. You keep telling me you love me…"

"I didn't want to rush things…"

They just clung to each other for ten minutes.

Tanya

Periodically Tanya appeared in the Jetstar to collect Mark, spending days at a time in the military establishment in Canberra briefing military prosecutors assigned by Jonathan. After several visits, cases had been established against all the people taken captive from the Morton village. Tanya, Stephanie and Mark, four others from The Settlement, a recovering Virginia and another from Kanangra attended the trials as witnesses. At the conclusion of the trials Jonathan met with Tanya in Canberra. As usual Tanya kissed Jonathan chastely on the cheek as she was shown into his office. As she sat down she looked at him expectantly, saying nothing.

"Five men have been sentenced by an army judge to be executed by firing squad for rape and murder," said Jonathan, shifting uncomfortably in his chair.

"Who?" asked Tanya.

"The elder Dunstan, together with four others. I can read out their names if you wish," he responded, ruffling through a sheaf of papers, "but they were the men who tortured, raped and killed your three troopers."

"Don't worry. I didn't know them. Have the sentences been carried out?"

"Yes."

Tanya wondered why Jonathan wouldn't look her in the eye as he answered.

"And the rest of them?"

"Have been sentenced to 20 years in a military prison; this includes Bruno, his wife and son."

Tanya nodded wondering why the sentences were so uniform. Again, Jonathan appeared to be avoiding her questioning glances.

"There are no rights of appeal," added Jonathan, again looking away.

"What the hell is he up to?" she thought. "He's hiding something."

JONATHAN

A few days earlier Jonathan had paid a visit, in the Sikorsky, to a secret base he had set up in Wagga Wagga, less than an hour's flight from Canberra. The Bandstand prisoners had already been ensconced in the facility for some weeks and had recently been joined by all the prisoners from the conflict at Morton, after their trials. There was a small cadre of trainers led by Major Moody, one of Jonathan's most trusted officers. Jonathan spent time going through the detail of a training programme for the prisoners.

"I want you to make sure these people can give a very good account of themselves in conflict. We don't have time to train them to the same level as our army recruits, of course. I intend to use them as a sort of irregular force, as I instructed you from the beginning. Also, all communication is to be through me personally. There is to be no general awareness in Canberra of the existence of this facility. I trust that is clear."

Jonathan toured the base, which had in the past been used as a small training facility for special activities. He saw with satisfaction that the small group of women who had been imprisoned at the same time as their respective menfolk were running the kitchens and the vegetable gardens.

"I want this place to become self-sufficient as soon as possible, so the mornings should be spent on military style training and the rest of the day tending the cattle, the horses and the vegetable gardens."

"All in hand, Sir, as you can see. The solar installations are now all working; we should be self-sufficient within a few months," said Major Moody.

"Okay Major, the nightly truck with provisions will continue until you give me the word. I will in any event be here at least once a week. As was the case today I will be able to provide you with appropriate small arms and ammunition on my visits."

"We need another 40 or so sets of saddles and bridles for the horses," added Moody.

"Raid a few nearby farmhouses and see what you can find. I will of course see what I can do. What have you told the people here? Do I need to say anything?" Jonathan asked.

"No Sir. I've told everyone that they are being trained for special assignments and if they behave, their sentences will be reviewed. The trainers and security personnel have been told the same thing."

Jonathan returned to Canberra well satisfied with his initiative, and ready to prepare for Tanya's visit. What he did not know was that one of the trainers, a Lieutenant McGrath, was a member of the ten Settlement Academy personnel now embedded with the military in Canberra; McGrath kept well out of the way during Jonathan's visits.

With the way the Morton battle had gone and the comparatively severe casualties The Settlement had sustained against a supposedly untrained enemy, Jonathan felt much more confident with his strategy of training and using enemies of The Settlement as a sort of mercenary force. He still hoped he could persuade Tanya to voluntarily bring The Settlement under his control, but he knew in his heart of hearts that this was a forlorn hope. Jonathan also realised his authority was under threat, confirmed by his own observations and further discussions with his personal pilot.

Tanya

As his meeting with Tanya continued, Jonathan announced, "I will make sure every community throughout the country is made aware of these sentences. Our job now, over the long term, is to re-establish the authority of the Australian Government throughout the country."

"Mnn," said Tanya, "there'll be some resistance to the restoration of the authority of the Australian Government," she said bluntly. "I'm sure that for starters such a move may provoke Thor.

"Apart from security," said Tanya quickly changing the subject, "we must find another source of fuel, as we have discussed before. What we have won't last forever."

"We have people trying to refurbish what's left of the oil refineries in Victoria, at Geelong and Altona," Jonathan responded. "Unfortunately, these facilities were severely damaged in the flood. Also, only a few of the 20-odd wells in the Bass Strait were capped at the time of the flood, so the remaining wells have been pouring crude oil into the sea for the last ten years or so. We've now managed to cap some of them, but the flow of oil continues. Anyway, within a few months we should be able to pump crude into the terminal at Longford in Gippsland and after that maybe we will have a refinery going in Melbourne, for military use in the first place of course. Anything over and above that can be directed in small quantities to other uses."

"We'll also look for other sources not inundated by the flood," responded Tanya, looking uncomfortable. "There's too much military this and military that for my liking," she thought. "Getting out from under that has to be a priority, and the sooner the better."

Jonathan looked at her uncomfortably. He wanted her under control, not taking initiatives that would maintain and reinforce the independence of The Settlement.

"While we are talking about how to recreate our civilisation, one possibility would be to take a leaf out of Virginia's book, Tanya, and run your operation on more democratic lines," said Jonathan, changing the subject and thinking Tanya would be opposed to a full scale democratic process.

"What we have now is very practical; it allows people such as me to get on with things without having to consult with every halfwit in the community," she answered.

"I wonder what he's up to," she thought. "He's talking out of both sides of his mouth. He doesn't believe in the democratisation process any more than he believes there's a man in the moon. I'm going to have to keep an eye on Jonathan and his cronies; maybe there's already something brewing."

Jonathan was about to say something but Tanya continued.

"I know, I know, unless there is some mechanism for people to have their say resentments could be building up without us being aware of it."

"Has it ever occurred to you, Tanya, that some Settlement people may not want you as their leader?" Jonathan added.

"I suppose it has occurred to me on very rare occasions. I can't say that I dwell on it much," said Tanya after a moment's reflection. She smiled. "I have spent all my energy for more than a quarter of a century on ensuring the success of our Settlement. I am quite certain, just between us, that if it were not for me, and of course David, that The Settlement would never have come into being in the first place. There have been watershed incidents during that period where, if others had been in charge, they probably would have fucked the whole thing up and we would all have drowned or starved."

Jonathan laughed. "Every dictator since the beginning of time could and probably did make such a speech."

Tanya nodded, "I'll work on it." She hesitated, wondering how she could put Jonathan off balance.

She then said, "Jonathan, is there room in the military establishment for some lunatic to take over from you and create a dictatorship all of his own, backed by the firepower of the military?"

"You're not the only one who's thought of that. I'm aware of the contingency and it's dealt with internally," he responded, looking uneasy.

"Okay, I'll think about the democracy thing," Tanya responded without much enthusiasm. She thought to herself, "Whatever we do, we need to pre-empt anything Jonathan is planning. He's also worried about something—I wonder what the hell it is."

Before she left, Tanya managed a half hour conversation with Chas.

"Your Uncle Jonathan is behaving peculiarly," she told him. She went on to explain how the people at Morton had been dealt with and that a number of the 'bad-eggs' from that establishment had either been jailed or executed as a result. "All courtesy of Jonathan and the military establishment in Canberra. During my discussions with him, today, though I got the feeling that I was not being told the whole story. I would like you to keep your eyes open…What?" Tanya exclaimed. "You look as if you have seen a ghost or something."

Chas looked very uncomfortable. "Mum, I can tell you categorically there have been no executions in Canberra for years now."

"Shit," thought Tanya, "so the bastard IS playing games."

"Anything strange going on?" she asked.

"Funny you should ask that. I thought it was nothing but a very select group has been sent to Wagga recently. Most of us have been told nothing of this, but I hear that a number of people who are serving long prison sentences have been included in this group for 'rehabilitation', whatever that means. One of our Settlement embedded guys was chosen to be one of the people in charge of the programme. I'll ask around and let you know."

"Also, you need to know," Chas continued, "that Jonathan's authority is under pressure. There is a Colonel Jacobs, a nasty piece of work in my opinion, who seems to have managed to usurp much of Jonathan's authority, at least in Canberra. Appointments are being made without consulting Jonathan. These people are taking advantage of their own positions; they are indulging in raucous parties and some of the more senior people are driving about in fancy reconditioned four-wheel drive vehicles. Jonathan, though, still has control of the military outposts outside Canberra, mostly on our northern coasts, which he visits regularly, using one of two private jets rescued after the flood."

Tanya was thoughtful for a moment. She then told Chas about Jonathan's idea for a military government for the whole country.

"What does Dad think about all this?"

"I haven't discussed it with him. He's helping the Kanangra people settle themselves into the Southern Highlands area. Do you see much of your dad?"

"No, I've seen him once since deploying down here; he said he was in Canberra for the trials you just mentioned. Anyway, what do you want me to do?" asked Chas.

"Just keep your eyes and ears open and let me know of any irregularities. I'll pass whatever you tell me on to your father. Despite everything we still have a good working relationship; we both know that the future of The Settlement depends on us. Also keep tabs on all Settlement people in the military here. You may all need to redeploy back home if things go haywire."

CHAPTER 5
Chloe

Despite her responsibilities in dealing with the large number of guests at David Bower's funeral, Tanya had noticed Chloe taking far more notice of Thor than would normally be warranted. After asking a few judicious questions and keeping her eyes open, it became clear to Tanya that Chloe and Thor had become lovers. Chloe had moved to the Viking village with Susan and Hercules and their son, Mars but stayed behind to be with Thor when Susan, Mars and Hercules moved on to the new areas north, as part of the dowry payment deal Tanya had made with Thor at the time of Jason and Venus's marriage.

Chloe found Thor surprisingly sensitive and intelligent, and without any word from her he paid a great deal of attention to his personal hygiene. Chloe had insisted she be allocated her own individual hut, but she often spent the night in Thor's large spectacular palace with its thatched roof and beautiful views over the surrounding bushland with the village's beehive style huts, all uniform, lined up neatly behind the palace almost as if paying homage. She had said to him during one of their early encounters, "Thor, if you think I'm prepared to be one of several bints available to you on a regular basis, you are mistaken; it's either me and only me or I will go and join Hercules and Susan."

Thor, clearly taken aback by Chloe's forthrightness, replied with some amusement, "'Ow toimes 'ave changed. Before the flood I wouldn'a 'ave got within a bull's roar o' the loikes o' you; me being par' o'what yer proberly fort to be the lowest of the low an' a member of a bikie gang dealing drugs. Yer probly considered yourself part of the elite in Sydney."

Chloe, saying nothing, merely smiled at the observation.

Early on during her sojourn at the Viking village, Chloe would sit on the wide verandah of the spectacular palace and wonder how she could genuinely make a contribution to the place. During her first two years there, Chloe had arranged for several mares and a stallion to be transferred from her stock of horses at The Settlement, with the idea of upgrading the stable of horses at the Viking village. Her other initiative was to get Thor to agree that the women in his establishment were badly treated. Knowing this was a sensitive subject, Chloe said to him one day in bed, "I think that we could make more of the women here; they don't take any initiative, they just do the bare minimum. If you let me, I am sure I could help them be much more useful than they are now."

"Wha'dya mean? If oi catch any of 'em slackin' they will be beaten; they know that. An' oi don' want any of this training 'em to be soljers and stuff, which is a man's job."

"No, no I wasn't suggesting that they be part of the security regime or anything," she said soothingly. "I am sure that if they had more of a say in what they did for the community, it would run better."

"I' runs perfecly well now," said Thor.

"Trust me, Thor; I can already see some things that would make an improvement, let me show them. They all know of our relationship so they will assume that what we are doing has your approval. Give me three months."

"Okay," he grunted.

She had persuaded Roger to provide her with a solar powered tractor and some implements, and she arranged for a woman from The Settlement to train people to maintain the village's solar installations.

Thor, once he saw the solar tractor, said to Chloe, "This is sommin' fer the men, wimmen can't manage technical fings."

"We could try but I'm sure the women will manage as well as any man, if they're properly trained. The trouble with the men is that they know all the bloody answers before they've even heard the questions," said Chloe. She had asked Roger to show her how to temporarily disable the tractor so after a few minutes the motor would peter out. She artfully then gave the man Thor had selected double the amount of training she had given to any of the women and sent him off to plough a patch leaving him alone. Hours later a very forlorn looking man sought Chloe out saying the tractor had broken down and he was unable to get it going again.

"Okay, don't worry," Chloe told him with a straight face, "I'm busy at the moment but I'll see what I can do."

An hour later Chloe, accompanied by one of the women, and the frustrated man, approached the tractor. She opened the hood and, unseen, flicked a little switch. The woman started it up with the motor running smoothly and completed the ploughing with the man looking on in confusion. The woman smiled at Chloe, understanding that she had played some sort of trick on the man but not understanding what.

Later that night in bed Thor asked how the man had performed with the tractor. "Oi'll bet 'e did twoice the acrage of any of the wimmen," he said.

"No,' said Chloe sleepily, "he really made a mess of things, I'm afraid. Within minutes he'd stalled the machine and was unable to restart it. I fixed it later and one of the women finished the job. The problem is that the men don't listen. Send the stupid bugger hunting or herding cows or something."

Thor looked nonplussed, but was thereafter prepared to leave Chloe to manage the women as she saw fit. Over time he came to see significant improvements in the amount and quality of available vegetables and for the first time they were cultivating grains. Thor could also see the women tended to be more cheerful and happy. "Oi don' know wha' you've done to all these wimmen, but they're all runnin' around makin' jokes and laughin'," Thor commented one evening in bed, "but I don' want 'em to be gettin' any ideas about their persisin 'ere. Anyways, wha' are you doin' to 'em?"

"None of them have been beaten since I became involved," Chloe answered. "I occasionally ask them if they have any ideas about how they might go about certain tasks, that's about it really. Anyway, forget about all that, just come here, I need a little bit of care and attention provided by you of course, as a special reward for all my hard work."

What Chloe had actually done was to divide the women into small groups and to give them certain tasks. She told them all to work out how best to do the task and, if they needed any advice, to ask. Roger delivered a milking machine. Thor didn't even discuss it; milking cows was most definitely a woman's job. He didn't care how it was done.

Chloe for her part loved Thor's big strong body; he was every-thing she wanted in a lover. She never gave any consideration to what David or any of her other former lovers might have thought of her new liaison.

During one of her regular visits, Tanya had said to her, "Be careful of Thor, he's a fucking sight smarter than he looks."

"I realise he is really very smart, but he can't deny me much, if you see what I mean," Chloe responded whilst giving Tanya a meaningful look.

"Okay. I don't want to frighten you but here's a revolver and two homing pigeons in case you get into trouble."

Chloe looked at her without saying anything. Her safe untroubled world had suddenly taken on another seemingly dangerous hue.

"He told Jason that Harold had been executed," Tanya continued. "I'm bloody sure he wasn't; we think Harold was sent away as a sleeper somewhere and if Thor can see a way to use him against us he will."

"You mean that Harold, the one who almost put paid to The Settlement in the early days? I didn't know he was still around," said a now wary and surprised Chloe.

"He kept out of sight, during our visits here, but I caught a glimpse of him a couple of times and mentioned it to Thor. Thor then saw how he could kill two birds with one stone, so he sent him away and got Hercules to tell Jason the big porky. We got the better of Harold but I bet the fucker is still out there somewhere, thirsting for revenge. So keep your eyes open. Also, make a plan to get the hell out of here if things get tricky."

A very thoughtful Chloe watched as Tanya took off again and waved as the helo circled the village and flew away. Chloe felt a new sense of isolation. Whilst she had made progress with the women and they obviously trusted her, she had no real friends among the Vikings even though she had been in the establishment for more than two years. She enjoyed Thor's attention and their time in bed, but she listened to Tanya and decided to be more alert and keep her eyes open for anything out of the ordinary.

One evening when Chloe was alone in her hut one of the women crept in, giving Chloe a fright; Chloe had always kept the women at arm's length, not wanting to alarm Thor. "I'll be quick," said Helga, as Chloe made sure the bed was between her and her visitor, "nobody knows I'm here, but don't be frightened. You need to be very careful though; the men are planning something very big. Most of them will be leaving here on horseback in three weeks or something like that, according to my husband. They are to meet up with another group and they will then attack your people; there was some mention of

Newcastle, but I don't know anything beyond that. My husband says it is my job to capture you and put you in the dungeon."

"When, when is this to happen?" Chloe asked, now on full alert.

"Three weeks or so, I am to come and take you the night before they leave."

Chloe quietly acknowledged the information, but said nothing more. Her first thought was that she might release the homing pigeons first thing in the morning.

"You have been very good to all of us women," her visitor continued, "given us our lives back. None of us want to return to what it was before, with Thor behaving like some sort of medieval king and treating us like slaves and, whether we liked it or not, being taken to his bed. Since you have been here that hasn't happened any more. I must go now. Please don't discuss this with anyone else, but I will be back from time to time to see what we can do." The woman slipped away into the night.

Chloe sat down heavily on the bed wondering what she should do. The homing pigeons were one idea but there was no guarantee they would arrive safely. She also knew Tanya was not planning to visit within the next month or longer. "Letting the homing pigeons go will alert Thor that I am aware there is something in the wind, so I won't do that just yet," Chloe thought. She felt badly let down by Thor; it now seemed to her that Thor had been using her in order to try to establish dominance over Settlement-controlled areas and she felt foolish for not having seen through him. She also felt frightened at Thor's apparent ruthlessness. She couldn't go to Susan's since she was sure her husband Hercules would immediately inform Thor. She would have to try either to get to Newcastle and her granddaughter Kim, or to Banksia. Until she had a plan she would have to behave completely normally with Thor. She also worried about how she would cope on her own on horseback riding to any of those places. She didn't really know the way and, although she had some skills in the bush, she didn't think she could kill snakes or wallabies as Kim had done during their escape from the flood in Sydney. "I'm too bloody old for all this," she thought.

After the conversation with Tanya and the visit from Helga, Chloe had put herself on high alert while still behaving normally during her encounters with Thor. One evening Thor, as was his habit, had gone to have a shower after they had had sex. Earlier Chloe had noticed a scrappy piece of paper lying on a table next to the bed, so as soon as Thor had left the room she picked it up keeping a sharp eye out for Thor's return. She read it with growing concern. It was from a Morton man called Jerry, who had now been re-established at The Settlement. It read:

almost all Settlement forces are occupied in moving the Kanangra establishment to the Southern Highlands so The Settlement is virtually undefended. This must create an opportunity for you to put in place your plan to take it over.

Chloe returned the note to exactly the same position as it was when she picked it up. She feigned sleep when, a few minutes later, Thor returned.

As part of her normal routine, Chloe had often gone for rides around the Viking property so she knew it well. Now her rides had much more purpose. She established that the hole in the fence which Jason had used to leave the property and call Roger and the troops during the first visit to the Vikings was still there. As a precaution, she cut another hole 200 metres further along the fence away from the guardhouse and the main gate. She also found a place in the bush, not very far from the guardhouse, where she could hide food which she would need on her journey.

A few days later Chloe found her two homing pigeons in their cage, dead, with their necks wrung. There was no subtlety and it was obviously intended as a warning. Chloe sought Helga out at the evening milking which took place twice a day, morning and evening. With an almost indiscernible nod she indicated that another meeting was in order. Helga crept into Chloe's hut later that night, "I can't stay long in case I'm missed," she said.

"I'm going to leave to warn Tanya and the others, but I need a bit of a head start." Chloe shuddered at the thought of what Thor would do to her if she was ever caught having run away from the Viking village, as she handed Helga a bunch of deep green leaves.

"You make some sort of hooch for them, don't you? I know Thor seems to like it." Helga nodded uncertainly. "Boil these leaves in water and then add some of it, say about one litre to every four, to the hooch. All it does is make them sleep for 24 hours. That will give me time to really get away. Three nights from now; it's the night the men have arranged one of their usual drinking sessions, isn't it?"

"This won't kill them, will it?" asked Helga.

"No, definitely not."

"Pity, I need something that will kill the bastards. What will happen to us? The women here. When you leave, they may blame us."

"Won't the men still be focussed on meeting up with that other group? They don't think I know anything of their plans."

"Maybe, but they may get suspicious."

"Someone killed my homing pigeons. You could tell them that I was scared and maybe that frightened me off," said Chloe.

"If we come up with shit like that Thor will definitely think we've told you something," Helga responded.

"The only thing that I know that will kill them is a bullet," Chloe continued. "Is there any possibility that some of you could escape at the same time as me or the day after?"

"Where would we go?"

"If you are serious about leaving, make for Newcastle. We have a big operation up there. My granddaughter Kim is in charge; she'll look after you."

"How the hell do we get to Newcastle?"

"Horseback; just go straight up the coast road."

"We'll see," said Helga. "I'll tell you our plans before you leave."

In the intervening days Chloe spent one night with Thor as usual and was on high alert to see if there was any change in his behaviour. She concluded that he was a very good actor as he was just as genial and welcoming as always. He had provided a light snack, which he knew she liked, and a pot of tea. This was flattery indeed as far as Chloe was concerned since tea supplies were running low and were reserved for Thor's exclusive use. She undressed him slowly, which she knew he enjoyed as it obviously turned him on. She almost persuaded herself that her worries were unnecessary and that Jerry's note and what Helga told her was fantasy. The next morning, she had left Thor's palace and returned an hour later to fetch something she had left behind. There were three of Thor's lieutenants in the main bedroom with him, talking while Thor attended to his ablutions. "Has the whore cottoned on to our plans, is she suspicious at all?" asked one of the men. "I killed those bloody pigeons a few days ago and left them in their cage, did she say anything about that?"

"No, nuffink, everythin' was normal," answered Thor with a laugh, "she's still bloody good in bed, we had fun. She's the ideal 'ostage. Those stuck-up bloody Bowers will do anyfink to rescue 'er and oi will enjoy havin' that too clever by 'alf Tanya in my clutches. Oi've wanned to fuck her from the minnit oi saw 'er. Oi'm quite sure the whore, as yer describe her, thinks..."

Chloe didn't waste another second listening and quickly left; the men unaware of her fleeting presence. Her feelings were partly of humiliation but mainly anger. Once she was back in her hut she mentally went through her escape plans. Helga had told her that some of them would leave on horseback to Newcastle the day after Chloe had escaped. Helga had said the men would be fed the doctored hooch as planned. "I have done a little experimentation," she told Chloe, smiling, "even when they wake up they won't be very mobile for a few hours."

After dark, once the men's drinking session was in full swing, Chloe crept out of her hut making quite sure she was not seen. She tapped the inside pocket of her warm jacket and felt the comforting weight of the .38 Smith & Wesson revolver. She was wearing dark clothing and taking, her horse's bridle, she crept towards the small paddock where she had tethered her horse at dusk. Feeding the horse some small treats she slipped on the bridle and led the horse to the stable yard where she saddled the animal. Chloe looked around carefully trying to make certain that she could not be seen. The night was dark; there were a few small points of light around the village as people moved about and a dull glow and sounds of laughter from Thor's palace. Chloe quietly led her horse away from the stables and down the track; she mounted the animal once she was out of sight of the village and quietly cantered towards the gate.

As she was loading her horse up with the provisions she had hidden Chloe was suddenly confronted by another rider. Chloe made a grab for her revolver. A young female voice said, "Please, please, don't hurt me, I think I can help."

"Who the hell are you and what do you want?"

"I've been watching you over the past week or so, I can see you're trying to leave. I saw that bastard, one of Thor's lieutenants, wring the necks of your pigeons. When they start that drinking it spells big trouble for all the women in the village. They have been behaving better since you arrived and took up with Thor, but I can tell you once they get going tonight none of the women will be safe."

"One false move and I'll plug you," said Chloe firmly. "So what do you want from me?"

"I want to get out of here, maybe to the place where Venus is, I hear she is very happy," the girl whimpered. "Please let me go with you, I have two horses and quite a lot of food. We can use the second horse as a pack horse."

"Okay," said Chloe, wondering what she should do. The last thing she wanted was a passenger and what if this was some kind of trap?

"As I have already told you, any buggering around and I will unhesitatingly shoot you."

"It's not a trap, I promise. My name is Annabel, by the way. I know you are Chloe Bower."

Chloe knew the girl from one of the work groups she had established and decided she would take her at face value. "We had better get packed up and not waste any more time then," she said.

They spent 20 minutes in the dark rearranging and packing all the food and equipment they had between them.

"It's lucky you thought to bring that spare horse," offered Chloe.

"While they were here I watched the people from your military Academy training our men, and spent time talking to one of the trainers, so learnt a lot from him; Thor wouldn't let women join the programme. As you know the trainers went home more than a year ago now."

"I'll bet that's not all he taught you," thought Chloe. "What was his name?" she asked.

"Adrian. He said he was based in the Blue Mountains."

"Yes, he is, I taught him to ride. He's a very good horseman, as are many at The Settlement." Chloe thought she now understood Annabel's motivation and became less suspicious.

With Chloe leading the way and Annabel leading the pack horse, they emerged cautiously from the bush and found the original hole in the fence, which they navigated easily. An hour later, under the dim light of a quarter moon, Chloe found what she thought was the path leading to Banksia. "We should be heading just west of north," she told Annabel.

"I've hardly ever been outside the Viking village," said Annabel. "I was only seven when the flood happened. We moved here about two years before the flood. I'm 17 now. So I won't be much use in helping to navigate I'm afraid."

"I should be alright," said Chloe more confidently than she felt, "we just need to keep going in the right direction, and we must put as much distance as we can between us and the village. When they find we are missing as sure as anything there will be a pursuit."

They kept going in a north westerly direction for the rest of the night and most of the next day, guided by the path that had developed between the Vikings and Banksia. They stopped occasionally to rest the horses and to let them graze and drink in the various streams they crossed. Chloe had spent some time in the bush with the younger riders due for Academy training and had found she had an instinctive sense of direction.

"We must be careful not to overdo it with the horses," said Chloe. "If they become lame we really will be in the soup." Whilst the path was well defined they noticed the surrounding bush was tangled and overgrown. "Because of the higher rainfall," Chloe pointed out. Both women were nervous and frightened by the crash of the occasional wallaby running away. Once, a snake slithered across the path. It was the fear of what lay behind them that kept them going.

"You can bet that Thor and the other men will not bother with the niceties of taking care of their mounts," Annabel said.

"No, I suppose not, but we must be a bit smarter than they are. I think any pursuit will make for Banksia in the first instance but if they have seen no sign of us, maybe Thor or whoever he sends after us will think we might have made for Newcastle. So when we rest from now on, it must now be well off the track in the hope they might just tear on past us."

Helga

Back at the Viking village, Helga had taken Chloe's advice and she and five others left on horseback at dawn following Chloe's departure; Helga decided not to try to take any other horses, partly because most of the women lacked skills with horses and handling one horse each would be as much as they could manage. They were armed with a motley collection of pistols and small-bore rifles Helga had filched from their menfolk; she herself owned a .256 Mannlicher with a scope. None of the women had much experience in the bush and, with the exception of Helga, only had a rudimentary notion of how to handle the weapons. While they had some food for themselves, it was insufficient for a journey that would take the best part of four days and they had not made any provision for the horses at all, expecting that they would be able to graze on the way.

Thor and the men gradually came to from about midday. "What a great night," observed one of Thor's henchmen, shaking his head in an attempt to clear it. "What I need now is cunt, preferably young cunt," he muttered. Wandering off he found the village women in a high state of panic. In his still soporific state it took him a few minutes to understand what the problem was. When he realised that a number of women had left the village during the night he half ran and half walked back to Thor's palace, "The women, the fucking women have run away," he announced breathlessly.

"Wha' you talkin' about?" asked a still-sleepy Thor. The man repeated himself. "'Ow many?" asked Thor, rapidly waking up. Anything threatening his leadership caused a rush of testosterone into his system and he was almost back to his aggressive best within minutes of understanding what was being said. "Wher'd they go?" he asked. The man shrugged. Thor, now fully dressed went outside and found the gaggle of women. "Wha' is all this about some of the wimmen leavin' the village?"

"Helga and five of them took horses and ran off, I think maybe towards Newcastle," answered Venus's mother who was still loyal to Thor despite her mistreatment at his hand. "Why didn't you stop 'em for Chroist's sake?" he grabbed the woman and shook her.

"I just saw 'em gallopin' off, I had no idea."

"Likely bloody story," Thor thundered and pushed her roughly away. He held his head. Another woman rushed up. "Annabel, my daughter, is also gone."

"Did she go wi' the uvver five?" asked Thor.

The new arrival shook her head. "I don't think so, she didn't sleep in her bed last night; I thought she might be with one of you, but all her things are missing as well as two horses."

Thor stood still for a second. "Oi'll jus' check on the Bower woman. 'As anyone seen 'er this mornin'?" The bemused expressions surrounding him and the lack of any kind of answer made him rush off and tear into Chloe's hut. He rampaged around throwing everything around in his frenzy to find her, completely trashing the inside of the hut. Thor raced over to a group of men who had enjoyed the drinking session with him the night before.

"Six of the bitches, includin' Helga, 'ave gone off towards Newcastle; I wan' a posse to go after 'em. Bring 'em all back here; Oi'll deal with 'em personally." He glared around, "Go on, off you go!"

"The Bower woman seems to 'ave lef' on 'er own," Thor mused, pacing up and down. "Maybe to Banksia. Oi'll take two others to bring 'er back 'ere, but I will personally visit Hercules first. God help anywun if they 'ave done anything to 'elp 'er."

Helga and her companions made good progress for the first day or so until one of the horses started to go lame. They continued, now more slowly to allow for the lame horse, following the main road where rusty old road signs showed the way to Newcastle. Most of the women had not left the Viking village since they had arrived there before the flood and were horrified to see the road littered with the now dilapidated wrecks of old abandoned vehicles. One of the women, Alice, plucked up the courage to peer into the cab of one of the cars, and was instantly sick. "We think we are hard done by," she said. She glanced at Helga, "Give me the lame horse, I'll go back, I don't want any more of this. At least we're alive."

"Okay," said Helga after a moment's hesitation, "you know what they will do to you when they find you, don't you?"

Alice nodded, "I've been fucked by half the men in the village. You know how they behave after one of their drinking sessions. At least I'm alive. If they catch you they will probably kill you."

"If you are certain then go; I suggest you take a route away from the road," continued Helga. "If there is anyone following us they will probably use the road, as we did. Maybe keep the road in sight so you don't get lost, and take it easy with that lame horse." Alice tearfully exchanged her horse for the lame one and turned around to return to the Viking village.

"We had better keep going," said Helga. "I wonder how long it will be before we see the pursuit?"

Within another day two more horses became lame. None of the horses had ever done much work and were quite unused to the hard ride they were now experiencing. Helga stopped the group near a stream and after some thought said to them, "Two of you must continue on and find Kim as quickly as you can, it will only take another day or so; they have helicopters up there and will be able to get to the village within minutes once they know what's going on. If there's a pursuit it won't be long before we see them here. We need to make sure we are partially visible and then we are going to ambush them and shoot the shit out of them. The youngest and smallest of us should go on to Newcastle, it gives the horses a better chance. Now go," she said, pointing at the two youngest. "We want you out of sight before there is any chance of the pursuit appearing."

They watched as the girls rapidly disappeared over the horizon on two of the still able-bodied horses. "Now we need to find a place where we can ambush anyone following. Here at the crossroads," announced Helga. She placed her two very nervous companions in a small copse on the side of the road, having tied their horses up a short distance away. She gave them a very brief lesson on how to handle their weapons. "I'm going out onto the road where I'll be certain to be seen," she said. "None of them will suss out that we have split up so I expect that however many there are they will come charging up towards me. Let them get to within about 50 or so metres and then let them have it. You're both lying down, so they'll have difficulty seeing you."

"Where will you be?" asked a quavering voice.

"On the other side of the road, behind one of those large trees. Even if you can't see very well, keep shooting; it will keep them off balance."

CHLOE

Chloe and Annabel continued to make good progress. Chloe, remembering some of the lessons from her journey with Kim all those years earlier when they had escaped Sydney at the time of the flood, said to Annabel, "We need to get off the path, but if there's a pursuit and if they are smart enough to follow our tracks, we must make it look like we have gone one way and then make camp well off the path on the other side. Lead your horse through the bush and then walk up the stream about four or five hundred metres up there," she pointed. "Make sure you walk the horse in the stream where they won't be able to follow your tracks. Just camp, absolutely no fire." An hour later she joined a very nervous looking Annabel, who had competently set up camp.

"We need to keep very quiet," Chloe said, "as this is the path to Banksia."

Chloe busied herself making a small meal from their supplies that needed no cooking, while Annabel made sure the horses were safely tethered. Chloe noticed the pretty, slim brown-haired Annabel was easy and comfortable round the horses. She was dressed in a suitable pair of jodhpurs and was wearing riding boots. There was no conversation except for essentials. When they had finished the meal, Chloe said, "You take the first watch, Annabel; call me either when you are tired or if you hear anything."

Chloe crawled into the two-man tent and feigned sleep. She still had some suspicions regarding Annabel's motivations so unobtrusively watched her companion walk a few steps and park herself on a convenient rock a short distance away from the tent. Instinct made Chloe crawl out of the tent on the side where Annabel couldn't see her. She moved to a place behind a small outcrop of rocks with a stunted bush poking out of the top, where she had a good view of the tent as well as Annabel. Although it was dark, she could see the shape of Annabel with the help of a half moon.

Some faint sounds came from the direction of the main path. Annabel moved uneasily but to Chloe's surprise, instead of coming to the tent to wake Chloe, she saw Annabel creep off in the direction of the path. Chloe followed her at a safe distance; she moved from tree to tree keeping Annabel's dim shape in sight, while carefully placing her feet as she walked, trying desperately not to tread on a stick or make any other noise. It took almost half an hour for Annabel to reach the main path. Again, much to Chloe's surprise, Annabel stood in the path making sure she was clearly visible in the moonlight. A minute later, two of Thor's lieutenants jumped out of the nearby bushes and took a shrieking Annabel down. This all looked pretty strange to Chloe. She wondered if the whole episode was just a set up to confuse her or was Annabel just so stupid as to make herself an obvious target.

"Okay, gotcha, yer bitch," muttered one of the men. "Now take us to the whore, or there'll be trubble." Thor had detoured to Hercules' place to see if Chloe was there.

Chloe wasn't able to decide if this was all part of an elaborate charade. She had the absolute advantage of surprise; whether the girl was a protagonist or not she would certainly have no idea that Chloe was nearby. The two Vikings were standing in a patch of moonlight with Annabel now kneeling and whimpering at their feet. Chloe, still hidden, was less than ten metres away. She levelled the .38 and fired two shots, one each, into the bodies of the men and then another two once they had fallen to the ground. Not waiting to see if she had killed them Chloe leapt out of the bushes, grabbed Annabel by the arm and within seconds had dragged the whimpering girl out of sight. "Quiet, silly bitch," whispered Chloe through her teeth. "Another sound from you and the next bullet will be into your head." Chloe stayed where she was, a few metres off to the side of the path, for a good half an hour, with the reloaded gun stuck firmly into the ribs of the young girl. She was certain there would be more men in pursuit, other than just the two oafs lying in the path, but there was no movement. One of the men groaned and tried to crawl away, the other one lay ominously still. Chloe eventually hoisted Annabel to her feet and they made their way back to their small campsite. Without a word, Chloe bound and gagged the terrified girl. "You, young lady, have plenty of questions to answer, but we'll leave that until morning. I would be very careful how you behave from now on. It would be the easiest thing in the world to put a bullet into your thick skull and leave you for the dingoes."

Wondering what to do, Chloe eventually decided it was possible there were at least one and possibly two more members of the pursuit team, so she crept back to the main path. Peering out from her hiding place in the bushes she could see three horses tethered to a nearby tree and the huge figure of Thor trying to attend to one of his lieutenants. She had a fleeting feeling of guilt but then considered what would have happened to her had the tables been turned. Thor clumsily lifted the bleeding man up on to one of the horses.

"'Old on vere," he mumbled. The man responded by losing consciousness and falling heavily to the ground. A forlorn looking Thor then went over to the other man who was obviously dead, picked him up and strapped him on to one of the horses. He then looked at the first man and did the same for him.

Looking about her Chloe considered taking Thor out there and then. "It'll save us a lot of trouble down the track," she thought. However, she was quite unable to make herself shoot the man in cold blood; he had been her lover. "Maybe he has learned his lesson and won't trouble us anymore," she muttered unconvincingly to herself.

Within a few minutes Thor had mounted his own horse and, leading the other two, moved off into the night heading back in the direction of his village.

Chloe decided she would be unable to sleep after all the activity so she packed up the camp, untied Annabel's bonds, saying to her as she helped her mount her horse, "One false move and I will have no hesitation in putting a bullet in you."

"I can explain everything," said a weeping Annabel.

"You certainly will, but not now. You will ride in front of me and my gun is loaded, so be very careful."

Chloe confidently headed up the main path towards Banksia. The path was clear due to the traffic it carried with the constant movement between Banksia and the Vikings; the surrounding bush was thick and overgrown. The one night they spent on the way to Banksia, Chloe tied and bound Annabel after they had eaten their meal and left her inside the tent. Chloe slept next to the small fire they had allowed themselves, Chloe now confident there would be no further pursuit. She made sure that they camped well off the track and that nobody would be able to tell where they had left the path.

By mid-afternoon on the fourth day after leaving the Viking village they rode into Banksia, a collection of cottages erected haphazardly surrounding a rough patch of open ground. They were greeted warmly by Joseph and Cath and the other residents, who all stopped what they were doing and came to greet the visitors. Despite the ramshackle appearance of the place the operation had benefitted hugely from the security provided by The Settlement, and the solar installations had helped to transform their lives.

When they had unsaddled Chloe briefed Joseph and the six Academy members, who Mark had stationed permanently at Banksia, leaving Annabel under guard.

"What do you want to do?" asked Joseph and his wife Cath, who had enjoyed the security provided by their association with The

Settlement but were now nervous. "The idea of having Thor and his thugs rampaging across the district is very worrying."

"Access to this place, from the east, is only through the narrow steep gorge, the path you just took," said one of the Academy people addressing Chloe. "It's easy enough to defend. I'll set up a permanent defence patrol of four or five people. This is only a short-term solution though; we'll need more people from the Academy to deal with Thor properly if he's intent on going berserk, which is the message I'm getting from you, Mrs Bower."

Chloe nodded. "Priority is getting word to Tanya. We can get to the Bandstand in four days, where there's telephone contact with Tanya. I need one of you people from the Academy to come with me please."

Chloe had deliberately not questioned Annabel regarding her antics until they arrived at their destination. "I had enough to think about in getting to the safety of Banksia and making sure we were safe from any further pursuit," she explained to Joseph. She spent half a day interrogating Annabel in a spare hut she had been allocated. She simply could not understand Annabel's apparently bizarre behaviour. To start with, Annabel would answer no questions. Chloe then said to her, "I think we should just send you back to the Vikings, you were obviously some sort of a plant. You can go back to your friends."

Annabel fell to her knees at this suggestion, desperately clutching Chloe's ankles, "No, no, please, I will be raped and then left in the dungeon!"

"What the hell were you doing, then? We were quite safe and the pursuit would not have found us."

Annabel continued to look confused and said nothing.

"If you don't answer the question we will do as I said and send you back to Thor and his cronies."

"I was scared," said Annabel. "I thought the men chasing us would eventually catch up and they would have beaten, raped and even killed us. I thought if I helped them they would see me as being on their side. I'm sorry, very sorry," she wept, looking down.

"The priority is getting word to Tanya as soon as possible about Thor's plans," said Chloe, talking to Joseph and the leader of the Academy detachment at Banksia once she had dealt with Annabel. "We'll leave Annabel here, but I'll try to get someone to pick her up in one of the choppers and take her to The Settlement. What we do with her after that is up to Tanya. She's confused and has hardly been out of the Viking village since she was a small girl. Maybe we can somehow make her into a useful citizen. The problem with the Vikings is that because of the way they treat the women there, all they think about is their own survival."

Joseph and the Banksia people reluctantly agreed to the situation. The last thing they needed was Thor rampaging around looking for one of his escaped women.

Before she left with the one Academy person who could be spared, Chloe had a long conversation with Annabel over a meal, telling her, "I don't really understand why you behaved like you did. If you behave yourself here, I will arrange for you to be transferred to The Settlement and we can then see what we can do to help you become someone who is valued by society. You may even be able to meet Adrian again." Annabel smiled at the mention of Adrian and nodded. She didn't say anything.

Alice

Alice, having taken Helga's advice to travel away from the road, made slow progress back towards the Viking village. Half the time she walked, leading the badly limping horse. During one of these periods she heard and caught a glimpse of a group of half a dozen men galloping furiously along the road, obviously in pursuit of her friends. Alice kept hidden. "They will kill them all," she shuddered to herself.

Two days later Alice arrived back at the main gate which, unusually, was unmanned. She made her way on foot through the bush leading her horse and making sure she wasn't seen. She released the horse into the main paddock and stored its tack. She nervously went to her hut expecting to have to answer some awkward questions from her husband, but there was no sign of him either. Alice returned to her normal duties collecting eggs from the henhouse and making sure the vegetable patch was properly watered, made much easier in the last few years with the solar powered pump and sprinkler system provided courtesy of The Settlement's re-supply programme. After a day Alice thought she had got away with her indiscretion. She was wrong. Thor barged into her hut the next day and unceremoniously gave her a huge clout, which sent her flying across the room. "Oi know you lef' wi' all the others!" he bellowed. "Where were you goin'?"

Alice tried to deny everything but was locked in the dungeon. "Yer, 'usband, when he come back from Newcastle, will sort yer out," she was told.

Helga

Helga had placed the two nervous women in a clump of bushes facing the road to their south, making certain they both had a clear view of any pursuit. She hid herself in a copse on the other side of the road. The three women did not have to wait long. They saw what soon turned out to be six men on horseback galloping frantically towards them. The two young women on their way to Newcastle had been gone for half a day and Helga briefly showed herself on her horse before she withdrew to her hiding place. There were shouts from the men who appeared to redouble their efforts. Helga tied her horse to a tree and waited. As the posse approached there were a few desultory shots from the hidden women, altogether missing their targets. The men came to a confused stop. Helga took careful aim and fired, knocking one of the men off his horse. There was another flurry of shots from the hidden women, again doing no damage. The remaining men quickly disappeared from sight. A few minutes later Helga saw three of the men jump up out of the scrub. They rushed into the bushes, having identified the women's position. The screaming women were disarmed, and savagely beaten with fists and horse whips. Helga felt helpless; she couldn't shoot at them for fear of hitting one of the women. Uncertain of the position of the other men, Helga remained hidden whilst making sure she could see what was happening. Having completely subdued the two women, the three men gestured and two men appeared from a position not far from where Helga was originally hidden.

At that moment, to Helga's amazement and relief, a Land Cruiser accompanied by an open backed three-ton lorry came tearing down the road from the north. Both vehicles were packed with what Helga determined were soldiers. She then noticed one of the young girls who had been sent on ahead to The Settlement's Newcastle base waving from the back of the lorry. The vehicles stopped and within seconds the troops had all rapidly dispersed into the surrounding bushland. One shot was fired into the air and a woman's voice yelled, "Everyone stay still and do not move! Drop your weapons!"

One of the men turned from attacking the two women, aiming his rifle at the sound. He was shot dead. Everyone else including Helga emerged from their hiding places with their hands up. Settlement troops stood up from their hiding places, now much closer to the conflict zone. The Viking men were bound with cable ties and their weapons dumped into a pile.

"You must be Helga," announced the woman who led the rescue. "I'm Kim, Tanya's niece. It looks as if we arrived just in time." Helga's rifle was returned to her. Bemused by the turn of events, she said nothing.

"You three can return with us in one of the trucks," said Kim, indicating Helga and the two injured women. "I'll get the women to hospital as soon as possible."

She instructed three of her troops to gather all the horses up and ride them to the Newcastle base. "Some of the horses look like they are in a pretty bad way," Kim observed, "so take it slowly." The two dead men were placed in graves already dug for them by the Academy troops. The two women, despite their injuries, wept and muttered some half-remembered prayers over the graves. The surviving Viking men just sat there glowering.

The next day Eustace landed one of the big Merlins on The Settlement parade ground, having picked up the injured women and the four Viking prisoners from Newcastle, as well as Annabel from Banksia and Susan and Mars from their outpost to the east of Amazonia. Hercules had been ordered to join his father Thor's expedition to attack The Settlement. Tanya was on hand when the helicopter doors were opened to disgorge its incompatible group of passengers. Chloe had arrived by this time and rushed up to hug Susan and take charge of Mars. Chloe also immediately took charge of Annabel. "You'll come and live with me for the time being," she said, "and I'll talk to Tanya about a programme for you." Annabel said nothing but looked around in wonderment at the neat and well-kept Settlement village.

Nursing staff collected the injured women, who looked about themselves in astonishment as they were whisked away on gurneys into the hospital. As the prisoners were about to be unloaded Tanya said to Eustace and the Academy escort, "Leave the fuckers where they are, I'll get Jonathan to agree to keep them in prison in Canberra."

"Canberra?" yelled one of the prisoners, "What the fuck are you talking about?"

Tanya looking in through the door of the chopper said to him firmly, "You are going to a military prison, in Canberra, where I expect you will spend a very long time. The days of you running around attacking your own people are over."

"Fucking bitch, just wait until Thor hears about this..."

"If I have anything to do with it, you will be able to report to Thor directly, from a neighbouring jail cell," answered Tanya with a half-smile on her face.

CHAPTER 6

The Battle with the Vikings

-Vikings 1. Preparation
Tanya

Tanya, racing back to her office on her own, left the prisoners in the Merlin under guard. She immediately phoned Jonathan.

"Jonathan, Tanya here. Please listen. There's a large force of Vikings on the move, they plan to join up with the people from Taree to come and attack us at The Settlement."

"How do you know that? Could be just another rumour."

"No, Jonathan, just hear me out. Chloe, your mother for Christ's sake, has just escaped Thor's clutches. The only goddam reason she decided to run was to warn us."

Tanya briefly explained how Chloe had escaped and the risks she had taken.

"It's solid info, fuck it, Jonathan. We also have a group of women who've escaped the Viking village. They've confirmed Thor's plans. He's already on the way…"

"Mnn. What do you expect me to do about it?"

129

"Jesus, Jonathan. This is dead serious. I expect your help for Christ's sake."

"Can't. We have a major op up north. I have no spare people. If you have over-deployed your troops, then pull them back. Stop empire building. There's your problem solved right there."

Most unusually, Tanya was struck dumb for a few moments.

"I don't fucking believe I am hearing this, Jonathan. There is a serious threat to the very existence of what we have built up over the years and you say you won't help."

"Can't. Sorry."

Tanya felt she had been slapped in the face. Jonathan and the military had always supported The Settlement. She now knew she was really on her own. Despite her churning emotions, then calmly explained the situation with her four prisoners. "Prisoners, sure," said Jonathan, "you'll have to drop them off here, we'll look after them and set up a trial like we did with the Morton people, but we can't do anything else."

Tanya rang off shaking her head. She asked Eustace to wait while she briefed Jason, her nephew and one of the stalwarts of the Academy. Jason had arrived in her office and had heard most of the conversation with Jonathan.

"Jonathan won't help?" he asked.

"Nope. We can still sort Thor out though. Once and for all," said Tanya more confidently than she felt.

"Take the 40 troops we have left here at The Settlement," she told Jason, "and try to make contact with the Taree people. See if you can persuade them to stay put. Take Derain with you. If they join up with Thor, we may be in real trouble. I'll deal with Thor, but I need to get our people back from Kanangra for that." Tanya hesitated. "Oh, and there's one other thing."

"Tell Venus as little as possible," said Jason quietly.

"As always, one step ahead of the sheriff."

When Tanya eventually returned to the helicopter she said to the escort, "We're short of people, so join Jason's group and I'll escort these pieces of dingo turd to Canberra." She carried her Steyr carbine with her and a holstered handgun. "Before you go can we just check the bonds on these assholes?"

There was a lot of swearing from one of the prisoners. Tanya shoved an old piece of cotton waste into his mouth as a gag. As they took off the man started to struggle against his bonds. Tanya opened one of the helicopter doors. "Go on with that shit," she said to the man, "and I'll tip you out of here for the birds and the dingoes to eat." The man glared at her and quietened down.

On arrival in Canberra, they were greeted by a sergeant who took the prisoners into custody and handed Tanya a note from Jonathan which read, "Please keep me in the picture. I can't see you today."

"Bowral," she said to Eustace, as they took off. She sniffed the air, "It smells better now." She smiled at Eustace.

They found Mark at the camp in Bowral near the centre of the area he and Virginia were now trying to settle. His troops were camped in the large grounds of what had been a five-star hotel not far from the centre of the deserted town. Having circled the area twice, Eustace was directed to a landing area. Mark, accompanied by a limping Virginia walking with the help of a stick, came to greet them.

"I'll be fine in a few weeks," said Virginia smiling. "All the hard work over the years has kept me fit and strong."

After further discussions about the progress in re-establishing the Kanangra settlement in the local area and what had happened to the remaining Morton villagers, Tanya explained the problem with Thor and the Vikings.

"I see; you need more troops," interrupted Mark.

"Yes, I need as many as possible to go north, with you leading them please, Mark." This was said more as an order rather than a request. "Don't worry Virginia, you'll get 'em all back when this little episode is over," she said looking at Virginia's anxious face.

Eventually they settled on 70 of the troops to be sent north, leaving just ten of the Academy people to deal with any issues arising from the resettlement of the Morton village. 40 of the troops would be taken by helicopter to the Bandstand, where they would be met by Roger with spare Settlement horses. Mark would ride with the 30 remaining troops with the intention of joining Roger's group at Banksia.

-Vikings 2. Thor

Thor, upon returning to the Viking village, wasted no time on returning from his pursuit of Chloe. He called what trusted lieutenants he could find to a meeting in his palace. Three men were sent to make contact with the group near Taree where, years earlier, he had sent Harold as a sleeper while he was originally trying to come to terms with David and Tanya. "They fink they 'ave me all tied up wiv their clever-dick type of inter-marriage stuff an' all that," he said to two of his closest lieutenants, "but they don' know what'll hit 'em and then we can all move to their smart village." Neither he nor any of his confidants could see beyond occupying The Settlement, which they all knew was a much better development than the Viking village.

Thor believed he still had Harold safely ensconced with the Taree group and was further cheered with the news on the bush telegraph that the survivors from Barrington Tops had also joined the Taree group. He had no doubts regarding the authenticity of this information, despite its age and uncertain origins. Thor had also found out about the clash with Settlement troops and how the Barrington group had been dealt with. "Vey'll be firsting for revenge," he told his lieutenants. "The Settlement people are soft; if they 'ad any sense they would've killed all the Barrington people, but wiv their holier than thou attitude they even treated some of 'em in 'ospital and let 'em go again."

As Thor was making his plans, Jerry arrived at the Viking village after ten days hard riding through the bush. Jerry, a Morton settler, now re-established at The Settlement, had kept in touch with Thor over several years while he was still at Morton. He had already sent Thor one message telling him that most Settlement troops were helping to move the Kanangra settlement to the Southern Highlands. He had watched the new arrangements with bemused anticipation. He felt he had no status at The Settlement, being a new resident, although he had no complaints about his treatment since his arrival. He now saw a golden opportunity to redress the situation, so shortly after Jason left with his 40 troops, Jerry, in the dead of night, saddled a horse and crept out of The Settlement enclave to join Thor. Jerry had no fears in the bush and knew where to find Thor and the Viking village. During supposedly casual conversations over the weeks he had been based at The Settlement, he knew exactly how to get to the Vikings. All he needed to do was to follow the well-worn paths to the Bandstand, St. Andrews and Banksia making sure he avoided those villages and all human contact...

Initially Thor took little notice of Jerry, being consumed with his own plans. He had almost finalised his plans when one of his lieutenants urged him to talk to Jerry, saying, "He says there are no troops at all left at The Settlement."

"I alreddy know vat," was Thor's response. "Vat's why we're plannin'..."

Unusually the lieutenant persisted, "We may not need the Taree people and Harold at all," he continued, "we can just go straight to The Settlement and walk in."

It took Thor a few seconds to understand what was being said. He then took the trouble to fully debrief Jerry, who was beginning to wonder what his role would be.

A week later Thor gathered up his more than 100 warriors. They stood in well-organised platoons below the steps of Thor's palace, with Thor standing on the top step looking down. He was satisfied with what he saw, although he gave no recognition to the transformation Settlement trainers had wrought on what, in the past, had been an unruly rabble. Most of this group had been through the training provided by the Academy; they were well-directed and well-led.

In a brief harangue he said to them, "We're now in a persishen to go and take wha' roightfully belong to us. No more kow-towing to them patronising arseholes at The Settlement. Led by women, for fuck's sake. I 'ave some very secret knowledge about their troops, vey even call their women troops, for shit's sake. Wimmen who should be cooking, milking cows and lying on their backs... We'll walk in there wivout a shot bein' fired and take over. Roight, let's get goin'!" There was a wild cheer from his men.

The Academy-trained people helped Thor ensure they knew the route and that they had a good supply of rations for themselves and their horses; aided by Jerry, they planned a quick way through the bush directly to Settlement boundaries. There was a general air of optimism. "We'll take 'em by surprise," was one observation. There was no recognition of the fact the Chloe had escaped and may have been able to warn Tanya and The Settlement people of Thor's intentions. Most thought he had somehow dealt with Chloe and that she was dead. He had not brought the two dead lieutenants back to the village but had buried them in shallow graves in the bush. Thor's demeanour ensured there were no questions.

-Viking 3. The Women

As soon as the men had left, several of the women, encouraged by the lead Chloe and Helga had given, immediately gathered in Thor's palace. They released Alice from the dungeon. "I am not prepared to revert to what we had before, with the men behaving as if we're a bunch of slaves, and with them believing they can rape us whenever they're in the mood. If they think that's what they are coming back to I'll burn this whole place down, right now," Alice announced.

"Does anyone know what happened to the women that left here with you, Alice, and the men that followed them?" asked a voice.

"I think we can assume some of the women, at least, made it to The Settlement's development at Newcastle," said Alice. "The fact that nobody has returned here also suggests the men may have run into trouble and may even have been captured by the people in Newcastle."

"What do you think we should do?"

"There are still a few horses left, so say two of us go to Banksia and two of us go to Newcastle," offered Alice. "The rest of us should carry on here as usual, but we should all be ready to move at short notice. I have no intention of being here when Thor returns."

Gabriella, a large, forceful woman in her late-30s added, in a loud voice, "Did you all hear what Thor just said, about women? He just sees us as a bunch of slaves, nothing else. We can't let this go on. The relationship with The Settlement seems to have created a few options, so I'm sure they will take us in. There is Banksia, Amazonia, and some other places too..."

"There is also the Bandstand; and I've heard talk about a small settlement near Kurri-Kurri," added Alice.

"You, Alice and one other will go to Banksia," announced Gabriella. "You probably know the way, and we'll send another two to Newcastle. I'll keep watch and control over the armoury and some of the women here who may want to revert to the old ways." She made a move to where she knew Thor stored all the Viking weapons. "There are a few guns and things the men left here, which we'd better take charge of. If any of those women play up, we have the dungeon of course. I will, however, try to persuade as many as possible to join us and not let Thor back in to control our lives."

-Viking 4. Discovery
Tanya

Within four days Alice and her colleague arrived at Banksia. She was pleasantly surprised to see Settlement troops, who had been established for a few days, under Roger. "They seem to have understood Thor's up to something," she muttered to her companion. The two women sent to Newcastle also arrived safely. When Kim was told Thor had left with his large force, she phoned Tanya, who was trying to keep tabs on all her troops movements with Eustace flying one of the Merlins. Tanya and Eustace flew to Banksia via Amazonia, where they picked up Stephanie and were briefed by Alice and her colleague.

"How many armed people are left at the Viking village?" asked Tanya.

"None," answered Alice, "mostly only women are left there now, although there are a couple of men who were too ill to go with Thor."

"So you're telling me the place is completely undefended."

"Yes, and most of the women there are quite fed up with the regime that Thor has run for so many years. They may want to burn the place down before they let Thor back."

"What are the women planning to do after that?" asked Tanya.

"Well, Chloe showed us another way, bless her. So, we were hoping you would let us join one of your establishments. We are all hard workers…"

"Yes, yes," said Tanya excitedly. "We'll find a place for you all somewhere. Just let me think for a few minutes."

"Okay," said Tanya, calling Kim from the Merlin, now parked at Banksia, as she barked her instructions. "This gives us the opportunity to shoot the living shit out of Thor and his thugs. It's the last thing the stupid fucker'll be expecting. Get the other two Merlins ready, as we did for Morton. Joe knows what to do. Have a couple of sharpshooters in each machine. I'll tell you when I've found Thor's men." Tanya briefly repeated the conversation she'd had with Jonathan. "So we're on our own," she said, "there won't be any help from the military."

"What should we do with the women we now have here?" Kim asked.

"Set them to work. We'll find somewhere else for them after this is over, if they want. You need to keep them calm."

"And tell them that we admire their courage and that they will be welcome to be a part of the society that we are trying to create," Kim finished off the sentence for Tanya.

Tanya laughed, "Way ahead of me," she said. "Jason, Derain and 40 of our people are on the way to see the group in Taree. Help him if he needs it."

-Viking 5. Tanya's forces ranged against Thor Derain

In the meanwhile, Jason had managed to persuade Derain to join him. Derain was the leader of the Aboriginal group who had been instrumental in helping The Settlement Academy understand how to survive in the bush. Derain, together with a companion and Rebecca from the Academy, patrolled some days ahead of the main party, their main purpose being to see if they could find the messengers sent by Thor to the Taree settlement. Several days were spent ranging through the deserted towns of Singleton and then Gloucester. As expected the streets were littered with the broken-down wrecks of vehicles scattered haphazardly in every corner. They paid no attention, knowing what they would find in the houses and vehicles.

While making their way carefully through Gloucester, something made Derain take a closer look as he stopped to sniff the air. "Woodsmoke," he muttered. They dismounted and carefully led the horses through the streets, their weapons at the ready with Derain in the lead. He left his horse in the care of one of his companions as he scouted the next street. They soon traced the faint odour to a hotel in the town with a dusty broken sign reading, 'Roundabout Inn'. Derain and Rebecca kept watch while their companion led the horses away to a patch of grass several streets away, where he tethered them before he joined the others. Soon three men emerged and sat eating on the front step of the hotel. "Thor's people," said Derain, "we'll wait."

As darkness descended the men went into the building, making no effort to shut the doors. "They'll sleep," announced Derain. Waiting another 40 minutes Derain made a hand signal indicating that the others should follow him. The trio crept into the hotel building, making absolutely no noise, using all their bushcraft skills to feel their way and making sure they didn't bump into anything unexpected. Derain successfully found two of Thor's men in the main room. There was a small fire in the fireplace, giving off some light; he swiftly removed their rifles. Rebecca found the third man in an adjoining room. She found and removed his rifle also, despite the dark. None of the men stirred. Derain's group each stood by one of the sleeping forms and, operating as one, stuck a rifle into the face of their chosen victim. Thor's trio each made an instinctive grab for their own weapon, no longer there. There were several scuffles before the trio were subdued, bound hand and foot with cable ties, and dragged out into the street. Derain lit a fire.

"Who are you and what are you doing?" asked Rebecca. There was no answer.

"Bring a horse," Derain told his Aboriginal companion. "We'll hang one of them," he said conversationally to Rebecca. "There's no time." He produced a piece of rope and tied it around the neck of one of the prisoners. A horse with a bridle but no saddle was brought into the firelight. Derain handed the reins to Rebecca, which she tied to a nearby tree while he and his companion hauled the man onto the skittish horse. They tied his hands behind his back and Derain tossed the end of the rope over a sturdy branch and tightened it. "Ask again," said Derain, looking at Rebecca.

She repeated the question. "Tell him, Dave," muttered one of the other prisoners. Again, there was no response. Derain signalled to Rebecca who held tightly onto the reins as Derain gave the horse a mighty whack, with a stick, making it jump away. There was a sharp yell from the man on the horse, and the man was left hanging in the tree, kicking, gurgling and gasping for breath. Rebecca intervened. "Cut him down," she said, "he'll talk now."

Derain pulled out a knife and cut the man down, who dropped heavily to the ground coughing and spluttering. He was violently sick.

There was a shattered silence. "The same thing will happen to you two unless we are told who you are and what you're up to. We can't afford to stuff around," Rebecca said.

Within an hour they had the whole story. They tested it several times with the men out of earshot of each another.

"Thor has now planned to go straight to The Settlement," muttered Derain. "We need to get word to Jason and Tanya. We have to be quick."

"What do we do with these pieces of shit?" asked Rebecca, indicating the three men.

Derain looked at her, "We'll take their horses, guns and shoes and leave them here. They won't be able to go anywhere. We can come back and fetch them later. If they run away, they'll die in the bush." He shrugged. He would have shot all three of them.

They searched the hotel and some of the houses in the surrounding area, making quite sure there were no firearms or shoes left. They left some food for their prisoners.

"You'll stay here," Derain admonished, pointing at the terrified men, "we'll come back later."

"One of us should go ahead," suggested Rebecca, "because leading the prisoner's horses will slow us up. I know the way; I'll go if that's okay with you Derain."

Derain nodded; he had no concerns about Rebecca becoming lost in the bush. "You go, you're the lightest of us. It'll be quicker that way." He smiled.

Rebecca cantered off to warn Jason. She knew a balance between getting to Jason's camp as soon as possible and looking after her horse was essential. Once the daylight started to fade she decided to stop for the night. As she approached a stream near the unused and damaged road, she dismounted and led the horse into the stream and walked for ten minutes in the water. "Just a precaution," she muttered to herself. The horse was tethered in a patch of grass, so it could reach the water and graze as well. She fed the animal a small amount of the fodder she had brought with her and fell asleep next to the small fire. Rebecca was not so fortunate the second night; it was pouring rain. After seeing to her horse, she ate some of the cooked food she had with her and spent an uncomfortable night wedged in the fork of a tree. Soaking wet, she set off just as the sky started to lighten on the third day, knowing it was a good day's ride to Jason's camp outside Bucketty. It rained all day. Both she and the horse were exhausted. Rebecca, knowing she was close to Jason's camp, kept going through the day and well into the night. Close to midnight, as the showers stopped, she heard the welcome voice of a sentry, "Halt, who goes there?"

"Rebecca," she answered, as she slipped off the horse, "Quick, get Jason, we've got a big problem."

A torch was shone in her face. "Rebecca, so it is. You look done in. I'll look after the horse."

"Bugger the horse," responded Rebecca, "get Jason, quick, now!"

The sentry ran off, knowing that Jason was in his two-man tent, near the smouldering fire. "It's Rebecca," he said as he shook Jason awake. "Come quick, she says it's really urgent."

Jason clambered out of his sleeping bag and, half-dressed, accompanied the sentry to where Rebecca was standing next to her horse.

"We found Thor's messengers on the way to the Taree place," a breathless Rebecca told Jason. "Thor is headed straight for The Settlement. He's cottoned on to the fact that all our forces are elsewhere. He sent messengers to Taree, who they think are under Harold's leadership, telling them to take their forces directly to The Settlement."

Jason knew he had to get back to The Settlement post haste, otherwise everything they had built up over the past 30 years would be destroyed. He shuddered, "Thor, in charge there, no way," he growled to himself. He reflected on his loving marriage to Thor's daughter, Venus. He shook his head, "The survival of The Settlement is paramount," he muttered, "everything else is a sideshow."

Taking the time to decide what he could best do under the new circumstances, Jason consulted with his platoon commanders and Rebecca. His troops were a good three days ride from home and the troops at Banksia under Roger were five days away. "We'll have to wait until dawn before we do anything, but I'll get two people ready to make a dash back home," he said to Rebecca. "We must get hold of Tanya. Hopefully she knows where we are…"

At dawn the next day, to everyone's relief, the camp was woken by the clatter of helicopter rotor blades. It was Tanya in the Bell.

"There's no sign of Thor anywhere," a worried Tanya announced, as she disembarked from the machine, removing her flying helmet.

"No sign of Thor,' said Jason, "but Rebecca has some news. She came in during the night." An exhausted and filthy looking Rebecca appeared. She told Tanya what she and Derain had unearthed.

"We need to find the bugger and his troops then," said Tanya after a moments contemplation. She returned to the helo and raised Kim on the blower. Having explained the situation, she said to Kim, "Thor has understood our forces are away from home. He took his troops south of Banksia and north of Amazonia. Get two copters scouring that area."

"And the third one?" asked Kim.

"Shift as many of Roger's troops from Banksia to The Settlement's eastern gate as possible; I just hope we're in time. I'll be going straight back home to organise resistance from there."

"Where do you want us?" asked Jason.

"Let's not panic," answered Tanya. "We have the big Merlins to shift troops around if needed. Move your force nearer to Singleton, which is closer to home if we need you. Thor may try to escape that way if we manage to nail him before he finds his way into The Settlement."

Tanya asked Rebecca if she wanted to come with her to The Settlement. Rebecca shook her head, "I'm okay now. I'll stick with Jason."

Tanya returned in the Bell Jetranger to The Settlement. "So far, no sign of Thor," she thought, as she landed on the parade ground.

-Viking 6. The ambush

Thor, leading his force through the bush, had hoped that by moving at night he would avoid detection. He caught a glimpse of Tanya's small helicopter racing back towards The Settlement and then realised the forces opposing him may have rumbled his strategy. Bold action was now required.

"If we can get into that bloody Settlement it'll all be over, they won't attack us if we're in the village itself, they won't want to shoot their own people," he said to his lieutenants.

With the help of one of the Merlins, Roger had successfully moved 20 of his troops, half his force, to positions close to but outside Settlement boundaries and in a place where they could stop anyone from entering The Settlement's eastern gate. He had no time to move the balance of his force. The eastern gate was on the top of a ridge some three hours walk downhill to the village, over very rough terrain. The country approaching the eastern gate was open, for several hundred metres in each direction, but with rough ground and rocky outcrops and a few stunted bushes through the whole area, providing excellent cover for Roger's troops. To the east and south was dense forest. Roger had time to individually place each one of his troopers in the best positions to defend the critical entrance to The Settlement. He made sure the gate was well-barricaded.

Before he could move the balance of his troops from Banksia, Roger's attention was drawn to a sudden flurry of gunshots, to his south, from first one and then another of the Merlins, tearing backwards and forwards towards targets on the ground a few hundred metres away. He knew they must be directed at what could only be Thor's forces. He saw one of their own falling from a chopper door. Roger moved from person to person to keep them calm.

"Wait until I give the order to fire," he said "and then give them everything you've got. We must stop them from getting through the gate." Roger knew the Vikings would substantially outnumber his own contingent.

The firefight between the Vikings and the Merlins approached at speed. All Roger could see was an enormous dust cloud. With a hand signal, he made sure the Merlins were aware of his position. Thor suddenly emerged from the dust and mayhem, leading his men on his white stallion and charging towards the eastern gate. Roger yelled, "Open fire!" as the Viking mob got to within about 100 metres. The Vikings kept coming and coming, despite the devastating fire from Rogers hidden troops, with men dropping from their mounts and horses stumbling and falling. The helicopters swerved away. A group led by Hercules of about 30 Vikings, seemingly overawed by the overwhelming fire, escaped and fled north, continuing their wild ride. Thor's horsemen came charging through Roger's men trampling several of them on the way.

Thor galloped up to the gate and, to Roger's great surprise, leapt off his horse and using his immense strength tore the gate off its hinges. He jumped back onto his mount and with a yell led some 40 of his followers into Settlement grounds. Roger and his men and women stayed where they were and continued to fire at the disappearing backs of the Vikings.

-Vikings 7. The attack on The Settlement

Tanya had, in desperation, earlier mobilised all Settlement children over the age of 13. She was struggling up the hill to the eastern gate with her two platoons of youngsters and was relieved by the sudden appearance of the two big Merlins firing volley after volley at targets some way outside Settlement boundaries. She called Eustace on their one operational walkie-talkie. One after another the Merlins roared over the village, banking steeply and returning rapidly to continue their pursuit. "Eustace, Tanya," she said. "What've you got?"

"Tanya, Thor just emerged from the bush to the south-east. We're giving 'em hell. I've identified Roger and his platoon, just east of the gate. Out."

Tanya could see the choppers continuing their pursuit, with ragged volleys emanating from Thor's Vikings. She continued to focus on getting her two platoons up the hill and into place. The choppers then seemed to withdraw just as Tanya heard a sustained burst of Steyr volleys, interspersed with dozens of ragged shots from what sounded like a variety of weapons. "Roger's troops and the Vikings" thought Tanya. She knew she had to hurry to get her last line of defence into place— there was no time to lose. She hurried her youngsters along. "Come on, come on, not far now," she urged.

As they dropped into several places Tanya had chosen, there were more Steyr shots and then a brief silence followed by a whoop and a yell as a large group of Viking horsemen led by Thor came clattering down the hillside. Enveloped in dust, they stopped briefly in confusion. The raiders were less than 100 metres from the well-hidden group of youngsters. "Let the bastards have it!" yelled Tanya as she fired burst after burst from her Steyr, until it was almost too hot to hold. The devastating fire from her and the youngsters caused the ragged band of horsemen to waver. Many were knocked off their horses either dead or wounded. Through the dust and cloud and gunsmoke Tanya thought she caught a glimpse of Thor, on his white stallion, dashing off back towards the gate. A dozen horsemen succeeded in breaking through, clattering down the hillside and finding their way to the centre of the village, where they set fire to two of the houses. Over the next hour, one by one, they were all shot dead by the continuing volley after volley of shots from those hidden in the houses, the final stage in the defence of fortress Settlement.

Amid the dust, noise and chaos, Roger, assessing the damage done to his small force, thought he saw a shadow of Thor galloping away back through the dismantled gate and away into thick bush. He led the remnants of his own force on foot through the gate, picking off the occasional Viking survivor. Most of the Viking invaders lay either dead or wounded within 200 metres of the gate.

Tanya, in the process of checking all her young charges, became aware of a man with no horse creeping about and making his way down to the village. As Tanya approached he stood up and was about to say something when Tanya emptied a full magazine from her carbine into the man's body. It was Jerry. "How many fucking chances do you expect to get, shithead," she said quietly.

Roger met up with Tanya and her youngsters before they returned to the village. "We lost at least two," he said, "I must go back and pick up the pieces. We were only just in time. A few hours earlier we would have nailed them. A little later and we were done for."

Roger explained he had seen a group of the Viking raiders escaping north with Hercules. "Okay; Jason's in place to stop them," said Tanya, "but I'll get Eustace to follow up."

She called Eustace on the walkie-talkie, who was still within range. "Roger tells me a group of Vikings disappeared northwards. Track and follow them please."

"We have a little time," she said to Roger. "I'll deal with them. You need to regroup, get your casualties back here to hospital and then get all your troops back to Banksia; we still have to deal with the Viking village and the women there."

Once the dust had settled, with the pervasive smell of death, cordite and blood gradually clearing, Tanya quietly led her young charges back to the village. Because they had been so carefully hidden the only damage sustained was one broken arm and many cuts and bruises. The group was very excited about the confrontation; they had no concept of the danger they had been in, so once the injuries had been attended to, she collected them together as a group on the parade ground. She was more expansive than usual, "I don't want you to think it's always going to be like this. This time we were lucky but some of our other forces did not come out of the situation quite so well; Roger looks as if he has lost several of his people, the same could have happened to us. You need to reflect on why we came out of the situation as we did. Always be modest about such victories and try to imagine what might have gone wrong."

-Viking 8. The wrap up

Tanya, having refuelled the Bell, flew north to find Jason as they had agreed, outside the small deserted hamlet of Milbrodale. Once she had landed and disembarked, she explained what had occurred at The Settlement. "You mean the kids saved the situation?" asked Jason with a look of horror on his face.

"Yup, and we shot the few Vikings who managed to get into the village."

"Is Venus okay?"

"She is; she shot one of Thor's lieutenants."

"Jesus. We were very lucky."

"I'll find Hercules and the rest of the Viking force. We'll shoot the bejesus out of them with the 'copters but we'll need you to do some cleaning up," said Tanya. "I still want you to stop the Taree people from doing anything stupid, so still plan on going there afterwards."

Eustace, piloting one of the Merlins with the other following, found Hercules' rabble, chasing them towards Jason's 40 troops who were lying in wait a few kilometres south of Milbrodale. Hercules had several furious conversations with his men.

"Where are we and where are we going," he was asked.

"Taree, that place near Taree, that was what dad said."

"Do you know the way?"

Hercules was silent.

Within a day the two big Settlement Merlins were hovering overhead shooting at them.

"It's those bloody helicopters again," yelled a voice. "We've got no chance. We should just surrender."

Hercules ignored him and continued leading his men north.

Jason carefully planned his ambush tactics. He sent four people away, each with a string of horses. "Keep well clear," he instructed. Most of his people were hidden along one side of the road. Derain and his Aboriginal companion had now rejoined the group. They and four others remained mounted and stayed in the bush on either side of the road to prevent anyone escaping.

Led by Hercules, the Vikings came tearing up the road. Jason had placed a red piece of cloth on a tree 200 metres from where his troops were waiting as a sign to the Merlin pilots. The Vikings came clattering on, relieved the relentless pursuit had ceased for a few minutes. Jason's well-disciplined troops held their fire until Jason aimed a volley of shots once the now-ragged remnants of the Viking expedition had galloped past his forward position. The following burst of fire utterly devastated the surprised and fleeing Vikings. Many of them lay either dead or wounded on the road. Four of the bolder Vikings saw where the fire was coming from and galloped down the side of the road firing as they went; they trampled several of Jason's troops before they were all shot dead. The others, still alive, stopped and raised their hands in surrender. One of Thor's lieutenants shouted, "Stop, please stop, we surrender!" He had his hands high in the air and had dropped his weapon. Out of his peripheral vision Jason thought he saw a wounded Hercules galloping away. With his hands full, he made no attempt at pursuit.

Jason and six of his men emerged carefully from the bush with their weapons levelled at the ten surviving Vikings, still mounted, but looking confused. "Do as I say and you won't get hurt," he said. "First, drop your weapons, all of them." There was a clatter as weapons were discarded. "Now, one at a time, dismount as I tell you. Remember you are all covered, any funny business and you will get a bullet in the head." He moved from trooper to trooper; the men dismounted and one of Jason's Academy troopers led their horses away. Soon all were sitting forlornly on the ground with their hands on their heads. "Okay," said Jason, "search each one for hidden weapons." Inevitably one man made a grab for a pistol hidden in his pocket. A short burst from an Academy trooper added the man to the numbers of dead. The bamboozled and thoroughly intimidated prisoners were then searched and bound with cable ties, with their hands behind the backs. They were made to sit under a tree while Derain and the troopers scoured the surrounding bush and emerged with another three prisoners, one wounded. Jason said to his two medics, "See what you can do for the wounded. The helicopters will be here soon; the priority will be to get the wounded to hospital … our people first."

"Why don't we just shoot the bastards? That's what they would have done to us."

"No," said Jason in a quiet but forceful voice "you know the answer to that and the reason." There was no dissent.

An hour later the two Merlins landed on the road. One had signs of significant damage as well as a lot of blood near one of the open doors. "Took a hit," explained Eustace, "we lost one there." He shook his head. "What about you?"

"One of ours is dead, four others need to be transferred to hospital. The rest are Viking rabble. Hercules got away but I think he was wounded," Jason reported.

"There are six Vikings wounded," announced Jason eventually, "all to go to hospital once ours have been seen to. The prisoners should be taken to the military prison in Canberra. We'll deal with the dead."

Half an hour later the helicopters took off again. The dead trooper was returned home for a formal funeral. Jason's troops busied themselves with collecting enough wood for a large bonfire, on to which the dead Vikings were piled. The bonfire was lit and tended by two troopers while the remaining soldiers set up camp a few hundred metres away. There was a sense of relief among the troopers, but no sense of triumph. Nothing was said. Jason decided to leave everyone with their own thoughts. He said to himself, "Thank God for the Academy and the foresight that created it."

-Viking 9. Jason and the Taree Village

Some days later, Jason and an advance party found what they called the Taree village which was set up on a small hillock some 50 kilometres west of the deserted town of Taree. Jason's group had not yet become accustomed to the much higher rainfall over eastern Australia since the flood, making the going difficult. The bush thrived under the wet conditions, growing thick and impenetrable in many places, so they generally had to stick to the roads which was also heavy going, with the tarmac crumbling and potholed. Any vehicles were left well alone; they knew what they would find in them.

"What are we going to do now?' asked one of Jason's troops. "If we all just wander in there we might be walking into a hornet's nest."

Jason nodded, "Of course. I will lead a group of six of us to reconnoitre and make contact. The rest of you should take cover, with very clear views of the Taree camp, but it's critical you remain unseen. They probably won't be expecting anyone so won't be on full alert. If we get into trouble you may have to come and rescue us." Jason selected five others, "Jim, you saw many of the Barrington people, including those we treated at our hospital; you need to come with us and keep your eyes peeled to see if you recognise any of them. They may try to duck away when they see us coming."

Jason selected three others to lead those remaining behind and spent half a day ensuring that the access to the village was understood. "The place is cleverly hidden," he told his companions, drawing maps in the sand to orientate them. "If you go wrong you may end up on the edge of a cliff or facing an inaccessible rock face."

It was midday when Jason, with considerable apprehension, led his little group into the encampment. The village was a motley collection of huts, constructed from local unsawn timber and grasses. Jason could see a small community centre and a toilet block. He could also see a herd of cattle and a thriving vegetable garden, where several people were working. There was a substantial stream on the northern boundary of the establishment. Initially there was no reaction to their presence, and then one of the women in the camp looked up, shrieked, and ran off to a hut, slightly larger than the rest. A moment later a tall dark, man in his late 30s or early 40s emerged from the hut. He was heavily bearded and dressed in animal skins and rags. He seemed untroubled by Jason's arrival. "What do you want?" he asked. "You're the first visitors we have had for years now. You government?"

Jason laughed. "No, we are not government and there is no government anyway. We are from a place called The Settlement, where we have been established for nearly 30 years."

"Ah yes—The Settlement, the uniforms. I've heard tell of you."

"Good things I hope?"

"No, not entirely. You've dealt harshly with people you didn't like."

"Only if they deserved it," said Jason. "You must be talking about people from Barrington Tops who moved off in this direction."

A troubled look came across the man's face. He gave a barely visible nod.

"Maybe we should chat. You can unsaddle over there," he pointed to a nearby water trough, "and water the horses."

"I'm Jason Bower, by the way." Leaning down Jason held out his hand which was reluctantly taken.

"Louis," was the response.

Jason and the troop dismounted, four of the troopers took the horses' reins and Jason and Rebecca followed Louis to his hut.

"I can offer you water, but not much else," said Louis.

"Water is fine, we couldn't offer you much more at home either," said Jason, admiring the spacious and light-filled room they were ushered into. There was a table, two upright chairs and a comfortable chair made from local timber and sheep skins, in the lightly furnished room. Louis poured them each a cup of water. He was alone.

"I've heard colourful stories regarding your outfit," said Louis, "something about a military training Academy, a well-appointed hospital and a ruthless leader called the 'white goddess'." He smiled, "Is there any truth in that?"

"Yes, of course, but that's only part of us. We no longer refer to her as the 'white goddess' by the way. The Aborigines sometimes refer to her as NgalaTanya, as a term of respect. It means…"

"Mother Tanya," responded Louis to Jason's surprise.

Jason finished off his briefing by saying, "We have no wish to harm anyone and we have done a great deal of good in many instances. We established the Academy knowing we would have to defend ourselves and we would not have survived had we not done that. As you can see or may have heard, women and men are treated equally. You mentioned our leader. That is Tanya Bower, my aunt. She has led the organisation since my grandfather David Bower died." He explained Tanya's role in developing The Settlement and the association with the Aborigines. "They believe that they have been told by their ancestors to protect her and The Settlement, and they take that duty very seriously. We would've been in trouble if they hadn't."

"What do you want from us?" asked Louis.

"Live and let live mainly, but there are a couple of immediate concerns."

"Like what?"

Jason took a deep breath, "I have mentioned the Barrington people."

Louis looked uneasy.

"Some years ago, we did a deal with a group called the Vikings. We thought they had accepted our live and let live philosophy, but apparently not. They sent a man here as a sleeper assuming he would take the place over together with a group we had chased out of Barrington Tops. The Vikings, under their leader Thor, was preparing to bring a force here, join up with you and then attack us at The Settlement, with the idea of taking it over."

Jason looked at Louis who remained impassive.

"We have just more or less destroyed the military capacity of the Vikings," Jason continued.

Louis looked slightly shocked, trying to absorb all he had been told. "What was the name of this sleeper that supposedly was sent here?"

"'Harold', 'Monckton', 'Godwinson'; he uses a number of names." Louis looked unconvinced. Jason then described him.

"He called himself 'Norman' when he was here, you don't have to worry about him any longer," said Louis guardedly.

"You mean he has left?"

"In a way, yes."

"And the Barrington people?"

"Some of them are here still, mainly the women. You don't have to worry about them any more either."

"They left as well?"

"Again, in a way, yes."

Jason was beginning to understand what he was being told. He almost asked what Louis meant by this remark, but didn't. Louis' demeanour indicated that any further questions of this nature would be less than welcome.

"Have you heard anything from Thor's messengers?" asked Jason.

"Nuh," said Louis dismissively. "If we had they would have been sent packing. Look, I have few things to do, but you and your people are welcome to stay here. It would be useful to continue our discussion. We have nowhere for you to stay. You'll have to camp," said Louis.

"There are another 30 of us outside," said Jason, not wishing to appear deceptive, as Louis rose from his seat.

Seeing Louis' look of horror, Jason laughed uneasily. "Sorry, from experience we don't take chances. We had no idea what to expect when we came here. If I may I'll tell them to come into camp."

When Louis had recovered his composure he said, "Mnn, I wondered how six of you had dealt with the threat from the Vikings. I now understand. Okay, I was going to invite you to eat with us, but we can't feed an army, as there are only about a hundred of us here anyway."

"No, we have all our own supplies, but we could join with you and help prepare a common meal, if that suits."

"Yes, certainly, I'll arrange that. Maybe Rebecca can come with me, while you get the rest of your army."

When Jason's troop rode into camp, Louis was on hand to reassure his people, who were naturally apprehensive with the sudden incursion of so many well-equipped people on horseback. There was the usual inspection of arms and horses. Any defects were listed and attended to. The Taree group looked on in amazement.

"It's all about the Academy," Jason explained to his bemused looking host. "It's our elite group. Strict discipline is enforced, and there is no doubt it's necessary and has helped our survival. We have not found any group outside The Settlement who can touch us."

Louis just raised his eyebrows.

Jason's people got to work in the disciplined manner they were used to. Some erected the familiar two-man tents on a patch of grass on the edge of the village. Others gathered supplies together and, with humour, were soon working with the Taree group preparing a meal in the kitchen adjoining the community centre. Some of the troops tended the horses, watered and fed them and made sure tethers were all in place.

"Snake! Great," one of the Taree women exclaimed, "Louis sometimes brings one back for us."

The Academy people laughed, relieved no explanation was needed in relation to their diet. Halfway through the meal Derain and his companions appeared in the half-light with the three Viking messengers as captives. Jason stood up to greet him and make the introductions; to his surprise Derain and Louis, after a brief handshake, embraced each other and said a few words in a language Jason did not understand.

"You know each other?" asked Jason in surprise.

"No, no," answered Louis, "but I have some Aboriginal heritage in my background. This helps in journeys around the bush. What surprises me is your close association with Derain's group."

There was some further discussion about the defeat of the Vikings and what they should do with their captives. Jason had had time to think about what had been done to the Vikings. He had withdrawn slightly from the conversation, worrying about Venus. Derain looked at him, realising his concern. He said, "Ancestors tell us that Venus is okay, you'll look after her anyway. Derain can help if needed." The conversation meandered on into the night. Derain's arrival reassured Louis he could trust Jason and The Settlement people, reinforced by the demeanour of Jason's troop. Jason left Louis and Derain deep in conversation when he retired to his tent.

In the morning Derain said to Jason, "This man Louis is okay. These people will be good for The Settlement and for Tanya."

"We'll go home soon, maybe tomorrow," Jason said. "Are you coming with us?"

"No, no I must go and talk to the ancestors, there are many things to discuss. I'll go today," Derain responded. "You must bring NgalaTanya here soon, maybe in the chopper."

Jason nodded as Derain and his Aboriginal companion disappeared having said their farewells to Louis. Jason was left with the problem of what to do with Thor's messengers.

Jim came to Jason saying, "You asked me to keep a lookout for some of the Barrington people. I have wandered all around the camp and introduced myself to as many of the people here as possible. Some of the women make themselves scarce when any of us approach; I guess they're frightened of us. I've caught glimpses of a couple of Barrington men who made the raid on us in Kurri-Kurri. They scuttle off when they see me."

Jason nodded, saying nothing. He now thought he understood what appeared to have occurred at the Taree settlement. He decided to tell Tanya and ask no further questions.

In his perambulations to all parts the primitive settlement Jason could see everyone working very hard. There was a large herd of cattle which appeared to be well looked after. It was all hard labour though; they had no mechanisation to speak of, no solar, and water was collected by hand from the stream in a motley collection of containers. He could see that with some help things could be improved very quickly. Some of the residents approached him shyly to ask more about The Settlement, others scuttled off as soon as they saw him.

Louis and Jason continued chatting during the day. "We would welcome a closer association with you people," said Louis. "I'd like to meet Tanya, or whatever you call her having heard so much about her. Derain is very fond of her in a protective sort of way; I'd like to understand how she is able to engender that sort of loyalty. We can clearly benefit from your technology, especially the solar stuff. We may also have things to learn from your cattle and sheep breeding programmes and your agriculture. Our medical facilities are primitive to say the least and certainly the standards you maintain with your military Academy are impressive," Louis summarised.

"How do you think the rest of the community will react? You seem to have been very independent for years now."

"They won't be a problem; I can promise you that. Anyway, I am asking for cooperation from you, not a takeover. Your live and let live philosophy which you told me about yesterday," Louis answered.

Viking 10. The demise of the Viking village

While Jason was dealing with the remnants of the Viking forces, Tanya flew the Jetranger to Banksia to pick up Alice who had been kicking her heels there awaiting developments. "I've told Mark to go directly to the Viking village," said Tanya. "He has 30 of our troops with him. I'll take you there."

After some thought she then added as sensitively as she was able, "You need to know the Viking force sent to attack us has been defeated, I'm sorry to have to tell you this, but most of them are either dead, wounded or in captivity." She said nothing about the close call they had had and how Thor very nearly succeeded in his quest to take over The Settlement.

Tanya could see Alice looking at her blankly trying to understand the enormity of what was being said. Had her whole world suddenly been turned upside down? All Alice and the women really wanted was a change to the slavish regime Thor had created, but she now understood that the whole Viking society was in the process of being destroyed. She braced her shoulders. "So be it," she said to Tanya, "it's got to be better than what we had."

Tanya landed the chopper in the Viking village relieved to see Mark and his troop had already arrived. She and Alice disembarked and went into Thor's palace to meet Mark.

"What happens now?" asked Alice.

"You need to decide what happens to this place," said Tanya. She waved her arms about, indicating the whole village. "Anyone who wants to, will be looked after at one of our other establishments."

Alice looked at her disbelievingly, "You mean we can choose which place to go to?"

"Not all in one place, but within reason you'll be able to choose. You know about The Settlement, Banksia, the Bandstand, St. Andrews, Amazonia, Kurri-Kurri and Newcastle. We have recently created an association with a settlement that's moving most of its activities to the Southern Highlands, the Bowral Moss Vale area."

"Where's Moss Vale?"

"South, halfway to Canberra."

"Sounds ideal; gets us away from Thor and all his bad habits."

"You won't have to worry about Thor too much if we have anything to do with it," said Tanya. "He will either be six feet under or in jail, preferably the latter."

Alice's expression was a combination of fear and relief.

Tanya and Mark spent an hour walking around the village while Alice and Gabriella talked to all the women gathered in Thor's palace. At the end of the meeting Alice approached Tanya who was standing next to the horse paddock, admiring the few horses left there.

"We all want out," she said to Tanya, "before any of the men return."

"All?" questioned Tanya.

"There are one or two holdouts, but yes most of us want to go."

Tanya and Mark spent most of the rest of the day helping the women decide where they could be accommodated. The three Merlins arrived during the discussions.

"Okay," said Tanya, "one to Newcastle, one to Amazonia and one to The Settlement." Each chopper was loaded with a number of women and children. There were some tears as the women took a last look at what had been their home for more than ten years.

"Come back in the morning," she said to Eustace. "Those that are left can go to the Bandstand and the Southern Highlands."

Two women had refused to go anywhere. Tanya spent an hour with them, trying to understand their motivation.

"Why do you want to stay here?" she asked.

"Thor gave us our lives," one of the women eventually answered, "but for him we would all be dead."

"And this gives him permission to treat you as his servants or slaves."

The women shrugged. "It's not that bad."

"We can't let you stay here. We're going to remove everything of any value. Mark has already taken steps to shift all the remaining livestock to Amazonia and then we're going to burn this place down."

The women eventually reluctantly agreed to move to Banksia, which they knew was only four days ride away.

A section of Mark's troops was left in the village to apprehend any of Thor's men who managed to return. A few days later Tanya, on her own in the Jetranger, circled the blackened ruin of the Viking village. There were a few wisps of smoke feeling their way into the azure blue sky. She had arranged to shift 20 of what were now referred to as Thor's refugees to prison in Canberra and Mark had burnt the Viking village to the ground once any items of value had been rescued. Some of Mark's troops had driven the stock to Amazonia and Mark was now well on his way back to Moss Vale with the balance of his force. In a few days Tanya would arrange for the troopers originally transferred by air from the Southern Highlands to return there. As far as Tanya could see the village was deserted, but she was still worried about what had happened to Thor as so far there had been no sign of him. She flew lower to get a better view and was just about to fly away and return to The Settlement when she saw him.

There was a white stallion tethered near the entrance of what remained of Thor's magnificent palace. Tanya landed as near as she could and, armed with her Steyr carbine, began walking up the stone steps which led to the entrance of the palace. And there he was, standing on the top step as he had been all those years earlier when she and Mark first sighted him. There was an emptiness in his eyes this time though, all the fire evident before was now gone; he looked completely defeated, empty. Tanya thought although he was physically alive, he looked dead inside.

"Thor," said Tanya. There was no answer.

"Thor!" shouted Tanya. He looked at her blankly. "Come with me now." There was a flicker of recognition on his face.

She took him by the hand and led him gently down the steps to the machine.

"I'm going to have to tie you into the seat." There was no hint of resistance and Thor allowed himself to be bound into the seat.

Tanya did a final walkthrough of the establishment, calling out as she went. There was no response. She cautiously approached Thor's white stallion who looked at her curiously. She removed the saddle and bridle and patted him, with the magnificent beast looking on benignly. Released from his bonds the stallion trotted over to the helicopter's open door and sniffed at the figure hunched there, he then backed away, gave a short whinny and cantered off. Tanya put the stallion's tack in the back of the machine before she closed the door for take-off.

The flight to Canberra took more than an hour. Thor made absolutely no response to Tanya's attempts to talk to him through the headphones, although he left them in place on his head. Tanya, after several attempts, raised Jonathan on the radio and told him what was happening. "Don't approach him under any circumstances, he's probably dangerous," he said once she told him she had found Thor.

"Jonathan, just listen for a moment, for Christ's sake," Tanya shouted. "Thor is all tied up here in the seat next to me in my bloody helicopter. I am about 30 minutes away from you in Canberra. Meet me at the fucking airport with an escort please."

"What. Who tied him up?"

"I did."

"But, but..."

"Just meet me, are you listening?"

"Yes, yes, we'll meet you." The connection was cut.

Tanya, on the final approach, saw the squad Jonathan had assembled. She landed the machine, switching off the engine. She hopped out, and started to untie the bonds holding Thor. She led him meekly by the hand to the reception committee. Jonathan was standing nearby. When Thor caught sight of them he went completely berserk, dropped Tanya's hand and attacked the nearest man who was knocked unconscious. Eventually, with men trying to hold on to his massive arms and legs and being shaken about like rag dolls, Thor was shackled and dragged, yelling, into a prison van.

"I don't get any of that," said Jonathan to Tanya, as the van drove off with Thor still yelling blue murder. "He allowed himself to come with you, quietly, when with his strength he could have broken you in two or at least done you an awful lot of damage. He then behaves like a lunatic when he arrives here. What did he say to you?"

"Nothing, not a fucking thing," replied Tanya.

The next day Jonathan phoned in a state of high anxiety, "That bloody man Thor, we simply can't control him. It's taking almost a dozen of my men to deal with him and he's disrupting the whole place. I need your help. You are the only person he listens to."

"I'll get back to you," Tanya answered as she put the phone down.

"We'll have to bring him here," Tanya announced after talking the matter over with Venus and Jason.

Tanya spoke to Jonathan on the two-way radio during the short flight to Canberra early the following morning. "We'll bring Thor back here to The Settlement. Just have him ready at the airport."

Jonathan didn't hesitate, "Okay. I have about a dozen men trying to look after him; he has broken several arms..."

As they approached Tanya could see Jonathan standing a short distance away from a prison van, which was surrounded by a dozen guards.

Once they had landed they all became aware of a constant noise in the van parked on the apron. Yelling, roaring, and the sound of banging on the inside of the van caused Tanya to wince and Venus run towards the van. The back door was opened to let Thor out. The noise continued until Thor caught sight of Tanya and Venus. To everyone's amazement, Thor immediately stopped and stood quite still. He held out his arms to his daughter. The guards tried to intervene, but a sharp word from Tanya held them back. Venus hugged her father. Tanya asked the guards to move back a few metres.

"Thor, would you sit down please," asked Tanya. She gestured with her hands. He immediately sat down in the back of the van, with his shackled legs on the ground. "We won't be long. Venus will sit with you for a moment, then you can come home with us," she said. Thor looked at her, without appearing to understand.

"Are you completely out of your mind?" asked Jonathan when Tanya told him what she was proposing. "Do you have any idea what you are taking on?"

"No other option," replied Tanya tersely. "What else can we do?"

To Tanya's surprise Jonathan failed to express any interest at all in what had occurred between Settlement forces and the Vikings. When Tanya raised the subject he said, "I've accepted a few more prisoners. What more do you want?"

While Jonathan was getting the paperwork signed for Thor's release Tanya explained that she and Stephanie were in the process of setting up an election process that would result in The Settlement and its domains being run on a more democratic basis.

Jonathan wouldn't look her in the eye. "Too early for that, much too early," he said.

"We discussed this at Kanangra," responded Tanya, "encouraged by you for Christ's sake. It's too fucking late for objections. We're ready and within a few months all will be in place."

As he handed the papers over Jonathan said nothing more except, "Best of luck with this animal. Best of luck." He turned away without looking at Tanya.

"He's up to something," thought Tanya. "All that behaviour is most unlike anything I've ever known from him. He really is up to something; I wonder what the hell it is."

Tanya said to Thor as they got him to clamber into the helicopter, once his shackles had been unlocked. "We'll have to tie you in like we did before."

Thor said nothing.

"He hasn't uttered a word, not a word," Jason announced as they took off. "Nothing since we arrived this morning."

There was a mixed reaction to the arrival of Thor at The Settlement. Chloe and the women from the Viking village were horrified and all made representations to Tanya. "He'll try to create the same regime that existed at the Viking village," was the universal theme. Chloe went to great lengths to avoid him.

"No chance for that," Tanya answered, "just stay out of his way." She justified her actions saying, "He was out of control in Canberra. The only other option was to execute him. I take full responsibility, we may even get him to do some work, where his great strength will be an asset."

Derain came to the rescue, "Thor being at The Settlement, the ancestors don't like it."

"What should we have done?" asked Tanya. "Shoot him?"

"Yes, that would be best, but I'll help as always. I've given Venus some leaves to boil in water, which Thor should be made to drink every day. That'll keep him quiet."

Without saying anything to anybody else Venus sought Derain out. All her instincts told her that Thor was play-acting. She explained her feelings to Derain, "Can you help me get him out of here? Nobody wants him in this place, including you. His white stallion appeared here yesterday…"

"What do you want me do?" asked Derain.

"Maybe we could put him on that horse. I have a rifle at home which he can have. He needs a spare horse for food and so on and then he needs someone as a guide for a couple of weeks."

"Where do you want him to go?"

"West, somewhere west. Far, far from here. If he stays here there'll be trouble."

It took a few days to organise, but very late one night, Venus and Derain escorted Thor out of The Settlement's western gate, riding his white stallion and leading another horse. An Aboriginal guide on foot led the way. As he left, Thor hugged Venus saying, "You're a good girl. Oi'm not sure when oi'll see yer agin." Those were the first words he had spoken since Tanya found him.

Jason popped in to see Tanya a few days later, "Have you seen Thor anywhere? He seems to have disappeared."

"Isn't he staying with you?"

"Venus and I have looked everywhere, he's nowhere to be seen."

Tanya immediately went and found Derain, "Thor has disappeared. Have you seen him? There is also a horse missing and some tack…"

"I've seen nothing of him," answered Derain, shaking his head. He avoided her questioning stares.

"Mnn," she thought, "somehow he's dealt with Thor, maybe that's the best solution. Venus doesn't seem to be particularly worried. I think I'll leave it at that."

CHAPTER 7
Louis
(A week later)

TANYA

After all the activity in dealing successfully with the Vikings, Tanya was relieved to be able to sit in her home office for a few days and think about the continued development of the area controlled by The Settlement. She had called a meeting of all the enclaves falling under the security blanket of The Settlement: Kim from Newcastle, Joseph from Banksia, Irene and Stephanie from Amazonia, Isaac fron St. Andrews, Caroline from the Bandstand, and Virginia, without Mark, had managed the journey from the Southern Highlands. Jason, Roger and Derain were also included. Jonathan was also invited.

Earlier, before the general meeting, Virginia had managed a brief meeting with Tanya in her office. "You need to know that Jonathan has paid us a couple of visits, while you were dealing with the Vikings. He's up to no good," she said.

"Go on," said Tanya.

"He's telling Mark that what's really needed is for Mark to take over the leadership from you. Something about having a 'Real Bower' in charge. He's been twice. He also muttered something about having 'that bloody Academy' to use his words, under the direct control of the military."

"I know he's up to something. So what's Mark going to do about it?"

"Mark just thinks Jonathan has rocks in his head. We are fully engaged in developing our new areas. Mark has no interest in anything else."

"What do you think we should do about it?" asked Tanya.

"Before I answer, there is one other thing," said Virginia. She produced a Steyr carbine from a bag at her feet. "Mark found this in one of the areas, from outside the village, that was attacking our people during the Morton business. With all that was going on he forgot to mention it. We also found a few more of them, buried underneath the floor of one of the houses in Morton we burnt down, based on info given to us by one of the Morton people who are now being resettled with us in the Southern Highlands."

"It's the same fucking model as the Academy is armed with," said an angry Tanya, taking the proffered weapon from Virginia. "This must be Jonathan's people, or Jonathan himself. Does Jonathan know about this?"

"No. I thought we should discuss it with you first."

"He's due here later today. He or someone in his organisation is playing a double game. Where are the rest of them?"

"I have one more here." Virginia handed the weapon over. "We have another five at home in Bowral. Hidden away, together with magazines and ammo."

"Anything else?" asked Tanya, frowning.

"Yes, there is. I'm not sure how seriously we should take this, but he talked glibly about a military government, with The Settlement firmly under Mark's control."

"Military government. Shit. Thanks Virginia. He can fuck off on that one," said a worried and thoughtful Tanya. "Okay. We'll get on with the meeting. We'll deal with Jonathan when he arrives."

Tanya spent a little time worrying about the relationship between The Settlement and the military. Despite the fact that Jonathan was still accepting prisoners, such as those he had accepted as a result of the defeat of the Vikings, there was now no guarantee the military would come to their assistance if needed. "We'll get an understanding of his attitude, at the meeting," she said to herself.

The meeting started promptly at ten am in the community centre. "Should we not wait for Jonathan?" asked Caroline.

"No," answered Tanya. "He has had notice of the meeting for a while now. I half expected him to arrive last night, which is what he usually does. This morning I got a garbled message that he might be late."

Tanya shrugged, "The stupid bastard is playing games. I'll let him stew in his own juice," she thought to herself.

Tanya gave the gathering a detailed account of all the recent conflicts. Most of them had some knowledge of what had occurred, but were pleased to be included in the full briefing. She concluded, "The close call with the Vikings and the attempted coup at the Bandstand indicates the need for a more democratic process." Jason was then asked to brief everyone on his visit to the Taree enclave.

"There is no threat from the Taree people. Louis, the leader there, would like some help with various things." Jason concluded following his short briefing.

"What about Harold and the thugs from Barrington Tops?" asked Tanya.

"He wasn't saying much, but I think Louis and his people may have killed or expelled most of them. He's no fan of the Vikings, either."

Jason went on to explain the rapport between Derain and Louis, nodding acknowledgement in Derain's direction.

"If it can be arranged, I think including Taree in some way would strengthen our organisation," Jason concluded.

"About Taree, Jason, you'll have an idea of what might be needed there in terms of solar etc. Take a look at what we rescued from the Vikings. Most of it will be quite usable. Kim," Tanya said looking at her, "deliver it to Taree, by truck. Anything left over can be kept in Newcastle."

"There are two more urgent issues we need to discuss," Tanya continued. Firstly, as mentioned we need a more democratic process. Stephanie has agreed to mastermind the issue. She will come and discuss our proposals with each one of you before we do anything. Does anyone have any difficulties with this?"

"What does Jonathan Bower think about it?" asked Caroline.

"He encouraged the initiative," said Tanya, disingenuously, "based on Virginia's experience." She looked at Virginia, who said nothing. Tanya knew perfectly well that Jonathan had only raised the issue to try and unsettle her. She said nothing further, knowing that Jonathan had no interest in a more democratic process.

There were general murmurs and nods of assent around the table. There were no objections.

"The other really important issue," announced Tanya, "is the question of fuel supplies."

Tanya knew that with the hard-working use of the three big helicopters and the increased number of reconditioned vehicles, they would run out of fuel in less than three years. She knew they would have to make a concerted effort to find another substantial source of fuel, independent of the military, otherwise the whole project of recreating their civilisation would come to a grinding halt and would revert to a primitive form of subsistence. She also felt the pressure of continuing to provide improvements for the communities in the wider settlement or it might start to disintegrate.

"I have recently asked Roger to take charge of that issue," she said.

At midday, in the middle of the discussion on fuel, the noise of another helicopter landing announced Jonathan's arrival. He was ushered into the meeting a few minutes later. He briefly said hello to all those present, just as a tray of sandwiches were brought into the meeting for lunch.

"We were just discussing fuel supplies," said Tanya for Jonathan's benefit, as she munched on a sandwich and took a drink of water.

He acknowledged her without saying anything. Tanya noticed him glancing uncomfortably in Virginia's direction.

"Roger has or will ask everyone here if they have any inkling where there might be fuel dumps we can commandeer. Kurnell was completely inundated as was Greenwich." She continued looking at Roger, "There may be a dump in western Sydney somewhere; we could try Bankstown Airport. Kim's people should be scouring Newcastle. Have a look at all the mine sites in the Hunter. There was some industrial activity at Kurri-Kurri in the past so look there. Old trucking businesses may still have supplies. First prize will be a place in the area we control. Also, Derain, you might know something." She looked in his direction. "Jonathan, is there any progress in reinstating the refining capacity in Victoria?"

Jonathon wasn't particularly forthcoming.

"Yes, of course," he said. "Any fuel produced there will initially be for military use, as I have told you."

There were some uneasy glances around the table.

"Well, we have actually come to the end of our agenda for the day," Tanya said to Jonathan, looking at her watch. "Is there anything you wish to raise? We still have time."

"Just a couple of things of things I would like to raise with you personally. I can chat informally to everyone else at dinner, later."

Once the rest of the group had left the centre and Tanya and Jonathan had moved upstairs and settled down in Tanya's office, she looked at him, saying, "You had some things you wished to discuss?"

"Yes. I think we need a closer association with your Academy."

"Like what?"

"Mark, who I assume is still head of your security, should report to one of my senior military personnel in Canberra."

"Who?" asked Tanya. She had no intention of acceding to such a request, but she wanted more information.

"I have a Colonel Jacobs, reporting to me, who I think is ideally suited to such a role."

Tanya remembered Chas telling her how a Colonel Jacobs was in the process of usurping some of Jonathan's authority.

"That's never going to work, for fucks sake, Jonathan," responded Tanya. "The Academy people are part timers. The person in charge needs to have an understanding of how any deployments will affect the smooth running of our establishments around the country." She did not tell him that, with the increased population, that particular problem had been resolved and that during longer deployments of Academy personnel, many of the people concerned were able to make arrangements for their civilian responsibilities to be taken on by someone else.

Before Jonathan could say anything further, Tanya said, "I have something interesting to show you." She produced the bag Virginia had left with her earlier and pulled out one of the Steyr carbines. Jonathan looked at her blankly. "This weapon and a few others were found in the Morton village. They tried to hide them."

"Your careless part time Academy people must have lost them somehow," was the glib answer from Jonathan. "That illustrates the need for better discipline…" He hesitated for a moment, "Anyway what do you think any of that has to do with me?"

She held up her hand. "Jonathan, that crap won't wash with me. The weapons you supplied us with were from two or three batches, with sequential serial numbers. The serial numbers on the two weapons I have here are from a completely different batch; the serial numbers are not a match with anything we have. I've had them checked. The only possible source of these weapons is from you, the fucking military. There is no possibility they came from us. I can also assure you that we run a very strict regime regarding our weapons. We have never, not once, lost a weapon."

Jonathan maintained his composure. "I'll look into the matter," he said eventually. "You had better let me have the weapons concerned."

"You can have one of them," she said handing one of the rifles over, "I'll be keeping the others."

The buffet dinner was held at Tanya's cottage organised by Nanny with help from a few others in the community. Jonathan circulated around most of the members of the surviving enclaves represented there. Tanya could see Jonathan becoming more and more agitated as the evening wore on. As the dinner came to a close, an angry looking Jonathan buttonholed Tanya on her own, saying, "What's all this rubbish I hear about a more democratic process? You know it's much too early for anything like that. Much too early."

"We discussed that very situation, in Canberra, after those trials you held for the miscreants from Morton. You suggested we should take a leaf out of Virginia's book and operate on a more democratic basis," said Tanya evenly. "Anyway, I'm not sure what it has to do with you. Since the very beginning of our efforts to set up The Settlement, we've operated as we thought fit. I'm damned sure your father never discussed governance issues with you at any time, and I don't intend to either."

Jonathan stormed off at that point and 15 minutes later Tanya heard the sound of a helicopter taking off.

Tanya, with heightened suspicious regarding Jonathan's motives, and concerned about his behaviour, motioned to Stephanie hovering nearby. She had overheard snippets of the conversation with Jonathan.

"A more democratic process will put a spoke in plans he may have for a military dictatorship. So I think we should accelerate the process," said Tanya. "We'll deal with it in the morning."

"Military dictatorship?" asked Stephanie.

Tanya nodded. "That's what he wants apparently." She told him about her earlier conversation with Virginia.

During a lengthy discussion the next day in Tanya's office, Stephanie said, "I was impressed by what we were told by Virginia during the visit to Kanangra. We could easily use what they've done as a model."

Tanya sat silently for a few moments wondering what she was letting herself in for. Then she looked up and said, "We'll have to do this sooner or later, so it had better be sooner. It's probably bigger than either of us think. I'll need you to return permanently to The Settlement to take charge. I'll need to be involved at every major step, but you know how I work, so you will be left to get on with things. You've been at Amazonia long enough, and with Thor out of the way you can be more use elsewhere. We'll have to find someone to take over your role at Amazonia. I have a few things to sort out here, but as soon as that's done, we'll pay a visit to Bowral to talk to Ron, the man who organised the election at Kanangra," added Tanya. "We'll go tomorrow or the next day."

JONATHAN

Jonathan was bedside himself with fury when he left The Settlement after the row with Tanya. He was silent while his personal pilot completed the final checks and they took off to return to Canberra. Once the aircraft had levelled out, Jonathan produced the Steyr carbine which he showed to the pilot.

"Do you know where they found this? he asked.

The pilot shook his head. "Looks like one of ours, or possibly one belonging to The Settlement."

"I think it's one of ours."

"Where was it found?" asked the pilot.

"Buried in one of the houses at Morton."

The pilot was silent.

"On another occasion, you mentioned a couple of out of the ordinary flights from Canberra in the past few months." said Jonathan

The pilot was silent.

"Well?"

"Maybe there have been. I'm not sure."

"What the hell is that supposed to mean?"

"There have been a couple of flights at night. When I asked what they were for I was told it was none of my business. The person who said that was quite threatening."

"Have you any idea what the destination was?"

"No, Sir."

There was no more conversation during the rest of the flight.

The following day Jonathan asked for the flying log from the airport. There were no night flights recorded.

The day after the row with Tanya, Jonathan paced around his Canberra office with the door closed. The only subject on his mind was how he should handle the situation with the Steyr carbine. He knew it represented a major challenge to his authority. He stared unseeingly at the large map of Australia partly covering one wall of the office and the framed photographs on the other walls of him as a cadet at the officer training facility at nearby Duntroon, and a succession of photos detailing the highpoints of his career, including two photos of Settlement troops on exercises. Jonathan was thoroughly conflicted. On the one hand, he desperately wanted to lead a programme to reunify Australia. He was furious about the way he had been outma-noeuvred by Tanya. He thought that unless he could stymie the move towards democratisation, his ambitions would come to nothing. Also, he knew that he had to unearth the mole within his organisation and deal with him or her.

Jonathan swore under his breath, saying to himself, "With every-thing that's going on, The Settlement will soon be out of reach of the military. I urgently need to get the bitch under control."

Jonathan had already arranged to have his senior officers to attend a meeting in his office to deal with the issue. Colonel Jacobs was a notable absentee as the others shuffled in. Jonathan waved at a large table in the office indicating they should sit there. The only item on the table was the Steyr carbine. After formal greetings, Jonathan explained the situation.

"Does anyone know where this weapon was found?" Jonathan asked, as he passed the weapon around the table.

"It is obviously one of ours, unless it came from that group you've supported over the years, somewhere in the Blue Mountains," was one senior woman's response. Otherwise there was deathly silence.

Jonathan then told the gathering where it had been found, and what led to its discovery.

"There is no doubt the weapon came from here," added Jonathan. "I've had the serial numbers checked. The Settlement people have also uncovered another five or six of these weapons, which they have hidden somewhere."

More silence from the group. Colonel Jacobs appeared suddenly. He saluted Jonathan sloppily and found a seat.

Jonathan, although angry at the show of insubordination, explained the situation to the newcomer without showing any signs of his displeasure. After a few more minutes and some unhelpful desultory comments from the group Jonathan could see he was not going to get anywhere.

"I have decided we need an enquiry," he announced finally. "Colonel Jacobs, would you stay behind for a minute please."

"A thief to catch a thief," Jonathan thought to himself.

"Sir," said Jacobs when the others had left.

"Colonel Jacobs. You will head the enquiry. You have four days. When it is completed and before anything is published you will come and discuss it with me. Is that clear?"

"Terms of reference. I need terms of reference, Sir."

Jonathan produced a handwritten half page, which he had in a drawer in his desk.

"Here," he said as Jacobs stood up. "Four days."

Jacobs, looking concerned, stood up, saluted smartly and left the office.

Jonathan then immediately phoned Tanya.

"I want to know the name of the person in whose shack in Morton you found the Steyr," he said without offering any greetings. Fortunately, this was during Tanya's trip in the Bell to Bowral, so she was able to call him back within an hour of landing. She gave him a name provided by Mark. He contacted Major Moody in Wagga Wagga.

"Do you have a man called Gregory there?" he asked Moody after a perfunctory greeting.

"Certainly, Sir, he's one of those from Morton."

Jonathan explained what he wanted.

"Tell Gregory that if he gives us the name of the army person he dealt with, I will see if I can get his sentence reviewed."

"Solleveld, is the name you want," Moody told Jonathan, the next day, "Gregory tells me he thinks he is a junior officer…"

"Okay, thank you Major." He cut the connection.

Jacobs was back within the stipulated four days. As he entered Jonathan's office, he gave a desultory salute and sat down when invited to. He handed over a three-page report. Jonathan glanced at the conclusion at the end of the report which read: 'Without being able to interview any of the personnel from Morton, some of whom may be deceased, it has not been possible to determine how the weapon came to be in the possession of the people in the Morton village.' Jonathan briefly read the rest of the report. He noted that it confirmed the weapon originated with the army.

"Should we take action against anyone?" asked Jonathan.

"I don't see how we can," said Jacobs.

"You have an officer called Solleveld on your strength, don't you?" asked Jonathan.

Jacobs tried to hide his amazement and concern. "Yes. Good officer, but what has that got to do with anything?"

"Possibly nothing," said Jonathan. He looked Jacobs in the eye before adding, "yet."

Jonathan saw Jacobs moving uncomfortably in his chair, "Got you," he thought.

"I have something else to discuss with you," he said to Jacobs, "before you leave."

Jacobs looked surprised.

"It seems to me that you and I have a similar agenda. We are just coming at it from different directions," offered Jonathan.

"What do you mean by that? Sir."

"I'm sure we both want the civilian population, that now exists, to be fully under the control of the military."

Jacobs nodded.

"I think it would be easier to achieve if we cooperated…"

"What do you have in mind?"

"The key to getting control over the civilian population is control over what is known as The Settlement. I have a very close relationship with that organisation."

Jacobs knew what had happened to the Morton establishment. No mention was made of the demise of the Vikings.

"How many people are we talking about in total," asked Jacobs, as they both stood in front on Jonathan's wall map. Jonathan indicated the extent of the area controlled by The Settlement.

Jonathan quickly added up in his head what he knew of the numbers in all the areas coming under the security blanket provided by The Settlement.

"About 12–15,000."

Jacobs looked surprised.

"How many in this so-called Academy?"

"About 400 at The Settlement itself, but each one of the surviving enclaves has Academy trained personnel on their strength."

"How many altogether?"

"About another 700–1000, I'm not quite sure of the exact numbers."

"How well trained are they?"

"The Academy personnel based at The Settlement are trained to a high standard. The rest are at least competent."

Jonathan was becoming slightly uncomfortable with the detail being asked of him.

"How mobile are all these troops?" Jacobs continued.

"Many are very good horsemen, others again are at least competent, and all are well mounted."

"Anything else?"

"They have a small Bell Jetranger," Jonathan decided not to mention the three Merlins.

"So presumably the key is to get the leadership here in our hands in Canberra," Jacobs reflected. "Just remind me of the woman's name again."

"Tanya Bower, my sister-in-law."

"How did a woman get to be in charge of a place like that?"

Jonathan provided a brief explanation.

"Why don't we just move people from the bases you have all the way around the country and nail The Settlement that way?"

Jonathan had no intention of allowing Jacobs to get his tentacles into what was still safely his own area of influence and control.

"No need," he said, "I've told you about the base in Wagga. Also, it's very dangerous to reduce the manpower in any of our bases in the North. There are still many incursions which we need to deal with on a weekly basis and we never know where a problem is going to occur next."

Ostensibly he was now an ally of the colonel, but he didn't like him much and was concerned with some of the misbehaviour emanating from Jacob's close associates. At the conclusion of the meeting he raised the issue with Jacobs about several parties held in the base, and the use of some of the reconditioned vehicles.

"It all seems to be wasteful and unnecessary," Jonathan protested.

Jacobs replied, "You have to understand, the people we have here in the base are bored out of their minds. To maintain discipline, we have to provide other attractions."

Jonathan decided to leave it there. As far as he was concerned the die was cast.

Jacobs had very little knowledge of what had occurred in the remote bases and very little interest. The way he talked, it seemed to Jonathan he believed that control of the Canberra operation, and now adding control of The Settlement, would achieve everything he wanted.

TANYA

With Stephanie and Virginia as passengers, Tanya flew the Jetranger to Bowral. She had taken the call from Jonathan on the way. They landed in what had been the gardens of the previously five-star hotel on the outskirts of Bowral. As a result of Jonathan's call Tanya immediately sought Mark out, who told her the name of the Morton man in whose house the Steyr carbines were unearthed. She immediately phoned Jonathan back with the info.

Tanya and Stephanie had a meeting with Ron, who had managed Virginia's election process. When she was satisfied that Ron was the right person to help them, she left Stephanie to discuss the details and joined Virginia, still using a stick to get about, who enthusiastically showed Tanya all the developments since her last visit.

"When can you release our troops?" Tanya asked.

Mark, who had just joined them, said, "Half can return as soon as you can arrange transport. We'd like to keep the others for another month, when I'll release them to return with the horses belonging to The Settlement."

It was obvious from his statement and demeanour that he intended to stay where he was and not return to The Settlement. Tanya did not pursue the issue. She and Stephanie returned home.

The following day Tanya flew the Jetranger on her own to Newcastle. The main Newcastle base had by now been moved closer to the old City and was established in some reconditioned houses on Cook's Hill overlooking the harbour to the north. Stockton and almost everything north of the harbour had been inundated by the flood. The new establishment was 15 to 30 metres above the new water level. The helicopter base, the horticultural area, and the cattle and sheep paddocks remained where they had first been established to the west of the city. Kim had ensured that there was a corridor cleared of any old vehicles and other debris between the two areas of their establishment. Tanya admired the energy that had gone into the neat workman-like haven that now existed.

Some of Kim's people were living in the houses near the original helicopter base, now run by Eustace, but the majority of the substantial community were now living near Cooks Hill. They were all living off the previously established vegetable gardens. There was a herd of cattle they had been able to tame from the beasts gone wild after the flood and occasionally people went hunting and supplemented their diet with kangaroo. Kim took her on a tour of the developments since it was some months since she had paid a visit, due to the issues of dealing with Morton and the Vikings.

"As we agreed we've almost completed one berth for a large ship to be able to dock here," Kim told her.

"Who do you think will use it?" asked Tanya.

"Don't know, but we might be able to rescue a vessel from Botany Bay and bring it here. We could then start shipping coal around the country. Joe and I have had a look at some of the abandoned coal mining operations in the Hunter Valley, near here. With a bit of effort, we should be able to recondition one of the power stations up there and then get the mine working again. We'll need lots of people to do that of course."

"Wow," said Tanya. "How is Joe by the way?"

"With Mum over here now, he is in his element. He loves all this technical stuff, and Mum has started the school here as she did in the early days of The Settlement."

"How will you load and unload ships?" asked Tanya.

"Well you can see there's a crane there. Dad found an old one near the harbour not under water. He painstakingly dismantled it and re-erected it in the new berth. He is working on building a big enough solar unit to drive it, which he says will take another few months."

"Joe's a marvel; you are so lucky to have your Dad with you. This really opens up some options for us. What are you doing about security? Your establishment is a bit scattered."

"Most people here are Academy trained. We're probably okay from that point of view."

"And from the sea?" asked Tanya.

Kim shook her head, wondering what was coming next, "We've assumed we're quite safe from that point of view. After all, everyone else round the world has been as badly affected by the flood as we are. It doesn't seem to me to be an immediate threat."

"Maybe not. You talked about refurbishing one of the ships in Botany Bay and bringing it here?"

Kim nodded uneasily, saying nothing. Tanya looked at her curiously but didn't pursue the matter. She knew there was something being hidden that would need to be revisited at a later date.

"What do people do for recreation? Now that you are so well established?" asked Tanya, having completed the tour. She was sitting with Kim in her small and comfortably furnished cottage. All the furnishings for the cottages had been sourced locally from shops and various warehouses. There was no evidence of any other occupant, male or female.

"Not much at the moment," answered Kim uncomfortably. "We have discussed it from time to time. It's been all work over past years."

"Is there a worry about having two residential areas so far from each other, and each in control of different infrastructures? Couldn't this cause trouble in the future?"

"No," she said dismissively, "we operate as one business."

Tanya saw Kim was irritated and uncomfortable with the turn of conversation and didn't pursue it.

"And you?" asked Tanya, "Is there any romance in your life? Or is it all just work?"

"I'd rather not discuss it," said Kim.

"If you need someone to talk to don't hesitate to call me. Your Mum and Dad are here too; maybe they are worth confiding in."

Kim shrugged.

Tanya made certain she spent time at all the various worksites and spoke to everyone. She mentioned her democratisation initiative to some of the people, which sparked some interest. In every case there was a feeling of a job being done well, but she had a feeling of something hidden, of wariness, perhaps an underlying sense of unhappiness or a need for change.

When she mentioned her concerns to Patricia, who was having fun recreating a school based on the one she had started at The Settlement, she was quite straightforward. "Although a very good job has been done here, Kim has turned out to be a bit of a slave driver, which causes resentment. There was a fellow we thought she might marry, but there was a bust up and when he returned to The Settlement he took up with someone else. He resented Kim's authority."

"Dear God, these men...I've had the same problem with Mark for years now." She explained the termination of her relationship with Mark and how he had now re-established himself in Virginia's life.

"I wonder if Kim knows any of this; maybe she would listen to you if she knew," said Patricia thoughtfully.

"You tell her. I'll leave it alone for now and try to talk to her next time I'm here. I'll be here a bit more often in the future, now the security situation is more settled."

It was with mixed feelings that Tanya took off the next morning to find the Taree establishment. "I'm planning a short visit, maybe just one night," she thought. She circled the encampment before landing. When the villagers spotted the Jetranger, they directed Tanya to a place near the centre of the small village. She knew what to expect from Jason's description. There was an attempt at keeping the place neat and orderly but it gave the impression of a plant just surviving, not knowing whether to give up the ghost or to soldier on. "Looks as though we may have arrived just in time," thought Tanya.

"Ah, NgalaTanya or whatever they now call you," said a man, matching the description Jason had given her, as she stepped out of the machine removing her flying helmet and dropping it on the front seat. There was no mistaking the electric shock that went through Tanya as she took his outstretched hand. "Welcome!" he smiled. "We weren't sure of the timing of your visit, so are quite unprepared, but welcome, we are delighted to have you here."

"Thank you," said Tanya laughing uneasily. She was not prepared for the very handsome man in front of her, "You must be Louis, Jason mentioned you."

"Ah, yes, Jason. He's been very helpful."

"I know you weren't expecting me today, so I have my own camping stuff. If it's okay, I'll set up under the trees over there."

"Mnn, that's what Jason and Roger did. I guess it's best for now as it is only for a night or two. In future if we have a bit of notice I'm sure we could find you a bed somewhere. Anyway, you'll eat with us?"

"Thank you."

"Can I show you round? I'm sure you would like to see what your people are doing here. We found beds for them by the way, so they have not had to camp."

"Lovely, I'll get out of my flying gear and set up the tent. I'll be about half an hour."

"Okay, I'm over there," he pointed to a shack, slightly larger and in better condition than the other visible shacks in the village.

She was able to stand up inside the tent, and it was easy to erect. Instinct made her lightly apply some make-up, something she rarely did these days. Some of the villagers nearby cast admiring glances at the stunning looking woman, with short blond hair, dressed in a pair of jeans, a shirt, and a pair of calf-length riding boots, as she emerged from the tent. On the way to Louis' shack she secured her flying gear and firearms in the helicopter and locked the machine.

Louis was waiting for her when she knocked and looked at her in admiration. He was in the same light airy room that Jason had seen, with a small kitchen on one side and a large bedroom on the other. Tanya knew that there were communal showers and toilets. He showed her around the village with an easy and friendly manner. He introduced her to everyone they came across. There was no sense of him showing off as the boss. It was clear that everyone had their own place and set of responsibilities and Louis' attitude reinforced that.

They came across Kim's two technicians installing solar in one of the houses. They both came and hugged Tanya, and showed her what they were doing.

"This solar," exclaimed Louis, "will really make a difference here. Just having decent light means that we can continue with all sorts of things at night. It extends the day; we can now cook after dark so work can go on until dusk. And the water pump has freed two people up altogether. These two you've lent us have got the tractor going and I can see what a difference that'll make."

"My uncle Joe made himself an expert in solar, even before we built the first house in The Settlement, so we've always had that," said Tanya.

"Jason says that he will try to get us a milking machine on his next raid..."

"Re-supply expedition," corrected Tanya with a smile, "we don't go on raids."

"Re-supply expedition, I stand corrected," laughed Louis. "That would make a huge difference. There seems to be an endless array of improvements available, courtesy of someone up there." He pointed skywards.

They covered the whole village. Tanya allowed Louis to hold her hand climbing a stile and going down a very steep incline. It was unnecessary but Tanya enjoyed the feel of his hand and the notion of being cared for, something that had not happened to her for as long as she could remember. They looked in on cows being milked by hand. There were people tending to the sheep, docking lamb's tails and paring overgrown hooves. Further away there was someone ploughing a large area with the newly supplied solar powered tractor.

"We'll plant oats and barley there, for animal feed. Jason provided us with some seed when he brought the tractor," explained Louis.

They admired the small herd of beef cattle grazing contentedly, near the fast-flowing stream. Once the tour was complete they returned to Louis' shack and he poured Tanya a cup of water. They both sat down.

"Is what you've done for us how you normally operate? It seems very generous."

"Most of the time yes. All we do is to provide the labour and transport. The items we find come for free. The same applies to the helicopters and the fuel to run them. What we gain is a much more secure establishment."

"You say most of the time?"

"There have been occasions when we have had to defend ourselves against people who wanted to take away everything we have built up, such as the Vikings, and there have been others, like the people from Barrington Tops."

There was silence for a minute.

"Can this continue for ever?" asked Louis.

"For a while. We're running out of fuel. But we're in the process of resolving that issue. Sooner or later though, we are going to run out of machines we use on a daily basis like helicopters, road vehicles, milking machines and so on. I have no idea how we replace them economically or even at all. Certainly, in the next ten years we are going to start going backwards unless we find other solutions."

"Jesus," exclaimed Louis, "and here we are just crawling out of the hole we thought we were in."

Both laughed easily, enjoying each other's company.

As the light started to fade Tanya said, "I could use a shower…"

"Of course," responded Louis. "There's a communal shower, which you are most welcome to use. There's plenty of water now your people have got the water pump going. Only cold water at the moment. Your people installed lights there within the past few days."

"I'll use it."

While showering Tanya thought about the day. She felt almost lightheaded. Her expectations of the visit had been low to non-existent. Reflecting on the time she had spent with Louis, it seemed special and she really enjoyed scrambling around the village with him. She shook her head, "Wake-up woman," she said to herself, "this is not reality, reality is The Settlement and its survival." Nevertheless, she allowed herself to think of the day and how she had enjoyed being with Louis and the feel of his hand on hers. Tanya emerged in a fresh pair of jeans and a clean shirt, with a pair of slip-ons on her feet. She again paid some attention to her makeup. Returning to Louis' shack she knocked on his door, looking forward to the dinner. "Looks like it might rain," he said, as he greeted her, "so they've moved everything inside to the community centre I showed you."

Everyone looked up as they entered the small community centre. Tanya could see people, including some quite small children, sitting and eating at several trestle tables crowded into the facility. There were men and women in the adjoining kitchen serving the meal. Louis and Tanya joined the queue. She had friendly conversations with many of the people, who were generally interested in The Settlement. Most commented on the transformation the solar installations had made to the community. She changed places a few times, to speak to as many people as possible. She did not notice when two people moved away when she found a place near them.

Towards the end of the dinner Louis stood up and made a short welcome speech, "Most of us here would like to understand the journey you began nearly 30 years ago and what has been achieved," he said to Tanya.

"Sure. I'll make it short. I know you must all be tired and ready for bed."

For a few minutes, she gave a brief description of the origins of The Settlement and what had happened since the flood. She included the relationship with Derain and his people and what they contributed to the survival of the community. She dealt very briefly with the recent security threats.

"To finish up, we look forward to on-going cooperation with you here, which will benefit us as much as you." She picked up a bag she was carrying. "I have a few bits and pieces of make-up here for the ladies. We can get you more of this if you want." She handed it to one of the women sitting nearby.

There was an immediate rush to see what there was and the women spent an amusing half hour sharing it all out.

"Well, that was lovely and fun," said Tanya to Louis, as they walked back towards his cottage, which was in darkness.

"No lights yet," said Louis, "I'll be the last cab off the rank. It sets the tone," he said almost apologetically.

They chatted for a few minutes once they arrived at the door to Louis' shack. Tanya felt reluctant to let Louis and the evening go but felt there was no option, so she kissed him lightly on the cheek saying, "Goodnight Louis, I have had a beautiful day, one of the best for a long time."

"Same for me," said Louis. "Look forward to seeing you in the morning."

Tanya made for her tent, the outline of which she could just make out about 100 metres away.

In the darkness, she quickly undressed, trying to put her clothes in an orderly way in her small suitcase. She normally slept naked, but on occasions like this she had an old tee-shirt that almost came to her knees, which she scrambled into before crawling into her sleeping bag. She tossed and turned, savouring every moment of the day. Unable to sleep, she looked at her watch for the umpteenth time noticing it was two am. "Bugger it," she thought. She hauled herself out of her sleeping bag. "Pants, I'm not going to need pants." Tossing them aside Tanya stepped out of the tent into the darkness and in her bare feet, ran the short distance, in the drizzle, across the rough ground to Louis' cottage. She opened the door without knocking. Louis was sitting there reading by the light of a smoky Dietz lamp.

"Another five minutes and I would have come to you." He rose and kissed her which Tanya deepened and deepened. They almost ran into the bedroom, where Tanya tore Louis' clothes off; as he lifted the tee-shirt over her head, he smiled in the dim light, saying, "You made that easy." They fell on to the bed with Louis whispering, "You on top?" "No, you," Tanya said urgently. Within minutes Tanya climaxed, followed by a flood of passion from Louis. Both fell into a dreamless sleep. Waking an hour later Tanya briefly wondered where she was and she then remembered, reliving every moment of their lovemaking while Louis still slept. She reflected, "We came together with no agenda, no promises, neither of us feeling inadequate in any way, as equals, as partners. My god, how wonderful. I have never felt so free in my life." Snuggling down next to Louis she felt him stir. "This time, me on top," she said as he opened a sleepy eye. Tanya made sure they had a much slower congress the second time around, finding maximum pleasure for both herself and Louis.

He looked at her in wonderment, "That was absolutely beautiful, beautiful," he whispered. "For me too," said Tanya.

They lay there each silently reflecting on the events of the previous 24 hours. "You are not leaving today, are you?" asked Louis, as the first signs of dawn started to lighten the eastern sky.

"What do you have in mind? If it's more of this," she stroked his strong body, "then how can I possibly think of going anywhere?"

"That's what I was hoping. We should get some breakfast, which'll be on in a few minutes, then I have a plan for the day that I think will surprise you. I promise it will be fun."

"Maybe one of your freezing cold showers will be my first port of call. That should dampen my libido for a minute or two. Then breakfast," Tanya laughed.

Tanya dressed in her skimpy tee shirt, dashed back to her tent and then to the shower. She and Louis were some of the first in the breakfast queue. There were a few curious glances from the other early risers.

"We're going for a ride," announced Louis, "to a very special place. You'll need a hat and a jacket."

Louis selected a big good-looking thoroughbred mare for Tanya, before saddling his own horse, a thoroughbred stallion. Tanya fed her mount a carrot she had filched from the kitchen as she carefully fitted the horse's bridle and saddle. She mounted, adjusting the stirrups. She tightened the girth again from the saddle, knowing that the horse would have held its breath to puff itself up, when she first saddled up.

"Okay, let's go," said Louis looking at Tanya with admiration. She was wearing the shirt from the previous day and a pair of riding breeches, which showed her slim figure off to its best, with a pair of riding boots and, as advised, a hat and a leather jacket. "All from our re-supply expeditions," she said apologetically. Louis glanced at her. "It's a fair way so we need to get a move on."

They cantered out of the yard, down a short hill into a well wooded area where Louis really put Tanya to the test. For 20 minutes, they galloped through the bush on what turned out to be an informal steeplechase course over bushes and fallen trees. Tanya coped with ease, following Louis at a safe distance; she really enjoyed the feel of the horse and she seemed to have created an immediate rapport with the strong, willing animal. She pulled up a minute after Louis, with the horses blowing noisily. Louis smiled, "As with other aspects of your performance today you ride very well."

"I've mentioned the Academy, we all have to ride well to stay in the programme," answered Tanya smiling. "Speaking of performances, you don't do too badly yourself." She moved her horse closer to his and kissed Louis firmly on the mouth.

For the next two hours they cantered the horses firstly through the bush and then into more open areas. An occasional kangaroo hopped off as they approached. Tanya noticed increasing numbers of cattle which ran away at the approach of the humans. "There are too many of the beasts now," said Louis. "We come out and shoot all the scrub bulls, or as many as we can find, but it's become overwhelming. We have some 10,000 head now as far as I can see and I have no idea what to do with more than a fraction of that number. They are also destroying the place. As you can see it's overgrazed in places." Tanya nodded not responding immediately.

"Is this still all your property?" she asked.

"Yes, my parents owned something like 80,000 hectares. We are still on the property they owned. I suppose I own it now."

Tanya looked at him curiously.

"I'll tell you the whole story later," said Louis anticipating the question.

Soon they were cantering along the side of a large dam. In many parts, the wooded areas reached down to the dam, looking it's very best with the bright sunlight reflecting on the still water. "My grandfather built this," said Louis, waving his arms in the direction of the water. "We'll be able to see the wall later."

"It's beautiful," said Tanya with feeling, "stunning." They stopped for a short minute admiring the view.

A few minutes later Tanya noticed a small paddock made with gum tree poles.

"Well, here we are," Louis announced, dismounting, removing his horse's saddle and rubbing the animal down with handfuls of grass. Tanya followed suit. He pulled two of the poles aside which opened as a gate. "We'll leave the horses here," he said. "There's plenty of grass in the paddock and they have access to the water from the dam over there," he continued, pointing. They released their mounts into the paddock and watched them rolling in the lush grass. Louis replaced the poles making the horses secure. He then leant down and kissed Tanya gently on the mouth, the kiss deepened and they stood enjoying the feel of each other for a few moments.

"Plenty of time for that," said Louis eventually. "It's time for a swim. We're going over there," he pointed at an island in the dam some 200 metres away. "Right! Everything off," he walked to the dam's shoreline and started stripping off. Tanya looked up, it was a warm day, still quite early; there was no possibility of anyone else appearing. She followed suit. Louis watched in admiration as Tanya removed the last of her clothing, "My god you are beautiful," he said, "I could sit and watch you all day." Unembarrassed, Tanya noticed his growing erection. She laughed, "If we're going swimming," she said, "that might slow you down a bit."

They hung their clothes over a nearby bush. "Come on," laughed Louis. He led her to the water's edge and dived in. After a moment's hesitation Tanya plunged in, enjoying the sudden shock of the cold water. Within a few strokes she had caught up with Louis and they swam stroke for stroke until they reached the island. "Careful, it's a bit stony," he cautioned. Still breathing heavily from the swim, he fished under a rock and produced a dilapidated pair of sandals. "Here, you have the sandals." She looked at them quizzically and put them on while Louis was stroking the water on her body away. She started to do the same for him. "Over here," he said and led the way to other side of the small island where there was a humpy, constructed from kangaroo skins and branches, not visible from the shore. They both gradually dried off in the warm sun. "Before you ask the question, you are the only other person ever to have come here with me. It's my private place," said Louis.

"I feel very privileged," she said simply.

"I'm privileged to have you here."

They kissed and he led her into the humpy where they lay down on a makeshift bed. They stroked each other; Tanya took his erection into her mouth for a brief few seconds. Louis rolled her over and they made love. Tanya noticed that despite its decrepit appearance the humpy appeared to be weather proof; the bed was soft and comfortable, made from cured kangaroo and sheep skins.

After a few minutes lying in each other arms Louis sat up on his elbow saying, "I have a story to tell you."

Tanya looked at him, as Louis continued, "I was quite happy and contented having been brought up on the property here. I am an only child and it was always assumed that I would take the place over in time. After completing school, and a stint in the navy, I worked every hour that God made, not that I cared. It was a wonderful life. I had no inkling of the catastrophe that was about to hit us though, none whatsoever. I often spent several weeks out on the property, mustering cattle, fixing fences and so on. I had a small crew that included two Aborigines, so we lived off the land and they taught me everything I know about the bush and surviving in it. My grandmother was part Aborigine, so I know something of the culture. I'd been in the field for three weeks, completely out of touch with the wider world. My crew had returned to their various homes and I was expecting to return to the big house, to a warm bath and a decent meal cooked by my mother." He hesitated. "I'm listening," said Tanya.

"I could see something was wrong a long way from home. There was a smoke plume which seemed to be coming from the direction of the house and when I got closer I heard gunshots and then complete silence. I tethered my horse 300 metres away and crept up to the burning house taking my rifle with me." He pointed to the roof of the humpy, where Tanya could see a good rifle secured into the roof. Her curiosity increased.

"When I crept into the yard, there were 40 or 50 cars spread about on the driveway and the yards. There were dead bodies scattered in all directions, none of whom I recognised. I ran into the blazing house looking for my parents; I found them both dead, riddled with bullets. By this time the fire was getting too fierce; I got out of the house just as a roof beam collapsed and the fire intensified. A shot was fired at me, missing by inches. I still had no idea what was happening and what had caused this invasion, but I knew my way around the yard and hid until I saw a man creeping about, probably looking for me. I shot him in the head, deciding to take no chances. I spent the night in one of the sheds, wondering what the hell to do. I managed to keep my head, although I was completely traumatised.

"Carefully walking around the next morning, in what appeared to be a deserted yard, I found the remains of a newspaper in one of the abandoned cars dated April 26th 2026. Once I read the article I realised that the world as we had known it had come to a shattering end." He pointed up to the roof of the hut. Tanya reached up and removed the now yellowed pages of the paper. "I still had no idea what all the people were doing on our property. Anyway, after creeping about for most of the next morning I could see there was nobody left alive, so I collected all the bodies I could find and put them into the still-smouldering house. I threw some more loose timber into the fire and watched it burn; by this time, I could see nothing of the bodies. I was getting very hungry. Luckily for me, I am able to survive in the bush because any food in the house had gone up in smoke. I hung around the homestead for a few days until another group of men arrived. I stayed hidden; they were obviously desperate. They left within a day but from the few snatches of conversation I heard they had almost run out of fuel and they had no food. Then I remembered this place and came here. There is a small boat, but from habit I keep it over here on the island. Whenever I left for more than a day, as a precaution I left the boat here and swam to the shore. Not one person, except me and now you, know of this place." He stopped.

Tanya leant over and kissed him. "And then?" she asked.

"I built the humpy, and improved it over time making it water-proof. I made the boat from a tree log and stayed here for about three months. Do you want some lunch by the way?"

"Sure," she said uncertainly, looking around for any signs of food.

He pulled a fishing rod from the roof of the hut, went outside, and she saw him picking up what looked like grasshoppers, which he attached to the hook. He cast the line out into the water and placed the rod carefully on a nearby stone. "If you could just hang onto that," he suggested, "I wouldn't like to lose that rod."

Louis busied himself making a fire, which was soon blazing merrily. He walked to the other side of the island, returning with some tropical looking leaves. By this time Tanya was struggling unskilfully with the rod that had something big tugging on the line. Louis took over and soon landed a decent sized fish which he gutted with a knife, retrieved from the roof of the humpy. He wrapped the fish in the leaves saying, "We'll wait until the fire has burnt to coals, the fish will then take about half an hour to cook. I promise something special." He grinned. "At last I have found something you don't do very well."

"I've never fished in my life, although some people fish in the dam at home. The first time I ever held a rod was now, today," she said defensively. "We didn't do fishing in Cabramatta, at least not for fish."

"I can teach you," offered Louis.

"If I'm with you, I won't need to worry," said Tanya, half seriously. "How did you come to set up the village?"

"Okay, where did I get to? Oh yes. After about three months, I started moving about the area. I still had the horse and gun. I built the paddock at about that time. I had no real plan and only a vague understanding of what had happened to our world. Then I came across this family of about half a dozen adults and children, close to where the village is now. They were in a bad way, but with my bush skills I was able to restore them all to health and we gradually built the place up from there. In various ways more people joined us; the Aborigines brought in some people, and I seem to have an instinct for where people might hide. I found one family living in holes in the ground. It's just grown from there. It's been a while since we had anyone new now, except for babies born."

"Who delivers the babies?" asked Tanya.

"Oh, I do. It's no different to dealing with a horse or a cow or any mammal for that matter, and I've had plenty of experience of delivering calves and foals and lambs. The only difference is that humans can speak, and they do, believe me." He grinned. "I also do most of the doctoring, helped by one of the women. We've lost people who would have survived with a proper doctor, so your hospital sounds intriguing; we've never had any access to western medicine. Common sense and some Aboriginal herb medicine is all I use. I would like to hear something about how your settlement survived." Tanya noticed that Louis avoided any mention of Harold or the Barrington people.

"Mere bagatelle, compared with what you've done. Before I start, you've never married or taken up with any of the girls in the village?" asked Tanya. "Some of them are very pretty."

"No, I have always been seen as the leader. I decided right from the beginning not to touch any of our girls despite the temptations that have arisen from time to time. This is now respected. Any other approach would have created divisions in the community; we might not have survived had I acted differently. Enough of that; let me get the fish and then let's hear your story."

They sat near the fire sitting on the lush grass. Each feasted their eyes on the naked body of the other. They ate the fish with gusto. Tanya spent the early part of the afternoon giving Louis chapter and verse on the history of The Settlement, filling in the details left out in her brief speech to the village community the previous evening. Just before three o'clock Louis said, "We'd better make a move. What a fascinating story, you can finish it later."

They cleaned up the site. Tanya buried the fire and Louis stored all his bits and pieces in the roof of the humpy. When they left only an expert would have known there had been anyone there that day, or anyone who had seen a column of smoke. Tanya ran to where they had originally landed; she dived in and beat Louis to the shore by a few strokes, "Bitch," he said laughing, "you took me by surprise. I'll get you next time."

She kissed him, smiling, "I'm happy to hear there will be a next time, I've had a wonderful day."

They dressed, and tacked up the horses, who were pleased to see them. They walked into the community centre, just as dinner was being served, having tended the horses and stowed the tack. They made no attempt to hide their affection for each other. Most people were pleased for Louis in particular. "If he trusts her then so do I," was a typical comment, followed by, "They've helped us with all this solar stuff," and "If it wasn't for him we would be dead and buried by now," or "It's time he did something for himself. He's spent the last ten years looking after all of us." The only word of disquiet was, "What happens if he leaves? What will happen then?" Nobody knew the answer to that. Unnoticed by either Tanya or Louis there were some uneasy glances shared by some of the surviving people who had come from Barrington Tops.

Louis spent an hour or more after dinner playing magistrate. He resolved a few issues. Tanya spent time with the Newcastle people; they needed no advice on how to do their jobs but were glad of news from home and the rest of The Settlement. Their eyes stood out on stalks when she told them about the security issues with Thor and what had happened to him. "Hot water in the showers, that's what I would welcome when I return," she said laughing as they finished up. "A 5:30 am cold shower is a bit too bracing, even for me."

"You'll be back soon?" she was asked pointedly by Vanessa, one of the two Newcastle girls assigned to help the Taree village.

She looked at the girl, and then glanced at Louis, "Soon, very soon. Frankly, wild horses won't be able to keep me away for long." They all laughed. They liked Tanya's straightforward and honest way of dealing with potentially awkward questions. The two girls glanced at each other.

"I need a shower," said Tanya as she and Louis walked, arm in arm, back to his cottage, "and then I am assuming your bed. I am pleasantly tired, but if you like I will try to finish the story of The Settlement."

"I'll see you over there," answered Louis referring to the shower.

Tanya fell asleep in Louis' warm bed before she had uttered two sentences of her continuing story. She was aware of Louis kissing her gently on the forehead as he snuggled into bed next to her.

Tanya spent an hour the next day finishing off the narrative of The Settlement.

"You are one mighty tough lady," said Louis after some reflection. "To suggest that what you have achieved is 'mere bagatelle' compared to what has been done here is ridiculous. Many more people have survived the flood as a result of your actions. I can't wait to see it all." He kissed her.

They spent time walking around the village for Louis to deal with the few issues that arose daily. Tanya said, at length, "Louis, to say that I have really enjoyed the last couple of days would be a massive understatement. I've loved it and being with you is very special. I do have to go home though. I think I must leave tomorrow, but I would like you to come to see me and the whole set-up at The Settlement."

"Okay, can you pick me up in the chopper?"

"Of course, just name the day and I'll be here."

"We'll settle on a date before you leave. I too have loved having you here. You are a very special lady."

"Enough of the lady stuff," Tanya joked. "By the way, how old are you? I wouldn't like to be accused of cradle snatching."

"43," he said, looking at her speculatively, "you look and behave like someone my age, although from what you've told me, you may be a year or two older than that. You have obviously kept yourself in great shape over many years and it shows."

Tanya opened her mouth to reply but Louis held up his hand, "Please, it's not important, not to me and anyway there is nothing either of us can do about it." Tanya looked at him gratefully.

Tanya packed up her tent and soon after breakfast the following day took off for the one-hour flight back to The Settlement, after a long hug and a deep kiss from Louis in front of the open door of the chopper. Most of the village were present to see Tanya off, hoping she would be back soon.

CHAPTER 8
Development

TANYA

Jason was waiting on the parade ground for Tanya when she returned.

"Auntie, we didn't think the visit to the Taree people would take so long," he said playfully. He only called her 'auntie' on rare occasions when he wanted to tease her. Jason could see from Tanya's demeanour that something special had happened during her visit.

"Yes, well, I was interested in what they were doing. Did you realise that they have about 80,000 hectares there?"

"No, but they must use only a fraction of that." He decided to back off, the reason for her extended visit would emerge in time. He added, "By the way, Roger has unearthed five fuel dumps. There are security issues involved in a couple of them, which we need to talk about."

"Okay." She quickly found she was back into the hurly burly of attending to the myriad of Settlement issues. When she had a moment to herself she was able to savour the few days she spent with Louis all the more, days without any immediate pressure or responsibility;

something that had not happened in all the time she had been involved with The Settlement. She made a note to repeat the experience.

Kim came to see her later in her office, with a very apprehensive look on her face. "I've been here a couple of days. We were expecting you back from Taree sooner than this."

Tanya shrugged. "Okay, what's the problem?"

"I have to tell you that I have rather over-extended my remit, without telling you. I'm sorry. I will resign if you want me to." Kim was almost in tears.

"I like people to take on more responsibility," Tanya grinned, "Go on, tell me what naughtiness you've been up to."

"Well you know that ship in Botany we were going to refurbish?"

"What of it?"

Kim drew a deep breath, "We've been working on it for more than a year now, Dad in particular. It's almost ready to be moved to Newcastle." Kim looked fearful at Tanya's possible reaction.

Tanya walked around the desk, took Kim's hand playfully and gave it a very light tap, saying, "Naughty, naughty girl!" She looked at Kim. "Have you the faintest fucking idea that's the best news I've heard in months? It's much bigger than you think. I'm thrilled, to be honest with you. Someone after my own heart." She stopped for a minute with Kim looking on, relieved and bemused. "It's how I worked with David; I would go off and do something, half expecting a slap on the wrist when I told him. Provided it moved the development of The Settlement on I got nothing but support." She hugged Kim. "Resign? Don't be bloody stupid, what the hell would we do with you if you did!" Tanya then added more seriously, "How long before you'll be ready to move the vessel?"

"Two or three weeks, maybe a month or so, something like that."

"Don't for God's sake stop working on it. We can talk later. Don't shift the boat until you've spoken to me. If you do, you really will have pooed in your nest."

"On the phone," said a relieved Kim, laughing uneasily. "There are some things I need to attend to in Newcastle."

Tanya nodded; she was already thinking ahead. "I'm sure Louis said something about being in the navy…" she thought.

Roger excitedly came to see Tanya in her office with Jason. "There is plenty of unused fuel about if one knows where to look," he announced.

"Tell me," said Tanya.

"Three mine sites in the Hunter coalfields, and maybe more, we haven't been to all of them yet. There's a substantial store of AVCAT, helicopter fuel, at Bankstown Airport, but we need to secure that as soon as we can."

"How?" asked Tanya.

"I'll come to that," said Jason, "let Roger finish his story."

"Well, there's an enormous depot at Jervis bay, where the navy had a base. The flood missed it altogether because it is up on a headland."

"Any sign of anyone having been there recently? At Jervis, I mean," asked Tanya.

"No, there are no ships there now and no evidence of anyone being there since the flood," answered Roger. 'The access is overgrown, but we eventually found the tanks. There is a safe place to land," Roger said, "but it's a huge quantity though."

"Just diesel at Jervis I suppose; navy vessels use diesel I think," said Tanya thoughtfully. "Okay, tell me about Bankstown. That's probably the priority."

"I decided to secure the place since it's on the boundary of what we can safely say is our territory, so we have ten of our people there now," answered Jason.

"And then?" asked Tanya impatiently.

"Much of the airport is flooded. Just the main buildings and the fuel tanks have escaped the flood. There's an abandoned fuel truck. It's half full, so people must have left in a panic. The tanks at the airport are almost full. We've tested the samples I took and it's all quite usable. Our people are in the process of reconditioning the tanker, which will take a month or so. If we are to make that source of fuel secure, I decided it had to be in the secure helicopter base in Newcastle."

Tanya nodded in approval, "How long will it take to shift all the helicopter fuel to Newcastle? Once you have the tanker operational?"

"Five or six weeks. The roads, as you know, are crumbling and we'll have to clear vehicles out of the way in many cases."

"You've started doing that?" questioned Tanya.

"Yes, today actually. There's a crew working from the Newcastle end, and another one will start from about half-way, moving south. We are collecting IDs from the vehicles where possible, and we bury the bones properly which takes time. It would be much quicker if we didn't have to do that."

"Still do that. Come back and tell me if you want to change anything," answered Tanya. "What about Jervis?"

"We'll need some sort of tanker ship to get to it," said Roger.

"Well done, both of you. This gives us fuel security for a few more years, if we can pull it off," said Tanya. "I've a couple of other things for you."

"So do we," said Jason. "I've just heard, from Joseph in Banksia this morning, that they have found Hercules, or rather his remains. Half eaten by birds and dingoes. He has now been buried and they've marked the spot. They couldn't do much else."

"Have you told Venus?" asked Tanya.

"No, I only heard a minute before we came to see you."

"Tell Venus, and then we should go and see Susan. Unless you need me to come with you now."

"No need. Venus is pregnant by the way, three months. The hospital says all is well," said Jason happily.

"Wonderful; congratulations!" Tanya leant over and kissed her nephew. Roger gave him a hug. "Fatherhood, the best thing in the world," he observed.

"You had something else for us?" asked Jason.

"Yes. The solar installations in the Taree village have already made a difference. A couple of washing machines and a dishwasher would also help. So on one of your trips to the Bankstown site maybe you could also pick up some stuff up and take it directly to the Taree village. I've invited Louis here for a visit, in a couple of weeks, so you could bring him back with you. I also found a cold shower at 5:30 in the morning a bit too chilly even for me."

They all laughed. "Louis told us that the lighting and water pump were priorities, I expect the water heater will be installed in the showers by the next time you visit," said Roger.

"Louis can stay with us if needs be," said Jason with a mischievous look.

Tanya looked at him, smiling, and without the hint of a blush, said, "Thank you. I expect he'll find it much more congenial to be staying with me. In my bed, since that seems to be what you're asking."

Jason laughed; he always liked the direct way that his aunt dealt with everything, even personal issues. Roger couldn't believe he was listening to such a conversation; blushing, he found a spot on the ceiling which captured his interest.

"One other thing," said Tanya. "How much contact do you have with our people in the military?"

"Some," said Roger, "it's not that easy..."

"Mnn, Jonathan's behaving strangely. There's something going on. Is there any way you can have a face to face with some of them, without drawing too much attention? Maybe Chas, who always has a nose for anything untoward going on."

"I'll bear it in mind. I'll be going to Canberra within the next few weeks and will see if I can sniff anything out," said Roger.

When the meeting finished, Jason said, "I'll come and fetch you when I've spoken to Venus. She'll be upset about Hercules, although I think she's anticipating the news because we haven't heard anything of him for weeks. She and Susan have become quite close, by the way."

An hour later Jason and a red-eyed Venus came to fetch Tanya and they silently walked the 50 metres to Chloe's cottage, where Susan and Mars were now firmly established. Looking at the downcast faces of the visitors Chloe realised immediately the likely subject of their visit. She picked up the yelling three-year-old Mars and took him outside.

Jason and Venus held Susan's hands, "It's about Hercules," he said, "I'm afraid it's not good news." He told her about the discovery of the body.

Susan was silent for a minute and allowed a tear to escape down her cheek, eventually saying, "He was actually a very kind man, you know, but too much under the influence of his father. When we were away from the Viking village we were quite happy. He was no fool and realised that Mars was not his. It is obvious who his father is anyway, one can see by his looks." Another tear escaped down her cheek. "He never took it out on either me or Mars; he treated Mars like his own son and he was always kind and considerate to me. I'm sorry." She looked at Venus and squeezed her hand.

"We know where Hercules is buried," Jason said after a few moments silence. "We could pay a visit, if you like. I can take you there in one of the choppers."

Venus and Susan looked at each other. Venus squeezed Susan's hand saying, "Yes, we would both like that."

Days later Jason took the two women in the Jetstar to a site in a very remote bush location. Joseph had thoughtfully hung a few ribbons on a tree so the place was easy to find. During the intervening days Susan had had a small plaque made from stone, which she took with her. The simple inscription said: 'HERCULES' together with his birth date and his assumed date of death.

"The Bowers are a bit of a mixed blessing," Venus confided to Susan one day, in the cottage she and Jason occupied, while they were planning the visit to the gravesite. "On the one hand, I've been given the love of my life in Jason. Otherwise, I would have been forced to marry one of dad's ghastly lieutenants. Also, most of our Viking women have been rescued and have much better lives here. But to achieve that they had to burn the whole Viking village down and kill most of the men. As I said, a mixed blessing."

"I wouldn't be alive if it hadn't been for Chloe and Kim," answered Susan, "although life has not all been plain sailing since then. Maybe it's because we now live in a much more primitive society and survival is what drives us. I do have Mars, which makes up for a lot."

The party spent 30 minutes placing the headstone at the site. Susan had asked The Settlement's Buddhist priest for a short prayer that she could say when they were at the gravesite. "I can come with you if you like," he offered. She shook her head, "It's not necessary, he had no religion, it's just that I feel so inadequate in such situations." When asked why she didn't ask the Anglican priest for a prayer, Susan could only shudder.

Ten days later, unable to concentrate, Tanya dashed out of her office on hearing the clatter of rotor blades from the chopper landing outside. Today was the day that Jason was to fetch Louis for a visit. "Calm down woman," she said to herself, "you're behaving like a bloody teenager." She was waiting on the edge of the parade ground when the Jetstar landed. To her consternation she could see no sign of Louis. She dashed up to the machine once the rotors had come to a halt and wrenched the door open. There he was crouching down, out of sight. "Ha, got you," she said laughing and much relieved. "He wasn't sick or anything horrible like that," she said to a grinning Jason. Louis hopped out and they clung to each other, kissing for a full minute.

"Welcome, it's lovely to see you," she said to an overwhelmed Louis, who was looking around in awe.

"It's wonderful to see you again, and to be here at last. I had no idea of the extent of this place," he said. He kissed her again. "All that buggering around was Jason's idea, he seemed to have some idea you'd be pleased to see me," he laughed.

She pulled a face, smiling, "I'll get him back one day."

"We'll get your luggage and then I'll show you round," said Tanya, moving back towards the machine.

Louis laughed, "Luggage? I don't have any luggage! Even if I had a suitcase I have nothing much to put in it. Jason said that maybe I could benefit from some clothes you have here from your re-supply expeditions."

Tanya put her arms around him, "Sorry, I forgot you had become a real bush baby. Come, I'll show you round."

Tanya showed him her own cottage first, laughing as she said, "I was going to suggest you put your luggage in here," ushering him into her bedroom. "Here is Nanny's room, and Didier sleeps here," she said moving about the house. "I told you who they were when I was with you, and just in case there is any doubt, Mark, my ex, if you want to use that ghastly expression, lives in the Southern Highlands."

"It's beautiful," said Louis, looking out of the sitting room window. "It seems so well organised and clean. I look forward to you showing me around. There is one thing though."

Tanya raised her eyebrows.

"I haven't had a hot shower for more than ten years..."

Tanya looked at him, laughed as she hugged him saying, "Of course, I'll tell you what. Let's first fix you up with some clothes and a razor. Then the shower and the royal tour."

They had an amusing half hour fitting Louis up with two hard wearing outfits, including boots for use in the Taree village. "How about something a bit dressier?" suggested Tanya, holding up a shirt, a pair of casual trousers and a pair of slip-on shoes. "Mnn, what would I do with them? I don't have anywhere much to keep stuff like that."

"Leave it all here; you can wear it on your regular visits to see me." She smiled and the young woman whose responsibility it was to look after the clothes store, giggled.

While Louis was in the shower Tanya popped over to fetch Chloe and Mars. "Susan is out at the moment," explained Chloe.

"He'll be out of the shower shortly," said Tanya, "then I'll make us a cup of tea." Mars was busy with a box of toys Tanya kept handy.

Hearing the shower had come to an end, Tanya walked proprietarily into her bedroom saying to Louis, "We'll probably ride later," indicating that he should wear something suitable. Unable to resist she spent a few seconds admiring his naked strong dark-skinned body, she kissed his now clean-shaven cheek.

They spent 30 minutes chatting easily. Mars clambered on to Louis' lap insisting on being read to. As Chloe left she gave Tanya a gentle hug saying, "Bless you dear, I hope he makes you happy. You deserve it if anyone does," while Mars led Louis outside to show him something. The rest of the morning was spent walking around the village, Tanya demonstratively proud of both The Settlement and Louis. Louis was very engaging and charmed all the people he met. He was particularly enamoured with the hospital and he watched fascinated as some Academy recruits were being put through their paces. As they sat comfortably in her kitchen while Tanya made sandwiches for lunch, Louis said, "What you have here is marvellous and it's unbelievable how you've all pulled together and built this place. It's lasted, which is even more admirable."

Tanya nodded, "I think I know what you are about to add."

"Go on," said Louis.

"The big question is, how sustainable is all this? What has been built mirrors the civilisation destroyed in the flood. We are to some extent self-sufficient but are becoming more and more dependent on re-supply expeditions."

"That's pretty much what I was going to add. The re-supply might give us another 20 years. Jason told me that he thinks the fuel problem has been solved for a few years. We need to think beyond that."

Tanya was thrilled and surprised by the use of the inclusive way he had framed his comments. "It would be useful to know what you think we might concentrate on to help resolve that issue," she said.

Their deep kiss was interrupted by Nanny, who said, "Oops, didn't mean to interrupt anything." She bustled about the kitchen after being introduced to Louis, who she looked at approvingly. "If you have anything you wish to get on with, I can clear up here. You'll all be in for dinner?" Tanya had told her about Louis' visit and where he would be sleeping.

"Have you seen Didier?" asked Tanya.

"Hospital. He'll be at the hospital this afternoon." She then whispered to Tanya, when Louis was out of earshot, "Be careful, he's feeling a bit left out I think."

"I'll take you for a ride around the property now," said Tanya, "but I would like to introduce you to Didier, who's training to be a doctor, so should be at the hospital this afternoon. Chas, my other son, is with what's left of the military in Canberra."

Tanya had explained to Didier who Louis was and had been straightforward regarding her relationship with him. They found him at the hospital where she introduced him to Louis. "I'm a bit pushed at the moment," Didier said in an offhand way.

"We'll hopefully see you at dinner," said Louis.

Didier nodded noncommittally and went on his way.

"Sorry," said Tanya, holding Louis' hand, "It looks as though I've cocked that up. I did explain the situation. He'll come round."

"It's natural," said Louis. "Come, let's go for that ride."

Tanya looked at him gratefully.

They were out until almost dusk. Tanya showed him everything: the livestock, the dams, the extensive cultivated areas. She took him through the bushland to the north. Tanya won the ten-minute race on what was still known as Chloe's cross-country course.

"Strange horse, strange course," said Louis with a laugh. "Give me some practice and I'll knock the spots off you."

They went home exhilarated and happy. Louis made for the shower again. "What, another shower?" joked Tanya, "I was just getting to like your smell."

While the shower was running Tanya followed Didier as he went into his room when he returned from the hospital. She sat on his bed and held him gently by the hand, "How was your day?" she asked.

He smiled, "Actually it was great, I removed my first appendix today and I think the patient will survive."

"Well, that's wonderful. I'm sure you'll make a brilliant doctor. Keep it up," she said rather formally.

She was silent for a moment, "I've explained something of Louis. There's water to go under the bridge, but he's becoming more and more important to me personally. It would be helpful if you were able to make a bit of an effort, that's all. I know it's difficult for you. You could show him parts of the hospital I know nothing about, for example. He does all the doctoring at his place, completely untrained, but they have no other option; he delivers babies..."

Didier's eyes brightened, "Good heavens, that's interesting. I'll see you at dinner. I do understand or at least I think I do." He patted her arm.

The conversation at dinner was somewhat desultory to start with, until Didier said to Louis, "Mum tells me that you do all the doctoring at your place in Taree. I'd be very happy to show you more of the inner workings of the hospital, if you like. I suppose all you got today was the standard tour."

Glancing gratefully at Tanya, Louis responded, "Yes, I'd love that. My doctoring skills are somewhat rudimentary. I actually need some help and possibly an arrangement where serious cases can be transferred to you here."

"If you come with me at 6:30 tomorrow morning," suggested Didier, "that might be best. Then we'll have the whole morning," he continued. He smiled at his mother, "If you can spare him for that long of course."

They all helped clear up. "Breakfast will be ready at six," said Nanny.

They all went to bed straight after dinner due to the planned early start and Tanya had determined she would go on her usual early morning run and have breakfast when it suited her.

"Come here," she said to Louis, as they closed the door. "This is going to be fun; I've been looking forward to this all day."

"All day?" said Louis in mock seriousness, "there must be something wrong with you, I haven't been able to think of anything else since you left our place two weeks ago." They both laughed.

"Oh, that was wonderful," said Tanya afterwards, "perfect," as she snuggled up to Louis in her nice warm bed. "You are the sexiest woman in the world," was his sleepy reply. "You can wake me anytime for more of that."

Tanya was up and about at five, ready for her run. "Hey, breakfast is only at six," Louis mumbled, "come back to bed."

Tanya leant over kissed him saying, "After lunch. Special treat after lunch, we'll have the place to ourselves then." She ran out closing the door quietly.

An hour later Tanya, dripping with sweat and still panting, came into the dining room where the others were having breakfast. She sat down on Louis' lap drenching him. "Hey," he said, "now I'll have to go and have another shower."

She kissed him full on the lips. "You'll wash yourself away altogether if you have any more showers."

"Mnn," said Louis, "that's almost better than scrambled egg."

"Careful, you said almost better, it had better be better."

"Just being tactful," answered Louis.

Didier and Nanny watched in amusement at the byplay. Neither of them had seen Tanya in such a mood before. Didier, in particular, started to understand what she meant by Louis 'becoming more and more important' to her.

"Can I get you some breakfast, Tanya?" asked Nanny.

"Lovely, but can it wait ten minutes? I need to get cleaned up."

"Good idea," said Louis.

"Now then, you two," said Nanny, smiling, "of course. The centre only opens at seven."

"Centre?" asked Louis.

"I look after the pre-school child care centre for the community. You should pay us a visit. We're all very proud of it."

After Louis and Didier left for the hospital Tanya emerged glowing from her ablutions to a wonderful looking plate of scrambled eggs on toast and coffee.

Nanny came and sat next to her, "Didier seems okay now."

"I feel such a clot; Louis had told me about his amateur doctoring when I was in Taree," said Tanya. "If I hadn't been thinking about myself and my relationship with Louis so much, I could have mentioned that to Didier long before Louis arrived. It would have saved us that little unpleasantness."

"You spend quite enough time thinking and worrying about others as it is," said Nanny fiercely. "It's time you spent a little more time on yourself, high time." Then she added, almost tearfully, "You and Louis are good together, he's strong enough to cope with your nonsense. I, more than anybody, hope it works out." Tanya leant over to hug her, but she had already returned to the kitchen.

Spending the morning in her office Tanya hurried back home just after one o'clock, hoping to arrive before Louis. He wandered in just after Tanya and without a word he picked her up and carried her to their bedroom.

"Make love to me," he said, "now! You on top."

"Would you like some lunch," she asked later as they lay together on top of the bed. "I can't cast a line out for a nice fresh fish, but I could make us a sandwich."

He rolled over and kissed her, "A sandwich would be good. You are the most beautiful thing, though, so don't put too many clothes on, they might spoil the view."

Tanya smiled. She loved this kind of flattery.

Sitting on barstools in the kitchen, both of them almost naked, Tanya said, "You were in the navy, right?"

"Yes," he said warily, wondering what sort of curved ball was now being directed at him, "for eight years."

"What did you do?"

"All sorts of things, I was an officer, so I can navigate, fire guns, I was often the officer on the watch so was responsible for the safety of the ship at sea and so on. Why do you ask?"

Tanya explained Kim's initiative of salvaging a ship from the wreckage in Botany Bay and the need for security in Newcastle. "You see, there's an abandoned warship in Sydney harbour and I thought we might just tow it round to Newcastle with Kim's boat, anchor it there and, with your skills, at least get the guns firing again."

Louis laughed and laughed, he was unable to stop himself for a good minute, "Woman, you are the most unusual creature I have ever known. We have just made the most wonderful love, and your next move is to ask me to help you steal a warship in Sydney harbour; as rare as rocking horse shit as they say. I half expected you to say something like would you like to go for a nice little walk down to the dam or some such thing, holding hands, but no, you want me to help you steal a warship." He laughed again.

"It's been abandoned for years," said Tanya pretending to continue the charade. She knew now that he would help her, "we could think of it as a salvage operation..."

"Shut-up woman, you know I'll help, all the tea in China wouldn't keep me away now." He kissed her. "What sort of warship is it, anyway?"

Tanya shrugged, "It's just a bloody warship..."

"Changing the subject again, did I hear you say something about making love?" asked Tanya. "Come on then, what's keeping you? You said that you'd been thinking about it for the last two weeks; let's get to it then." She rushed, giggling, into the bedroom followed by Louis.

"How was the visit to the hospital?" asked Tanya an hour or so later as they showered together and dressed. "It had better look as if we've been behaving ourselves," giggled Tanya.

"Who do you think we'll be fooling?" He smiled. "The visit was great, great," he said, "and I had a word with the chief surgeon who has a plan to help us, once you sign off on it."

Tanya responded, "She's a woman of great common sense, what did she have to say?"

"Periodic visits and an emergency arrangement. Something about homing pigeons."

"Sounds ideal. I'll discuss it with her when she comes to see me."

They sat in companionable silence for a few minutes waiting for Nanny and Didier to return.

"When are we going to steal this warship?" asked Louis.

"I thought tomorrow, unless you have a better idea," answered Tanya, not rising to the bait.

"Don't you have to plan anything for that?"

"Well the chopper was serviced today and I've asked Rebecca and Adrian to be ready for take-off at 6:30 am sharp. I know the way, having done the trip several times in past years. As far as I can see the weather looks benign. I can't think of anything else."

Louis looked at her, smiling, "Ask a silly question," he said shaking his head.

CHAPTER 9

Warship

(Three weeks after Tanya's visit to Taree)

TANYA

Rebecca and Adrian, dressed in Academy gear and armed with regulation carbines, were waiting next to the chopper as Tanya and Louis arrived at six the next morning. Tanya was similarly attired. Tanya introduced Adrian. Louis had already greeted Rebecca whom he remembered from her visit to the Taree settlement with Jason. Tanya performed the usual inspection on the two including a careful examination of their firearms. Rebecca made the same inspection on Tanya. Louis looked on in admiration.

"I have one of these for you," Tanya said to Louis handing him another rifle. She opened the breech and removed the barrel, indicating that the gun was safe. Louis similarly inspected the firearm. Tanya started her usual pre-flight inspection as the others settled into their seats. Louis, seated in the right-hand seat next to Tanya, chatted easily to the other two, "Ready to steal a warship?" he asked. Adrian and Rebecca just smiled. Tanya had briefed them the previous day.

Just after 6:30 Tanya started the engine and took off. As she often did, she flew a quick circuit right around The Settlement, admiring the neat well-kept houses and the contented looking stock.

Tanya asked Adrian, "Do you see anything of Annabel, the girl who helped Chloe escape?"

"Yes, certainly, I got to know her quite well when I was stationed at the Viking village. Our friendship has continued," said Adrian, giving nothing much away.

Conversation continued, through headphones, "Louis hasn't seen Sydney since the flood, so I will take a slightly circuitous route," Tanya explained. They flew along the length of the M4, still littered with the wrecks of old, rusting vehicles. "We have extensive records of all this," said Tanya to Louis, "as most of those vehicles contain the bones of those who died there either of starvation, thirst, or gunshot wounds if they were lucky."

Louis nodded. During past conversations with Tanya and his own experiences he had a reasonable idea of the extent of the catastrophe and the devastation it had caused. They flew over the deserted western suburbs and the flooded central city to Woolloomooloo bay where Tanya had seen the warship in the past. "I'm looking for a place to land," said Tanya.

"I served on a frigate like that," said Louis, pointing at the moored frigate, trying to hide his excitement. "We carried a helicopter; look, there near the stern, there's the flight deck. The ship's helicopter is long gone. You can probably land there." The frigate was the only ship moored in Woolloomooloo Bay.

Tanya looked dubious.

"I'll tell you what," offered Louis, "if you can hover just above the deck so I can rope down, I'll make sure it's safe."

Tanya smiled at his reversion to naval terminology.

"Okay, I'm sure I can do that; Adrian, you go with him."

During a precarious manoeuvre, Tanya managed to get the machine to hover ten metres or so above the deck and first Louis and then Adrian dropped down onto the deck using the rope. Tanya flew another two circuits, waiting for a signal from Louis.

"Look," said Rebecca to Tanya in amazement, "they seem to be talking to someone down there. It seems quite friendly."

After another two circuits Louis made a few hand signals. "It looks as if he thinks it's okay to land," said Rebecca. Tanya manoeuvred the chopper towards the deck. When she could see Louis, he raised both thumbs to indicate safety. Tanya settled the machine hard down on the deck, as Louis had instructed her, and cut the engine.

Louis, Adrian, and a very thin man with long wispy strands of grey hair and dressed in rags approached. The man was shaking, "Thank god, thank god, rescue at last," he muttered. He fell to his knees.

"He and his wife and daughter have been here since the flood," Louis explained. "I think they live on the ship."

"How the hell have they survived," Tanya wondered. "Still that story will be told in good time." She bent down to talk to the man, "My name is Tanya," she said, "we can take you to a safe place."

"Ted," said the man. Tanya could see he was emaciated and looked on the point of starvation. He scratched himself continuously.

"Where are your family?" asked Tanya.

The man looked confused for a moment, then smiled, saying, "Vegetables, we grow vegetables on roofs over there. They have gone over there to water them and pick what there is. They'll be back. There is only one boat; we'll have to wait for that."

Tanya thought for a moment, saying, "The first priority is to get these people back to The Settlement hospital. We also need to make an assessment of the state of this ship and whether we'll be able to tow it to Newcastle. We must contact Kim and her people in Botany so they can bring the ship they have salvaged out of Botany and into the harbour here."

"Maybe Adrian and I should stay here; I can start having a look at the ship," offered Louis.

"Good," said Tanya, "Rebecca and I can get these people to a place where we can look after them." She turned to Ted, "How soon will your wife and daughter return?" she asked.

Ted shrugged, "They'll have seen the helicopter, so quite soon I expect. Daughter maybe frightened. I'd like to show you downstairs."

"Okay," said Tanya, "one of us should stay and wait for Ted's wife and daughter. I think that should be me, the rest of you go with Ted. What are the names of your family, by the way?" she asked Ted.

"Eileen is my wife, Mary our daughter. Mary knows no other life apart from this," he waved his arms around. "We've not seen another person since the flood. She was born a year before the flood and has no knowledge of how we lived in normal times. We found a few magazines, here on the ship, and books in some of the flats that were not flooded, but it's difficult for her to comprehend it all. The only people she has ever spoken to are me and Eileen, so she'll probably be scared."

Tanya said, "I understand, I'll bear all that in mind." She handed Louis two torches that were part of the equipment carried in the helicopter. Ted led the way down through a door, followed by the rest of the party.

20 minutes later a very nervous woman hesitantly climbed up one of the steep steel ladders, attached to the side of the vessel. She was carrying a small bag, partly filled with something.

"Probably vegetables," thought Tanya.

Tanya was sitting in a deliberately non-threatening position on a nearby bollard, "Who are you?" asked the woman. Her terrified looking daughter tried to hide behind her mother, clutching on to her.

"I've come to rescue you," said Tanya, "there is no need to be frightened. Ted has gone downstairs; he'll be back soon. My name is Tanya."

"Dark, down there, there is no light," said Eileen.

"Torches, I gave them torches."

She tried to give the child one of the four torches always carried in the machine. She gave it to Eileen, who came a bit closer. Tanya noticed Eileen was in much the same physical state as her husband, but the daughter looked fine and well-fed. "They have obviously been making sure the girl is properly fed and have being going short themselves," thought Tanya.

"Can I see?" asked Tanya indicating the bag. After a moment's hesitation Eileen handed it over. There were a few carrots and a leaf vegetable that Tanya had difficulty in identifying. "Very difficult to grow anything now, the seeds have run out and the soil is no good anymore," explained Eileen. Mary was now constantly switching the torch on and off, on and off.

"We have plenty of food, so you won't need to worry anymore," Tanya told her.

"Where, where are you from?" asked Eileen, growing more confident.

"The Blue Mountains. You'll be safe there and we have a very good hospital where we will be able to look after you all. We can take you in the helicopter, it takes about an hour."

"One hour," said Eileen quietly. "This hell and you were only an hour away." A tear slipped down her cheek.

"When you can bear it, we would like to hear your story and how you survived. Many people died as you may know."

"Maybe it would have been better if we had died," said Eileen. "We had no idea we would be eking out this miserable existence for so long, and Mary has had a very bad start. I wonder if she will ever be normal."

"What did you do before the flood?" asked Tanya, trying to change the subject.

"We ran a restaurant, here in Potts Point. It was a very good restaurant. We lived in the flat above. We were planning on selling it in a few years and moving to a cottage we have down the coast. I suppose that has gone now with everything else."

Tanya nodded.

"One of the reasons we were able to survive is that we had food from the restaurant and Ted had always grown a few vegetables in the back garden, so we knew what to do. Ted realised everybody else round us was in a total panic so he found a source of seeds and saw it would be possible to grow vegetables on the roofs of surrounding blocks of flats, which is what we did, instead of trying to run away. Ted found a small rowing boat, so we were able to get about."

The others returned. Ted immediately ran to his daughter to protect her, "It will be alright Mary, these are nice people; they will look after you."

"Look daddy," she said cheerfully switching the torch on and off.

"Is there anything you need to take with you?" Tanya asked Eileen and Ted. "We won't be returning here."

They looked at each other, "No, not really, we don't own anything," said Ted.

"What, not even some old photographs or things like that?"

"No, no, we had a suitcase full of stuff like that, which fell in the water when we moved here, so there's nothing."

"Okay," said Tanya, "Eileen you might like to come in front with me. Ted, you will have to hold Mary on your lap with Rebecca sitting next to you. Okay?"

A nervous looking Ted nodded.

"Do you think Mary will be alright? Is there anything else we should be doing to keep her calm?" asked Tanya.

"We all probably need a pee," answered Eileen. "I'll just pop around the corner on the deck since we won't be coming back here."

"Ted, we'll be taking you to a place in the Blue Mountains. You'll be quite safe there and have somewhere to live. I'll tell you more once we are on our way," explained Tanya, as Eileen and Mary returned.

Everything seemed well while they took off. Ted and Eileen were fascinated by the transformation of their once vibrant city into the eerily silent place that confronted them. Mary was quite content switching her torch on and off. Suddenly there was silence in the rear of the chopper and then Mary let out the most unholy scream. She seemed to have realised that her world had altogether changed and she was now terrified. The torch was discarded. Glancing back, Tanya could see that Ted was not strong enough to keep control of Mary for very long. "Take over from Ted!" she said to Rebecca urgently. "You'll have to hold her and keep her under control. If she gets loose, we might have an accident."

After ten minutes of tumult, with Rebecca being bitten several times on her arms, she yelled to Tanya, "Can you put the machine down somewhere, I can't hold her for much longer! We need to do something else!" Tanya looked behind her again and saw the chaos, with Ted unable to do anything and Rebecca bleeding. She spotted a field and landed the machine with a bump. Tanya wrenched the door open and with her considerable strength, grabbed the still-struggling child. "I think there is some rope in the back somewhere," she said, "we'll have to tie her up with that." Between them they tied Mary tightly into the seat and gagged her. "Sorry," said Tanya to Ted and Eileen, "we don't have any choice; she might have caused us to crash. Rebecca, you will just have to sit right at the back there. Won't be long, only another 30 minutes."

They took off again, but Tanya flew in a circle over a gaggle of huts that Rebecca had pointed out when they were on the ground. There were signs of habitation but absolutely no movement, either human or animal. Tanya shrugged, "We can't rescue everybody," she muttered to herself. When they landed, Rebecca raced off to the hospital and returned with a gurney and the duty doctor.

Mary was still struggling against her bonds. "We're going to have to give her a sedative," the doctor said to Ted, when Tanya had explained the situation. Taking one look at Ted and his wife, he added, "You also need attention, so come with me."

"You stay here to explain the situation to the hospital and keep Roger informed; the bites on your arms also need attention." Rebecca looked disappointed for a moment, but saw the sense in what Tanya was saying.

"I'll find someone to take my place," Rebecca said and dashed off.

Ursula, a seasoned member of the Academy, appeared five minutes later, in full Academy dress. Maintaining the discipline, Tanya made her go through the inspection procedure. Rebecca returned saying, "I think they are all okay, the medical staff are looking after them now. They think they have arrived in heaven after what they have been through." She ran off.

"We need to refuel before we go back," said Tanya to Ursula.

On the return flight to the ship Tanya briefed her new companion. Flying over Sydney again Tanya decided only for the second time since the flood to see what had happened to their house in Mosman. She was unable to spot it on the first pass; the whole suburb was overgrown and returning to the natural bush that existed before the first fleet arrived. "There, it's that one over there," she said, eventually spotting the house which she pointed out to Ursula. Being born in The Settlement, Ursula had no concept of what it was like living anywhere else. She looked interested but said nothing. "It's almost waterfront now," observed Tanya, to the uncomprehending girl.

Landing under direction from Louis on the deck of the frigate; she jumped out and kissed him. Tanya told Louis and Adrian of the trouble they had had with Mary which explained their delay.

"I've had a look around the ship," said Louis, "somehow it's upright and floating. Ted said there was a second tsunami a few months after the first, which the vessel also survived. He told me that the ship had been securely moored so it has stayed put for all this time, about ten years I suppose. I had a look at the engine room, but it's difficult to see down there. I suppose from what you said the main consideration will be to see how difficult it will be to tow it to Newcastle."

"What do you think we should do now?" asked Tanya, thankful of Louis' presence and apparent expertise.

"There is no sign of anyone else around here and the frigate has been sitting here for all this time, so the possibility of any further significant damage is remote. I think we should go and see what your people in Botany are up to. Getting a big boat out of there and in here with what I assume is an unskilled crew is going to be interesting," he said. "Luckily there are no other ships, and there are tugs in the vicinity we could use."

"That's where you come in," laughed Tanya, "I had a feeling you would come in useful somehow." She stood on her toes and kissed him on the cheek.

"Mnn," said Louis, "don't push your luck."

Ten minutes later they were hovering over a large bulk carrier floating in the middle of Botany Bay. Several people waved and Tanya saw Kim pointing to the ship's flight deck where she could land. Joe emerged from the depths of the ship, wiping his hands on a lump of cotton waste. Louis was introduced.

"It's getting a bit late now, so we'll have to show you round in the morning," said Kim. "The good news is that dad now has the engine running and we have been able to briefly engage the props. I think we can raise the anchor. None of us have any idea how to steer this thing though. Joe has got one of the ships generators working, so we have light all over the ship."

Tanya explained Louis' background.

"Hopefully I can help," said Louis.

"Tanya, we have cleared a cabin for you," said Kim, "Louis will have to doss down with the boys; we have a men's area and one for the women." Louis had moved away and was chatting to Joe. Adrian and Ursula were securing the helicopter.

"Thanks; unless the cabin is very small Louis can share it with me," replied Tanya. Kim tried to hide the surprise on her face saying, "Okay, it's the captain's stateroom so is quite spacious."

During the evening meal Tanya was surprised to see that Kim had a crew of 20 people. She said nothing but gradually established that at least half of them had been on the ship for less than a month.

"With Louis' help we may be able to get the ship going within a day or two and it should be safely berthed in Newcastle after that," said Kim.

Louis looked at Tanya who smiled, saying, "I had a little diversion in mind. Kim, do you remember our discussions relating to the possible threat to the security of the port at Newcastle from the sea?"

Kim nodded, wondering what was coming.

"Well, I've found a warship in Sydney harbour," she said as if it was the most everyday occurrence. Heads raised at her announcement. She now had everyone's complete attention. "When we get this boat going, we could just pop into Sydney harbour and tow the warship back to Newcastle. Its appearance there will spook most people with bad intentions and in time we ought to be able to get the gun working again."

There was an incredulous silence for a minute or two. "Louis has said he will help," Tanya added, smiling.

"Are you serious?" asked Kim eventually. "Getting this thing up the coast is going to be an enormous challenge as it is. What you are asking makes it much more difficult. And what will Jonathan say?"

"I'm totally serious; the security threats are just as likely to come from the sea as anywhere. I'll deal with Jonathan but he hasn't taken any interest in the frigate for more than ten years now. As far as I am concerned it's a salvage operation, like this one here."

"You really are, as always, full of surprises," said Kim, glancing at Louis, and recalling the conversation with Tanya regarding security, continued, "We'll obviously see what we can do. It might be useful to have a look tomorrow, if you could take me up there in the helicopter?"

The next day while Louis and Joe reviewed and tested all the repairs that Joe had effected on 'the boat' as they were all now calling it, Tanya took Kim back to Sydney harbour. Landing on the warship together they spent two hours trying to assess the difficulty of attaching a hawser and then pulling the warship away from its mooring and getting it out of the harbour without causing any more damage. "You do give us impossible tasks," said Kim, "but we'll manage."

When they had finished, comfortable with each other and sitting on the deck eating a snack they had filched from the kitchen on 'the boat', Kim said, "You seem to be very fond of Louis."

Tanya laughed, "Yes, and I don't care who knows it. Actually, 'very fond' doesn't come close to describing how I feel about him and I've only known him for a month. During the few days I spent with him at Taree, I was able to almost completely forget about The Settlement and all the goings on regarding my responsibilities." She hesitated a moment before continuing. "Since David and I started talking about setting it up, all those years ago, I don't remember a single moment when I was able to do that," she said wistfully. "I'll probably try to go up to Taree a bit more often from now on."

"What about Mark?" asked Kim.

"That was over a long time ago," said Tanya carefully. "I was just not prepared to recognise it and was too obsessed with the survival of The Settlement. He's living with Virginia and their son in the Southern Highlands."

"Son?"

Tanya explained that Mark had fathered Virginia's son. Kim decided that the conversation had gone far enough.

Returning to Botany Bay, they saw 'the boat' slowly moving around the bay. Tanya saw 'the boat' straighten up and continue on a direct line when the helicopter was spotted. There was a wave from the foredeck indicating that she should land. She hovered over the deck for a few moments keeping pace with the slow-moving ship and then landed the chopper safely. "Whew," she said to Kim, 'that's a first."

"We'll need a week to do some training, so we have a chance of getting this vessel into Sydney harbour and then up the coast," Louis told them at dinner. "Actually, I've been thinking about this whole business," he added. "Even if we do manage to get the warship towed to Newcastle, with no power there is no way to manoeuvre it, and to have such a vessel floating round in the harbour not moored to anything will be very hazardous."

"What do you suggest then?" asked Tanya.

"Joe and I have discussed this," said Louis, looking down the table for support from Joe. "What we really need is to find a tug which we can recondition. While we can get 'the boat' up the coast to Newcastle from here, getting it out of the harbour once we have it moored will be difficult, so we will need a tug to help with that anyway. If we had a tug, then it will be easier to tow the frigate up the coast and get it into position. Also, as we know, at present there is no mooring for the warship in Newcastle."

Tanya summarised, "I think that was a very good conversation and may have prevented us from getting into trouble." Louis was impressed with the way she handled the issue and there was no hint of Tanya pressing her own point of view once it became obvious that towing the warship up the coast would be foolhardy with existing resources. Tanya continued, "Once we are all happy that we have the skills to sail 'the boat' up the coast and moor it in Newcastle harbour, we'll do that. Kim, under your supervision we'll establish a permanent crew for reconditioning other boats. We will start by finding a tug that can be refurbished. I have mentioned that Roger has unearthed a large store of diesel in the old naval base in Jervis bay. To access that we will need a tanker vessel, so we will try to find one as the next project and so on. I am sure that the skills we have acquired on this job here will stand us all in good stead."

"What happens if another party wants to do the same thing as we do?" asked Ursula expressing the sentiments of many in the gathering.

Tanya thought for a moment, "I think we all have concerns of that nature. We have developed and will continue to develop skills that will be in short supply which gives us both an advantage and a number of options. We could cooperate with a rival party for example. There are so few people around anyway that the likelihood of any rivalry is remote; nobody has been in Botany Bay or Sydney harbour since the flood, so I don't expect a rush."

CHAPTER 10

More Ships

Tanya

Louis spent time training a crew of ten how to sail 'the boat'. All the training was conducted within the safe boundaries of Botany Bay.

"I don't think it's wise to try to manoeuvre this vessel, in and out of harbours, on its own. We really need a tugboat to do it safely," Louis told Tanya on her next visit. "It will also be a little different when we move this thing outside into open water. We should try to avoid being out there when there's a storm brewing. I wonder how I can get a handle on the weather?"

"Try Derain, he seems to have more clue about weather patterns than the rest of us," answered Tanya.

"Okay," said Louis. "Can you bring him here?"

When she returned to The Settlement Tanya managed to persuade Derain to accompany her in the Jetstar to 'the boat'.

"Where are you going to land?" Derain asked anxiously as they circled the vessel with Kim waving from the deck.

"Down there," Tanya answered, pointing.

"Oh, my God, I knew this was a mistake, it's much too small," wailed Derain holding his head in his hands. He refused to look as they landed safely on the deck.

Tanya patted him on the arm once she had switched off the engine. and the helicopter had been strapped onto the deck, under direction from Louis. "It's all okay now," she said smiling. "Louis is here to talk to you." Derain looked up and clambered out of the machine as if he'd been flying about in helicopters and landing on the decks of ships all his life. He spent half a day talking to Louis about the weather which gave Louis an indication of when it might be safe to take 'the boat' out of Botany Bay and up the coast to Newcastle.

"It's not quite the same as having the sophisticated forecasts of the Met. I used to work with during my time in the Navy, but he has a surprising grasp of weather patterns and has been most helpful," he told Tanya. "We only need two or three days at the most."

"I think I've found a tugboat," said Tanya in conversation later with Louis, Kim and the crew on 'the boat'. "It appears to be jammed into the access of a deserted block of flats some way up the Parramatta River, in the suburb of Abbotsford. Roger and I have had a look at it and it still seems to be floating, although the superstructure is badly damaged."

"What do you mean by access?" asked Joe.

"The block of flats was built around a quadrangle and I suppose the residents drove in through the gap and parked there. The tug is jammed in the gap; there is at least one storey of the block above the tug, if you see what I mean. The tug must have become jammed in the gap when the waters rose." She drew a rough sketch.

"How do we get to this tug? Is there a road close by?" Joe continued.

"We managed to land the helicopter on the roof and worked our way through the building and actually stood on the deck of the tug." Tanya hesitated. "It's not a pretty picture by the way. There are bones strewn all over the place. The nearest road is a few hundred metres away."

"There would obviously be access by water," added Roger. "We've picked up a couple of small craft with outboards on our re-supply expeditions which we could use to get to it. The real problem is how we drag the tug away from the building."

"Would it matter if the building collapsed or partly collapsed?" asked Joe.

"No, that's going to happen anyway, as with many of the buildings in Sydney," answered Tanya.

"Okay,' said Louis, "a plan is sort of suggesting itself. We should try to release the tugboat and drag it down to Woolloomooloo where the frigate is parked, and then we can work on both vessels together, and then the tug will be available to get 'the boat' out of Botany and into Newcastle."

Roger decided the outboard motors they had would not be powerful enough to dislodge the tug so, guided by Joe, he found two big powerful Volvo outboards on one of his re-supply expeditions into Sydney, which they succeeded in fitting to the two small craft. Louis, in his earlier review of the frigate, had seen that the two rigid-hulled dinghies normally carried on such vessels were missing.

"We could spend weeks gradually taking down the block of flats to bits, brick by brick," speculated Joe. "Even then there is no guarantee there won't be a collapse and we could find ourselves in a worse position. Not to mention the danger to people trying to do the job."

"What do you suggest then?" asked Louis.

"I'll show you."

With Louis' help, Joe attached a long rope hawser with a steel bridle Louis had found on the frigate, to the two boats with the Volvo outboards recently fitted, making certain the boats were not in any danger of being hit by falling debris. "I'm going to set off three small explosions above the tug which should dislodge the concrete blocks holding the vessel. We should then be able to pull the tug out from where it is lodged without too much more damage."

Joe spent a day setting the charges. Louis had directed Kim and Roger who were manning the boats.

"Just you two in the boats, anyone else will be on the headland, over there," he pointed. "Well out of the way."

"Where will you be?" Louis asked Joe.

"With you. I can set the charges off remotely."

The outboards were gurgling away just using enough power to keep the cables taut as Kim and Roger had been instructed by Louis. Joe pressed the plunger and there were three small explosions emanating from the block of flats. The tug popped out like a cork from a bottle and would have swamped both boats if they hadn't accelerated away once the restraint had been released. Kim and Roger, in unison, gradually slowed down and turned upstream, as they had been taught by Louis, bringing the tug under control.

Nobody was watching the flats, all eyes were on the tug, hoping it would float. "My God look over there! the whole bloody place is going to collapse into the water." Louis shouted. With the tug gone, the side where it had been trapped fell slowly into the water, followed shortly after by the rest of the block. Soon there was nothing left except a few bricks poking out of the murky water.

"We'd better get on to that tug, to plug any leaks that might have developed over the past few years. We don't want to lose the bloody thing now," said Louis. Joe, Louis and three others were picked up by Kim and transferred to the tug, which they now saw was called Fern Bay. They spent several hours patching up the myriad of small leaks that had developed during the previous ten years.

Once they had the tug safely tied up with HMAS Perth in Woolloomooloo bay, Louis said to Joe, "How long will it take to recondition the tug's engine? It's lucky that Roger has thought to 're-supply' us with that mobile generator so that you'll have some light down there."

"'Bout a month," said Joe.

CHAPTER 11
Taree again

TANYA

While work continued on the tug, Louis and Tanya managed to escape to Louis' hideaway. Louis, anxious to strengthen his relationship with Tanya, had said to her, "Everyone has been briefed and they will be busy for a couple of weeks. Bearing in mind what you said to me recently about never being able to get away from Settlement issues, I was thinking that we should try to go away, maybe even for a week or ten days. We need to get away altogether, just the two of us."

"What do you suggest? Paris, London, Tuscany?" Tanya said dreamily.

Louis laughed, "There is only one possibility. You know where that is."

"How'll we get there?"

"We can take the Jetstar. We'll be completely on our own for a little while and come back here completely refreshed and full of new ideas."

They flew to what they regarded as their special place on Louis' property near the dam. They had some food with them. "Just the basics," said Louis, "we'll be able to fish and hunt and live off the land like Derain has showed you. We need to take some clothes, but it will be warm. I have my own rifle up there as you know, but I have taken your 30-06 from the old Academy days. And binoculars. Anything else?"

While Tanya was securing the helicopter, Louis swam over to the island and returned with the canoe. "Untouched," he said, "everything is as we last left it." They packed their supplies into the canoe and paddled over to the island. They were completely alone. Louis kept an eye out and periodically scanned the shore with his binoculars but there was no sign of anyone; there were a few cattle about, an occasional wallaby and not much else. They swam naked, made love, fished or just lay about doing nothing. On a couple of occasions Louis took the canoe and his rifle and sometimes returned with a wallaby, once with a large black snake, and always with a few berries.

In mid-morning on the day before they were due to return home, Tanya said to Louis, "This has been just what we needed, it's been perfect. I'm just going to pop over, in the canoe, to the chopper to do my flight checks and to make sure everything's okay. I'll be back in an hour or so." She took nothing with her; everything she needed was locked in the machine. She paddled over, secured the canoe, and spent 30 minutes making all her checks. She started the engine. "No problem, everything is just as it should be," she said to herself. She locked the helicopter, and turned to walk the 200 metres back to the canoe when she was confronted by a large man pointing a rifle at her: it was Harold. "Okay, bitch, you are coming with us," he said harshly. Harold, looking older and thinner than Tanya remembered, was dressed in a combination of rags and skins. His hair was long and unkempt. Tanya, although shocked by the intrusion, somehow kept her head; she tried to make a dash for it but she was taken down in a ferocious rugby tackle by another man. She was gagged and then dragged into the bush, 500 metres away, where her captors had established a small rudimentary camp. There was another man there and two women, who Tanya recognised from the Taree village. One of the women came up to Tanya and savagely slapped her across the face yelling angrily, "You thought you'd got rid of all us Barrington people and that we had turned over a new leaf at Taree! You killed my husband! You're going to find out what suffering means and then we'll deal with lover boy over there," she waved in the direction of the island. "You are just going to disappear; nobody will ever find you." She gave Tanya another vicious slap. The woman looked bedraggled and careworn. As with Harold, she was dressed in a few old rags and animal skins, many of her teeth were missing and she had sores on her arms and legs.

Harold looked on with a bemused look on his face. The woman dropped some kindling onto the fire. "We'll fix dinner and then we'll deal with that pretentious bloody cow over there. She's going to regret the day she was born when I have finished with her. Fuck her if you like," she added conversationally.

Tanya feverishly calculated the time she had been away. She'd said an hour— had she been that long? She must have. Louis would come looking for her soon. She hoped. The three men converged on Tanya and, after a fierce struggle, stripped her naked.

The woman attending to the meal said in a worried voice, "That Maureen, skiving off again, went for a pee 20 minutes ago..."

The men took no notice. "I'll hold the bitch down," said Harold through gritted teeth. He looked at one of the other men. He relaxed his grip for a split second to adjust his hold; that was all Tanya needed. As the man went down over Tanya she pulled her right leg back and kicked with all her might. The man's head went back and there was a crack like a bone breaking. Harold was taken by surprise, but he picked up a nearby log and lifted it above his head. There was a loud report of a gunshot and Harold collapsed onto her, his brains scattered all over Tanya and the nearby bushes. As Tanya pushed the remains of Harold away there was another gunshot and the third man fell down a few feet away, as he tried to run away. Tanya leapt up, grabbed the log and flung it full into the horrified face of the woman by the fire. Tanya was on her before she could recover, wresting the knife from her hand and sinking it to the hilt in her stomach. She dropped the woman where she stood into the fire. Louis emerged from the nearby bushes and ran up to the naked Tanya, who yelled, "Give me that gun! None of these fucking bastards will ever see the next dawn!" She grabbed the weapon from Louis and, making certain there was a round in the breech, fired a shot into Harold's dead body, followed by another shot. She repeated the exercise with the two other men and the woman in the fire. "Now where's that other woman?" she yelled, like a demon.

"I dealt with her earlier," said Louis, who was looking on, shocked at Tanya's ruthlessness. "Come here," he said, "it's all over now." He cuddled her. "Here are your clothes," he said. Tanya collapsed into his arms, shivering. "Where did these fuckers come from?" she asked as she struggled into the remains of her clothes, "I thought they were all dead."

"We need to build up this fire and burn the bodies," said Louis.

"There's a can of petrol in the chopper. That might help," offered Tanya, "and some more wood."

Louis started to collect wood and he built up the fire. He dumped the bodies of the five miscreants into the blazing fire. Tanya gave him the can of petrol. He unscrewed the lid and threw the container on to the fire, where it exploded. They spent the next two hours making sure that the bodies were completely burnt before they made their sad and uncertain way back to the chopper.

"Well, our special place has been wrecked as far as I'm concerned," said Tanya sadly. Louis had briefly returned to the camp to pack up their few possessions, which he loaded into the chopper. A very shaken Tanya was still able to fly. "I thought that all these assholes had been taken care of," she said, as she set course for The Settlement. "What's the real situation? We all just assumed from the way you talked that you had gotten rid of them all."

Louis sighed, "The ringleaders, except Harold, were indeed all hanged when I found out what they were up to. We had no choice. I did a deal with Harold; he and several others were freed provided they left the area altogether. He promised he would never bother us again. Those two women stayed in the Taree village; I thought they were still there. I'm afraid this business is not quite over; there are still some people in the village who were friendly with the two women. I wonder what their reaction will be when we return there."

"I now wish I had pursued the matter with you a bit more strongly," said Tanya. "I knew Harold and what he was likely to get up to. I blame myself." There was silence for a few more minutes. "We must not let this come between us, Louis, not in any way. I take full responsibility for all that happened to me."

"How many of the Barrington people are left in the Taree village now?" asked Tanya, after another short silence.

"Another five or six," said Louis, "not all of them were friends with the killers, though. We need to be careful about that."

The following day, two of the Merlins took off from The Settlement each one carrying 20 Academy troops. Tanya and Louis left in the Bell, two hours later. Tanya kept in touch with Jason and Roger, each one in charge of a helicopter. "Okay," Jason advised at noon, "we're all in place. You can land now."

20 minutes later Tanya landed in the village to be greeted by Alec, Louis' second-in-command, who had provisionally been left in charge. He greeted them both with a big smile, saying, "This is a pleasant surprise, what gives?" The expression on Tanya's face told him something serious was in the offing. It took her and Louis 30 minutes to brief Alec, in Louis' cottage, who said, "Yes we wondered about that, four people just disappeared one night a few weeks ago. I couldn't get anything out of anyone as to where they had gone; now we know."

"Nobody has ever said anything about Harold?" asked Tanya.

"Not a word," answered Alec.

"Okay," said Louis, "see if you can find these six people," as he gave Alec a piece of paper with six names scrawled on it. "When we arrived some of those may have tried to escape, but they'll have been picked up by Tanya's people surrounding the village." He explained to a surprised looking Alec that there were some 40 Academy people surrounding the village. "The others on the list who are still here should be asked to come to the cottage."

Within a few minutes a man and a woman came to the cottage and greeted Louis and Tanya with a broad smile. "How nice to see you," they chorused. Then the man added, "We don't see enough of you. Is this just a courtesy visit or do you have something special in mind?"

Tanya nodded at Louis who briefed the pair fully. They sat in their chairs silently with their mouths open. "But that bloody Harold left here years ago now, I just don't understand," said the man. "What happened to them?"

"They attacked us and are all dead, that is all you need know. There are four others here with a Barrington background whom we have been unable to find. If you wait here for a while, we'll see what we turn up."

An hour later the Academy troops converged on the village. They had four struggling captives, two men and two women. "Within half an hour of you landing the chopper in the village we found them trying to escape through the bush," reported Jason, "They were well prepared, mounted and had substantial quantities of food plus firearms and even some old maps. We've not been able to get any answers out of any of them."

Tanya shrugged, "The best thing is to cart them off to Canberra and a lengthy jail sentence."

"You wait, when Harold hears about this…" yelled one of the men.

"Harold? What about Harold, he hasn't been here for years now. We thought he had gone somewhere else," said Louis.

After a day and a half of relentless interrogation the story eventually emerged. Harold had never left the district and a number of the ex-Barrington people had clandestinely kept in touch with him and made sure he had enough to eat. Harold always had a plan; he knew about Louis' hideout and had seen him there with Tanya on her first visit to the village. Ten days earlier he had made contact with all his supporters in the Taree village telling them that Tanya and Louis were staying in the hideout and that he had a plan to capture them; four of them joined him in the bush. Not hearing anything from Harold made the remaining supporters apprehensive, hence their preparations for escape and the appearance of Tanya's chopper confirmed that somehow the plan had come unstuck.

"What were you going to do when you had captured Tanya and Louis?" asked a bemused Alec.

"Harold said he had a plan which would restore us to our rightful positions here," said one of the women.

"Mnn, would you like to know what he did when he did indeed capture Tanya?" asked Louis.

There was an apprehensive silence.

"Tanya would you mind telling them what happened?" asked Alec.

"They had no plan other than raping and killing me. They succeeded in doing none of that. They all died in the attempt."

There was shocked silence.

"What!" screamed the other woman, "You killed him?"

"Yes," said Louis, "he was on the verge of raping Tanya. He had stripped all the clothes off her..."

"Where, where is he?"

"He was cremated," said Louis.

The woman burst into tears.

"You're all going to jail in Canberra," said Tanya. "And you," she faced one of the men, "we saved your life once, all those years ago and even treated you in hospital. I will see to it that you are never ever released."

The four were manacled and escorted to one of the Merlins that had now landed in the village. One of the prisoners dragged herself to face the two who had come to Louis' cottage. "You, you bloody traitors, you've helped to mess all this up. We'll get you one day," she said as she was hauled away.

"Mnn," said Tanya watching the pantomime, "I wonder, that seems to be um...contrived to me. I wonder if those two are really as innocent as they make out."

Louis asked, "How many people were at the Barrington place?"

"There were 45 men who came on the raid to Kurri-Kurri. There were a couple of casualties; I suppose there were a similar number of women and possibly 20 or 30 children," Tanya reported.

"Nothing like that number ever came here to Taree; we might have had 20 altogether plus a few kids; three were hanged. This means that despite all this shemozzle there still may be some people out there wishing us harm."

"Maybe as many as 20 or 30," said Tanya. "Those two," she indicated the two supposed innocents, now out of earshot, "are going to have to cough up some usable information or they will also find themselves locked up in Canberra. We'll leave troops here as well, and run regular patrols through the bush. We have to nail this thing."

Louis nodded. "We could do with some help from Derain," he said thoughtfully.

The Academy troops were left in the village for a month; Derain joined them. Within a week they picked up five ex-Barrington people, none of whom had ever lived in the village. Intensive interrogation revealed they were told that more than half of the original Barrington settlers had genuinely moved on and had not been seen for eighteen months. "We've had no contact with them either," said one of the captives under pressure. The two 'innocents' seemed genuine and had no knowledge of the machinations of the other Barrington people in the village; they were allowed to remain. The five others were transferred to the military prison in Canberra.

CHAPTER 12
Election

TANYA

Stephanie met Tanya and Louis on the parade ground after their return from Taree. She started to brief Tanya on the short walk to her office. "I have some recommendations regarding the election process," Stephanie told Tanya, as Louis saw to the refuelling of the Jetstar.

"I think that each development area should have an elected mayor and four elected councillors," she said, after they had both sat down with a cup of tea, "except for Kanangra and The Settlement each having six councillors, because of their relative importance. Each development area would send one representative to a central council which would have a president and a deputy to be elected by all the adults in the wider community associated with The Settlement."

"Why do we need all these layers?" asked Tanya. "We could just have an elected council here at The Settlement and each satellite could then send one representative here every three months or so."

"I think that would focus too much power here in The Settlement," argued Stephanie. "I think the other enclaves would then want more self-determination, if they're going to go through all this hassle."

"The Settlement will be providing most of the resources, as we do now, so that seems fair to me," said Tanya.

"That might be fair at the moment but some of them might grow more quickly than others and then all I can see is a potential for friction."

"Hmm, maybe. Which do you think will be the independent development areas then?"

"Taree and Kanangra have agreed to join, and we have the Bandstand, St Andrews, Kurri-Kurri, Banksia, Amazonia, and Newcastle. That makes nine, including us," said Stephanie without looking at Tanya.

"Newcastle!" Tanya bristled, "We built Newcastle from the ground up— it's part of us!"

She asked Louis what he thought, as he joined the meeting.

"I'll think about it," said Louis. "I will probably need to spend a bit of time there to understand all the vibes."

"What are you going to do? I see Taree has agreed to be part of the scheme."

"Yes, certainly. I'm considering my own position anyway. Alec could easily take over from me now."

When questioned, he wouldn't elaborate. Tanya looked at him speculatively; she knew that for both their sakes their relationship would have to be formalised in some way in the not too-distant future. This would involve some possibly difficult discussions with Mark; she knew she would have to initiate those discussions realising he would do nothing to bring the situation to a head.

Louis, after a trip to view Joe's progress on rehabilitating the tug and spending a few days in Newcastle, said to Tanya, "You asked my opinion whether Newcastle should be included as a separate entity or as part of The Settlement, when we were talking about the election process."

"Yes," said Tanya warily.

"If one looks a few years ahead, Newcastle is likely to grow. In time, it could be considerably bigger than The Settlement."

"I see."

"It will be an active port and if one adds a couple of coal mines in the Hunter, which they are working on, it could be responsible for a few thousand people."

"So, what's your recommendation?"

"It should be included as a separate entity. They are all very loyal to you and The Settlement. I think having them as a separate entity actually strengthens your hand considerably."

They batted the issue backwards and forwards for several minutes.

"Okay," Tanya eventually conceded. "We'll have it as a separate entity."

There was silence for a short minute.

"I have something else to ask you," said Tanya.

Louis nodded.

"Would you stand as my deputy for the central council?" Before Louis could say anything, she continued, "Jason will stand as The Settlement's mayor and Roger will be put in charge of security, a post that is not subject to any sort of electoral process; I just need Mark's support for that, but I'm sure he's completely committed to Virginia and the establishment of the Southern Highlands enclave."

"Thank you," he said. "I would be glad to."

Tanya walked over and kissed him without saying anything further.

Before the elections, Tanya paid a visit to the Southern Highlands on her own. "Mark and I are standing as joint mayors," Virginia told

Tanya, "there won't be a deputy, so we'll run the place in much the same way as before."

"I need to talk to Mark on his own, if you don't mind, Virginia. I suppose you know of my relationship with Louis," she looked at her for an answer. Virginia nodded, saying, "Of course." She was obviously untroubled by anything that Tanya could or would say to Mark.

"Before that though, we both need to talk to you about Jonathan," said Virginia. Mark joined them, in the refurbished cottage they shared in Bowral.

"I've been over to Canberra a few times in recent months, and Jonathan is not his usual self," Mark said. "There are military people running about in fancy cars living high on the hog. All the principles we established at The Settlement about sharing and the egalitarian way in which we did things, and in fact the way we work here, seems to have been chucked out of the window. They are definitely creating an elite who treat the rest almost like medieval serfs. I've spoken to Chas and told him to keep his eyes open; it's lucky that he used another surname when he enlisted over there, so there is no overt association with The Settlement, either with him or any of the other nine from The Settlement embedded over there. By the way, Chas has recently been promoted to captain. Chas also told me that he has uncovered the existence of a secret training base in Wagga and most of the people there are refugees from Morton, the Bandstand, the Viking establishment and Taree. I don't like it at all. He said he had mentioned it to you…"

"What do you think they are up to?" asked Tanya. "I'm pleased about Chas; he did drop me a note. I didn't realise most the people in the place at Wagga were enemies of ours, although I knew none of the executions that were sanctioned actually took place."

"I'm not sure, but we need to be very careful. Jonathan keeps muttering something about absorbing The Settlement's military Academy."

"Jonathan has asked me in passing when I am likely to visit Canberra again. He wouldn't elaborate when I asked him what the agenda was. I can go after the election," offered Tanya.

"When you do go, please make sure you tell everybody what you are up to, especially us here. My instincts tell me that something rather smelly is about to happen," Mark concluded.

Tanya nodded.

Virginia left Mark on his own with Tanya in the cottage. He also seemed more relaxed than Tanya had ever seen him. As always, he waited for her to start the conversation.

"I need to talk to you about us; I have to say the way you and Virginia work together is very impressive. She is obviously the right partner for you."

Mark nodded, waiting for Tanya to continue. "Do you two want to get married?" asked Tanya.

"We haven't discussed the matter. As far as I am concerned the current arrangement suits me quite well."

"What about your security responsibilities?"

"Roger has effectively taken over with my blessing. I think that could be formalised now. I have enough to do here as it is."

Tanya rolled her eyes. As always, Mark was showing no regard for her feelings; he merely looked at everything from his own point of view. She kept her cool.

"It could suit me for us to have a formal divorce. There is no need for a lot of hoo-ha though; I don't want to upset you or anyone else."

"I'll talk it over with Virginia. I'm sure we can work something out."

Tanya spent a bit of time talking to all the Kanangra people. The settlers had stubbornly stuck to the name, although most activities had been moved to the Southern Highlands around Bowral and Moss Vale. While Tanya was admiring all the new developments, as she was being shown around, she was asked what she stood for. "Security, democracy and we must find the resources we need to maintain our civilisation. We need to establish constructive relationships with other groups that have survived the flood," she answered. "Is there anything else you want me to think about?"

She again sought out Virginia, still limping and walking with a stick. "I'm in some awe how you and Mark have now rekindled your relationship," Tanya said to Virginia, "I've never seen him so relaxed. You are a marvel, you seem to know exactly what to say to him and when."

Virginia shrugged, "I'm just me; I haven't contrived anything. I'm sorry to say this but I fell in love with him the moment I first set eyes on him. I tried to resist my feelings…"

They sat in companionable silence for a few minutes, "Mark says you mentioned a divorce. That would actually suit us both," said Virginia.

"I think it would be better if it were formalised. It means I have free hand. It won't be complicated. I'll draw up a brief agreement if that's okay with you," said Tanya guardedly.

After the Kanangra visit Tanya made a point of visiting all the enclaves coming under the security blanket of The Settlement and repeated the same mantra to all the groups involved in the election. There were some questions, but few objections. Most people had come to trust her and her motives. Ron temporarily moved himself to The Settlement for the duration of the election process. He was able to travel to all the enclaves and had appointed agents in each place, who had strict instructions how they should operate. On the day of the election he put himself in charge of the election process in The Settlement's community centre. He closed the poll at exactly six pm and locked the door. With three other personally selected people he counted the votes, three times.

By seven pm, Ron was satisfied that the counts were accurate, so he opened the doors of the community centre and about 100 people who had been queuing up came into the centre, including Tanya, Louis and Jason.

"I am only able to announce one result," Ron announced. "I will have to wait for counts from other centres before the results for the President and Deputy President of the Central Council can be announced."

There was an expectant hush.

"Result for the post of Mayor for The Settlement," announced Ron.

"Jason Bower. 395 votes."

There was some enthusiastic clapping. Tanya hugged Jason, who was standing next to her.

"Brad Thislethwaite. 57 votes.

"I can therefore announce that Jason Bower is elected as Mayor of The Settlement."

Jason went over and shook his rival by the hand.

A week later Ron told the community that he was now able to announce the results for the President and Deputy President of the Central Council.

"President of the Council.

"Tanya Bower. 7646 votes. There were no other candidates so Tanya Bower is duly elected as President of the Council."

There was wild cheering from the large crowd gathered in the community centre and outside. Almost everyone wanted to hug her or shake her hand.

"Deputy President of the Council," announced Ron, once the noise had died down.

"Louis McLeod. 3851 votes."

He read out two other names, but the details were drowned out by the cheering.

"Louis McLeod is therefore elected as Deputy President of the Council."

Roger did not stand for any elected post as he had been appointed as the new head of Settlement security, reporting to Tanya, as Mark had done before him. The other mayors elected were Caroline for the Bandstand, who had decided after much introspection to stand despite the trauma she had suffered from the attempted coup, Isaac for St. Andrews, Stephanie for Amazonia and surrounding areas, Richard for Kurri-Kurri, Joseph for Banksia, Alec for Taree, and Virginia and Mark for Kanangra.

The Central Committee suggested by Stephanie was constituted with Tanya as Chairperson, Louis as Deputy, together with all the mayors.

Immediately after the election results were announced, Tanya was persuaded to have her annual medical check-up. She knew she was, as always, in very good physical shape and had no concerns regarding the result. A few days later she met the chief medical officer, Dr Wickremasinghe, while walking through the village. "You'd better pop-in today," she invited, "there is one little issue that you should be aware of."

"Good news or bad news?" asked Tanya.

"Definitely not bad news," said the doctor, "probably more of a surprise, I would say."

"Can't you tell me now? I'm quite busy."

"No," said Jane firmly, "come and see me, this afternoon about three, please. You are not the only one who's busy," she smiled.

At three the doctor went through all the results of the various tests she had conducted: "Hearing okay, sight 20/20, cholesterol..." Tanya stopped listening, "...physical condition and this is just as well under the circumstances..." Tanya was suddenly on full alert. "I wonder what she's about to tell me," she thought.

"Physical condition, like a bloody 30-year-old. As I was saying just as well; you realise you're pregnant don't you?"

"What the fuck are you talking about, pregnant? I can't be."

"Well you are; couple of months by my reckoning," she said without the hint of a smile.

"I suppose you are wondering who the father is," said Tanya uncertainly.

"Immaculate conception?" said Jane looking at Tanya with an amused look on her face.

Tanya laughed despite herself. "You're having fun aren't you? As I'm sure you realise, the only possibility is that Louis is the father."

"Ah, yes. Louis, of course."

"How can I be pregnant?" asked Tanya after a brief pause. "I thought the potential for pregnancy had faded years ago."

"Well, only you will know how you became pregnant. I must admit it's unusual in a woman of your age, you must be over 50, but not unheard of. As I said it's just as well that you have looked after yourself so well. I need to do a full examination and I'll tell you what I think."

"As far as I can see, you are growing a big healthy baby," said the doctor after completing the examination. "At your age, there is some risk of the child having Down's Syndrome. We can do tests to establish whether this is the case or not."

"Yes, you'd better do that, before I tell Louis. I will then decide what to tell him."

"Don't make any decision regarding the baby all on your own. Any decision regarding possible termination, if that is indeed what you decide, needs to include the father; your on-going relationship with Louis is dependent on him being included," said Jane. She hesitated for a brief minute before continuing, "Seriously, we all know and welcome the change in you since Louis has arrived on the scene. You must understand that most in the community think you are a much better person for that relationship. Don't bugger it up, you are not alone in this. Louis needs to be a part of what you decide."

As she dressed and stood up to go, Tanya looked at the strong caring woman in front of her. She was not used to accepting unsolicited advice from anyone.

"Thank you for that. Okay, Louis will be involved in any decision; I've been used to making decisions on my own, since David died. You're right. Thank you again."

CHAPTER 13
The Frigate to Newcastle

Joe had, with the help of Roger's resupply expeditions, managed to recondition the powerful engine on the tug. "The superstructure is still a bit of a mess, but we can fix that when we get it back to Newcastle," he said. He and Louis sailed the tug up and down the harbour a few times making sure the vessel was operational, despite its shortcomings. 'The boat' was then towed out of Botany Bay by the tug and, with Louis in charge, also helped moor the vessel in the newly prepared berth in Newcastle.

Derain categorically refused to accompany 'the boat' on its journey up the coast, even after having been taken on a couple of trips in Botany Bay in the vessel. "This thing," he pointed at 'the boat', "will sink out there in the sea and then I will not able to look after you, Tanya," he explained. "I presume you aren't going on 'the boat' either'?" he asked.

"Maybe not," said Tanya smiling.

She managed to persuade him to accompany her to Newcastle to watch 'the boat' being successfully and carefully manoeuvred into its new berth.

"See, it's all quite safe," Tanya explained to Derain as they walked up the powered ramp onto the deck of the vessel.

"I have taken on the responsibility of looking after you, Tanya," said Derain firmly. "I know nothing about boats."

"Where do we go from here?" asked Louis later that night over dinner with Kim, Joe and the crew at a house that had been converted into a community centre for the Newcastle development, near the established headquarters on Cooks Hill. "What are you going to call 'the boat'? It has to have a proper name. It's very bad luck not to have a name."

"There's only one name that would be acceptable to all of us," said Tanya, "and that's the David Bower. I would be very happy with that. We need to have a naming ceremony. Louis maybe you could..."

"Me? No, absolutely not. The christening ceremony always has to be done by a woman; a man performing the ceremony creates bad luck. So it's either you or Kim. Maybe even Caroline."

"How about Chloe and Caroline, together, if they will agree?" Tanya added, "You seem to be obsessed with luck, what's all that about?"

"Mariner's superstitions."

Later back in Sydney, on examining the five-inch gun mounted forward off the stack on the frigate, HMAS Perth, Louis said, "I need power to be able to train and fire the weapon, but the ammo has been correctly stored and looks okay; it needs testing of course."

"I'll get one of the generators on the ship operational," responded Joe.

"What about the main engines?" asked Louis.

"Two gas turbines," replied Joe. "I've had a look. They need a great deal of attention having been sitting idle here for the last ten years. Now we have the tug operational, the best thing we can do is to tow the frigate to Newcastle, and work on it there."

"So are we into towing this bloody thing back to Newcastle?" responded Louis.

"Yes," said Joe. "I'm in the process of setting up a team there to refurbish this and any other vessels we might find."

"I might get the gun working first, if it is to be any use."

When Joe had provided the power, Louis was able to get the gun moving on its base. He found suitable oil on the ship and, with the help of a crane which Joe had made operational too, stripped the weapon down completely and reassembled it.

"We'll just load one round to start with, and hope for the best," said an apprehensive Louis, who was sitting with Kim in the ops room. He and Joe had worked out how to get the fire direction radar working. "That's a relief," he said to nobody in particular, "because doing this manually is almost impossible." He remembered the system was automatic, but managed to persuade it to load the one round. "If this works we can load a few rounds into the magazine which should make life a bit easier," he said to Kim who was watching with interest.

Louis showed Kim how to operate the firing mechanism. "We'll see if we can bang this round right between the heads," he announced. Kim pressed the firing pedal. The whole ship was rocked violently, although they could not hear much from inside the ops room.

Louis was looking through a pair of binoculars he had found on the ship. "There it is," he announced triumphantly, "right on target! We'll now load the magazine and see if we can fire a salvo in the same place. We don't want to waste too many rounds but they seem to have stocked it up very well, there must be 500 rounds in store."

The system automatically loaded the magazine and with Joe and his crew watching, Louis fired a salvo of five shots into the same target area.

"Done," said Louis, "we can now tow the frigate up to Newcastle."

"Okay," Joe announced pointing at the frigate, "we need a few practice runs with the tug to see if we have it all under control. Louis, you'll have to steer the bloody thing."

They had a number of practice runs out to sea, making certain that they had everything under control. Louis knew that if the worst came to the worst, there was a manual system that could be used to steer the ship in an emergency.

Under Louis' direction, Joe and the crew established three tow lines between the tug and the much larger frigate. They had again re-tested the powerful engine on the tug. Eventually Louis was satisfied all was in order for the 200-kilometre tow. Joe had three others on the tug with him and Louis had five people, including Kim, on the frigate. "Three days," said Louis confidently. Kim had found a berth in Newcastle where they could safely moor HMAS Perth. As Louis had directed, it was within line of sight of the Newcastle harbour entrance.

Louis was responsible for navigating the two vessels, which he did by dead reckoning, calculating the rise and dip of known landmarks, with Kim looking on fascinated. He maintained a constant watch on the tow and kept radioing course and speed to Joe on the tug. The first day was uneventful and they all relaxed, hoping the rest of the journey would be as easy. He had time to run through some basic emergency procedures with the scratch crew.

Louis knew that a warship is a treasure trove, and would be of great benefit to The Settlement, aside from the additional security it provided. He had checked everything in detail personally. The HMAS Perth included: fully stocked electronics, woodworking and metal-working workshops with complex and expensive tools, including the hand-held, gas powered broco cutters needed to cut through any door; a fully stocked hospital, including drugs and surgical equipment; a dry store in a watertight compartment containing enough dry food to feed 200 people for six months. The armoury would have over 200 rifles, ditto pistols and at least 10 .50 calibre machine guns, not to mention a collection of crew served minimi SAWs and more than 100 sets of ballistic body armour. The magazines would contain at least 100,000 rounds of small arms ammo, several pounds of C4, flares, and grenades. The CIWS magazine alone would have hundreds of thousands of rounds. Then there was the fuel lockers, stuffed with diesel, AVCAT and petrol, and a substantial collection of vital spares for helos and speed boats. All of this stuff was in double bulk headed, highly secure locked compartments. On top of this, there was more than 50 sealed life raft capsules, each containing enough emergency rations to sustain 30 people.

The first night out in the Tasman Sea, the wind started to rise uncomfortably and the waves became bigger and bigger. "Shit, this is not good. If this keeps up we'll never make it in three days," said a worried Louis to Kim. As the seas increased, the tug disappeared from view after every large wave and the hawser attached to the tug strained and jerked around. Louis knew the limits of the shackles and bridles and hoped the set-up would hold.

Derain had warned Tanya of a major storm developing along the coast directly in line with the frigate's course. Tanya immediately reacted. Roger, piloting the Bell with Tanya and Rebecca on board, flew over Sydney harbour to monitor the progress of the frigate. Flying up and down the harbour, Roger skilfully negotiated the blustery conditions but they couldn't find any trace of the vessels. "If they are out in this, they'll be in deep shit. Luckily, we thought to get the winching equipment installed," said Tanya. "Dammit why didn't they ask Derain about the bloody weather, like last time?"

They refuelled the Jetstar in Newcastle. Taking off they turned south on an interception course. Flying through ever worsening weather they eventually found the boats struggling through the storm.

"It all looks under control," Tanya observed, "they seem to be making progress although it's slow." Louis waved from the bridge wing of the frigate.

"Don't speak too soon," said Roger. "Just look at what's coming. Look at that enormous wave, it'll hit in a couple of minutes."

The wave smashed into both vessels, drenching the deck of the tug and partially obscuring the frigate. "Shit!" said Tanya. "Thankfully, the tow still seems to be holding," she said, "I wonder if they'll survive another one like that, though."

"Look!" yelled Rebecca, "Someone on the frigate is in trouble! Christ, its Louis! He's been swept off the bridge wing. He looks badly hurt!"

Tanya took one look at the situation and a feeling of desperation overtook her. She scrambled into the harness.

"I'm going down," she said to Roger. "You need to hover over the deck." He did as he was told, despite the risks, glancing uneasily though the perspex at the heaving deck and listening to the chop of the air as they descended. The chopper bounced up and down in the swirling rain. Tanya was quickly winched down to the heaving deck and scrambled her way to Louis, who was clinging desperately to a railing.

"Leg," he pointed, as Tanya approached. Tanya nodded. She tried to strap him into the gear so they could both be lifted to the helicopter, but was unable to. She unstrapped herself and with a monumental struggle managed to transfer the harness onto Louis.

"Can't do anything," he managed to say. "Shit, fucking hurts," he said as he passed out. Tanya waved at Rebecca to raise Louis into the machine.

Meanwhile Kim had dashed down from the bridge and handed Tanya a lifeline which she attached to the handrail. Kim quickly returned to the safety of the bridge. Another great wave crashed over the deck. Tanya managed to cling on, with the help of the lifeline, as a seemingly never-ending torrent of water tried to tear her from the ship. She looked up and saw Louis being safely pulled into the helicopter. Rebecca started to lower the harness again. Tanya desperately waved her away. "Go, go, hospital!" she yelled uselessly into the howling gale. Rebecca seemed to get the message and the equipment was returned to the aircraft and the door closed. Tanya saw the machine gain height and quickly dash off west. "He should be okay now," she thought as she made her way inside and up the wildly pitching bridge steps.

Another great wave boiled over the ship. Tanya was careful not to move without the lifeline being attached. She was pulled into the bridge and the door closed.

"Shit," she thought, "the baby." She closed her eyes for a moment, "Louis is safe now. That's all that matters."

"Jesus Tanya," said Kim. "we all thought you were a goner for a moment. Thank heaven you're safe." The others on the bridge crowded around her.

"How are we doing?" she asked. "Why did Louis fall down?"

"The tow parted …" said Kim.

"You mean we are completely adrift?"

"No not quite; Joe has another two hawsers attached loosely to the tug. Because of the weather we had decided to further loosen the tow. Louis was outside checking that what was being done from the tug was correct. It knocked…"

"Yes, yes, does that still need to be done?" asked Tanya.

"Yes," said Kim.

Tanya looked out at the enormous seas still furiously washing over the vessel. The tug was only visible on the crests of the waves.

"Do we have any contact with Joe and his crew on the tug?" asked Tanya.

Kim nodded, "It's intermittent, but we can try. He probably has no idea what happened to Louis of course. He may not even have been able to see the rescue."

Joe answered at first call, "Louis…"

"It's Tanya here."

"What, how the hell did you get down there? We saw the helicopter. What happened to Louis?"

Tanya tried to explain through the howling gale.

"What now?" asked Tanya.

"Maybe trying to fiddle with that hawser was a mistake," said Joe. "We're still attached and I have headed out to sea. Nothing could be worse than ending up on the rocks. This storm can't last too much longer. When it calms down we can make for Newcastle."

"Okay," said Tanya, "we'll ride it out."

"Is there any way we can find a dry set of clothes?" asked Tanya, realising she was sodden and very cold. She had an anxious moment about the baby growing inside her.

"Downstairs," answered Kim, "I mean down below. Louis kept insisting we use nautical terms," she mumbled awkwardly.

Kim disappeared below and reappeared with several bundles. "Clothes for you and me," she said to Tanya, "and food for all of us. We don't know how long this storm will last. We had thought that some of us might kip down below, but one can't see a thing, there's no light."

Without hesitation and to the embarrassment of the men on the bridge, Tanya stripped and carefully dried herself off before she clambered into the ill-fitting clothes provided.

"We don't know how long this storm will last," said Tanya. "Some of us should try to sleep, however uncomfortable that might be. You obviously have established shifts. I'll take the helm now. The rest of you try to get some sleep. I'll wake you in two hours."

Within 12 hours the wind had eased and another 12 hours later, Joe came on the line saying, "we can now tighten that tow line now and make our way into port." A day later they were safely tied up in Newcastle harbour.

Tanya was surprised to see Dr Wickremasinghe on the pier, waiting. As Tanya came down the gangway, she was taken firmly by the hand and into a waiting vehicle. Within minutes Tanya was on an examination table in the Newcastle medical facility. Nothing was said until the examination was complete. "You are very tough and very lucky," said the doctor kindly. "When Roger told me of your antics

I really wondered if you and the baby would survive. Most would say you are completely crazy; frankly, nothing you do surprises me anymore."

"Two questions," said Tanya, looking gratefully at the doctor. "Is Louis alright, and is the baby alright?"

"Louis is fine, badly broken leg, that's all. He'll recover. The baby seems to be fine and although you haven't asked, you are also okay. I'm going to keep you here for rest and observation for at least 24 hours. Don't argue, it's for everyone's sake. I am personally going to look after you."

"Those tests you did for Down's on the baby...?" asked Tanya quietly.

"The baby should be quite normal," said the doctor.

24 hours later, Tanya said to Dr Wickremasinghe, "I'm ready to go home. I feel perfectly alright."

"The helicopter will be here tomorrow; Roger said something about servicing it. You might as well stay where you are," was the response.

Tanya looked at her and smiled, "Thank you for being here and thank you for looking after me, it's much appreciated."

"To use your language, it's the least I can fucking do. You now need to make sure that baby is looked after for the next few months. The birth may not be that easy in view of your age. You need to take things a little bit more calmly, if you can..."

Tanya, nervous and almost silent, was sitting next to Jane in one of the rear seats of the chopper, with Roger piloting. She longed to see Louis and wondering how he was despite all the reassurances she had had from Jane. As they landed, and as soon as it was safe, she jumped out of the machine and headed straight to the hospital. She found Louis, propped up in bed, dozing. She gently kissed him awake. They clung to each other for a few moments.

"Don't know what we would have happened if you hadn't rocked up," said Louis. "I probably would have carked it. Anyway, here I am; I owe you my life."

Tanya told him briefly about the rescue of the frigate. "The ship is now tied up beside the now flooded Kooragang Island, a place you chose with Joe." Louis knew in days gone Kooragang Island was the major coal exporting terminal servicing the coalfields of the Hunter Valley and that water levels there were fifteen metres above where they had been before the flood. "The important thing is that in daylight from the bridge of HMAS Perth we have a clear view of the harbour entrance."

"I'll have to test the gun on that frigate again, when I get the chance," said Louis.

They chatted for a few minutes before Tanya said, "I have some other news for you, by the way." Louis looked at her suspiciously and raised an eyebrow.

"I'm pregnant, three months. The baby is fine."

Louis looked at her wonderingly. "Come here," he said. They hugged each other tightly in silent joy. When they relaxed, Tanya told him about the doctor's ministrations and what tests had been undertaken. "Dr. Wickremasinghe has told me the baby is going to be fit and healthy, that's all that matters." She hesitated for a short minute before adding, "When I saw what had happened to you on that ship, I didn't care what happened to me. If you had died my life would no longer have been be worth living anyway."

Louis shook his head, "I don't have anything to say. If the occasion arises, and I trust it doesn't, I hope I will have the courage to do the same for you."

Ten days later, as Tanya was preparing dinner, since Nanny was busy elsewhere, Louis stumbled in, having been discharged from the hospital. He was still on his crutches. "I have a question for you," he said smiling.

"Oh, what's that?" was the disinterested response.

"Will you marry me?"

"What?" she dropped everything, "Say that again?"

"You heard; will you marry me?"

Tanya nearly knocked him over as she rushed at him and kissed him firmly on the mouth.

"Marry you? Yes! Yes, yes, yes, yes!" She danced around the room. "When?"

"Well, I hadn't got quite that far," replied a smiling Louis, "I thought we should agree on the principle of the exercise first."

CHAPTER 14

Military Coup

Tanya now felt more secure having HMAS Perth safely moored in Newcastle and under Settlement control. She phoned Jonathan. She was somewhat apprehensive since the only contact between the pair in the past few months was the brief exchange regarding the Steyr carbine. She was in her office at The Settlement and had asked Louis to listen in on another line, on what was likely to be an important conversation.

"As I told you during your last visit here," she said, "and as we agreed, during our mutual visits to Kanangra, we have conducted and completed a fully-fledged election process."

"I told you it was much too early for such an initiative," Jonathan shouted down the phone. "Much too bloody early."

Tanya continued as if she hadn't registered his anger. She gave him the results. "We have had the first meeting of the Central Committee; it was very productive. We have good people on the committee."

"It's much too early for all that stuff," repeated Jonathan, "I should have been consulted."

"What the hell are you talking about? We discussed it when you were last here and you were the one pushing the election agenda only a couple of years ago. I've heard nothing from you for months now."

"As I said then and I say it again, it's too early," he said in a combative tone, knowing he had actually encouraged the initiative in the first instance. "I repeat; you should have talked to me about it before you proceeded."

"I've never talked to you about any fucking thing before I proceeded and I'm quite sure your father didn't either."

"Who is this fellow Louis who's been elected as your deputy?"

"He set up and ran the Taree establishment."

"I thought they were a bunch of thugs, intent on destroying you."

"It turns out that we were mistaken; they are very much part of our wider remit now."

She smiled at Louis, who was sitting next to her. There was silence for a minute.

"You've stolen a boat," Jonathan continued. "That has to be illegal."

"Crap! I happen to know the rules of salvage quite well. The boat had been abandoned for years. We cleaned it up and got it working again. You may be interested to know we've formally christened it the David Bower after your father. It's based in Newcastle." Tanya decided not to tell him anything about the tug or the frigate, but she did add, "Louis was an officer in the navy."

"What do you need it for?"

"We are working on getting one of the coal mines in the Hunter going again. The David Bower can then deliver coal to survivors in other parts of Australia."

"You should have discussed all that with me first."

"Bullshit; that's never happened in the past and won't happen in the future."

"We need to conserve the resources we have for the benefit of the whole of the country..."

"Crap! You mean leaving a boat floating around in Botany Bay, bumping into things, and allowing a coalmine in the Hunter Valley to rot away while you get your act into gear, is conserving resources? You know it isn't. What the hell is going on, Jonathan? I don't like it. You assholes are up to something, I know you are. Come clean with me for Christ's sake."

There was silence at the other end for a minute or two. Tanya thought for a moment she had gone too far but then heard a muffled conversation in the background which made her all the more uncomfortable. Jonathan came back on the line. "We think you should pay us a visit; there are a number of things that need discussion."

"Who the hell is we? I am not now, and never was, responsible to anyone in the military, although as I have said your own personal support has been invaluable over time."

There was another muffled discussion at the other end.

This time a more conciliatory Jonathan said, "Tanya, there are a number of issues that need discussion. Even you will appreciate that, in order to rebuild, we need a coordinated approach. You certainly represent one of the more developed settlements and we would appreciate input from you on the subject."

Tanya listened suspiciously. "Okay. I'm flat out at the moment. I'll let you know when it's convenient."

"Is it unusual for Jonathan to have another person with him when you call him?" asked Louis, once the conversation with Jonathan had ended.

"It's never happened before."

"What do you think they are up to?" asked Louis.

"I don't know, but we are going to be one hundred percent prepared for the worst, the very fucking worst," said Tanya.

"What do you think we should do? I can help with the planning, despite my leg." Louis pointed at his leg which still had a plastic boot on it and was heavily strapped. "I can travel around and brief people. If we're to plan for the worst, I should make sure that the frigate in Newcastle is at least capable of defending the place from the sea."

"We're going to have to make considerable preparations. I need your help and I need to find Derain. We'll work up a plan, together with Roger, and then make sure everyone is aware of what's going on." Tanya continued, "Dear God, this whole exercise burns my arse! The very fact we are discussing our relationship with the military in Canberra in terms of defending ourselves is ridiculous. It should be a cooperative relationship as it always has been. I have always trusted Jonathan; I've known him since he was a kid. He's either gone loopy or is being manipulated," said Tanya.

Tanya, Louis, Derain and Roger spent the next week travelling to all Settlement development areas in the Jetstar. They explained their dilemma and rapidly put a plan into place. Roger flew Tanya Louis, Derain and Dr Wickremasinghe to Bowral in the Jetstar, for a meeting with Mark and Virginia to explain her plans in detail and the reasons for putting them in place.

During the flight Tanya said to the others, through the headphones, "I've arranged a meeting with Jonathan. You'll have to just drop me, and I suppose Jane, off. She has insisted she accompanies me on some of my trips now. Then return home. If you don't hear from me within two days all our plans are to be put into place; all of them."

They were greeted on arrival by Mark and Virginia, who ushered them into part of the old hotel which they were now using as a community centre.

"We're not absolutely sure what Jonathan and the military are up to, but we need to be certain we have every possibility covered," said Tanya opening the meeting.

Tanya, Louis, Roger and Derain then explained their plans in detail and went through every aspect twice so there were no doubts.

During the meeting Mark added, "I've kept in touch with Chas and he keeps tabs on the other nine of our people embedded with the military there in Canberra. There are rumours that a group is being trained to ride through the bush to take us on directly at The Settlement. He's well briefed and knows what to do if it's true."

"Is Jonathan a part of all this?" asked Tanya.

"I don't know. He gives me the feeling that he's not all that comfortable with what's going on though. Chas says he is cooperating with Colonel Jacobs though," Tanya looked at Mark, hearing the doubt in his voice.

At the end of the meeting Virginia looked at Tanya speculatively, having noticed her slightly expanded waistline, "I suppose it's necessary for you to go to Canberra?" she asked.

"We've cooperated with the military almost since the very beginning of The Settlement and it makes sense for that to continue. I'll see what I can negotiate," responded Tanya.

The following day once the Jetstar was airborne Tanya phoned Jonathan.

"We'll be there in 30 minutes," she told him.

"Okay, I'll be there to fetch you. I've set meetings up for 11 am and then after lunch," he said.

"It all seems quite normal," she thought to herself.

Through the headphones she said, "Roger, drop Jane and me off. You and Louis should return home. As I have already told you, if we haven't called in two days, you are to activate our plan. All of it. All the satellite communities have been well briefed. You and Louis should keep in touch with them as best you can."

"What about you two?"

"We can look after ourselves," she smiled, not betraying her deep concerns. "Don't worry, I'll be in touch."

They circled the airfield in Canberra. Spotting Jonathan standing beside a new Range Rover, Tanya said, "Okay, Roger, land, we'll hop out as quick as we can and then you skedaddle. We should waste no time."

As the rotors slowed, Tanya and Jane quickly left the machine, each with a small overnight bag. Keeping their heads down, they ran towards the airport buildings as Roger revved the helicopter engine and took off again. Tanya watched the machine climb quickly, rapidly heading northeast. Tanya was dressed smartly in her Academy uniform, with colonel epaulettes and a bush hat. Jane was dressed in civilian clothes.

Tanya noticed Jonathan's agitation as he greeted her with a light peck on the cheek. "What's all that about?" he asked, waving at the fast disappearing helicopter.

"The machine is required for other duties. He'll return when needed. You remember Dr Jane Wickremasinghe who runs our medical facilities? She comes with me on some of my longer trips now."

Jonathan, looking uncomfortable, shook Jane by the hand, "What's the problem, are you sick or something? I must say you look very well, blooming even."

"I'm not sick," said Tanya curtly.

Jonathan anticipated Sergeant Harris, who was in charge of the airport, approaching as he and Tanya walked over to meet him. Jane waited next to the vehicle.

Tanya, as she always did, said a polite 'hello' to Harris who said to her, "If you need anything, ma'am, please let me know." He glanced at the helicopter disappearing to the north-east.

Tanya nodded.

"So, what's the programme?" asked Tanya into the silence that followed after they had all clambered into the truck.

"There is a meeting set up right now. We'll go straight into the meeting. There is no need for the doctor to attend."

"She does or I don't," responded Tanya.

"But she has no knowledge of our business…"

"She will attend the meeting," said Tanya firmly. She decided to try to put Jonathan off-balance, saying, "What's with all these fancy Range Rovers I see around? I thought the idea was to conserve fuel."

"We've found them in various places and had them reconditioned," he said, defensively.

Tanya just shook her head.

On the way into military headquarters now located at what had been the Royal Military College at Duntroon, they were made to wait as a troop of 50 or 60 horsemen clattered past. Tanya was suddenly on full alert. "Fuck," she said, "Jonathan, what the hell is going on here? There's one of those murderous Dunstan bastards and bloody Bruno! Why have they been released from jail? And look there! Animals from the Vikings! And Morton! My God and the Taree prisoners and those thugs from the Bandstand. They were all sentenced to life in prison or execution. How come they are free? Were any of the fuckers actually executed?"

"Times have moved on, we are short of people, so we use all the resources that are available. They've all been retrained," he said. His manner lacked conviction.

"Including criminals!" Tanya shouted. "I suppose that bunch of thugs we sent you from the Vikings are now part of your elite?"

"Some of them have been repurposed into a training programme, yes. As I said we use all the resources that are available."

"I don't believe I am hearing any of this. Everything we've been building up over the past God knows how many years is being compromised here. How the hell can we possibly trust you ever again?"

"Well, we're here now; we had better go into the meeting. I expect they'll be waiting for us," said Jonathan with resignation.

"Who the fuck are *they*?" asked Tanya.

They were led into a large, well-appointed boardroom in the Military College, which Tanya had never seen before. One side of the table were a dozen or so male officers, unknown to Tanya. Jonathan parked himself at one end of the table. Tanya and Jane sat themselves at the centre of the table. Tanya placed her bush hat on the table.

"My name is Colonel Jacobs," said a well-built, athletic looking man in his mid-fifties, seated in the middle of the row of people opposite. He wore a military moustache and his short thinning hair was brushed to one side with a parting. He gave Tanya the impression of a man in a hurry and of ruthless indifference to others. "We know who you are, Mrs Bower, but who's this?" he asked, waving his hand in Jane's direction. Nobody else was introduced.

"This," Tanya said slowly as she looked at all those in the room, "is Dr Jane Wickremasinghe. She is the chief medical officer at The Settlement and she accompanies me on some of my longer trips."

"Why is that necessary?" asked Jacobs.

Tanya looked at him for a long tense moment before responding. "Colonel Jacobs, I have come here in good faith at the invitation of General Bower. Neither he nor you have taken the trouble to introduce any of your colleagues and nor do I have any indication of what this meeting is about. We have had a very good relationship with the Australian military over the past 30 years. If you no longer want that association, tell me now and we can all move on."

Jacobs glared at her without saying anything.

"Do you have an agenda, Colonel? asked Tanya.

"We would like to extend the nature of our cooperation with your group," Jacobs responded eventually. "The Settlement I believe it is called."

"Why should we do that when you are not honouring agreements you had with us?"

"What do you mean by that?"

"On our way here from the airport we came across a group of horsemen, led by two people who had been sentenced to life imprisonment by your military court. Included in the group were others from various organisations who are hostile to us. We were led to believe that these people had either been executed or were sentenced to long periods of imprisonment."

Tanya glanced at Jonathan, who looked away. She assumed he was comfortable with the structure of the meeting and how Jacobs was running it.

"We run operations here, not you, and will take the action we think fit with anyone under our jurisdiction," answered a furious Jacobs.

"Let me continue," said Tanya. "These particular individuals wished us a great deal of harm and our colleagues in a nearby settlement would not have survived but for the action we took. I will not be cooperating with any organisation that treats them as anything but criminals." Jacobs tried to interrupt. Tanya held up her hand. "Hear me out Colonel! I have also seen some people here, wandering about as free men, from an outfit called the Vikings. They also had plans to destroy us, which we foiled. General Bower supposedly had them all jailed for extended periods. It seems that a large part of your undertaking here is fundamentally hostile to us. What do you have to say to that?"

"Mrs Bower," said Jacobs, now more calmly, "the people you're talking about have been deemed to be rehabilitated after a period of correction. It's not a conspiracy, it's the process of military justice. I think you can trust us. What we are looking for is to extend our cooperation."

"How?" asked Tanya bluntly.

"We would like a closer association between your military capacity and ours."

"What do you have in mind?" asked Tanya.

"Well, for maximum efficiency your military should report directly to me here."

"I already keep General Bower informed of our activities. Why do we need to duplicate things?"

"What I had in mind was that your military people should actually be based here in Canberra."

"You obviously don't understand that our military personnel, as you describe them, are part-timers. All of them have significant duties, outside their military responsibilities, within the various communities we have jurisdiction over. Remove them and you destroy their ability to defend themselves and take away skills that are essential to our everyday survival. I am not prepared to put at risk what we have built up over many years. General Bower is well aware of how we operate."

She again glanced at Jonathan, who looked away.

"There is no possibility I'll contemplate any such move," Tanya continued. "If, on the other hand, you need us to take action to assist you with particular missions and projects, we would be able to cooperate for short periods. You will however, as I have pointed out, have to deal with the people within your organisation who wish us ill, before we agree to anything."

The conversation continued for more than an hour, to Tanya's surprise. One or two other men in the entourage said a word or two but the conversation was led from the military side by Jacobs. Sandwiches were produced for lunch. As Tanya and Jane took a toilet break and when they were alone, Jane said, "To some extent they are playing along with you, Tanya. I think they're waiting for something to provoke their true agenda."

When they returned the room was deserted, except for a junior officer, who had not been at the meeting, and who introduced himself as Second Lieutenant Ohlsson. He said, "Colonel Jacobs has been called away. The meeting will only commence again tomorrow. I'll show you to your rooms." Tanya took a selection of sandwiches from the tray and they followed the officer into another part of the building, where they were shown to two interlocking rooms. The rooms were comfortably furnished each with a double bed and a set of comfortable chairs. Each room had a private bathroom and toilet. The officer said, "If you want anything I or someone else will be outside." Once they were seated alone inside, Tanya said to Jane, "The windows are barred. I wonder why?"

Since it was still early afternoon and once they had eaten some of the sandwiches and there was no word from anyone, they found their way out of the building. They were acknowledged by Ohlsson who was seated in a chair immediately outside their rooms. The Royal Military College at Duntroon was a short walk down to the nearby lake. Across the water and high on the hill opposite they could see the bare flagpole on the newish Parliament building, built as part of Australia's bi-centenary celebrations. There was, however, no sign of any activity on the opposite bank which appeared to be completely deserted. There was some activity on their side of the water. They couldn't help noticing that wherever they went there were military personnel flitting about.

"What time does the canteen open for dinner?" Tanya asked Ohlsson on returning to their rooms.

"The canteen is not open to visitors," was Ohlsson's answer, "but I have been advised that dinner will be provided at seven pm. Here."

"I've eaten in the canteen dozens of times, on previous visits," Tanya answered.

Ohlsson shrugged. The two women looked at each other and Jane made tea from the facilities provided.

"I don't really like what's going on," said Tanya. She went out of the room to remove keys she had seen in the doors earlier. They were missing.

Tanya went up to Ohlsson. "The keys please, Lieutenant Ohlsson."

He looked at her and then reluctantly took the keys from his pocket and handed them over.

CHAPTER 15
Newcastle and Kanangra

Louis and Kim

Louis and Roger sought each other out every few hours once they had returned home. "Nope, nothing yet," said Louis, the first several times he was approached by Roger. He tried to busy himself with little things, but he grew more and more anxious as time wore on. He was unable to sleep, "It should have been me that paid that visit to Canberra," he said to himself. "I hope the baby is alright."

As the 48-hour deadline approached, Louis and Roger met on the parade ground.

"Not a peep," said Louis, still hobbling about on crutches. "We'd better put the plan into action. "I'll get Eustace to pick me up. You'll be busy enough here and might need the Jetstar. I'll keep in touch."

Louis was waiting for Eustace on the parade ground when he arrived in one of the Merlins later. As he often did, Eustace pumped much of the contents of the Merlin's fuel tanks into the AVCAT tank near the parade ground. "It pays to keep the tanks here full," Eustace explained, "I'll fill up again back in Newcastle."

"What gives?" asked Eustace.

"Tanya told us to activate the plan if we hadn't heard anything for 48 hours, so that's now in progress."

"Everything?" asked Eustace.

Louis nodded. "I'll get the gun on the frigate set up. You need to get the choppers in the air to see if there are any major troop movements."

There was little further conversation, Louis' thoughts alternating between what he had to do to defend the harbour and worrying about Tanya's welfare.

Eustace put his hand on Louis arm, "Don't worry too much," he said, "she's pretty good at looking after herself."

Kim came hurrying up as they arrived back at the helicopter base in Newcastle.

"Any word?" she asked.

"Sorry, no. We're activating the plan."

"Okay," said a worried but well in control Kim "What are the next steps?"

"We defend the port. Everyone approaching by sea or by land is now a threat. Tanya thinks there is possible danger from the sea so we must make certain we are in position to blast anyone out of existence who tries to attack us from there and possibly from inland as well; I can't imagine where the danger from the sea will come from though," said Louis.

"I hope you're right, but we've been told to be ready for anything."

"I need a couple of people to help me to get the gun on the frigate operational," said Louis.

"Okay," said Kim. She found three people to accompany Louis, before saying to Eustace, "Make sure the Merlins are fully fuelled up, armed and manned. As per the plan we discussed with Tanya, do a few sorties inland to see if there's any action, such as major troop movements, and check on all the other satellites."

Kim also made sure her Academy contingent was put on full alert. She sent a group to the headland, overlooking the harbour entrance, where wood had been collected for a bonfire. Louis and his scratch crew boarded the frigate. He activated the fire direction radar, which he had tested while the frigate was still moored in Sydney, and again during a recent visit to Newcastle. He aimed the gun seaward. He fired a few salvos from the frigate, making certain of the ranges.

Mark and Virginia

Eustace landed the Merlin, fully armed with two door gunners and machine guns, in the grounds of the hotel in Bowral. Mark came rushing over.

"There are a group of horsemen coming up the main road from Canberra," Eustace reported. "They all scattered into the bush when they saw me."

"How far are they from Moss Vale?" asked Mark.

"At least 100 ks."

"Were they in uniform?"

"Couldn't see."

"As Tanya told us, we had better be ready for the worst. We've never had a visit from a large contingent of the army before. In the past it's just been Jonathan on his own."

Virginia joined them. Mark quickly explained the situation.

"We anticipated something like this might happen," said Virginia. "There's an ideal ambush spot about 15 ks south of Moss Vale. I'll mobilise our troops. We'll be leaving in less than an hour. They'll have to continue up the main highway," she said referring to the insurgent horsemen, "it's impossible to make any headway through the bush now."

"Take a couple of spare horses with you," said Mark as Virginia, still limping, raced off. "I'll go with Eustace to mobilise the people in Moss Vale and to survey the ambush spot." Eustace nodded confirmation.

During the brief flight to Moss Vale, Eustace contacted Kim to report on the situation. He told her he was going to stick with Mark to help if needed. Moss Vale, still overgrown and with potholed roads was gradually being cleaned up and resettled, so some of the houses were now occupied and there was now a large cultivated area in one part of the old town. Cattle had been tamed and were corralled in paddocks on the edge of town. As it was in the process of being resettled by people from Kanangra, Eustace was asked to land in the main street. A small crowd gathered. Mark explained the situation to Michael, who had been left in charge of the area. "Virginia will be here in a couple of hours. We need your ten Academy troopers to join her, fully armed and mounted," he said. "I'll be just down the road."

Mark directed Eustace to the well-chosen location about 15 ks south. Together they surveyed the ambush position and then found a place a few hundred metres away where Eustace could wait the outcome of any conflict.

"I'll remain here," said Mark. "I'll fire a red flare if we need your assistance. Keep the door gunners with you. You'll have to spend the night here. You can feed with us; I'm sure Virginia will have provided for that."

Virginia's choice for the ambush was ideal; on the top of a hill on a section of what had been known as the Hume Highway. There were a number of boulders on each side of the cracked and potholed road. Mark was able to identify at least 30 positions where their troops would have a clear field of fire and plenty of cover. Mark could see right down the Hume; looking to the south there was a gentle downhill slope facing them, where the old road ran to a dip, when it then rose quite steeply up to where he was positioned. "We'll be able to see them for 500 or more metres," he muttered to himself.

At dusk Virginia and the contingent of 30 arrived. Horses were tethered and corralled under guard, not far from Eustace's helicopter.

The troops settled down for the night. They ate what they had brought with them. Virginia told them, "No fires."

Mark kept a careful look out from dawn onwards, the next day. At about mid-morning he tapped Virginia on the arm. All the troops had been in position for more than an hour.

"Riders— 50, 60 of them, I think," Mark said, as he handed her the binoculars.

"Okay..." Virginia began. Her injury meant she struggled a bit to move around the rough terrain comfortably. She rubbed her leg.

"Maybe they're military," said Mark.

"No," said Virginia, when she got into position and peered through the binoculars. "There are no uniforms."

Mark took the binoculars back and, a few minutes later, said, "Virginia! I simply don't believe it, you look." He handed the binoculars back to her. There was a group of 60 horsemen trotting up the road, five abreast. They were all armed with Steyr carbines and were well mounted. They wore a motley collection of clothing.

"That bastard Dunstan and, unless I am mistaken, Bruno is with him," she whispered. "I don't care whether they're friendly or not, I should have shot them all years ago. I'm not going to make that mistake again."

"Okay, you take Dunstan and I'll take Bruno," said Mark. He had already told his troops to hold their fire until he either fired or gave the word.

Mark watched the hostile troops quietly trotting along the main road, and as they came closer he heard Rudolf Dunstan say loudly, "The turnoff is somewhere along ... arrrrgh!" Dunstan clutched his throat as Virginia's shot took him there. He was dead before he hit the ground. Bruno had less than a second of shocked surprise when Mark's shot hit him in the side of the head. Mark laid his rifle aside as the rest of his squad launched a devastating volley on the intruders, and fired a flare in Eustace's direction.

The murderous fire from the hidden Kanangra troops continued for 20 minutes with Eustace's chopper hovering overhead and his door gunners adding to the mayhem. Two men managed to escape back down the road; the rest stopped and raised their hands. Once the shooting stopped, Mark signalled for half his troop to advance, while Virginia and the other half stayed hidden, giving cover. Some of Mark's force disarmed and secured the surrendering troops while others took control of horses that hadn't run off.

"Have a closer look at some of these people," Mark said to Virginia after she had cautiously approached with the balance of the Kanangra force. "Some are from Morton; they should be in jail and the rest of them don't look like soldiers…"

Eustace landed the helicopter nearby, on the road. "I'll take the wounded to The Settlement hospital," he said. "I'll ask Roger where he wants the prisoners."

They collected weapons scattered about and bundled them into the aircraft, together with seven of the wounded raiders, who Eustace flew to The Settlement hospital under the guard of one of Mark's troops.

Each one of the remaining prisoners, now sitting in the middle of the road under guard, was questioned at length. Soon a garbled story emerged: they had been promised they could settle at Kanangra once 'that stupid bitch' had had her comeuppance. While he was waiting for Eustace to return, Mark made his captives dig graves for their dead companions. When Eustace returned in the Merlin, he told Mark, "Roger wants the prisoners to be held at The Settlement."

"Why did you do this to us?" asked a plaintive voice, "We were only paying you a friendly…"

Mark flattened the man with punch to the face. "Any more bright remarks?"

The manacled captives were dumped into the machine. One man managed to attract Mark's attention; something in his demeanour made Mark listen to him. "Just watch out in Newcastle," he whispered, "something is planned for you there as well."

Two of Mark and Virginia's ambush party accompanied Eustace in the chopper to keep an eye on their captives. "You'll notice there are no doors on this machine. Anyone who fidgets or misbehaves in any way will be tipped out of here," one of them said.

"Mark, I overheard what that man said to you about Newcastle; I'll tell Kim, but I expect they'll be well prepared anyway," Eustace said. "I'm going to drop this pile of shit off," he said, jerking his thumb at the prisoners, "and then return to Newcastle."

Mark, Virginia and the Kanangra troops retreated to Moss Vale together with three dozen captured horses to spend the night.

Louis and Kim

Louis and his crew had stayed on the frigate. One man was constantly on watch. When Eustace returned with his news Kim popped over to tell Louis about the plan to attack Newcastle from the sea. She also briefed him on what had occurred and what the outcome was in the Southern Highlands.

"So the game is on," said Louis. "Looks as though all of Tanya's instincts were correct. We're well prepared here." He tried to put out of his mind his now-heightened worries about Tanya. With Kim, Eustace briefed the other two Merlin pilots.

"I just need a bit of shut-eye," said Eustace, "but we'll be on full alert by dawn."

Kim returned to her contingent of Academy troops. She repeated what she had been told by Eustace. "One person on watch," she said, "Everyone else to try to get some sleep; we need to be on full alert an hour before dawn."

As the sky lightened in the east Louis was alerted by the watch. "Bonfire, headland!" he yelled. "Something must have entered the harbour!"

"It is not yet light enough for me to see what's on the way," said Louis, outwardly calm but the action had set his pulses racing. "I'll fire a salvo into the darkness to warn them off. They can't be friendly if they're arriving like this before dawn."

Once it was light they knew they would have clear view of the harbour entrance, due to the rise in sea levels. Sitting in the ops room, Louis fired a salvo of three rounds, which he knew would land just inside the entrance.

"That should get them to back off," said Louis.

After the shockwaves had stopped echoing off the surrounding hills, there was a few minutes silence. Even though he was ready for it, Louis jumped when the first rattle of machine gun fire burst out of the darkness. Bright orange muzzle flashes showed in the old opening of the sea wall and lines of tracer arced up towards the signal bonfire, their red and green lines searching along the edge of the headland.

"Yeah, good luck to you, boys," Louis said as he watched them light up the position. "They'll be long gone. I'm going to let them have it. From the sound of those guns it's two of the navy's ACPBs, no match for this baby though."

"What's an ACPB?" he was asked.

"Patrol Boat," he said as he made some minor adjustments to the elevation of the gun. He could now see silhouettes of the patrol boats against the horizon, with their antennae making them look like angry insects. Louis pressed the firing pedal directing another salvo of three rounds at the enemy. Seconds later there was a massive explosion, and the sky and surrounding area was lit up like daylight for a minute, as two of the rounds scored a direct hit on one of the two patrol boats which had become visible in the early light.

Louis fired another salvo. He quickly made his way to the bridge of HMAS Perth. He activated the LRAD loudhailer system.

"Heave to, heave to and reverse your gun. Reverse your gun and wait for direction. All personnel above deck and wait for direction. Comply or we will fire on you." Louis' voice echoed across the harbour.

Louis could see two of the Merlins hovering above the remaining patrol boat, enveloped in a pall of smoke with twisted metal jutting out of its mangled superstructure. The vessel came to a gradual stop, flaming oil leaking out into the clear waters of the harbour. Louis heard a single shot as the surviving patrol boat made its way slowly towards the frigate escorted by the two helicopters.

Louis thought they had everything under control, but was shocked into action by another burst of machine gun fire echoing across the harbour. He was horrified to see one of the Merlins cartwheeling into the sea with parts flying off it as it descended helplessly, with a large splash, into the water.

"Shit," said Louis, as he rushed back to the ops room in the frigate. "Another goddam patrol boat," he said to the crew member waiting there. The vessel was just coming through the heads. He made a minor adjustment to the elevation of the gun. "I'll see if this'll nail him."

There was a quick exchange of fire between the first patrol boat and the remaining helicopter, with patrol boat crew members rushing about the deck trying to take cover. Louis fired another salvo; "Just missed," he said. Making a small adjustment he fired a further salvo. "Got the bastard, now there won't be any more crap from these assholes," Louis responded to the massive explosion as one of the shells hit the incoming patrol boat.

The pilot of the surviving helicopter escorted the one surviving patrol boat as Louis repeated his instruction from the bridge of the frigate through the loudhailer. "Heave to, heave to and reverse your gun. Reverse your gun and wait for direction. All personnel above deck and wait for direction. Comply or we will fire on you."

As the patrol boat slowly made its way to the indicated berth, Louis surveyed the devastating scene in the harbour. The smoking wrecks of the two patrol boats; some of the oil that had leaked into the water was now on fire; bits of debris floating about and what appeared to be some body parts; and the wreckage of the helicopter was still visible.

Kim threw one of the crew a rope and the vessel was tied up under the watchful eye of Louis, Kim, Eustace and the Newcastle Academy, personnel all of whom had their rifles pointed at their captives. Silently the 20 able-bodied crew members climbed the gangway with their hands in the air. One of the party was being helped; he appeared to have been wounded in the leg. They all looked utterly terrified, looking around in wonderment, especially at the frigate.

Tanya

After breakfast had been served in their rooms, Tanya and Jane were escorted by Lieutenant Ohlsson to the meeting room where they waited for nearly an hour before Colonel Jacobs and his entourage appeared.

"Where is General Bower?" asked Tanya.

"The General is indisposed today," answered Colonel Jacobs curtly. Tanya could see his eyes glittering, like a snake poised to strike.

"Just one question," asked Tanya. "Are we prisoners or are we entitled to leave?"

Without answering, Jacobs looked at Tanya with a self-satisfied look on his face.

"We have a considerable amount of information regarding some very serious matters which you personally have been involved in Mrs Bower. Murder, in particular."

Tanya just looked at him.

"Well, don't you have anything to say about that?"

Tanya said nothing.

Tanya could see Jacobs responding to her goading as he said, "I will detail some of the information that has come into our hands, and this is only the tip of the iceberg:

"In 2029, you murdered Demetriou Smith and some 30 of his followers."

He looked at Tanya to see if there was any reaction. There wasn't.

"More recently you murdered Harold Monckton together with four others."

There was still no reaction from Tanya.

"Again, in past months, you were responsible for ambushing and killing some 40 or more people from what I understand is called the Viking village, who were innocently attempting to pay a friendly visit to another group of survivors. You were also responsible for attacking and killing several members of the same group who were trying to pay you a friendly visit. You were also instrumental in illegally burning down the Viking village."

Tanya merely raised her eyebrows.

Jacobs continued, "You personally, illegally, and without legal sanction, were responsible for the execution of a Mr. Owens.

"You illegally apprehended and incarcerated one Samuel Barnes…"

Tanya looked confused.

"Also known as Thor."

Tanya smiled.

"I could go on," said Jacobs. "Apart from some of your crimes just detailed, I think I have some news that may persuade you how much trouble you really are in." He turned to a messenger who had just entered the room. The man stood for a few moments looking completely panic stricken. Jacobs was sufficiently alert to quickly usher him out of the room. A few minutes later, based on a signal from outside, all the officers attending the meeting left the room.

"Time for us to go as well, I think", said Tanya.

Before they could make a move three soldiers arrived, all pointing rifles at the pair. "You are under arrest, orders from Colonel Jacobs."

"Oh, on what charge?" asked an unfazed Tanya, refusing to look at them.

"Out, come with us," said the leader, appearing to be uncomfortable with the developments, without responding.

Tanya recognised his voice as that of her son, Chas. He winked at her behind the backs of his two companions, when she looked up. Tanya and Jane were returned to their rooms, the door was locked and a guard posted outside. Before the door was locked, Chas said to Tanya within earshot of the others, "Sergeant Harris will be the guard relief in two hours."

Chas returned with Sergeant Harris. They had both heard the reports about the attacks in the Southern Highlands and Newcastle and the results. As part of a developing plan, Chas also brought Jess, the wife of one of the embedded Settlement people.

"You take over guard duty on Tanya at midnight," Chas told Harris. "We can then get Tanya out of there, leaving Jess in her place so they think they still have Tanya in captivity. In the meantime, you and I should eat; we can use the canteen. None of us will provoke any attention. Jess should probably eat separately. I have explained to her what her role will be."

Chas and Harris arrived just before midnight. They unlocked the door and brought Tanya and Jane up to date with their plan. Tanya pleaded with Chas to find Jonathan, "See if you can get bloody Jonathan to come with us; I can't believe that he's a willing partner in all this crap." Tanya spent a few minutes with Jess, who she knew from The Settlement. "I really appreciate you standing in for me and the personal risk you're taking. We'll make sure you're looked after when all this is over. I really need to get on top of things now."

As Tanya and Jess were in the process of swapping clothes there was a scuffle outside the room and a lot of shouting. "We've come to take the prisoner to another location!" yelled a voice. Jess didn't hesitate. "Quick, under the bed," she whispered. "They may not know what you look like." Tanya dived under the bed and pulled a cover down concealing her. A man in a sergeant's uniform pushed his way into the room and seeing Jess in Tanya's colonel's uniform assumed she was the prisoner. "You are to come with me, Ms Bower, and you," he said to Jane politely and they quickly left.

Harris hurriedly re-entered the room and was momentarily unable to see any sign of Tanya, until she crawled out from under the bed.

"Quick, we'd better get you out of here," he said. Tanya and Harris went outside and waited for a few minutes. "I'm expecting Chas and a vehicle," explained Harris.

"Mnn," said Tanya after a few more minutes, "It's dark, there's nobody about. If you can find a water bottle and some food, I'll walk out of here. By dawn I'll be well out of Canberra. Sooner or later they are going to find that Jess is not me so I need to be well away before then. If you do manage to get hold of a vehicle I'm going straight up the main road, so you can pick me up, and please remember Jane. It's about 200 ks to Moss Vale, so it'll take me three days to walk there.

Harris hesitated for a minute and then disappeared, returning 30 minutes later with two water bottles and a back pack. "E-rations that will last you a few days and some fruit in there."

He handed her a Steyr carbine with a spare magazine.

"Where is Chas?" Tanya asked.

"He's gone to catch-up with the main body of the troops sent to attack The Settlement. There were a few stragglers who he took with him."

Tanya nodded. She knew she urgently needed to get to Bowral.

He watched until she disappeared into the dark.

CHAPTER 16

Wentworth

Roger, Chas and Derain

Roger had collected 400 of the best Academy trained troops. Some from The Settlement itself and others from surrounding surviving satellites, resulting from the briefings provided by Tanya. Everyone was gathered at The Settlement; they were well mounted and well equipped. They all knew they were about to engage in the most serious confrontation they had ever contemplated. Derain led them out of the western gate saying to Roger, "I'm now going to find Chas. Amaroo will guide you through the bush."

Three days into his journey, Chas had caught up with the main force and it soon became clear that the officers leading the military expedition were having trouble with the overgrown bush and needed help, so Chas approached Colonel Wetherall, who was in charge saying, "If you will let me, Sir, I'm sure that I can find a short cut through the Blue Mountains to our destination, it will save at least a week." Privately he had no intention of helping; his plan was to lead the force into a blind gully.

The colonel looked at Chas with disdain, "Captain, if I need your advice, I will ask for it, now return to your position."

"Sir," answered Chas. He turned on his heel and returned to his unit.

Chas had made sure that he was visible on the fringes of the combined task force whilst seeing to the welfare of the men in his platoon. Soon his efforts were rewarded when Derain whispered from a nearby bush during one of his nocturnal perambulations, "Chas, Chas, It's me, Derain."

Ensuring he was not seen Chas crept behind the bush. He embraced Derain. As with most of the people in the Academy almost everything he had learnt about surviving in the bush was the result of Derain's skill and training. Chas had a closer relationship with Derain than many others, because he was Tanya's son. "How did you find us?" asked Chas.

"Aboriginal man in Canberra," he said shortly.

Chas explained how his offer of help had been rejected by the officer in charge.

"These people obviously know the location of The Settlement but they don't know the tracks through the bush," said Derain. "Especially now it has grown so much. I will track the force for a day or two and then let the man in charge stumble on me by accident. Perhaps he'll listen to me."

"We don't want them to be running around for too long. We want them back in Canberra as soon as we can get them there," replied Chas.

Derain grinned in anticipation, "I have a plan, and all these people will be back in Canberra in two weeks. Roger's not far, Amaroo is bringing him south. He'll be here in a day or two."

Derain made sure the colonel was the one to appear to stumble across him; he was carrying his traditional weapons and had a dead snake slung over one shoulder. Derain made a friendly gesture. He had a brief conversation with the colonel and made as if to disappear into the bush again.

Wetherall was by now conscious of the fact that he was not very clear about the route to The Settlement and felt that the arrival of Derain was a signal from on high that he had been right in rejecting Chas's offer of help. Derain seemed like a godsend.

"Are you one of those blacktracker types, eh? Me plenty good bloke, yes? Alright, then. God knows you people weren't good for much before the flood— may as well make yourself useful now," said Wetherall.

"Yes. I can help if you like."

After another short conversation Derain led the huge troop on. When the colonel next saw Chas he said uncharitably, "I have now engaged an Aboriginal guide, he probably knows a helluva lot more about finding his way around here than you do."

"Sir, I am sure you are right," answered Chas without a hint of a smile on his face.

Within a few days the force had entered the southern fringes of the Kanangra Boyd National Park. During his regular clandestine meetings with Derain, Chas said to him, "You will keep away from the village here, won't you?"

Derain nodded. He told Chas, "I'm going to lead them into a narrow gully, where there is no way out. I've explained the plan to Roger; he can surround the soldiers there." He was also clutching a large pile of deep green leaves, "Tomorrow night boil these leaves and put the water in the soldier's tea. It will put them in a deep sleep." Tanya had told Chas about the use of the green leaves and how they had used them to destroy Demetriou and his raiders.

There was uneasiness among some of the troop as they entered the narrow gully and made camp. "We're being led into a trap," was the observation of one of the junior officers. Wetherall ignored him. Chas made sure all The Settlement embedded people knew of the plan; importantly, not to drink the tea and to keep on the fringes of the troop. They were all instrumental in putting green leaves into the boiling water. One or two of the military personnel asked what the leaves were for so when questioned Derain said to them, "It's very good for stomachs, bush food sometimes disagrees with people." Chas judged that about 450 of the 500 had drunk the tea, including Colonel Wetherall.

Most in the troop, including the senior officers, had come to trust Derain and his charming ways. The colonel had introduced him round as 'my Aboriginal guide' so he was well accepted. By midnight the camp was well and truly asleep. Roger found Chas and Derain on the fringes of the encampment.

The junior officer, Lieutenant Henderson, refused to drink the tea and had kept a separate watch on the camp; by the early hours of the morning it was obvious to him that something was seriously amiss, since most of the men appeared to be in a deep sleep. He quietly searched the camp for those who were still awake, directing them to a niche in the rock face on one side of the gully and instructing them to bring all their equipment. He explained what he thought had happened, adding, "This all has something to do with that Aboriginal guide. It's a trap, I'm sure there's no way forward. We'll try to find a way out of here. Let me think. Ten of us should try to go out the way we came in here earlier; if that is clear, the rest of us can follow. A couple of us should stay back in case of an ambush and then quickly come back here to warn us. Don't do anything rash."

As soon as Chas and Derain were certain that the main camp had settled down, Roger was alerted and he and The Settlement troops were positioned near the entrance to the camp, out of sight.

"Some of your people need to collect the horses and tack," said Chas. "We don't want to lose the tack. Also, we need everything, horses and tack, back in Canberra, so we should arrange to get that moving as soon as we can."

"Canberra?" asked Roger, "Shouldn't we just take them back home?"

"No, we need the horses and all your people back in Canberra, with the troop as prisoners," answered Chas. "Something Mum cooked up with Derain. For the moment, I think the horses should go to the old settlement at Kanangra and await developments. We can then shift them all to Canberra when we're ready."

"Okay," answered Roger, who implicitly trusted anything Tanya had planned. He gave orders for some of his troop to collect the military horses.

One of the embedded Settlement soldiers returned, in a hurry. "Not everyone drank the tea, and as far as I can see one of the officers has cottoned onto the fact they're in trouble. I expect him and a few others will be coming down the track shortly, trying to get out of here."

"Okay," said Chas, "let's get the horses away as quick as we can, but don't go too far; we'll need them to carry all the military weapons." 50 Settlement troops were each made responsible for a string of six or seven horses. They drifted off into the moonlight night under the guidance of the ever-capable Amaroo. Roger selected 30 Settlement troops to set an ambush near where the horses had been corralled. The remaining troops were left in reserve, "We need to sort out the people who have seen through our trap and then we'll deal with the rest of them," he explained.

Ten of Henderson's men walked gingerly into the clearing where the horses had been corralled, under the supervision of a sergeant who said, "I'm sure this is where we left the horses," in a very uncertain voice. "Yes, there are hoof marks all over the place, but…"

"Keep very, very still," Roger said in a loud voice, "You are all covered with rifles pointing directly at you…"

All the military men stood stock still and raised their hands. A signal was sent back to Captain Henderson indicating they had been ambushed.

"Drop your weapons, all of them," said a still-hidden Roger.

All the men dropped their weapons. Ten of Rogers's troop picked up the weapons, secured the men with cable ties and tossed their weapons into a pile and made their captives sit back to back facing outwards.

The Settlement man, who had originally raised the alarm, said to Roger quietly, "There were at least 50 in this group. I think these were sent to test the water. There are at least another 40 still out there, maybe thinking how to attack us." Roger thought quickly. He walked out into the clearing and picked out the sergeant. He had already sent 50 Settlement troops back down the path anticipating a possible attack from the rest of Henderson's men, who had not consumed the tea.

"Sergeant, I need to explain to you who we are and what we are about. We actually wish you no harm, in fact as far as we are concerned all of you are a fundamental part of what we consider to be the rebuilding of Australia." He then spent a few minutes explaining in detail the philosophy and strengths of The Settlement.

"You need to understand, Sergeant, all your horses and all your supplies are now under our control. The rest of the troop will wake up sometime in the next twelve hours, but they won't be able to function for a few hours after that. We think it is in the best interests of everyone that you and your other colleagues surrender and return with us to Canberra. Your colleagues could certainly fight their way out of here, but they will all probably die in the bush, without horses or supplies and they will be pursued by our people who all have considerable bush skills. Colonel Jacobs was leading you all in a very bad direction. I sincerely suggest you join with us with the clear objective of rebuilding the Australia we once had."

The sergeant turned to his colleagues and after an animated discussion the sergeant said, "You and I need to go and talk to Henderson. Carry a white cloth or something."

They walked unhurriedly to the niche in the rock-face where Henderson and his men were hidden.

"Who are you?" asked Henderson.

"I'm from The Settlement, the people you were intending to attack. Our troops have surrounded you. All your horses and all your supplies are under our control. As I have explained to the sergeant here we wish you no harm, no harm at all. As far as we are concerned you and the rest of the military set-up are fundamental to the rebuilding of Australia. Colonel Jacobs is intent on feathering his own nest and would have done a great deal of damage to that objective. All I can suggest is that you surrender to us; we will then return to Canberra and if you are willing, you can play a constructive role in re-establishing the civilisation we once had."

"I need to discuss all that with these men here."

"Go ahead, just remember every man has a rifle aimed at them."

Henderson returned after 30 minutes.

"Okay, we surrender."

"One at a time, file out of here and drop your weapons in a pile over there," Roger pointed.

To the consternation of Henderson and his men a dozen of Roger's troops slipped silently out of the bush and covered the prisoners with rifles pointing at them. Another group picked up all the weapons and others secured all of Henderson's men with cable ties. Roger's men then marched Henderson's troops to join the other ten.

Roger said loudly to anyone within hearing, "The boss said, 'no bloodshed if possible,' we need all these people. Hopefully it will stay that way."

Roger organised the remaining Settlement troops to walk the 200 or so metres to the soldier's camp, where all the soldiers were still soundly asleep. Their weapons were collected and all the soldiers' hands were tied behind their backs with cable ties. The horses were returned to the camp and the captured weapons loaded onto them. A thorough search was made of each soldier making sure there were no hidden weapons. By dawn the horses were on their way to the original Kanangra village with their captured booty.

By mid-morning the drugged soldiers started to wake, finding themselves captured with their hands behind their backs. The officers were separated from the other ranks. When Wetherall woke, to his utter amazement he found Roger in front of him with a revolver pointing directly at him. He said, "Colonel Wetherall, you are under arrest for treason. You do not have to say anything but anything you do say will be taken in evidence and may be used against you at your trial."

Wetherall gradually came to and could hardly believe his eyes, "Who the fuck are you?" he demanded. "Just wait until General Bower and Colonel Jacobs hear about this—you'll be in trouble. You'll be executed on the spot."

"You'll find out soon enough who I am. You just need to listen to what I said, anything you say will be taken down in evidence and may be used against you at your trial for treason."

"You don't have the authority to do this…"

"I do and just did. Starting today you and the surviving members of your army will be walking back to Canberra. I assure you we will stand for no resistance; if you behave you will come to no harm. Any nonsense and you will get what's coming to you. I suggest you ask Lieutenant Henderson for his opinion."

Roger said to Derain, "We'll be able to manage now, Chas will lead us back to Canberra. Maybe see if you can find Tanya; the first place to look will be Canberra, it's possible they will have detained her. If you take a horse it will be quicker."

"I'll start looking for Tanya in Canberra" replied Derain as he set off on a horse, "at night always give people small amount of green leaf tea to keep them quiet," was his final advice to Roger.

TANYA

Leaving Canberra, Tanya walked for most of the rest of the night. The late hour ensured she saw nobody at all. She drank some of the water and ate sparingly from the supplies Harris had given her. Tanya was confident her fitness would allow her to walk the whole distance to Moss Vale or even Bowral which she knew was only ten ks beyond Moss Vale. "I must not hurt the baby," she thought, so periodically she detoured off into the bush and found she was able to catch two or three hours sleep, often in the fork of a tree. During these rest periods she always placed stones across the road, between the wrecks of old cars which partially blocked the road, hoping that anyone coming along the road would stop.

After a day she needed more water, and there was no sign of any rescue vehicle, so she diverted off into the bush, thinking about what Derain would do under the circumstances. She found a small stream from which she filled her water bottles; she hoped the ten years since the flood would have eliminated any nasties that might have polluted the water in the past. As she was about to resume her journey, the sound of a vehicle several hundred metres away on the road disturbed the silence. To create a diversion, she lit a small fire. Making her way to the road she watched. She could see an army jeep, stopped on the road. It was manned by two soldiers she didn't recognise. "Smoke, I saw smoke," one of the men said. "There must be someone there. We should go and have a look."

The two men moved off into the bush to see who had lit the fire. She decided she could easily hijack the vehicle and drive it to Bowral. She waited ten minutes as the noise of the men crashing through the bush faded. Tanya quietly left her hiding place and crept towards what she assumed would be an unattended vehicle. To her horror she saw there was another man leaning against the side of the vehicle looking around disinterestedly. She fingered her Steyr carbine for a second or two and then thought better of it. Tanya picked up a large stone and hurled it into the bush on the side of the vehicle away from her and away from the man's colleagues. The man moved off to investigate. All Tanya needed was a minute or two; as soon as the man had rushed off into the bush she quietly opened the door of the vehicle. Almost immediately, a voice said, "I saw you, come out with your hands up."

Tanya looked around wondering what to do. "Was this it? Was the game up?" she thought. To her relief she noticed the keys were still in the ignition. Tanya dived for the driver's seat, fumbled frantically for the keys and twisted them violently in the ignition. The windscreen shattered outwards as a single shot rang out. She rammed the vehicle into gear and took off as a couple more shots hit the body of the vehicle before she was safely around the corner.

"No choice now," she thought as she drove as fast as the conditions would allow towards Bowral. The road was still littered with the broken-down wrecks of vehicles abandoned at the time of the flood. After 20 minutes she noticed the fuel gauge dropping down quickly. "Shit," she thought, "fucking fuel tank." Wasting no time stopping to investigate, she drove for another ten minutes until the engine coughed, spluttered, and died. She parked the vehicle downhill facing the bush.

"I'm probably 30 ks or so from those soldiers," she thought. She looked through the vehicle and found more food in a knapsack; she had her water bottles and the Steyr. "I'm still 20 or so ks from Moss Vale." She took everything she needed out of the vehicle, put it in gear, took the handbrake off and, standing next to the vehicle, turned the starter key, quickly jumping away. The vehicle slowly moved and then, gathering speed, ran off the road crashing into the bushes before turning over. It was just visible from the road. She continued her walk.

Eventually Tanya thought she must be getting closer to Moss Vale. She walked down a long slope and then up a steep hill where she saw several fresh mounds of earth on the side of the road and large quantities of shell casings nearby. She picked one up. "Steyr," she said to herself. She looked around. There was no sign of anyone.

There were some nearby boulders which she clambered through. More casings. She continued on her journey.

By late afternoon she arrived in Moss Vale and came across one of the new settlers, who recognised her.

"Good heavens, Mrs Bower. How did you get here?" he asked.

She briefly explained. "I need to get to Bowral as soon as possible," she said.

"It's too late tonight. Just stay the night and we'll get you there in the morning."

"Thank you. I saw what looked like the signs of some sort of clash, just down the road. Lots of shell casings…"

"Yes. Mark and Virginia ambushed a group of men. Some dead, I believe, and many taken prisoner."

DERAIN

Derain found his way into Canberra, making contact with some other Aboriginal residents at the base. He spent a day unobtrusively talking to as many of them as he could. He wasn't particularly concerned that the presence of an unknown Aborigine would attract much attention, thinking that most of the whites would barely see him and merely think of him as another harmless oaf. He recognised Jane, who was with Sergeant Harris.

"She started walking to Moss Vale a couple of days ago now," Harris told him. "We'll be going to Bowral as soon as we find General Bower."

"I must get on," said Derain. "I'll see you in Bowral." Harris then suggested he take one of the reconditioned four-wheel drives from the military pool. "They're unused since most of the personnel are on the expedition to The Settlement." So he and an Aboriginal colleague did as was suggested and took the road to Moss Vale.

Derain was keeping a lookout for Tanya and every few kilometres he stopped to look for any signs of her or any other signs of trouble, such as campsites, possible tyre tracks and fires. About 150 kilometres outside Canberra, he thought he could smell a faint trace of wood-smoke. They proceeded with caution, just using the parking lights.

"May not be Tanya," he explained to his impatient companion. After more than an hour Derain signalled to his companion to park the vehicle, "Maybe Tanya," he said again, "maybe not."

He returned an hour later, "There are three soldiers. There is no vehicle and they are all asleep. We need to drive slowly until I say so and then go like hell."

They drove slowly for ten minutes, then Derain said, "Lights up now. Go as fast as you can."

The driver looked worried for a moment but did as he was told. They bumped into some stones on the road but managed to get past what Derain had determined was the soldier's camp. There were a few shots once they were well out of the way. "Okay, you can drive normally now." The journey took them far longer than anticipated due to Derain's caution. As they were driving through Moss Vale at midday the following day, to his amazement Derain thought he recognised a tired looking figure standing by the side of the road. It was indeed Tanya. He told the driver to stop the vehicle.

"Can I give you a lift ma'am?" he asked cheekily.

Derain got out of the vehicle. They looked at each other for a few seconds and then Tanya walked over and hugged him.

She explained briefly, "We need to get to Bowral, quickly."

Derain shrugged. "Sure; that's where we're going."

Derain was unknown to her hosts so they were very surprised when Tanya told them she would travel to Bowral with what to them looked like a rather untidy and disreputable Aborigine. "It's a long, complicated story," Tanya said, smiling. "I'll tell you about it one day," she said as she got into the vehicle.

TANYA

They arrived in Bowral within a few minutes and found their way into the office in the five-star hotel where Mark had established himself. Tanya could see Mark was having a very difficult discussion with someone on the phone. "Tanya, a prisoner…" he did a double take when he saw Tanya. "Kim," he said, "I'll get back to you, Tanya's just walked in."

Once they had been able to locate Jonathan, Sergeant Harris, Jane and Jonathan left Canberra half a day after Harris had helped Derain secure his vehicle. They had been flagged down by the three soldiers standing forlornly on the side of the road. Harris said, "Let me handle this," as he stepped out of the four-wheel drive.

The soldiers all shuffled to attention when they saw Harris in his uniform. "What are you doing here?" he asked.

"Routine patrol."

"Where's your vehicle?"

"It was stolen."

Harris looked at the man, "Likely bloody story," he thought.

"How long have you been here?"

"Two days," the man lied.

"Okay, we're on our way further north with General Bower," Harris indicated Jonathan, sitting in one of the rear seats, with a jerk of his thumb. It shouldn't take long. We'll pick you up on the way back this afternoon. I suggest you start walking though."

"All our food and water was taken when the truck was stolen."

Harris handed the senior man a full water bottle and a ration pack.

Jane went into overdrive when she spotted Tanya on arrival in Bowral, "You bloody walked here, are you nuts? I need to do a full examination just to make sure you're alright."

"No, you don't. I'm fine," responded Tanya.

Jane didn't listen and she took Tanya firmly by the hand to a small cottage in the grounds of the hotel and she spent an hour doing a careful examination. "Well you seem to be alright, but you need rest, proper hydration and a proper feed, and probably someone to examine what's in your head," she added acidly.

When Tanya rejoined the meeting, Derain told everyone about the ambush in the forests of the Blue Mountains and that they had captured all the military's horses, equipment, weapons and men. "The horses are now holed up in the Kanangra village, and all the prisoners are walking back to Canberra, with Roger and The Settlement people in charge. There may be some soldiers needing to go to The Settlement hospital."

An hour later they managed to return the call to Kim, who said, "I had a Colonel Jacobs on the line from Canberra. He reckons he's got troops in place ready to take over The Settlement, and he claims to have you, Tanya, in custody. He wants us to surrender or he'll green light them to execute you."

"Takes a lot more than what they had to lock me up; call me the new Scarlett Pimpernel!" Tanya laughed easily, not betraying the close call she had had, "I am back in the saddle here so to speak. So bloody Jacobs wants us to surrender to him; from what I understand the position is that Jacobs' troops have actually surrendered to us."

Derain nodded his agreement.

"Does Jacobs have any contact with his forces?" asked Tanya.

Derain shook his head. "Roger has taken it all away. No contact anymore."

"When you next speak to Jacobs, tell him we agree to his terms," Tanya said to Kim. "Make it clear we have surrendered, and our troops are marching to Canberra, under the direction of his forces."

"And then?" asked a troubled Kim.

"He's going to get a very nasty surprise."

Tanya managed a short conversation with Louis. "I need you here with me. It's now urgent," she said.

"I'll get one of the choppers to fly me to Bowral as soon as I can. Be careful of the baby."

"Jane is here, looking after me," replied Tanya, smiling. Jane just glowered at her.

"What happened on the Hume?" asked Tanya. "I saw what could have been graves and a whole pile of shell casings."

Virginia and Mark briefed the new arrivals.

"We buried Dunstan and Bruno on the side of the main Hume highway, together with half a dozen of their companions. We sent 40 or so prisoners to The Settlement. At least two of the force sent against us escaped; until you arrived we have been a bit apprehensive about what might happen. We thought they might come over in force and try to sort us out, perhaps with helicopters," said Mark.

"If they had come they would have got a lot more than they bargained for," growled Virginia.

"Okay," said Tanya, "So far so good. What happened in Newcastle?"

Mark gave her a brief explanation about what he knew.

Later, Tanya managed another conversation with Kim and Louis. Kim was surprisingly calm regarding the loss of the helicopter. "Without your frigate we would have been in real trouble," she said. "As things stand we lost real friends and colleagues in that 'copter, but we will survive."

Louis continued, "By the way, we managed to get the captain of the captured patrol boat to speak to Colonel Jacobs, in Canberra, on the blower. He really gave him a piece of his mind, said that he had put them all in danger quite unnecessarily and as a result lost the whole complement of 42 and two patrol boats. The captain and crew are in custody here, we sent one man who was injured to The Settlement hospital."

"So, to summarise," said Tanya later, "we have 40 prisoners at The Settlement, many of whom should be in jail in Canberra and we will return them there as soon as we can, and another 20 in Newcastle. Derain has told me what happened in the bush, so we're on top there.

We also have Jonathan who has a lot to answer for. He is still very groggy, but Jane says he ought to be able to answer a few questions in a day or two; even now he barely knows where he is."

"So, Derain, there are 500 captured soldiers walking towards Canberra under guard by Settlement troops?" asked Tanya.

"Yes, but the bad men are still in Canberra; what are you going to do when the prisoners get there?" asked Derain.

"Roger and Chas need help to make a plan," Derain continued. "I told them I would find you so they are waiting for you."

"Where are they?"

"We'll go in the old chopper; I'll find them easily enough."

"Okay," said Tanya, "the Jetstar is here, we can go as soon as possible. Louis is on the way in one of the Merlins. We can use that for any wounded soldiers."

They made another call to Newcastle.

"Okay, now what?" Kim asked.

"First, keep Jacobs thinking he has us on the hop. You deal with him; if he asks where Mark is, tell him he's somewhere in the bush between Canberra and The Settlement," said a more than usually effusive Tanya. "Tell him to put in writing all his demands and somehow send them to you. If he asks to speak to the captain of the patrol boat again, tell him the man has been moved to The Settlement. He'll obviously try to get hold of Wetherall, he's the colonel in charge of the military expedition sent to destroy us. I'll contrive some sort of response to that."

"What happens if they use helicopters to try to confirm what's going on?"

"Good point. I'll see if I can do something about that. Now, for the rest of it. I need two of the big Merlins," Tanya told Kim, "and as many Academy people as you can spare."

"As you know we are one helicopter short," Kim informed her, "and I still have the navy people here, under guard. I can let you have five people, but I'm sure that Stephanie will be able to spare at least a dozen more. I'll give Eustace a note and he can drop into Amazonia on his way over. I can still send two choppers, but that leaves us with no spare."

Derain pointed when they had been airborne for less than 30 minutes, "There you can see, all walking to Canberra."

Tanya circled and, directed by Roger, landed in a glade within a few hundred metres of where the forlorn looking troops were camped.

"I'm planning on infiltrating the base in Canberra with our own people," Tanya said to Roger. "I've about 20 coming from Newcastle and Amazonia, so I need 20 uniforms from your prisoners here. Also, I want another 20 from your Settlement contingent, to be dressed in regular military uniforms; they can swap uniforms with some of the soldiers. I've brought with me 20 or so outfits the soldiers can change into while we take their uniforms. Eustace will be here within two hours to take any wounded to hospital. In the meantime, I need those uniforms, so we had better get on with it."

"Where do you plan to be?" asked Louis.

"I will lead one of the groups," said Tanya.

Louis looked at Tanya and whispered, "Is that smart? Mark or Virginia should lead one of the groups. I'm sure that Dr. Wickremasinghe won't approve."

Looking slightly disappointed, she nodded in agreement.

"You think you're going to be able to take over the whole military outfit in Canberra?" added Louis, after a moments silence.

"Yes. Just watch me." ·

"What do you want from me?" asked Louis.

"Just watch my back," she smiled.

CHAPTER 17

The Reverse Coup

TANYA

After the initial conversation, Roger guided Tanya, Derain and Louis, still hobbling about in his moon boot, around the 500 Canberra troops platoon by platoon who were being readied to continue their walk through the bush back to Canberra, directed by mounted Settlement troops. The two Merlins arrived shortly after.

"One of the choppers is to take anyone requiring treatment to The Settlement hospital," Tanya advised. "I have asked him to return and run daylight patrols over the entourage once he has done that."

"And the other Merlin is to help me with something really urgent," said Chas, who had now joined the group. "We need to get control of the airport and disable their choppers. I'm very surprised they haven't used them at all up to now. I have a team ready to go."

"Changing the subject: Has there been a formal handover of control?" asked Tanya.

"Not yet. We were waiting for you," answered Roger after glancing at Chas.

311

"Okay Chas, before you move off, we'll have a ceremony where officers should formally hand over control of each platoon to me. It reinforces the position they are in and it also means the troops are not beholden to obey any orders given by their erstwhile commanders. We'll start with Colonel Wetherall, who I understand is in overall charge."

Tanya prepared a short, handwritten, surrender document for presentation to Colonel Wetherall as Chas gathered his airport team together. Wetherall did a double take when Tanya approached, "What are you doing here?" he asked.

"Yes I know Colonel, seeing me here is, I am sure, a big surprise," Tanya smiled.

She handed Wetherall the surrender document, which Wetherall tried to push away, "You wait," he said, trying to recover his composure, "until I tell Colonel Jacobs..."

"Colonel Wetherall. Look around you. All the people under your command have been disarmed and all your equipment is under Settlement control. Just sign the fucking document before I lose patience." Wetherall then reluctantly signed the surrender document, as did every other officer, who then formally handed over each platoon to individually selected Settlement officers.

"I've been speaking with the prisoners, in a planned and organised way," said Roger once the formalities were concluded, "as has Chas and the other Settlement people who were embedded, and my feeling is most of the troops will cooperate. There is a sense among the troops that Jacobs was leading them all up the garden path. Wetherall is a bit of a problem though, maybe you could take him away somewhere and lock him up."

By now, Chas had gathered a 30-man team led by himself, and one of The Settlement personnel embedded with the military, who was familiar with the set-up at Canberra Airport. They were all dressed in uniforms which they had swopped with the military captives. Eustace, directed by Chas and flying in low over the trees, landed in a glade some ten kilometres from their target.

"Some of the satellites servicing the GPS system seem to have failed," said Eustace, "so there are blank spaces in the service. I suppose when the functioning satellites are on the other side of the globe…" So now, as had become routine, they made certain of the route and the destination with the use of an old map. With some difficulty they found the glade; the pristine bush was much thicker resulting from the increased rainfall since the flood, and they spent nearly half an hour flying up and down, looking for it. Once they were certain they had identified it, Eustace flew low over the area, scaring off the many kangaroos that had come out to graze in the late afternoon. The disciplined troops disembarked in full battle dress and assembled in three sections on the edge of the glade. "We'll be in touch," said Chas to Eustace before the Merlin took off again. Chas led the men on a fast march to the airport perimeter, where they arrived just after dusk.

Chas cut a hole in the protective fence, with a set of cutters Eustace had as part of the regular equipment in the Merlin. The hole was large enough for the men to crawl through, one at a time. He tied a ribbon onto the fence ensuring they would find the place if they needed to retreat. One man had been sent a little way ahead as a lookout, but they were still some way from the main airport buildings so there was nobody about. There were eight large troop-carrying Sikorsky S 92 A helicopters parked on the tarmac, similar to the one Jonathan used regularly, and two small Cessna 650 Citations, used to ferry the Canberra leadership to some of the more remote places under military control.

The group waited in the long grass, 50 metres from the parked aircraft. Soon a two-man patrol appeared, a sergeant and one other, who together quickly looked over each individual aircraft.

"All under control, we need to get back to the hangar," said the sergeant. "I'm uncomfortable about the manpower shortage." Chas allowed the small patrol to return to their base in the airport buildings.

"I want you to temporarily disable the starter motors on all these machine, just the choppers, not the jets," Chas instructed. "The jets won't be much use to them if they want to attack us from the air, they are unarmed." He left five men to complete the job. The 25 others carefully made their way around the perimeter fence to the fuel storage tanks. There was one guard, who they crept up on, disarmed and tied up. "Again, temporarily disable all the pumps on the tanks. Tanya said she'll want to refuel our own machines here rather than at The Settlement or Newcastle." Within 30 minutes the job had been completed.

Leaving one man to guard the tanks Chas, still dressed in his official army uniform, then led the rest of his platoon on a roundabout route to the main entrance gate of the airport. He marched up to the duty guard saying, "We've come to better secure the airport. Orders from Colonel Jacobs. He says our men have captured all Settlement troops, but we don't want anything to go wrong." The guard was relieved, having had to complete two shifts in a row due to the lack of personnel, most having been commandeered to go on the expedition to attack The Settlement.

As dawn broke, Chas confidently marched his platoon to the nearby airport hangers, having detailed one of his men as guard to take over duty at the entrance. The sergeant in charge of airport security was greatly relieved to see Chas's platoon, and he knew Chas. With Chas and all his men, wearing army uniforms, no questions were asked regarding his authority.

Chas repeated what he had said to the gate guard.

"I've been asking for additional personnel for some time now," the sergeant said.

"You and your small contingent can return to barracks for a few days," Chas instructed. "We have sufficient personnel for guard duty for the time being. I will be in contact later."

Once the troops were again wending their weary way to Canberra, Tanya, Louis, Derain and Roger spent several hours planning their next moves, sitting inside Eustace's Merlin which had returned from delivering Chas' group to take over the airport. The machine was parked near the slowly moving entourage of captured troops. Once all the plans were in place, Tanya and Virginia took Wetherall to Bowral in the Bell, instructing the guards, "If he gives you any trouble, plug him. I'm sick of all these nincompoops. I just need to think about the best way of dealing with him."

As Wetherall was being led away, Virginia said, "The simplest thing would be to string him up on that tree," she pointed. "Dealing with all these people in a semi-humane way as we did with the Morton people merely got us into more trouble."

"Maybe; as I said I'll think about it."

A day or so later, in one of the small cottages that had been cleaned up in Bowral, Tanya had Wetherall brought to her. The cable ties on his hands were removed. Tanya had made sure the jury-rigged phone worked properly.

"Jacobs thinks he still has me under lock and key and that our forces have surrendered to you," Tanya said to him when he had been seated opposite her. The guards were still hovering.

"In a minute, I am going to arrange for you to speak to him. You are to speak to him as if this is actually the case. If you put one-foot wrong or even create the faintest suspicion that the opposite situation is true, I will blow your fucking head off." Wetherall winced as she produced a large long barrelled Webley.45 revolver. Through the open window of the room they were in Tanya aimed and fired the revolver at a nearby tree branch which shattered into several pieces. "Just in case you thought I was bluffing. There are five more rounds left in this baby, I'll only need one, if you see what I mean..."

Wetherall visibly blanched at the action. After a few minutes, a phone was thrust into his hands, "Colonel Jacobs," he was told. During the conversation Tanya held the revolver within a foot of his face.

"Just remember, Colonel Wetherall," said Tanya "I can hear both sides of the discussion and one word out of place..." she waggled the revolver in his face.

"Yes Colonel, all under control. They've all been disarmed and are being marched under guard to Canberra," stammered Wetherall.

"Good. When do you expect to arrive?" Jacobs asked.

"Five days or so. We'll let you know."

"The leadership. All firmly manacled and under control?"

"Yes, of course, Sir."

"Do you need any help? I can send a couple of choppers along, maybe pick up the leadership, so they can join that bitch on heat in her little jail cell."

Wetherall flinched.

Tanya shook her head firmly.

"Not necessary, Sir. The choppers would have trouble finding somewhere to land anyway."

"I might just fly over you, once or twice to see if everything is okay."

Tanya nodded.

"Good idea, Sir. That will be good for morale."

"Okay, Colonel Wetherall. You have done well. Thank you."

The phone went dead. Tanya looked at the shivering wreck in front of her.

Before the sergeant had left the airport with his detachment of security personnel, Colonel Jacobs and an aide arrived in a pristine Range Rover. Chas marched up to him and saluted smartly as he got out of the vehicle so any doubts the sergeant may have had about the changes to the security regime at the airport were dispelled by this action.

"Captain Bolt," he said, [he only knew Chas by the name he had enlisted with] "I thought you were a member of the group that accepted the surrender of the rabble from The Settlement?"

"Yes Sir, I was, but Colonel Wetherall was concerned about security at the airport and instructed me to return here to bolster it. We originally needed the manpower to increase troop numbers moving against The Settlement and he knew this had created a shortage of security personnel here; but now that issue is resolved so he asked me to return here to ensure all is in order. There is no doubt it's necessary; the remaining security here is very overstretched."

"How did you get here?" asked Jacobs.

"One of the opposition choppers, Sir. They are being extremely cooperative."

Jacobs nodded as if this was well within his expectations.

"A day or so ago I had a call from Colonel Wetherall, who has asked me to overfly the troops," said Jacobs. "Can you now organise that for me please, Captain."

"Certainly Sir, just allow a few minutes for me to make a final check on one of the choppers. Then we can go. There's a pilot here and I will accompany you, to help with navigation. The GPS system is becoming less and less reliable, Sir, as you know."

Chas commandeered a vehicle and drove the short distance to where the army choppers were situated. Unobserved, he told his men not to disable the helicopter fleet as instructed earlier but to actually make sure all the aircraft were serviceable. "While I am away with the Colonel, and while the technicians are here, get all these choppers refuelled and ready to go." Within an hour, with Chas making sure everything was under control and that there was no suspicion as to which side he was on, he retrieved an impatient Colonel Jacobs from a waiting room in the airport buildings.

"Apologies for the delay, Sir," said Chas. "Having just taken over the security I felt I had to ensure there had been no incursions while so many of our men had been involved in the exercise in the bush, Sir."

Jacobs merely nodded as he and his aide climbed into the machine.

Chas had carefully discussed with his second-in-command further details as to how they could secure the airport. "Just make sure all the old security personnel are back in barracks and away from here, and then get all the choppers fully operational. If you are able to get hold of Eustace on the blower, without being overheard by anyone, tell him what's going on. They may be surprised to see one of the military choppers overflying all the people walking back here."

It took them less than an hour to find the entourage, with Chas sitting in the right-hand seat of the Sikorsky helping to direct the pilot. "I'd advise not flying too low," said Chas, "although they have all been disarmed, one can't be too careful." Jacobs nodded listening through the headphones. They flew over the entourage several times, just high enough for nobody to be able to see any detail. On the third pass over the huge slow-moving troop a green Very Light was fired arcing its lazy way through the azure blue sky, away from the aircraft but clearly visible.

Chas kept his mouth shut, but after a short delay Jacobs said, "Looks like a signal that everything is under control. We can't contribute anything more. Take us back home now please, pilot."

Chas nodded and the chopper returned to Canberra.

As Jacobs disembarked, he said to Chas, "It all seems to be under control, Captain. When do you think the troops will arrive here?"

"I'll keep an eye out, Sir," Chas answered, "and I'll report to you on a daily basis."

Once Jacobs and his aide had left the airport, Chas' second-in-command said to him, "A couple of people seem to have sussed out that we are not kosher. They and the guard we apprehended are all confined, but we need to deal with them…"

When Jacobs returned to the office normally occupied by Jonathan, he was well satisfied that all was under control. He had started to remove Jonathan's memorabilia from the walls and his desk. There was a sudden interruption, with a filthy and dishevelled Lieutenant Henderson suddenly appearing unannounced.

"What the hell?"

"Sir, we are in trouble."

Henderson then hurriedly proceeded to explain what had occurred in the bush. Jacobs went pale as he listened, without interrupting, to everything Henderson was telling him.

"How did you get here?"

"Horseback. We stole some of their horses."

"We?"

"I have 18 men with me here, Sir."

"Unnoticed?"

"Yes. I think so, Sir."

"We still have that bloody woman in custody here."

"No, Sir, we don't. She appeared in that small chopper of theirs and took control, just before we managed to escape."

"I spoke to Colonel Wetherall yesterday. He told me all was under control."

"Maybe," said Henderson, "but I can tell you he is a prisoner, just like the rest of us."

Jacobs remained icily calm. "Lieutenant, we need a new plan. What do you think our options are?"

By this time Jacobs' senior officers, those that had remained in Canberra, were standing around having been called into his office.

"We have a problem which needs dealing with," said Jacobs. "Lieutenant Henderson, please brief everyone on what you have just told me."

Henderson repeated his story.

Jacobs knew he was in trouble, but he was desperate and determined. After a brief discussion, he said, "We still have control of the airport and the helicopters, so we need to get them in the air as soon as we can. We also have…"

"How do we know that this Lieutenant Henderson is telling the truth, Sir? He looks like a plant to me," a Colonel Templeton interrupted. "Sir, you said you had just spoken to Wetherall and he told you all was well. You also overflew our people with the captured Settlement troops walking back here. What Henderson is saying has no credibility. For God's sake, Sir, we have 500 well-armed and well-led troops, against their puny force."

He looked Henderson up and down. "This bloke is obviously a turncoat and a spy. He's leading us into a trap. He should be dealt with accordingly."

Henderson tried to say something.

"If what Henderson said is correct," Templeton continued in a loud voice, "why would they all be coming back here to Canberra? Surely, Sir, they would be trying to get everyone back to their wretched place in the Blue Mountains, so would be walking in the opposite direction. This is nonsense. We know we have Mrs Bower here safely under lock and key—I made sure of that this morning. We should just lock Henderson up and deal with him when all this is over."

The rest of Jacobs men breathed a sigh of relief and they looked at their colleague with admiration. Henderson tried to leave, but Jacobs called security, saying, "Lock him up, we'll deal with him later."

Back at the airport Chas knew he had to act quickly. "I'll get hold of Eustace as soon and the technicians have all left for the day. I assume that all the security people here are our own people?" he asked his second-in-command.

"Yes."

At that moment, there was a call from the gate. "The sergeant from this morning and six others are demanding entry. Something about no instructions were ever given about changing the guard detail at the airport."

"Let then through," instructed Chas.

"Get ten of our people," Chas instructed his second-in-command. "We have to nip this in the bud."

The sergeant in a dilapidated old Range Rover appeared a few minutes later to find themselves surrounded by ten of Chas' Settlement troops, all pointing their rifles at the surprised security detail as they emerged from the vehicle.

"Drop your weapons," instructed Chas. One man made an attempt to resist. One shot was fired and he dropped dead next to the vehicle. Absolute horror crossed the faces of the remaining security personnel, none of whom were in the prime of youth which was one of the reasons that they had not been included in the troops going to take on The Settlement. The rest cooperated.

"Lock them up with the others;" instructed Chas, "I'll get hold of Eustace."

An hour later Eustace arrived in the dark, after all the technicians and other non-security personnel had left the airport. The men in custody, with their hands tied behind their backs, were bundled into the Merlin under the guard of three of Chas' personnel. They were sent to The Settlement.

"Ask Roger for another 30 Settlement troops," Chas said to Eustace. "If there are any more problems, we need to be able to hold on here until all our people arrive. Also, do you have a pilot who can fly army Sikorskys?"

"Yes, two. What do you have in mind?"

"We need to get the Sikorskys out of here. If you could borrow the Bell, the pilots can be picked up to return here for another flight. They can fly backwards and forwards all night. Take them all to The Settlement. We need to be ready for anything."

By midnight Eustace had delivered the promised additional personnel in one of the Merlins. By dawn, two of the Sikorskys were parked on the parade ground at The Settlement, and the process of removing the remaining Sikorskys continued throughout the rest of the day.

"If you run out of room for the Sikorskys at home, take a couple to Bowral and a couple to Amazonia," Chas instructed.

When his colleagues left the office, a desperate Jacobs called security and ordered them to return Henderson to him.

When Henderson reappeared, Jacobs said, "As I mentioned we have control of the airport. It's under the control of Captain Bolt. We need to get the choppers in the air and then, if what you say is correct, we can use the choppers to attack. It will give our people the chance to overwhelm Settlement forces. You go to the airport and I will collect three or four pilots and meet you there."

Henderson did as he was told. He returned to his men and had a brief discussion. They quickly made their way to the airport on horseback.

The guard at the gate phoned Chas, who was busy arranging to remove the last of the Sikorskys to a place controlled by The Settlement. "There is a Lieutenant Henderson here, under orders from Colonel Jacobs, with 18 men. He says he has been told to get the choppers ready to attack the troops coming south." The guard managed to provide Chas with as much info as he could without alerting Henderson to the fact that the military no longer controlled the airport.

"Right, let them through," ordered Chas, who quickly assembled his own force, which now consisted of more than 50 well prepared Academy troops, all with their weapons ready. As Henderson and his troops appeared and halted, Chas emerged from the buildings, saying to Henderson, "I suggest you tether your horses, over there. I have been told what you propose, but I need some help with such short notice." He stopped and looked at them closely. "You all look as if you have had a difficult few days," he observed.

Henderson explained tersely how they had escaped, "I'm sure we were not noticed. We'll be able to take them by surprise, if we can get the choppers in the air."

"When do you expect Colonel Jacobs?"

"An hour or two, he just needs to find the pilots."

"Okay," said Chas. "Time for some food and then we can get the Sikorskys operational. They have all just been refuelled. I suggest you all make your weapons safe and I'll see you in the canteen over there," Chas pointed.

When Chas could see that Henderson's men were seated in the canteen and busy eating, he assembled two sections of his troops who quietly filed into the canteen.

"Be upstanding!" Chas yelled before Henderson could do anything, "And do not move, you are all under arrest!" A surprised and shocked group of men unsteadily stood up as instructed. They were all instantaneously disarmed and hands were bound behind their backs with cable ties. They were all locked up.

"I'll wait for Jacobs at the gate," announced Chas.

An hour later Jacobs and three others, whom Chas assumed were pilots, arrived at the gate in a four-wheel drive, and were admitted. Chas and a small detachment made the vehicle halt and everyone disembark.

"You are all under arrest," he announced.

Jacobs looked at Chas with horror.

"You can't..." Before Jacobs could get the words out of his mouth Chas forcibly turned him around and slapped a pair of handcuffs on him.

"Lock him up with the rest," Chas instructed.

Jacobs was led away shouting obscenities.

Once they were certain that the prisoners had arrived in the vicinity of Canberra, Tanya, Louis, Jonathan, and Derain were dropped off at Canberra Airport in the Bell. Because of the very low number of flights in and out of the airport, air traffic control had been discontinued many years earlier. For safety, they hovered over the airport for a few minutes until they were given the all clear from the ground, which amounted to a thumbs up from Chas. They were greeted enthusiastically by Chas and his cohort.

Tanya watched Jonathan walk authoritatively, in his now freshly washed and pressed general's uniform, towards Chas, who saluted him. Jonathan did a double take, having not been informed of the takeover of the airport by Settlement forces. "What the hell are you doing here?" he asked in confusion.

"Tanya agreed we should secure the airport."

Jonathan still looked confused, "Whose..."

"I'm with Settlement forces," answered Chas, anticipating the question.

"Captain, would you kindly arrange transport into the base now," ordered Jonathan.

Chas quickly explained to Tanya that he had Jacobs locked up, at the airport, together with a number of other military personnel. Within five minutes, one of Chas' airport troop drove up in another pristine four-wheel drive and Tanya, Louis, Derain, and Jonathan climbed in with Chas taking over the wheel. There was no further word from Jonathan. The airport was left in charge of Chas' second-in-command.

"I said we would meet the troops in a nature reserve a few miles north east of the city," said Tanya to her passengers once they were on their way. "There's a bit of cover, and it has probably become overgrown since the flood, so they won't be noticed. I'll direct you. We'll have to take a roundabout route, to avoid being seen.

Colonel Templeton, looking for Jacobs, was alerted by what he mistakenly assumed was a message from Colonel Wetherall, but was actually sent by Virginia from Bowral on Tanya's instructions. He quickly asked his aide to again assemble all his colleagues.

"Here!" Templeton waved the note, once they had all arrived, "It's from Colonel Wetherall again; they'll be arriving within the hour. See, I was correct! That Henderson was a plant. We'll meet them on the parade ground."

During the night Tanya and Louis, on horseback, marched the captured troops from the pine plantation they had been settled in to the airport. All the troops had been fed and, although exhausted, by dawn they were lined up ready to march on the military headquarters. Tanya needed confirmation that the note supposedly from Colonel Wetherall had actually been received by the targeted military hierarchy, so a watch was set up at the college and, when it was clear that preparations were being made to review a major parade, she was advised. When Tanya was told the military hierarchy was in place on the dais, she gave the order for the troops to quick march from the airport.

"Kindly arrange a suitable reception party, to include Mrs Bower," Templeton had ordered in Jacobs absence.

A junior officer was instructed to fetch Tanya whom everyone thought was still in military custody. The officer had no idea what Tanya looked like, so he ignorantly fetched Jess.

Resplendent in their fresh uniforms, Templeton and his colleagues assembled on the hurriedly erected dais in the parade ground of the former Duntroon Military Academy. They left a space for the absent Jacobs in the centre of the front row. The officers started to become agitated when there was no sign of the troops after they had been waiting for 30 minutes.

"Where the hell are they all," muttered Templeton.

Under escort, Jess arrived just as the first troops started to march onto the parade ground. She was placed in a prominent position at the end of the group on the dais. Templeton did a double take. "There's something wrong," he thought. "That's not the bloody bitch!" He reflected on the information provided by Lieutenant Henderson, now wondering if it was correct. There was nothing he could do as troops started to make their way onto the parade ground.

The first few platoons were actually Settlement troops dressed in purloined military uniform. They were fully armed and lined up on the side of the parade ground, with arms at the ready. All the military hierarchy relaxed, all seemed to be well. The first platoons were immediately followed up by platoon after platoon of bareheaded soldiers, marching in good order behind Settlement troops. The first platoon wore Settlement uniforms, so initially it appeared that Settlement troops were indeed the ones under captivity.

"Here, here they are," said a relieved Templeton.

More unarmed bareheaded soldiers still marching in good order followed, platoon by platoon, but this group were all now dressed in full military uniforms.

"What's going on here?" muttered Templeton. "Must be some mistake."

Colonel Wetherall and Chas, mounted and flanked by 20 mounted Settlement personnel also dressed in purloined military uniforms, then made their way onto the parade ground. "They seem to have a helluva lot of prisoners," Templeton observed, as more of the bareheaded troops came into view.

Mounted and looking regal, Jonathan and Tanya, followed by Louis and Derain, came into view. They were followed by Jacobs, mounted, but bareheaded and with his hands bound behind his back, being led by an Academy soldier on foot.

Templeton went pale, "Oh my god, what the fuck! What happened to Jacobs and what's that bloody woman doing there, I thought we had her all safely locked up? Let's get out of here." He had time for another glance at Jess.

Mark, leading another 20 Academy personnel, had infiltrated himself and his troop into a position immediately behind Templeton and his fellow officers. Since they were dressed in regular army uniforms Templeton assumed they were part of the welcome parade. "Stay where you are," said Mark as his people, as one, cocked their weapons. "Colonel Templeton, you and all these people here," Mark waved at the reception committee, "are under arrest. One move and I promise you, you will receive a gut full of lead." One man made the mistake of going for the revolver on his belt. There was a short sharp sub-machine gun burst from one of Mark's crew and the man dropped down dead on the podium at Templeton's feet. There was a deathly hush as Mark's people rapidly cuffed the coup leaders. "You won't get away with this!" yelled Templeton. Mark just looked at him, saying nothing.

Over the next half-hour the tired and dispirited captured troops were gradually lined up in the middle of the parade ground, surrounded by well-armed Settlement soldiers, with rifles at the ready. Most Settlement troops were mounted, with a few still on foot. Finally, the horses loaded with the captured weapons were marched onto the parade ground. From the original Kanangra establishment, they had been directed to follow the main entourage to Canberra.

When all was in order, Jonathan, after a word from Tanya, and resplendent in his uniform, dismounted and silently walked over to the dais. Colonel Jacobs had been made to dismount and was obliged to stand to attention, in front of the dais, still bareheaded and with his hands tied behind his back. Tanya, Louis, Derain and Chas remained mounted just to the side of the men in the reception party.

Once all was quiet, Jonathan addressed the thoroughly demoralised troops. "We have come to the end of an unfortunate episode that does this organisation no credit at all," he said and looked up. "The leaders of what can only be described as an attempt at a coup, a forceful takeover of the most successful of the surviving organisations in this country, have been foiled and they will get their just desserts before a properly constituted court martial. The actions of each and every one of you will be examined in detail; my expectation is that most of you did no more than obey orders. If that is so, then you will be free to continue as before as members of our military organisation."

He hesitated, looking uncomfortable as he said, "I must also pay tribute to the people from what is known as The Settlement, who played a leading role in foiling the attempted coup against them." Tanya had earlier told him not to mention her own or any other names in reference.

Jonathan continued, "All military personnel are to return to barracks and are confined there until told otherwise. If you disobey this order, it will be assumed you were part of the attempted coup and will be dealt with accordingly."

Jacobs and his fellow conspirators, all now bareheaded and with their hands bound behind their backs, were hustled away by Mark's Academy troops. Tanya noticed Jacobs trying to say something to Jonathan. Jonathan had hastily turned his back. The exhausted troops shuffled off to barracks under the watchful eye of the full contingent of Settlement forces.

Tanya and Jonathan made their way to the same room in the military headquarters where Tanya had met with the now-disgraced

Jacobs and his people. Jonathan was left to his own devices for an hour, under guard, while Tanya planned her next move.

When Tanya returned, Jonathan was almost apoplectic. "What am I?" he blustered, "Some sort of prisoner?"

Tanya ignored the outburst. Once she was comfortably seated opposite Jonathan she said, "We must be very careful this does not blow up again." She handed Jonathan a document that stated that the Australian military swore under oath to subject themselves to democratically elected civilian rule.

"You and all your officers will sign the document under oath," said Tanya. "We simply cannot afford to have any of this nonsense occur again."

Mark and Louis now entered the room, followed by Derain.

Jonathan looked aghast at the document. "Tanya, it's much too early for this sort of thing. We have to continue as we did before until there are some genuinely democratically elected governments around the place."

Tanya could see a look of desperation on Jonathan's face. Only Derain saw the glance of pure hatred directed at Tanya that followed.

"The area under the security blanket provided by The Settlement is now under full democratic control," answered Tanya, staring at Jonathan. "If we cooperate, within a few years we ought to be able to get most of the country back onto a democratic footing."

Tanya looked at Mark for support. "You have no choice, Jonathan," said Mark quietly. "We still have a helluva job on our hands; somehow you allowed Jacobs and his minions to take control of the military. Control of the military needs to be much more broad-based than it has been in the past so the chance of another such military coup is reduced to zero."

"You are expecting me to report to Tanya, is that what all this means?" Jonathan protested. Although he had respect for what Tanya had achieved with the development of The Settlement, he had always seen himself as superior to Tanya and indeed any Settlement personnel;

he was unable to bear the idea that he, General Jonathan Bower, was to report to a person with such lowly origins as Tanya—and a woman at that!

"You've not read the document properly, Jonathan," said Tanya. "The document says that the chief of the defence force will be appointed by and will report to a military commission which will consist of representatives of all the democratically elected governments in Australia."

"At present you, and your so-called central committee, are the only democratically elected governments I am aware of, so it still means I will be reporting to you."

"I'm sorry you have so little faith in me, Jonathan. Surely I don't need to point out that if we hadn't done the planning and taken the action we did, you may not be sitting in that chair. I bet that you would probably be languishing in a jail cell or worse, lying in an unmarked grave somewhere out there in the bush." Tanya pointed vaguely out of the window.

"Jonathan, you really fucked up! You need to recognise that, really fucked up," said Mark. "The military commission has not yet appointed anyone as chief of the defence force, so if you don't want the appointment..."

Jonathan looked at him furiously; he could see that he was cornered. He said nothing, "Just bloody wait," he thought, "I'll get back at this lot in time."

Louis had said nothing up to that point. "It was Tanya who insisted on relocating that frigate to Newcastle, the rest of us thought she had gone overboard, forgive the pun, when she suggested it," he said.

This gave Jonathan time to regroup. He looked at Louis suspiciously, "I know nothing about you, who are you anyway? I thought you were headman of a couple of huts near Taree."

"My name is Lieutenant Commander Louis McLeod, retired. I have been elected as Tanya's deputy."

"Mark already knows this," said Tanya, "but now that he and I have finalised our divorce, I have agreed to marry Louis. Also, if you haven't already noticed, I'm pregnant with Louis' child."

There was an uncomfortable silence.

"So who will be on this military commission, as you describe it?" asked Jonathan, disdainfully.

"Mark, Louis, Virginia, myself, and the chief of the defence force, which for the time being I have assumed will be you, Jonathan. All the other elected mayors will also be represented," answered Tanya. "And Derain will represent the traditional owners of the land. The composition of the commission will change as other areas are democratised." She knew they really had no choice but to appoint Jonathan; his presence would help to reassure all the military outposts throughout the country that nothing had changed.

"Derain, what can he possibly contribute?" Jonathan glanced at Derain with distaste.

Tanya then spent more than half an hour detailing what Derain had contributed to the survival of The Settlement, including his role in foiling the recent attempted coup. "We would not have survived if it wasn't for him," said Tanya forcefully, "and, as you know, he taught all of us our bush skills."

"He is not democratically elected."

"Oh yes he is, and if his people ever get fed up with him he will be dumped and replaced."

Seeing Tanya's determination on the issue Jonathan reluctantly agreed to comply and he signed the document with bad grace. Tanya pointedly retrieved the document and placed it in a folder.

"What are the next steps?" asked Jonathan, with resignation, knowing that he would not like what was coming.

"Every one of your officers resident here in Canberra, will sign, under oath, a copy of the document you have just signed. We can complete the exercise with one ceremony under the jurisdiction of a judge; we will all of course be present. You will be leading the statement of oath."

"When?" asked Jonathan.

"Today or tomorrow morning," answered Tanya. "And one other thing."

"Yes?" said Jonathan warily.

"There will be no exceptions. The officers either accept the document or they will be locked up and prosecuted along with Jacobs and his fellow conspirators," said Tanya firmly. "And thereafter every person enlisted in the military around the country will be obliged to sign the same document, also under oath. This applies to all new recruits as well."

"We have people all over the continent," said Jonathan.

"Sounds like a job for some of your senior officers and perhaps some members of the military commission," said Tanya.

Jonathan just shook his head, knowing he had been out-thought and out-manoeuvred at every step of the way.

"One step ahead of the sheriff, as always," said Tanya, smiling, looking at Jonathan.

"How will the Settlement's military operation fit in to all this?" asked Jonathan.

Tanya reacted angrily. She just looked at him without saying anything for a full minute.

"Jonathan, for fucks sake, stop playing games. You know the set-up, nothing has changed. Liaise with Roger," was the very short answer. Tanya then glared at Jonathan, until he looked away.

Virginia and Sergeant Harris were ushered into the meeting.

"Of the 60 or so people being held in Newcastle and The Settlement," reported Virginia, "41 of them are from Morton, the Vikings, the Bandstand and Taree, and should never have been released from jail in the first place, and should go straight back there. Three people from the military will not cooperate. The rest can be included in your programme of rehabilitation."

"Where are these people?" asked Tanya.

"Here, we brought them all back here. The three military men I mentioned are locked up with all Jacobs' cronies and the rest are unarmed and confined to barracks with all the other military personnel."

"One other thing," Tanya said looking at Jonathan, "That so-called training facility in Wagga Wagga will be closed immediately. Is that clear?"

Jonathan looked blank. He blurted out without thinking, "How do you know about that?"

"I know about many things that you may not be aware of," she smiled. "I repeat, that place is to be closed. That is an instruction."

Jonathan looked at her trying to hide his hatred of her. "It will be done," he said quietly.

CHAPTER 18

Consolidation

(Weeks later)

TANYA

43 officers were eventually indicted for treason and all were sentenced to death by firing squad. Before the sentences were carried out, Tanya, as chairman of the military commission, said at one of their regular meetings, "I don't want us to impose the death penalty on all those people; it seems unnecessary..." The meetings were being held at The Settlement, with Tanya finding it more and more difficult to travel in view of her impending confinement.

"What's the alternative?" asked Jonathan impatiently.

"Jacobs should be executed; the whole thing was his idea, as we know." She looked at Jonathan for a good 30 seconds. "That is if you, you bastard, have told us the truth," she thought. He held her gaze for a few seconds and then looked away. "I'll be keeping an eye on you my friend," she again said to herself, "the jury is still out on that issue whether you realise it or not."

She then said aloud, "We should commute the other sentences to a lifetime of hard labour. All of those involved should be obliged to witness Jacobs' execution. The commutation should include the ability to impose the original sentence for any further transgressions," added Tanya, "and the death sentences imposed on the Morton people will still be carried out. I want that done immediately, is that clear?"

Jonathan nodded.

"Where will this bunch see out their sentences?" asked Mark.

"Any ideas?" asked Tanya.

"As we discussed a few weeks ago now, send them individually to various military locations around the country, but don't let them settle anywhere. They should be moved on every year or so. In time, some of them might be capable of rehabilitation," suggested Louis.

"We need to develop an intelligence apparatus," added Louis. "We need to know what's going on everywhere. Jacobs plan to subsume the whole power of the military for his own selfish ends demonstrates that. Also, if we had had an effective intelligence apparatus we would have known more about Thor and his plans and attitudes well in advance." He then added, "And keeping an eye on the people whose sentences have been commuted further demonstrates the need for such an apparatus. Some of them may still have ambitions of their own."

"Any such organisation would have to report directly to the military commission, not to the military," Louis added hastily, looking at Jonathan. "You must understand the reason for that, Jonathan, after everything that has happened. The chief of the defence force would be included in all briefings, of course."

"We are overcomplicating the issue," said Jonathan. "Any security apparatus should report to the military." He looked desperate.

"No, fuck no!" said Mark. He stood up pointing a finger at Jonathan. "That is just not going to happen, get used to the idea. For Christ's sake wake up, Jonathan, we are simply not going to allow the situation to get out of hand again." He glared at his younger brother. "You have to accept that civilian control means just that and nothing else."

Jonathan was surprised at the vehemence of Mark's outburst and wisely kept his own counsel.

Tanya brought the meeting under control again, "So are we agreed on the commutation issue?" she asked.

There were nods around the table.

"Louis maybe you could come up with a formal proposal for the structure of the proposed intelligence apparatus," Tanya concluded.

Against advice from Dr Wickremasinghe, Tanya insisted on being present in Canberra when the members of the military commission told the men sentenced to death, individually, that their sentences had been commuted and they would be sent to various locations around the continent. They were also told they would have to witness the execution of Colonel Jacobs.

"What about our wives and families?" asked one of the sentenced men, in tears.

"You should have thought of that before you decided to join the plot. They will remain here, in Canberra, continuing with their current duties," answered Tanya. "You were sentenced to death; you should clearly understand that what you are going to is not some sort of club med vacation. You have been stripped of any rank and entitlements you had and are sentenced to hard labour. You've not been exonerated from any crimes committed; what is intended is punishment for those crimes. The matter will be reviewed in five years. Dependent on your individual behaviour this commission has the right to further review sentences; including the imposition of the original sentence."

Tanya visited Jacobs briefly in his cell, which was clean and well ordered. He was then brought to the prison control office, without handcuffs, and told to sit down with Tanya sitting opposite him. There was a cracked formica table between them. Jacobs was dressed formally in his pristine colonel's uniform. He was clean shaven, upright and in full control.

"Colonel Jacobs, you have been sentenced to death, by firing squad, by a legally constituted court. I am here to tell you that the sentence will be carried out within the next week. What you had in mind is a disgrace to you your family and indeed the whole military operation and would have sent this country back to the stone-age."

Jacobs glared at Tanya, with an unwavering stare. He said nothing but didn't blink.

"I can also inform you that the sentences of your co-conspirators have all been commuted to life imprisonment with hard labour."

After a short silence, Tanya added, "Do you have anything to say, Colonel Jacobs?"

Jacobs continued to glare at her for a full minute before answering, "Fuck you, you bitch. You'll get your come-uppance one day..."

"Take him away," Tanya said to the guard. She held his unrepentant stare until he had disappeared down the corridor, back to his cell.

Tanya went to see Jonathan, now reinstated in the office he had previously occupied.

She told him of the meeting with Jacobs. "As chief of the defence force you are instructed to attend the execution," she said.

Jonathan looked uncomfortable, but said nothing.

Tanya left Canberra before Jacobs' execution, to attend to the imminent birth of her third child. At the final meeting of the military commission held there before she left, she said, "Jonathan, with the agreement of the commission, I would be grateful if you could provide us with an assessment of our total military strength, where they are located, and an assessment of their capacity to deal with any local difficulties. Also, and just as important, could you please provide us with an assessment of all the surviving communities around the continent with information such as numbers of people within each community and their military capacity, if any. Perhaps a comment on how they survived, what their political philosophy is and a view, if you have one, of their willingness to rejoin the Commonwealth of Australia, based on the democratic principles we have started to establish in the areas we already control."

Jonathan was about to raise objections, but one look from Tanya, was enough to persuade him to keep his mouth shut.

"Because I am unable to travel I want to see every commander within your jurisdiction at The Settlement within the next three months. I also want to see the leaders of the surviving clans around the continent. Again they will, for the time being, have to come to The Settlement. After that I will be able to travel."

"Won't the birth of your child interfere...?"

"No,' said Tanya, "we have the resources to make sure it doesn't."

"One other thing," she said. The other members of the commission, except Louis, looked at her tiredly.

"Louis," said Tanya, looking at him, creating an opening for what he was about to say.

"Tanya and I are getting married within the next few weeks," said Louis quietly. "There'll obviously be a bit of a party at The Settlement, but because of recent events, it's inappropriate for people from all over to attend. If people are present at The Settlement, in the normal course of events, they're welcome to come but otherwise not. Appropriate announcements will be made so the whole community knows what's going on."

"That should apply to everyone including members of this commission," said Virginia.

Tanya kept her mouth shut during this exchange, but nodded approvingly. Jonathan looked down at his feet.

Within the designated week, Mark and Louis were deputed to attend the execution of Colonel Jacobs as witnesses, together with Jonathan. Jacobs was led out from his cell, again dressed in his full colonel's uniform. He was bareheaded and his hands were handcuffed behind his back. He was tied to a newly erected post at one end of the prison yard. He stared ahead and remained upright and unrepentant. He shook his head when offered a blindfold.

Jacobs' co-conspirators were assembled on the opposite wall of the prison yard, just 30 metres away. All were handcuffed and dressed in civilian clothes, as befitted their new status. A major, unknown to either Mark or Louis, lined up the 12 members of the firing squad, 15 metres from the unblinking Jacobs. The judge stood in front of Jacobs and read out the sentence he had imposed on Jacobs.

"Colonel Jacobs. Do you understand?"

There was no answer from Jacobs who just spat in the judge's direction.

The judge moved aside and signalled to the major.

"Squad! Ready!" Muscles braced. Rifles were lifted to position.

"Aim!" Fingers touching triggers. Feet firmly anchored.

"Fire!" 12 shots rang out in unison.

Jacobs slumped against his bonds. Blood seeped out over his chest.

"Squad. At ease."

"Doctor, please examine the prisoner," said the major.

The doctor moved forward and after a brief examination said, "The prisoner is deceased."

"Burial party, advance," instructed the major.

The burial party cut Jacobs down and lifted his body onto a stretcher. The party marched out to a waiting four-wheel drive. Another officer took control. He had been instructed to bury Jacobs in an unmarked grave 20 kilometres from Canberra, in a heavily wooded area. Jacobs co-conspirators were returned to their prison cells. Three needed assistance.

CHAPTER 19

The Wedding

(Three weeks later)

Tanya

Tanya and Louis' civil wedding was held in The Settlement's beautifully decorated community centre. The centre was a mass of flowers, in every nook and cranny, either grown by the community or were wild flowers especially picked for the occasion. The centre was full to bursting, with many in the community being obliged to stand outside as an informal guard of honour.

"No reserved seats," Tanya had insisted, "just Chloe, Chas and Didier, otherwise first come first served."

"Who will give you away?" Chloe had asked.

Tanya had looked at her quizzically and then said, "I hadn't thought of that. Sounds like bullshit to me; maybe I'll give myself away."

"What about Jason? You can't give yourself away."

Not wanting to create any sort of argument, and after a moment's hesitation', Tanya said, "Okay, we'll settle on Jason."

339

Louis, looking resplendent in a full colonel's Academy uniform, entered the centre on his own just before the scheduled time of ten am. The 36 members of the honour guard, provided by the youngest members of Academy and made up of equal members of both sexes, presented arms as Louis entered the centre. A few minutes later Tanya, on Jason's arm, walked smiling and waving through the cheering crowd. She was also dressed in a full colonel's uniform, carrying all before her.

"Shouldn't you be wearing a white wedding dress?" Chloe had argued.

"Don't be bloody ridiculous," Tanya had replied, laughing. "A symbol of virginity, with me looking like I'm about to pop at any minute?"

The Academy honour guard presented arms as Tanya and Jason approached. The pair stopped immediately and stood to attention before entering the centre.

"Honour guard. Load," ordered the newly promoted sergeant in charge. Rifles were raised in unison to the sky. "Honour guard, fire." 36 shots were fired into the air as one, with two more shots following, again in perfect unison.

"Honour guard. Shoulder Arms."

Tanya acknowledged them by giving a smart salute.

"Honour guard. At ease."

The community band situated on the dais, inside the community centre, played 'Here Comes the Bride.' The senior community judge was standing immediately in front of the dais.

"Who gives this woman…" he began.

Jason stepped forward, with Tanya still on his arm, and then he stepped back.

A happy and smiling Tanya looked up at Louis. She was pleasantly surprised to see all the religious denominations represented on the dais. The judge said, "As discussed with you Tanya, I have been guided by parts of the Anglican marriage service."

Tanya nodded.

The judge addressed the gathering:

"As you all know, we are gathered here to witness the marriage of our great friend and leader, Tanya, to Louis.

"First, I am required to ask anyone present, who knows any reason why these persons may not lawfully marry, to declare it now."

There was complete silence throughout the centre. The judge waited a full minute before continuing:

"Louis, will you take Tanya to be your wife, will you love her, comfort her, honour and protect her, and forsaking all others be faithful to her as long as you both shall live."

"I will," said Louis.

"Tanya, will you take Louis to be your husband, will you love him, comfort him, honour and protect him, and forsaking all others be faithful to him as long as you both shall live."

"I will," said Tanya.

"Please face each other holding hands, and repeat after me:

"I, Tanya, take you, Louis, to be my husband, from this day forward, for richer, for poorer..."

Tanya had insisted that she should speak first at this juncture in the ceremony.

"It sends a message of equality right through the community," she had argued.

"I, Louis, take you, Tanya, as my wife, from this day forward, for richer, for poorer..."

"Now for the rings," said the judge.

Jason handed over the rings.

Again, Tanya started the process:

"I, Tanya, give you, Louis, my husband, this ring..."

"I, Louis, give you, Tanya, my wife, this ring..."

The judge said to them both, with a smile, "You may now kiss each other."

Which they did.

"I now pronounce you man and wife."

There was a cheer from the assembled community, matched by a louder cheer from outside the centre.

The judge then announced, "All the religious denominations within the community wish to bless this marriage."

So, in order, the Imam, the Buddhist monk, the Hindu priest, the Anglican priest, the Roman Catholic priest, and the Presbyterian priest, representing all the protestant churches, chanted blessings on the pair, to Tanya's absolute delight.

The sound of a digeridoo signalled the arrival of Derain and a small group of his Aboriginal colleagues, suitably painted with white and green stripes all over their bodies who advanced on the bridal pair.

First Tanya and then Louis had their faces partly blackened. The Aborigines chanted while white smoke was wafted around the pair and sticks clanged together then Derain, with his eyes shut, looked as if he was in a trance as he chanted special words that Tanya was unable to understand.

Tanya was suddenly forced to bend double. She grasped at Louis' hand saying, "You'd better get hold of Jane," she whispered, "the little bugger isn't waiting for anyone."

She grimaced further as birth pangs started to rack her body.

Just as Derain had completed his ritual, Jane appeared wheeling a gurney, having been alerted by Jason.

"On," she said, "and don't argue."

Tanya was lifted onto the gurney by Jane, Louis and two nurses as her waters broke, and the gurney was wheeled out.

Derain looked on as if this was what he had expected all along.

Three hours later Tanya, in the confines of the hospital, gave birth to a big bouncing boy.

Louis walked over to the centre where the party was still in full swing. There was silence as he entered the room, "Boy, nine pounds, David Louis Derain is what he'll be called."

There were shouts and applause.

Derain and his group paid an immediate visit to the hospital where they insisted, under the disapproving eye of Jane, in doing another short ritual dance, surrounding the bed and clicking their sticks. Tanya was thrilled, with little David, unaware of anything else, sucking furiously on one of Tanya's large and very full breasts.

Icefall

No Happy Valley
Book One of 'Winds of Change' Trilogy

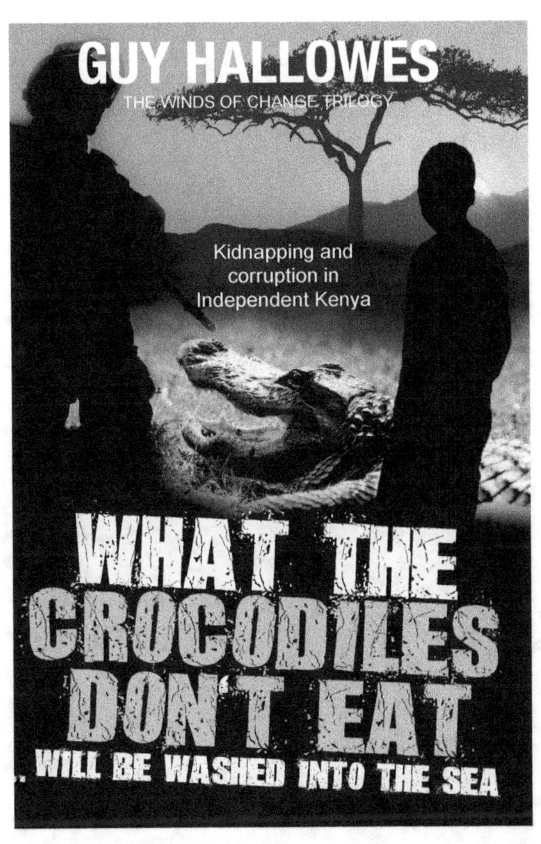

What The Crocodiles Dont Eat Will Be Washed Into The Sea
Book Two of 'Winds of Change' Trilogy

No Peace for the Wicked
Book Three of 'Winds of Change' Trilogy

Rough Diamonds

9 780645 179071